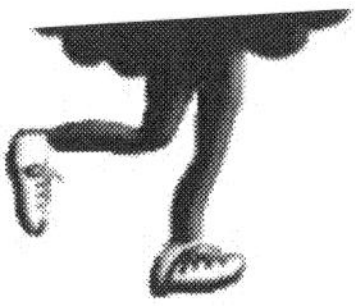

Other titles by Sherrie Hansen
From Beckoning Books and Second Wind Publishing
www.secondwindpublishing.com

Night and Day

Maple Valley Trilogy

Stormy Weather
Book One ~ Maple Valley Trilogy

Water Lily
Book Two ~ Maple Valley Trilogy

Merry Go Round
Book Three ~ Maple Valley Trilogy

Merry Go Round

Book Three ~ Maple Valley Trilogy

By
Sherrie Hansen

Beckoning Books
Published by Second Wind Publishing, LLC.
Kernersville

Margy,
To second chances,
Sherrie Hansen
The Blue Belle Inn

Beckoning Books
Second Wind Publishing, LLC
931-B South Main Street, Box 145
Kernersville, NC 27284

This book is a work of fiction. Names, characters, locations and events are either a product of the author's imagination, fictitious or used fictitiously. Any resemblance to any event, locale or person, living or dead, is purely coincidental.

First Beckoning Books edition published March 2011. Beckoning Books, Running Angel, and all production design are trademarks of Second Wind Publishing, used under license.

For information regarding bulk purchases of this book, digital purchase and special discounts, please contact the publisher at www.secondwindpublishing.com

Cover quilt, Almaaz, designed by Liz Schwartz & Stephen Seifert, www.equiltpatterns.com. Back cover photo by Rose Hill, http://rose-hill.artistwebsites.com

Manufactured in the United States of America
ISBN 978-1935171621

Dedication

To my friends in Colorado Springs - you saw me through a very difficult time in my journey, a time of transitions and learning about life. You taught me about true friendship, about love, about God's love. For that, I will always be thankful. Even when you hurt or disappointed me, you were there for me, challenging me to grow - in faith, in knowledge, in understanding - until I became the person I am today.

To Lisa Deyo, who read my first works in their earliest stages, and had the insight and courage to tell me what she really thought. Your candid suggestions and insights have helped me immeasurably.

Sherrie

Chapter 1

Tracy Jones Tomlinson stepped up to the front porch at her parents' house and turned to see if Theodora, Titus and Timothy had caught up to her. She was just ready to yell at them to quit fighting and hurry up when she heard voices.

"Did Tracy and Trevor say anything about being late, Mom?" she heard Rachael asking, probably from the kitchen. "The pork tenderloin's going to dry out if they don't get here soon."

Her mother responded. "I told you to use Tracy's recipe – you know, the one that came from Trevor's mother. It always comes out of the oven so melt-in-your-mouth tender when it's simmered in that heavenly gravy she makes."

"This is the recipe I use at The Painted Lady," Michelle said. "It always turns out perfectly. Everybody loves it."

"Well, Tracy didn't say anything to me, but I know Trevor's schedule has been extremely hectic lately," their mother said. "Every time I've talked to her recently he's been off on one errand of mercy or another. Such a dear man."

Tracy froze. She'd been keeping Trevor's secret and playing the part of the perfect pastor's wife for over two years. She was sick of it; tired of making up stories about where he was, covering for him at church, and having to pretend that they had the proverbial marriage made in heaven.

"I hope the church up in Blooming realizes how fortunate they are to have Trevor," their father added in a loud voice. "Trevor works night and day for that church. I'm sure the parishioners give them what they can afford, and of course they have the parsonage, but a man as hard-working and talented as Trevor could be making ten times as much money in the private sector."

She peeked around the corner just in time to see Rachael

and Michelle giving each other the look. Not one family gathering could pass without the traditional *Isn't Trevor Tomlinson wonderful?* speech being delivered by their father, their mother, or both. She risked another quick glance. Mac and Jake were probably down in the basement playing with the kids – at least they didn't have to be subjected to their dad's well-practiced oration.

"That Trevor has such a heart for shut-ins," their mother added. "He visits each one in the Blooming area at least once a week, besides his regular visits to the nursing homes and the hospitals in Austin and Red Oak."

"He's been up to Rochester to visit folks at the Mayo Clinic at least twice this month," their father added. "You just don't find men like him in the world very often anymore."

"I know I've said it a hundred times if I've said it once, but Tracy is so blessed to be married to a man like Trevor," their mother said.

Her sisters exchanged another look. Yeah. Well, for once, it appeared her sisters were right.

She heard the kids behind her and took her cue. "Hello! Sorry to keep you waiting." She held the screen door open while Theodora, Titus, and Timothy entered the kitchen single file, their mouths shut, their faces angelic looking.

Michelle wiped her hands on her apron. "Hi, Teddy! Wow. Did you do something different with your hair? I love the way it sweeps around in back."

Theodora beamed silently as her aunt spun her around to get the full effect of her new hairstyle, then turned and threw her arms around Michelle. "Thanks, Aunt Michelle. Mom still refuses to call me Teddy. And, she hates my new haircut."

Michelle returned "Teddy's" hug and smiled fondly at the boys. "How ya doin', Ty? Hi, Timothy. Nate and Josh are downstairs playing with Ian and baby Sarah if you want to go tell them dinner is ready."

"If everyone could please have a seat," Rachael said, looking impatient.

"Nate and Josh are here? All right!" Timothy crowed.

Even Titus' face lit up for a second. Nate and Josh, Jake's children from a previous marriage, lived three hours away, in Cedar Rapids, Iowa with their mother, and spent every other weekend with Michelle and Jake.

Their mother went to the door and looked out. "Did Trevor have trouble finding a place to park?"

"He's not here," Tracy told her with feigned surprise. "I'm sorry. I thought I told you he wouldn't be able to make it."

"I'm sure you didn't, dear."

Her mind went blank. Panic clutched at her side. What was wrong with her tonight? She was a master at keeping a straight face when she was trapped in a half-truth and had to find the right words to cover her tracks. She'd been practicing since she was what – eight or nine? She knew hundreds of ways to bend words, to get out of a jam without actually lying. Sadly, the web of deceit she and Trevor had woven since he'd asked her for a divorce had stretched even her reserves.

"Um..." She had already nursed the counseling-a-hurting-parishioner angle to death, and given the excuse about Trevor having to visit a very ill member of the congregation too many times over the last few weeks for it to be plausible. Their church wasn't big enough to warrant such never-ending pain and suffering among its members. Besides, the children were still within earshot. Whatever she said now would have to jive with what she had told them earlier.

"I'm sure I told you about the conference, Mom." She kept her tone light. "He's been gone all week. He did call the other night though, and he told me to give Ian a big birthday hug. Is he downstairs with his daddy?" Tracy was halfway across the spacious kitchen by the time she finished speaking and around the corner before her mother could formulate the words to disagree with her again.

"Conference? Something to do with the church?" She heard her dad ask.

"I have no idea," she heard her mother say.

Tracy gripped the handrail at the top of the stairs and stood concealed from the sight of the others. She could hear Jake's melodious voice, Mac's deep, rumbling laughter, and Timothy's high-pitched squeal of excitement mingling with the noisy clatter of the other children's voices.

It wasn't really lying, she tried to convince herself. Keeping your troubles to yourself was just what the Joneses did. Problems, personal flaws, shortcomings, and weaknesses of the flesh were squelched - squashed if necessary – and made to disappear long before they ever became public knowledge. These people lived victorious Christian lives even if it killed them.

Unless you were taken with a serious disease, of course. No one asked to be sick. There was no shame in sharing your woes when one of you was ill. She certainly didn't wish Trevor any harm, but him being sick would have been easier to explain than what was really going on.

She herself was feeling ill just imagining what people would say if they knew their perfect pastor / son-in-law / husband of the year was gay.

"Watch out for baby Sarah!" Jake's voice startled her when it suddenly resounded over the enthusiastic din. "She's not quite as big as you are, Timothy."

Tracy stepped to the bottom of the stairs. "Hello, everyone! Happy birthday, Ian." She knelt down and scooped her little nephew up in her arms. "Hi, sweetie." She had barely managed to kiss his chubby cheek when, in his eagerness to rejoin the bigger children, he squirmed out of her arms and slid the remaining distance down her legs to the floor.

"Wow. He's so strong," she said, shocked.

"He likes to move." Mac raised one eyebrow. "The only time he sits still is at night when Rachael reads him bedtime stories."

"Sarah sure has grown." Tracy nodded at Michelle's husband, Jake, who was sprawled at one end of the sofa, his long legs outstretched and his arms hooked behind his neck.

Jake smiled down at his only daughter. She lay on her stomach on the floor in the center of a rainbow-colored afghan Rae had crocheted for her. "She's our little snuggle bear."

Tracy felt a flash of envy. Her babies were all growing up so fast. Timothy still liked to climb into bed with her in the morning for a little snuggle, but it wouldn't be long before he'd be just as bad as Theodora, who acted as though she loathed her much of the time, and Titus, who stayed as far away from her as he possibly could when given the choice.

She sighed. Neither Jake nor Mac asked where Trevor was, assuming incorrectly that he was upstairs with the other adults. Tracy slumped down into her father's old recliner and curled her legs up underneath her. "I thought Luke and his mother were coming today."

"Rachael had a last minute call from a client from the Cities. Today was the only time her husband could come to see the house she's interested in. Luke volunteered to take the appointment. Uncle Luke and Grandma Zimmerman are going to come celebrate your birthday tomorrow night at our house, aren't they, Ian, old boy?"

Mac reached down and scooped the birthday boy off the floor just as he was about to jump into the middle of the Candy Land game board the older children were concentrating on. Mac whistled. "Close call."

Luke Zimmerman, who was Rae's partner in the real estate office she'd opened four years earlier, and his mother, a sweet, matronly woman with the complete antithesis of their own mother's personality, had become adopted uncle and grandma to Rae and Mac's baby, Ian, during the period Rae had been estranged from the Jones family.

Tracy's stomach churned, remembering the shock they'd all experienced when they'd learned of Ian's illegitimate conception. The whole fiasco Rae had gone through with Mac and Luke would pale in comparison to the bombshell Trevor was about to drop.

She resisted the urge to cry - again. No matter how

screwed up Rae and Mac's beginnings had been, Ian was a true gift from God. Much as she'd tried, Tracy could not see how any good could possibly come from Trevor's admission. Shame, embarrassment, and grief – yes. Total, utter humiliation – definitely. Devastation not only in terms of her life but the fragile development of her three innocent children – most certainly. But joy? No one could convince her that anything positive could come from Trevor's announcement that he was leaving her for someone else, especially when that someone else was a man.

"Supper's ready!" Rae yelled down the stairs. "Come and sit up to the table before it gets cold!"

Tracy stood and stepped back to let the children go ahead of her. For the first time, she felt a flash of compassion for Rae. Being the oldest – the trailblazer – probably hadn't been an easy role to play. But then, Rachael was the most logical, articulate, and gutsy of the three of them. It was almost as though she'd been chosen for the part.

Things that Rachael had argued herself blue in the face over, she and Michelle had done to little more than a raised eyebrow.

Sweet, obedient, middle child, Michelle had never had Rae's rebellious nature. Michelle had been so easy-going and even-tempered, and their parents, so busy arguing with Rae and gushing over her, that poor Michelle had practically gotten lost in the shuffle.

It hadn't taken Tracy long to realize, after watching Rae constantly butting heads with their parents, that the key to peaceful coexistence in the Jones household was to keep your mouth shut and toe the line. She'd had just as much of a wild streak as her older sister, but unlike Rae, she'd never had the urge to flaunt it.

Tracy's philosophy had always been *what your parents don't know won't hurt them.* She'd basically done whatever she'd pleased when she was in high school. She'd just made sure her parents were none the wiser. To the best of her knowledge, even Rae and Michelle didn't have a clue to most of the things she'd gotten by with.

She thought back on some of the escapades she'd participated in when she was younger - things she'd never admit to in front of her children. She'd been only a few months older than Theodora when she'd sneaked off to a concert to hear Rita Coolidge sing "Fever". Her parents thought she'd been at youth retreat at Bible camp.

She shuddered to think that Theodora was fast approaching the same tender age she'd been when she'd gone on her first date with Trevor. Her parents had been so thrilled that she was dating a "nice boy" from their church that they hadn't seemed to care that she was only fifteen to Trevor's world-wise eighteen years. She and Trevor had had sex for the first time when she was barely sixteen. If only she'd known then what she knew now.

She put her mother of three / pastor's wife persona back on and trudged up the stairs.

"We saved you a seat right beside Mom, Tracy," Rae said as she rounded the top of the stairs.

Tracy glared at her sister. Darn conniving Rae, she thought, taking note of her sister's spot at the opposite end of the table.

Mr. Jones cleared his throat. "Let's bow our heads for a word of prayer."

Tracy kept her head bowed and listened as her father proceeded to give thanks for the meal. She'd spent her whole life perfecting the art of camouflaging not only her actions, but her true feelings. As a pastor's wife, she'd become a pro at putting on a brave face for the world – more importantly, for her children. She'd had to. She would not let Trevor Tomlinson cloud her babies' lives with the knowledge that he had, quote, *an inborn preference for male companionship.*

"Amen."

Her mother passed her a bowl of mashed potatoes. "So tell me about Trevor's conference, Tracy. Was it something the church recommended he attend?"

Tracy took a deep breath. "No, just a topic Trevor was interested in. It's sponsored by a Christian organization in California. He took some vacation time so he could go."

Her father cleared his throat. “What denomination is this group with then?”

“I have no idea, Dad. I didn’t ask.”

“There are some pretty radical religious groups out in California. I’m sure Trevor knows better than to get mixed up in anything the folks at Fellowship wouldn’t approve of.”

Her shoulders tensed. What was it that gave her father such an uncanny sense of knowing when something was amiss? “You know Trevor as well as I do, Dad. The man doesn’t do anything that he hasn’t thought out carefully and thoroughly researched.” There, she had dodged the issue without actually lying. Well, maybe she had. She knew good and well that the conference he was attending was sponsored by a Christian gay rights organization. Trevor was pursuing his supposed calling to minister to gays and lesbians within the Christian community.

“Tracy, dear. Your father asked you a question.” Her mother’s voice penetrated her stupor like a knife.

Question?

Her mother reached over her plate and put her hand on her forehead. “Is something wrong? Your cheeks are all flushed. Are you coming down with something? It feels like you might have a fever.”

They were all staring at her now, from little Ian on up.

Her head started to spin, the room, too. Lights were flashing and Rita Coolidge’s husky alto voice was singing.

Don't cry out loud
Just keep it inside, learn how to hide your feelings
Fly high and proud
And if you should fall, remember you almost had it all.

“Sorry. I’m not feeling too well all of a sudden. Please excuse me,” she mumbled. She touched her napkin to her lips, pushed back her chair, and fled the room, as completely and utterly ashamed as if they’d been able to read her mind.

“Do you think one of us should go after her and see if

she's all right?" Mac looked at Rae, then her mother.

"I'll go," Michelle spoke up quickly. She didn't know what was wrong with Tracy but she felt certain that whatever it was, their mother – most likely Rae, too - might make it worse. Her eyes locked with Jake's for a second while she slid her chair away from the table. Aside from some occasional good-natured grumbling, Tracy never got upset - at least not in front of the family. She couldn't imagine what was wrong.

"Please don't wait on us. The food will get cold," Michelle insisted to the family's stunned silence. One did not get upset at a Jones family gathering. There was no reason one could possibly have to get upset. All was good and well; everything was always fine in the Jones family. (*And you'd better remember it if you know what's good for you.*) Their father's words rang in her ears as she headed up the stairs.

The door to the half bath her parents had added the year after Michelle went off to college was open. She turned to Tracy's old bedroom and rapped lightly on the door.

"Who is it?"

"Michelle." She held her breath during the brief silence that followed.

"Come in."

She opened the door slowly and smiled at Tracy.

Her sister pulled her legs up to her chest and leaned back against the headboard of a canopied bed her parents had brought home from a garage sale when they were girls.

"What's wrong? We were worried about you."

"I'm fine," Tracy said, looking anything but fine. "I'm feeling a little better already. I'm sure it's nothing serious."

"Maybe you're lonesome for Trevor. Has he been gone all week?"

"This week and part of last." Tracy's eyes narrowed and glinted with what looked like unaccustomed hostility. "You're lucky Jake doesn't have to travel too often anymore."

"Yes." Michelle hadn't been in Tracy's room for years.

A riotous field of blue, purple, and yellow paper daisies clung stubbornly to the sloped ceilings and walls of the old bedroom, a vivid reminder of days long past.

She looked back in Tracy's direction and caught her sister's eyes following hers.

"I suppose my choice of wallpaper offends your decorator's sensibilities," Tracy said.

"There's no accounting for some people's tastes," Michelle teased.

"This wallpaper was the rage back in the '80s! And who are you to talk anyway? You had lime green love beads in your room when you were in high school."

Michelle rolled her eyes. "Don't remind me."

"I've been after Mom to redo one or the other of our rooms so she'd have a decent guest room when company comes."

"You and me both. I'd do it as a designer, I'd do it as a daughter, I'd do it for free if she'd just give me the go ahead. She told me that the only people who stay overnight here are your kids and an occasional missionary who's speaking at their church. And according to her, neither of them cares what the room looks like as long as they have a comfortable bed to sleep in."

Tracy rolled her eyes. "Yes. We pastor's families and missionaries are so busy thinking about heavenly things that we pay no attention whatsoever to how people's homes are decorated."

Michelle smiled. "That certainly explains why your home is so lovely."

"What's sad is that the people at church feel the same way as mom. The only reason the parsonage looks the way it does is because I took the initiative to paint or repaper all the walls and sew new drapes for the windows. The church would have left it the way it was for another two or three decades."

"It was pretty awful when you first moved in."

Tracy smiled. "Thanks for helping me pick everything out. I didn't mind doing the installation but I wouldn't have known where to start when it came to coordinating designs and colors to match our hodgepodge of furniture. I know it wasn't fun having to scour bargain basements and remnant shops to find things that were in my budget."

"It was fun! We made a good team. Remember that mismatched paint we got at Sherwin Williams?"

"All thirty gallons of it - for a mere dollar a gallon. I can also remember you glopping a little from this gallon and a little from that gallon in a pail until you had the perfect shade."

Michelle giggled. "You did a great job using it all to its best advantage. You really have a talent for painting and papering. It must be the Jones perfectionist gene."

"That gene is probably the one and only thing all three of us sisters have in common." Tracy sighed.

"I think you're right. I try not to drive my subcontractors crazy with my high expectations but it's difficult. I'd give anything to have someone like you to contract jobs out to, Tracy. You've got such a good eye for detail." Michelle waved her arm around the room. "Look at these walls! The pattern match is perfect, the seams are indistinguishable, and the design is level – and this house is as crooked as can be. This stuff has been here for more than twenty years and it looks as smooth and flawless as the day you put it up."

"Now you sound like Mom. *Why should I replace it when it still looks brand new?"* Tracy mimicked.

They both laughed. "Well, call me if you ever decide to go into business, Tracy. You know me, I've got a million good ideas but I hate installation work. Hey - you could call yourself *The Handy Woman.*"

"Sure." Tracy giggled. "You know, I'm really starved all of the sudden."

"What are we waiting for then? Let's go eat."

Chapter 2

Tracy inhaled a breath of fresh, almost-autumn air and pulled her jacket more tightly around her neck. It had been uncomfortably hot and sultry for the last few days, but tonight the sky was clear, the moon full, and the air crisp. The remainder of Ian's birthday party had gone smoothly, still she was glad the night had come to an end. There were times she wished her family was one to discuss personal concerns, but tonight she was relieved that they hadn't continued to ply her with questions about Trevor's absence - or her mood.

It had helped simply to talk with Michelle even though their conversation had centered on the mundane and not the events that lay heavy on her heart. It was possible that at some point she might even be able to confide in Michelle. No one had ever talked about it openly, but Tracy felt sure that Michelle's one time beau, now friend, Dennis, who had driven out from Colorado to do her wedding flowers, was gay. At any rate, Tracy wasn't ready to share the anguish she felt over Trevor's betrayal. Not yet. Not with any of them.

The pungent scents of cedar trees and roses wafted east on the wind from her mother's garden. Deep in thought one moment, she stopped abruptly the next, turned her back to the wind, and stretched out her hand. "Please stop dawdling, Timothy. It's getting late and we've got church tomorrow."

"I miss Daddy."

"I know you do, honey."

"When *will* Dad be home, Mom?" Titus asked pensively.

"Sometime next week." Trevor had promised her he would be home to spend the long weekend with the kids. It had been their tradition to spend Labor Day at the Minnesota State Fair in St. Paul ever since Trevor had first asked her out. As teenagers, she and Trevor had spent their first date at the Mower County fair riding the roller coaster, playing ring toss, and gorging on cotton candy and Tom Thumb donuts dredged in sugar. She sighed. Until Trevor had turned traitor, the State Fair had been the yearly catalyst for the renewal of their love and commitment towards one another.

It was still hard for her to understand the transformation that had occurred in their relationship since Trevor's admission that he felt gay tendencies three years earlier, harder yet to fathom why he had sought her out in the first place if he was not interested in women.

"Getting married at a young age is a fairly common reaction to the realization that you have same sex desires, especially among men who have been raised in very conservative homes," Trevor had tried to explain when she'd questioned him. "You know how we were raised, Tracy. Differences were not tolerated. Nothing in my experience had prepared me to deal with my feelings. The first and only thing I could think to do was to find a woman to make love to, to prove once and for all that I was a man, capable of performing physically with someone of the opposite sex. It was my way of denying reality, pure and simple."

"You were so beautiful," he'd added when he saw the hurt look in her eyes, "so innocent. It was easy to fall in love with you."

Yeah, right. Probably because she'd looked like a boy. Three kids later and she still had practically zilch for boobs.

She dug in her purse for the car keys until she finally located the evasive ring. Oh, to have those easy, carefree days back again. To revel in the delightful knowledge that another human being loved you more than anything in the world. To laugh crazily, spin dizzily, and giggle yourself silly on the Tilt-a-Whirl or the Paratrooper until your insides were so scrambled that all you could do is look up and laugh.

She breathed a sigh of renewed disappointment. The fair wouldn't be the same without Trevor. She didn't understand how he could not realize it. The children had been looking forward to their yearly outing for weeks. But that hadn't seemed to matter when Kurt, Trevor's *friend*, asked him to lead a round table discussion at the conference when one of the speakers canceled at the last minute. Trevor had been so thrilled with the opportunity to make a name for himself among the participants at the conference that he hadn't thought one second about how disappointed the children would be that he wouldn't be back in time to attend the fair.

"Your dad said he'd talk to us again on Tuesday after school. Maybe he'll know what his plans are then. Did you get all your homework done so we can spend all day Monday at the fair, Titus?"

"Yeah."

"He hardly had any homework," Theodora pointed out. "His teacher is nice."

"She is not," Titus protested.

"I know both Mrs. Crabtree and Mrs. Hinklebaum personally and they're excellent teachers. Homework is a fact of life. You may as well accept it because it's not going to go away."

Titus kicked a rock and it scuttled along in front of them. "At least if Dad were here he could help me with my math."

"And take us to the fair," Theodora lamented.

"I'd be happy to help you with your math, honey."

"You're rotten at math, Mom," Theodora said in a blunt tone.

"Thank you, Theodora. It's too bad your memory isn't so clear when it comes to remembering what the Bible says about honoring your mother." She regretted the words the instant they were out of her mouth.

A gust of wind whooshed past them with a swirl of leaves and dirt as they reached their car.

"Why don't we just move to California so Dad doesn't have to be gone all the time?" Titus demanded out of the blue.

"California?" Theodora snorted. "Like I'm going to leave all my friends and move half way across the country."

Titus kicked the rear tire of the car. "At least you'd be rid of Mrs. Hinklebaum."

"Titus..." Tracy said helplessly. *Had she been right? Did Titus know more than he was letting on?*

"I don't want to move to California!" Timothy started to cry as he climbed in the back seat of the battered old Plymouth station wagon. "I want to go live with Josh and Nate at Aunt Michelle and Uncle Jake's house. They have a river by their house and we're going to build a raft and go swimming."

"Don't cry, Timothy. You're just tired. We're not going to move to California."

Titus slammed the car door closed behind them. "Josh and Nate don't live with their dad anyway. They live with their mom in Cedar Rapids. They only visit every other weekend. Their parents are divorced."

"I don't like anybody to be divorced." Timothy sobbed. "I want to see Josh and Nate all the time."

Tracy twisted around in her seat. "Honey, please don't cry. Just be glad you got to see Josh and Nate today. Think of all the fun you had playing hide and go seek with them!"

"But I miss them," Timothy cried.

She struggled to keep her own tears in check even as she consoled him. "You're going to be so busy with school that you won't have time to miss them, sweetheart. You'll make all kinds of new friends in kindergarten."

"A lot of good that will do if we have to move to California."

"Theodora Hope Tomlinson! Stop it right now! I won't have you upsetting your brother. We are not moving to California!"

Tracy turned the key and started the engine with a roar. The very thought of the children being subjected to Trevor's new lifestyle firsthand, say nothing about having to witness it on an ongoing basis herself, made her ill.

There was no way she was ever going to move to California. Of that much at least she was sure. What else the future held was anybody's guess, but of that much she was absolutely, positively confident.

Tracy steered the station wagon onto Highway 218 and focused on the faded center line of the old payment. Timothy's whimpering faded to a whisper. He'd be sound asleep by the time they reached Blooming Prairie. Trevor would carry him right to his bed and she would undress him and slip him into his pajamas without awaking him. Poor little thing. He was so tired.

The headlights of an oncoming car scanned their vehicle as they turned to head south from a gravel side road. A full minute passed before Tracy realized what was wrong with the familiar scene she'd painted: Trevor was gone. Timothy was too heavy for her to lift by herself. She would have to wake him up when they reached home. He would be cranky and upset. Hell, she would be cranky and upset. Damn Trevor. Damn stinking homosexuality. *Why did it have to touch her life? Why them?* Her children had done nothing to deserve having to grow up without the daily presence of a father. Nothing at all. Tracy clutched the steering wheel and drove north, wishing more than anything that she had some chocolate.

They were almost home when Tracy felt a familiar sensation. *Well, that explains why I've been so touchy all day.* She had stopped taking the pill over two years ago after Trevor had told her he couldn't continue to use her purely for his physical gratification when his heart wasn't in was she had thought to be lovemaking. Although it was nice not to have to take the drug any longer, she missed knowing exactly when her monthly blessing was due almost as much as she missed sex.

The flood lights illuminating the local convenience store and gas station came into view just moments later. "I'm going to run inside the Budget Mart for a few things," she whispered to Theodora, who was sitting beside her in the front seat. "Please stay in the car with the boys. I don't want to wake Timothy."

She turned into the parking lot and narrowly missed a Ryder truck that was jutting out into the parking lot at a precarious angle. "Idiot driver," she mumbled under her breath. She parked and turned to Theodora. "I'll be back in a second."

She climbed out of the car, keeping her legs clenched as

tightly as her movements would allow and tried to minimize her usual stride as she quietly closed the car door and walked towards the store.

Of all the predicaments. She hated purchasing feminine supplies at local stores and normally bought them in Owatonna, where few people knew her, after she'd dropped off the kids at school. Buying sanitary pads or tampons in Blooming Prairie was tantamount to putting up a billboard along Highway 218 announcing what time of the month it was.

She scanned the isles of the mini mart through the glass store front before she opened the door. A tall, blond-haired gentleman with a deep tan and broad shoulders stood at the end of the isle to the left just inside the door scanning the cold drinks in the refrigerator case. He was not from Blooming Prairie and most probably was the one who didn't know how to park a truck. The clerk on duty was Mrs. Mosier's oldest daughter, Clarice, a young woman Tracy knew only by name. At least there was no one she knew well in the store, and more particularly, no one from their church. It wouldn't do to have anyone from their congregation presented with such graphic evidence that she was a woman and not just *the pastor's wife,* now, would it?

The stranger looked up over the tops of the display racks and met her eyes when the bell announced her entry into the store. She returned his stare for a moment and tried not to be obvious about the fact that she was taken with his good looks before averting her glance and heading for the personal isle.

What was she thinking? She was the pastor's wife, for goodness sake. People were always gushing about Trevor and she being the perfect couple, about how wonderful and strong and loving their marriage was. She could hardly be going around ogling other men just because their eyes were the color of a sun-drenched sky, their hair as straight and soft and blond as corn-silk, their legs, amazingly well shaped and incredibly suntanned...

Her cheeks flamed. *Get a grip.* She'd always been horny – and out of sorts - the day or two before her period started.

That was all it was.

She looked again - this time at the curve of his backside - and felt a zing of guilt. She forced herself focus on the task at hand. She could have looked at him all day long.

The man moved across the end of the isle where she was standing. A fleeting image of the wispy blond curls that covered his legs from his Nike's to his thighs replayed itself in her mind's eye as she stooped to pluck an embarrassingly large bag of sanitary napkins from the shelf. She clutched the plastic swathed bale to her chest with one hand and reached for a box of tampons with the other.

She was half way to the counter when the craving for chocolate hit her with a passion so intense she was powerless to resist. She turned to the right and found her way to the next isle over. Milky Way, a Dove Bar, or her usual M&Ms? Maybe one of each. She could have devoured a week's supply in minutes. Should she buy a treat for each of the children, or smuggle something just for herself into the house to relish after they'd fallen asleep? The latter would be the cheaper course, but the question was, could she wait that long for a taste?

Her concentration was so intense she that she was oblivious to everything in the world but the package of M&Ms she'd so carefully honed in on.

She heard a burst of laughter a mere second before she felt a hand gliding unsuspectingly against hers. The stranger's fingers lingered comfortably on hers as he stopped their near collision in mid course.

"Sorry." He chuckled. "I should have seen that one coming."

"No, really. Excuse me."

"I think you dropped something."

"Oh." Her cheeks burned bright when she realized what he was about to do.

"Here. Let me."

"No," she insisted. "I'll get..."

Their heads clunked resoundingly as they each leaned forward to retrieve the embarrassing bundle.

"Ouch," he scowled down at her, grasping his head with one hand and gently restraining her with the other.

"Oh, I'm so sorry!" she stammered.

"That's what I get for trying to be a gentleman."

"Oh, no, don't think that. It was nice of you..."

"Forget it."

They both looked at the floor. The bundle still rested on the linoleum between them. Neither dared move.

"Should I?" he ventured.

"No, I'll..."

He laughed again.

"Be my guest." He waved with a flourish and stroked his head gingerly.

"I'm really sorry." She couldn't help but stare into his eyes for a moment. They were the blue of warm summer days, as fathomless as a pool of crystal blue water shimmering in the sunshine. Pastor's wife or not, she could not help being mesmerized by those eyes.

"No problem."

"Mommy," Timothy tugged on her sleeve, startling her.

She blushed. She was not feeling much like a mommy at that particular moment. She glanced at the stranger to make sure he wasn't about to make any sudden movements before she knelt down to greet her youngest son. "Timothy! How did you get in here? I thought you were asleep."

"I woked up." His voice belied his crankiness.

The stranger looked on with amusement.

Timothy's mouth opened and closed in a yawn as dainty as any cat's. "Mommy, what does *jerking off* mean? Titus said a boy at school went to the bathroom ten times in one day and stayed in there so long that everyone thought he must be jerking off."

Oh, my Lord, she thought. *What next?* She glanced over her shoulder to make sure no one but the stranger had heard his question. Clarice was occupied at the far end of the store. No other customers had entered. Thank God for small blessings. But Timothy was still looking at her expectantly. She opened her mouth but no words came out. She was too mortified to formulate a response. What must this man think? Her mind flitted from one possible way to inflict pain on Titus after another. She couldn't turn her back on him for one minute.

Laughter rumbled from deep in the stranger's chest. "Allow me?" he said to Tracy's open mouthed expression of dismay. She supposed she shouldn't have trusted him to... but for some reason, she instinctively knew that she could. She nodded silently.

"How old are you, Timothy?"

Timothy stared up at the stranger in awe. "Five. I'm in kinkergarten."

Tracy put her hand over her eyes and shook her head. He never could get the word right. Just her luck that he'd had no trouble pronouncing *jerking off* correctly.

"I bet there are some cute girls in your class."

"Girls are yucky."

"I see." The stranger crouched down beside her son and rocked back on his heels.

Her son looked puzzled. "Why? Do girls *jerk off*, too?"

"Not exactly."

"Well, what is it then?" Timothy was getting irritated.

Tracy cringed. She had a fleeting image of Timothy standing at the back door of the church asking the head of the deacon board if he *jerked off*. She felt compelled to interject a word or two. "It's something people don't talk about except in private, honey. Titus shouldn't have..."

"I just wanna know!" He pouted. Timothy hated being the baby. He didn't want to be left out of anything, especially if it involved his older brother.

The stranger leaned back. "Well, you see, it has to do with liking girls and dreaming that they'll like you back. Stuff you'd probably think was pretty yucky since you don't like girls much right now."

"It sounds gross."

"I thought that's what you'd think. You'll feel differently about it later on."

"Do you ever do it?" Timothy asked with such sweet,

curious innocence that even his mother had to smile.

Now it was the stranger's turn to blush. "Sure. Sometimes," he answered just as seriously. He looked up and met Tracy's eyes over the top of Timothy's head.

She was probably ten shades of red. She nodded her thanks and affirmed his efforts with a shy smile. He had done well. *Perhaps he had children of his own*, she thought, feeling a certain tenderness towards him that was incongruent with the fact that she didn't even know his name.

Timothy rubbed his eyes with his fists. "Maybe I'll do it someday, too. When I'm big."

"Sure you will. But I wouldn't worry about it yet, okay, big fella?" The stranger roughed Timothy's shoulders up a little in a gesture that overtly made Timothy feel like one of the boys.

"Can I go back out to the car, Mom?"

"Sure, honey. I'll be out in a minute."

The stranger held out his hand. "Clay."

She gave him hers. "Tracy."

"Nice to meet you, Tracy." His blue eyes focused on hers.

It was a strange sort of intimacy they shared in that moment. "Thank you for being so gentle with him. I might have made him feel bad... I didn't know what to say. I can get kind of blustery with the kids sometimes. Especially when I'm tired."

"How many do you have?" He raised one eyebrow.

"Three."

Sounds like a handful."

"They can be at times."

"Their father?"

Tracy glanced around the store with a furtive sweep of her eyes. She wanted to confide in someone so badly. This Clay didn't know her from Adam. In some ways that was comforting. Dare she trust him?

Clay Alexander cleared his throat. What was he

thinking? It didn't matter what, who, or where their father was. It was no concern of his whether the woman was divorced or not. He was in no position to get involved with a mother of three children he'd met at a convenience store in the middle of nowhere. It was too bad circumstances weren't different. There was something about her...

"Their father's just left me for someone else." She crinkled up her nose and pursed her lips in a grimace so unaffected he wanted to take her in his arms right then and there. "No one knows yet," she whispered, blinking back tears. "Not even the children. It's a small town." She shrugged.

"I'm sorry," he stammered. He could feel his eyes shining with a protective fire as he skimmed her boyish figure, the wispy blond red curls framing her delicate features, the freckles sprinkled here and there across her nose, the box of tampons clutched to her chest in an impossible effort to camouflage the obvious. She was very vulnerable. The last thing she needed was a lout like him to kick her in the stomach when she was down.

"Well, it was nice bumping into you," he said with a finality they both recognized.

"Thanks for taking the time to talk to Timothy."

"No problem."

The stranger nodded, hurried to the counter to pay for his purchases. He turned just before he exited the store. "Enjoy your M&Ms."

"You, too."

Tracy hung back for a moment, not wanting to prolong their encounter now that the man had dismissed her. She was grateful for his intervention, yet she felt a sense of loss. Is this what their lives would be like now that she and her children had joined the ranks of the broken family? Their needs met in piecemeal fashion here and there by one stranger after another? Tracy looked down at her M&Ms through teary eyes, certain she would find no comfort there or anywhere.

Chapter 3

"Good morning, Mrs. Tomlinson. How are you today?"

Tracy forced a smile and slipped through the front door of the Blooming Prairie Fellowship Church.

"Top of the morning to you, Mrs. Tomlinson. That's sure a pretty dress you're wearing." Evelyn Peterson spoke with a throaty, eighty year old voice as she hobbled along with the aid of a cane. "Those autumn colors really bring out the highlights in your hair."

Tracy bent to take the woman's hand. "Thank you, Evelyn."

"Way too hot out there to feel like fall today, isn't it, Mrs. Tomlinson?"

"Any idea when Pastor will be back, Mrs. Tomlinson?"

Mrs. Tomlinson, Mrs. Tomlinson, Mrs. Tomlinson! Why couldn't one blessed person call her Tracy? She knew and called them each by their first names. What was it about being the pastor's wife that elevated her above the rest in their minds? She just wanted to be treated like they treated each other.

"I bet I know someone who'll be awfully happy to see Pastor when he gets home," Patsy Crokkenbacker said slyly.

Tracy mustered another smile and turned before the other woman could see the hot red blush staining her cheeks. She didn't want their respect! She didn't deserve it! Mrs. Tomlinson, the reverend's wife, wouldn't have lain in bed last night thinking about a certain handsome man's blue eyes. The Mrs. Tomlinson these people adored wouldn't have even realized that Clay's hand had touched hers, say nothing about fantasizing about it like she had. Mrs. Tomlinson, the pastor's wife, wouldn't have even noticed the look of his blond, hair-covered legs doubled up under him, lean with pure muscle, as he'd squatted down to talk to Timothy.

"Mrs. Tomlinson, will Pastor be doing communion next Sunday since he's not going to be here today?" one of the woman from the altar guild asked.

"I assume so, Josie. When he left, he wasn't planning to be gone so long, so we didn't discuss it."

"Thank you, Mrs. Tomlinson." Josie moved away.

Well she wouldn't be Mrs. Tomlinson for long. She'd be Tracy Jones again soon enough. And she hoped - how she hoped - that she might have a real friend then. Someone to confide in. Someone who would see her for herself, instead of an extension of Trevor. Someone who would speak the brittle truth instead of the rosy, glossed-over platitudes that people so often reserved for the pastor and his wife.

"Mrs. Tomlinson, would you mind telling Pastor that I'd be happy to sing a solo next week during communion – if he'd like me to."

"Sure, Susie. I'll mention it as soon as he gets home."

Her cheek muscles were starting to ache, but she managed another smile. The people at church were always friendly, but never friends. She and Trevor were well liked and accepted as the leaders of the church, but no one would have dreamed of dousing a good time by inviting them to a social gathering. She could almost imagine the conversations: *The Tomlinsons are nice folks, but having Pastor at the party would put, well, a damper on things...*

"Hi, Karen! How are you today? Did your kids have a good first week at school?" she asked a woman about her age, desperate for some sort of personal interaction.

"Fine. Just fine," Karen said, looking uncomfortable. "The kids are all doing fine, too. We're all fine." She smiled.

Tracy knew that Karen's ten year old son, Jack, had been held back a year, according to Theodora and Titus, because he was too emotionally and academically immature to move on to middle school. She tried to look encouraging, to let Karen know that she could talk to her honestly.

"Well, I'd better go round up the kids before the service starts," Karen said, smiling again.

"Okay," Tracy said, with a fresh realization that the

members of their church simply didn't want Trevor and her to know their personal business. They intentionally kept them on a pedestal, well removed from the actual goings on in their lives. It was as if by shielding them from the facts of any truly meaningful situation or conflict, they could refrain from offending some imaginary Christian sensibility. Sadly, their attempts to appear perfect kept them from revealing the very humanness that made them lovable.

"Mom, do we have to sit up front since Dad's not here?"

She turned to Titus, and wondered if she was guilty of doing the very same thing. She'd played the role of the perfect daughter in her own family, a role created by her parents, who had nurtured such high expectations for Rachael, Michelle, and herself that not one of them had dared openly do anything that wouldn't survive public and religious scrutiny.

"I don't even get why we even had to come," Theodora said. "I mean, if it's okay for Dad to have a vacation..."

"It's not a vacation," Tracy said. "It's a religious conference."

"On the beach. In California," Theodora said.

"There's no reason for us not to be here," Tracy said.

"But Dad..." Titus started to say.

"We don't come to church because of your Dad, we come to worship God." Tracy sighed. Truth be told, she didn't much feel like being here today either. Her heart just wasn't in it. But how could she tell her children that?

It was a sad situation. To look at the people around her, one would think not one of them had any problems. They were all actors, actresses, masters of propagating the charade. No one admitted it when their children did something wrong, no one confessed their trials and heartaches, no one brought their anxieties or concerns past the front door of the church. And for what? For fear of being judged unworthy by the others? How sad when they could have been praying for each other, showing support and concern – loving one another. She was just as bad as the rest of them.

"I can't wait until I'm old enough to go to college," Titus said. "The first thing I'm going to do is to move someplace where no one knows I'm a pastor's kid."

"Maybe you should move to California," Theodora said. "No body around to check up on you – you could skip church every Sunday and no one would ever be the wiser."

"Cool," Titus said, grinning.

"You could like post on Facebook that you just love that song, *How Great is Our God*, or something like that. When people saw the post, they'd be like, 'Hey, he must have heard it at church'. You wouldn't really be lying–."

"It is lying," Tracy said. "When you know the truth, but you don't speak it, it's called a lie of omission." And she was as guilty of it as anyone. She and Trevor's marriage had been held up as the model for countless young couples embarking on the journey of wedded bliss, their family noted as a paragon for exemplary behavior on numerous occasions. And she hadn't said a word. She hadn't thought she was lying at the time, but she had been.

And she had to keep right on doing it. Tempting as it was to let Trevor tell his whole sordid tale, and in doing so, exonerate her, if she was to protect the children from knowing the true reason she and Trevor were ending their marriage, she would have to take the blame that should have been his upon her self. It would be a new experience for her. She'd avoided any pretense of guilt for decades. She had never once gotten caught doing something of serious consequence. When she'd come close, she'd had a million and one excuses up her sleeve designed to cast blame away from herself and on to others. But this time things would have to be different. The only way she could proclaim her rightful innocence in this whole mess was to reveal that Trevor was in love with a man – and she couldn't do that to the children.

"Front row like always, ma'am?" Ricky, their young, skinny-as-a-fence-post usher, glanced furtively at Theodora.

Without waiting for an answer, Ricky proceeded to show them to the front row pew on the left where they sat every

Sunday. "There are plenty of bulletins. You can each have one today."

"Thank you, Ricky."

"Attendance is always down when Pastor Tomlinson is gone." He beamed at Theodora. "No one can preach like Pastor Tomlinson."

Theodora finally gave Ricky a timid smile in return. Only then did he reluctantly move away from the end of their pew and resume his duties in the rear of the sanctuary.

Tracy noted his departure with relief.

"Teddy has a boyfriend," Titus whispered.

"I hate it when people suck up to me just because I'm the pastor's kid," Theodora said sullenly.

"How do you know he's not sucking up because you look so beautiful?" Tracy said. Much as she hated the role at times, she had to admit that there were also perks in being Mrs. Trevor Tomlinson. She'd tried without fail to do her husband right, to live her life in such a way that not even the nit pickiest of their members could find fault with anything she did or said. She'd done her best to earn the respect of the people in their congregation and to make Trevor proud of her. He always had been.

Like it or not, it was who she was - or who she used to be. Her whole persona would have to be restructured once the word came out that she would be reverting back to plain old Tracy Jones.

The organ swelled to a fine crescendo as the choir director made his way to the front of the sanctuary to lead the worship portion of the service. "Let us bow our heads in prayer," he said from the pulpit.

Brooke Adams, a friend of Theodora's, slipped into the pew just as they were closing their eyes. The two girls touched shoulders and smiled before they lowered their heads for the opening invocation.

Tracy lifted her heart to heaven. When Rae went through any kind of a rough spot in her life, she got mad at God and ended up bitter towards everything to do with the church. Conversely, Tracy's faith meant more to her than ever now.

If anything, losing the comfort and security of Trevor's physical love intensified her need for God's love. It was reassuring to Tracy to know that whatever happened, God's faithfulness was a constant in her life.

She looked at the people filling the pews on either side of her. She hoped having God in their hearts meant that they would be supportive when Trevor told them he was leaving. More importantly, she prayed that the children's friends wouldn't scorn them because of their father's actions. Theodora would need the constancy of Brooke's friendship, Titus, the camaraderie, however tenuous, of boys his own age to draw confidence from. Timothy would look to her. Tracy knew she would have to be strong for his sake. He would need her in the days ahead. They would all need her.

"Please turn in your hymnals to page number 384, *Count Your Many Blessings*. Let's stand while we sing."

Tracy stood with the others and listened as the voices around her wove melodious scales in four part harmonies. If there was one thing the folks at Fellowship were good at in the purest sense of the word, it was creating music that was glorifying to God. Slowly, she started to relax as she let the music wash over her.

"Count your many blessings, name them one by one, and it will surprise you what the Lord hath done." It was easy for her to identify the blessings of the past. The future was more uncertain. Would she be able to look back at this day one year from now, two years from now, and count her blessings as clearly?

Timothy sat quietly throughout the service, looking at a book on Noah's Ark from the church library while Mr. Studtveiler delivered his sermon. Titus, Theodora, and her friend Brooke behaved reasonably well. Whether they listened to the oratory or not, they knew what was expected of them. One could not get by with much when sitting in the front pew.

When the altar call was done the choir director announced that Reverend Tomlinson would be back for next Sunday's services. Tracy reached down and took Timothy's hand to try and mask the shudder that raced involuntarily across her shoulders. Poor parishioners, thinking everything would be back to normal by next Sunday, when in reality, everything would be different – every single thing.

She complimented the organist and lingered at the front of the auditorium as long as she could do so without seeming rude when the service was over. It was becoming increasingly hard for her to look people in the eye, knowing what she did.

"I think people are ticked at Dad for being gone so much these last couple of months." Theodora looked at her pensively.

"He's hardly taken a vacation in ten years. He's just using up what's coming to him," Tracy snapped, her worst fears surfacing. There were those who would probably always adore Trevor, and those who would turn on him very quickly once he announced that he was leaving. "I'm sorry, sweetheart."

"Some of the deacons were talking about it. I don't think they saw me standing there," Theodora said.

She rounded up the children as quickly as she could and headed for home. The thought of hiding safely away in the sweet haven of their home was an irresistible lure although she knew only too well that the structure they lived in was owned by the church. She wondered how long she and the children would have to get out once Trevor resigned.

They were in the car facing east, waiting to make a left turn onto Highway 218 when a Ryder rental truck flashed by, heading south. Perhaps she just imagined it, but she thought the driver waved.

*****

Clay shifted back into fourth gear and glanced out the rear view mirror as he left Blooming Prairie behind and headed south towards Iowa. He smiled as he remembered his somewhat comic encounter at the Budget Mart the night before. One had to feel for the woman – three kids and a husband who obviously didn't know a good thing when he saw it.

If things were different... he conjured up a momentary vision of the woman's bright green eyes, her cute freckles and pixie-like features.

But they weren't.

She was obviously embroiled in a sticky situation with her husband; his own life was a mess. Nothing good could come of trouble plus more trouble.

Not that it wasn't high time that he retook control of his life. His father's decision to send him to Iowa to reorganize Maple Valley's faltering woolen mill had not been a suggestion. He could have put up a fight, charmed his way out of his father's latest edict, or just laid low and let the whole thing blow over – tactics he'd used more than once over the years. But to be honest, the idea of escaping the social rounds in the Cities and his mother and father's overbearing intrusions into his life had been damn appealing. Being free of Lauren's clutches definitely held an allure he was loath to deny.

His supposed fiancée had thrown a major hissy fit when he'd broken the news that he was moving to Iowa, adamantly refusing to begin their life as husband and wife in what Lauren liked to refer to as "some God-forsaken hell-hole in the middle of nowhere". Conversely, he'd taken an immediate liking to the small Iowa village he now called home. And since he had no intention of marrying Lauren, her ultimatum hadn't hurt his feelings one little bit.

Lauren was right about the fact that Maple Valley was miles from anywhere that mattered, but he'd stumbled on a gem of a house – a classic arts and crafts design whose masculine, geometric lines and rich oak woodwork fit his tastes to a tee. Maple Valley's citizens seemed friendly and genuine and Elk Creek Woolen Mills wasn't half as shoddily maintained as his father imagined it to be.

His cell phone rang as though on cue, a lightning rod for the trouble he'd been reviewing in his mind.

"What exactly are you trying to prove now?" His

father's voice charged through the phone like a bull breaking free from a fence.

He tried vaguely to think of what it was he had done to offend his father this time. Could be anything. It didn't take much. "You'll have to tell me which vice you're referring to, Dad."

"Renting a Ryder truck? Moving yourself?" His father wasn't even trying to disguise his scorn today. "Good grief, Clay. We own a moving company. And asking the men at the plant to help you unload the truck? Buying them a few beers as thanks? What kind of a precedent does that set?"

"You made it clear that I'm in eminent danger of losing my inheritance. I figured I'd prepare myself, save a few dollars, see how the masses do it, experience life on a limited budget."

He'd also wanted to make good and sure the workers at the woolen mill knew that although he was his father's son, he had a completely different management style than they'd grown accustomed to. But he didn't tell his father that.

"Cut the crap and listen to me for once in your life," his father said, clearly not impressed by Clay's newfound thriftiness.

"It's bad enough that you intend to live in some dilapidated old barn on the main thoroughfare through town. First impressions mean everything, Barclay. You know that. If you act like a pauper, the employees – and the people of Maple Valley - will treat you like one. How you expect to gain their respect—"

"The house is going to be beautiful when it's done. And maybe if the employees at Elk Creek see me living frugally, they'll still respect me when I implement budget cuts and tell them we have to learn to do business more efficiently."

His father sputtered for a second – maybe he was getting through to him on some level. He wouldn't count on it.

"Lauren will never be happy in that house – who would be, with semis roaring by night and day? I told you a month ago that Wilbur's people had found a house that was perfect for you – a secluded acreage on the river, just vacated by a doctor who moved on to a bigger city. He had it custom built only six months ago... it would have been much more suitable than-"

The fact that Lauren had refused to marry him as long as he was living in Iowa was another of the many reasons he was considering making the relocation permanent. Lauren was as concerned about keeping up appearances as always – that's why she'd planned the housewarming party. But he hoped his move might prove to be the catalyst by which Lauren finally accepted the fact that he had no intention of marrying her, no matter how resolute their family's scheme to see them united.

Clay thought back to the day when his troubles had all begun. Well, the most recent set.

His father had first gotten wind of the fact that his only son had *flagrantly snubbed three generations of family tradition* and voted Republican in the last election via an old friend who had overheard Barclay talking at a pub he frequented in downtown Minneapolis. The way they'd carried on, you'd have thought he'd embraced Hinduism or run off to join a cult.

"I've been doing business with Wilbur Putt for two decades," his father railed on. "This Realtor you used, this Jones woman or MacPhearson, or whatever she calls herself, has only been in town for a couple of years, and from what my people tell me, she's done nothing but stir up trouble in the time she's been in town. Her sister – the one you hired to decorate the place - isn't much better from what I hear."

Clay focused on the road and zoned out ninety percent of what his father was saying.

The Republican candidate he'd voted for had been his roommate at Harvard twenty years earlier. And yes, Clay was fully aware of how many millions his father had contributed to the Democratic party over the years. He also hadn't agreed with his friend on every issue, but the man was honest, a true gentleman, and as hardworking as they come. In Clay's opinion, a man's character was a better measure of his worth than his politics, especially when the man was headed to Washington. His father had not been amused. And still wasn't...

"How the hell you can continue to make one erroneous decision after another when you've just seen firsthand the havoc your actions have created is beyond me.

"From the moment you were stupid enough to brag about the fact that you'd voted for a Republican in a place where the media are known to congregate..."

Clay had already tried to defend his actions, to no avail, so what possessed him to take another stab at it was beyond him. "I take my right to express my personal opinion very seriously. I voted for the candidate I believed to be the best man for the job."

"How you can hope to harbor any sort of political aspirations in this town when you don't even have the good sense you were born with-"

"I have no political aspirations. It's you who-"

"Your mother fears she'll be the laughingstock of Summit Avenue," his father said. "Is that what you want?"

"Of course not," Clay said, shifting into a lower gear as he approached Red Oak. He hated causing his mother grief. She'd been so distressed over his actions that she'd taken to her bed for a month and missed two meetings of her bridge club. He could still see her face when she'd heard the news.

"My God." His mother had wailed and wrung her hands disconsolately. "We're invited to John and Betsy's house for dinner next Saturday night. How ever can I face them? They're sure to have heard."

Clay braked, and the truck lurched to a halt at the stop sign on the north end of Austin.

"It's high time you grew up and shouldered some responsibility in this family, Barclay. Your shenanigans may have been cute when you were a young man, but I won't continue to tolerate this blatant disregard for everything your mother and I hold dear," his father thundered over the phone line.

His mind wandered back to his mother. While she had been predictably mortified upon hearing of Barclay's ill-advised faux pas, his father had been his typical, take-charge self.

"The only thing that can save us now is some quick-thinking, and a little swiftly-executed intervention on my part," his father had said, pacing the floor. "If we've any chance of making this incident go away..."

Incident? All I did was help vote a damn good man into office, Clay had thought to himself.

"I've just lost a manager at that woolen mill we own in northern Iowa. The place has been mismanaged for years," his father had railed. "Profits are in a free fall. Production quotas and employee morale have hit an unprecedented low. I've wanted to sell the damn money pit for years but I can't unload it under these conditions without taking a tremendous loss.

"My advisors think it would do you good to get out of the Cities for awhile, keep a low profile until this little aberration is forgotten. By the time you marry Lauren and start your family, all will be redeemed."

Clay eased his foot off the brake pedal and pushed in the clutch. Things had calmed down somewhat after the original hoopla. But even then, Barclay Alexander II had remained adamant about Clay's exile and the fact that he *would* marry Lauren.

Barclay felt a sinking sensation in the pit of his stomach as he listened to his father rage on. If it wasn't for the promise he'd made to his Grandma, he'd have disappeared years ago and made a new life for himself - someplace far, far away, someplace where no one knew he was Barclay Alexander III.

His grandmother's voice echoed in his head. "Your grandfather was as kind a man as there ever was. Why, he made his millions in the first place because he was so generous and caring. I wish your father no ill, but when he's gone and the company passes on to you, I'm counting on you to restore the family's reputation, to run the businesses the way your grandpa would have wanted."

His father's accusatory voice jerked him back to the

present. "The special events committee at the country club has withdrawn its recommendation to let you head up the golf tournament next spring."

"I'm moving to Iowa. I wouldn't have been able to do it anyway."

"If you appeal to them one last time, they may reconsider," his father advised him, his voice less angry and more serious with his concern for propriety. "Your mother and I can't coddle you forever, Barclay. It's high time you learned to stand on your own two feet."

Clay drove over the I-90 overpass and turned left on to the entrance ramp. The truck surged forward as he revved the engine into high gear. He'd always hated the country club.

Chapter 4

Tracy had been home for about two hours when the telephone rang. She'd heated some corn dogs up in the oven and made tomato soup for lunch. It wasn't much as far as traditional Sunday dinners went, but she was determined to watch her pennies while they were at the fair the next day, and reasoned that if she fed the children corn dogs today at the cost of thirty-five cents per serving, she could avoid having to pay four-fifty or five dollars each for pronto pups tomorrow on the midway. Her plan was to pack ham sandwiches on ice in the trunk instead. She'd even baked a cherry pie, the children's favorite, for a treat to eat at the rest stop along I-35 on the way home.

She hated having to pinch pennies but until she and Trevor met with their attorney and worked out some sort of settlement, until she found some sort of a job and a house where she and the kids could afford to live, she didn't want to spend so much as a dime frivolously. The rides at the fair would be expensive enough. She would just have to make it clear to the kids that they couldn't afford both junk food and entertainment.

It was Theodora's turn to dry the dishes after lunch. Timothy had fallen sound asleep on the floor in the family room while the Lion King droned on unsuspectingly in the background. "Do you know where Titus is?" Tracy asked casually as she put away the pot she'd heated the soup in.

"No. Is he in trouble for opening his big mouth in the car last night?"

Tracy was reminded that she needed to find some time alone with Titus to discuss what had happened. Half of her was tempted to say, "Just wait until your father gets home," like she usually did, and let Trevor deal with it when he returned, but then, she could hardly afford to fall into that pattern of handling problems with the kids, now could she?

"Titus is growing up faster than any of us realize. I just don't want him to cut Timothy's childhood short like my older sisters so often did mine by making him feel ashamed to be a baby."

"What did Aunt Michelle and Aunt Rachael do to make you grow up too fast?"

"Well, for starters, Rae used to call me a dumb baby because I liked to play with dolls. I couldn't have been more than six or seven at the time, but she was ten and saw things only from her perspective. Your Grandma made her apologize, but by then the damage was done. At that age I idolized her and believed every word she said. If Rachael thought it was stupid to play with dolls, there was no way I was going to do it."

"Are all little kids that gullible?"

"I don't know. You don't think you were?"

"No. I mean, I probably was, but I didn't have anybody to look up to but you and Dad and I trusted you guys."

Tracy tried not to look too pleased for fear of undoing the unexpected pleasantness that had arisen between them. "So you're glad you're an oldest child and didn't have to worry about older brothers and sisters trying to con you out of your innocent years?" she bantered.

"I always wished I had an older brother with a lot of cute friends who would come and hang out at our house."

Tracy laughed. "Well that doesn't surprise me. I used to wish that, too. Actually, it wasn't half bad having older sisters when it came to meeting guys. In fact, I first met your dad because he was a friend of Rae's."

"Did Aunt Rachael mind that he liked you instead of her?"

"Well, yes, now that I think about it, she probably did."

"I'm glad she has Uncle Mac now. I really like him."

"He's been good for her I think."

Tracy patted herself on the back as she walked down the hall to Titus' room. There were times when she really enjoyed being a mother. Of course she wasn't so naive to think that there wouldn't be many more fights between she and

Theodora before her daughter was grown and on her own, but an occasional period of easy rapport and a shared confidence or two made the rocky times easier to endure. Maybe this single parenting thing wasn't going to be so bad after all.

She rapped on Titus' door confidently but quietly so as not to risk waking Timothy. "It's me. Mom," she whispered.

"Yes?" He sounded none to eager to enjoy her company.

"May I come in?"

"I guess so."

Titus was stretched out on his bed reading a Sport's Illustrated, a pillow propped up behind his neck, his tennis shoe clad feet crossed in front of him.

Tracy slipped inside the door and closed it behind her. "If you were in the middle of something - like jerking off, or whatever - I can come back later," she said with as much nonchalance as she could muster.

"Oh, gol, Mom. I can't believe you said that."

She didn't say a word, waited, raised one eyebrow, looked.

"Okay. Fine. I'm sorry I said anything in front of Timothy. He's such a little baby," he ribbed derisively.

"That's exactly what he is. He's five years old. You're more than twice his age - almost a teenager. I expect you to know about certain things. I also expect you to use a little common sense when it comes to deciding what topics of conversation are appropriate when Timothy's around."

"If he doesn't hear it from me he'll hear it from someone else."

"Not if I can help it. Not yet."

Titus glared, albeit somewhat sheepishly.

"I'm serious, Titus. Do it, talk about it, tease your friends about it all you want, but let Timothy be a five year old. Let him be a little boy. Let him be happy being a little boy. The next few weeks are going to be hard enough on him as it is..."

She felt the tears springing to her eyes just as she realized what she was saying. Titus froze, his whole stance filled with sudden, unforgiving suspicion.

"I'm sorry, Titus. The truth is, I sometimes wish life didn't dictate that you had to grow up so quickly either. But you will. You'll have to. We'll all have to." Tears streamed down her face. She half turned and groped for the door knob. "I love you, Titus."

"I'm sorry, Mom. I'll try to be a little nicer to Timothy."

"Thanks, Titus. I appreciate that."

It was the phone that had rescued her from the revealing corner she'd boxed herself into. It wasn't that she didn't want to be honest with them, she told herself as she backed out of his room into the hallway. She was ready to tell them. But she couldn't. Not yet. She'd promised to wait for Trevor. They'd promised to do it together.

She assumed the call was for Theodora when the phone stopped ringing. She peered into the dimly lit hall mirror and tried to wipe her eyes without smudging the faint bit of mascara she used to outline her eyes. She heard Theodora just as she'd finished drying her tears.

"Mom, Aunt Michelle wants to talk to you!"

"I'll be there in a minute, honey." She knew her daughter and her sister would find no lack of things to talk about if she took a second or two to compose herself. Theodora would be able to tell she'd be crying whether she went to the phone now or in five minutes anyway. Tracy brushed her hair back from her face and marched down the hall.

She kept her face turned away from Theodora's as she took the receiver with her hand. "Hi, Michelle."

"Oh, Tracy. Thank goodness I reached you. Listen, I'm in a big bind and I'm hoping you can help."

"Me?"

"It has to do with what we were talking about last night except I just found out this morning that Roger, the man I use to do ninety-nine percent of my paint and wallpaper work, broke his ankle playing basketball at the high school gym last night."

"Oh, no. Sorry. I hope you're not right in the middle of a big project."

"Unfortunately, the timing couldn't be worse. I've got three major house renovations going on at the moment. Bud, my back-up painter, has been working on the Alexander house because Roger was already working out at the Zimmerman farm, but then Mr. Alexander complained about the repairs Bud made to the plaster ceiling in the parlor and I had to switch them around. Bud is a good worker but Mr. Alexander is really a perfectionist and Bud just isn't as painstaking as he should be. I should have had Roger on that job from the beginning. Well..." Michelle stopped briefly to catch her breath. "Thank God Roger finished all the plaster work at Mr. Alexander's before he broke his ankle because I don't know who I else I could have gotten to do the kind of quality work Barclay expects at the last minute. But anyway, the bad news is–"

The whole sordid scenario sounded like bad news to Tracy.

"Barclay Alexander needs to have all the painting and wallpapering finished in three weeks because his girlfriend or fiancée or whomever she is has invited a group of their friends down from the Cities for a housewarming party. Tracy, I'm just between a rock and a hard place. I've phoned everyone I can think of trying to find extra help and no one's available for at least a month. Roger's doctor forbids him even to be on his feet for the first two weeks he's wearing a cast, so ladders and scaffolding are definitely out. I just don't know what to do."

Tracy was starting to have an idea where Michelle's dramatics were leading but she didn't feel inclined to take the problem on herself. Not now, when there was so much going on in her life already. Besides, she had never done anything like this professionally. If Mr. Alexander was as picky as Michelle claimed, the last thing she'd want to do was start out working for someone like him. "Sounds like quite a mess."

Michelle, who could probably sense Tracy's mounting skepticism, sighed loudly into the phone. "I'm not exaggerating the situation one little bit, Tracy. I know you're not interested in doing anything like this on a regular basis and I'm sure Trevor will have a fit if you agree to help me out - even if it is just this once," she added for good measure, "but the only possible solution I could think of was that if Laurie covered for me at the shop, the two of us could do it together."

There was dead silence on Tracy's end of the line. Her mind raced over the pros and cons of accepting Michelle's offer. The timing was rotten, but she did need a job. Maple Valley was a good hour south of Blooming Prairie, but if she was painting walls in Iowa instead of Minnesota she'd be spared the indignity of every one in town talking about how far down the rung the pastor's wife had fallen. She could probably get Brooke's mother to pick up the kids on the mornings she had to drive to Maple Valley, and they already had a way home from school every day.

There was no reason Michelle had to know how hard up she and the children would be for money in the weeks to come, but Michelle's interior design business was flourishing and it sounded like there might be more work for her if things went well at Mr. Alexander's. It was pure coincidence that she and Michelle had ended up discussing wallpaper the other day in the first place. Maybe this was meant to be. God had been known to work in stranger ways.

"If I say I'll help you will you promise not to leave me in the lurch halfway through the project? Because I'm not kidding, Michelle Jones Sheffield, I will not be left to do this job by myself. I have no tools and no recent work experience, say nothing about having to deal with a perfectionist home owner who's already kicked one workman off the job."

"Don't worry about a thing. I promise you I'll have everything in order."

"I hope that means Jake is going to be involved." Okay, so that was a slam, but Michelle was one of those people who was always running a day late and a dollar behind. Jake, who was an engineer, was the methodical right brain to Michelle's creative but haphazard left.

"We'll be so well organized that it'll go like a dream. I may even send Sarah up to Jake's Mom and Dad's house for a few days so I can concentrate on nothing but this job. They've been pestering me to have her all to themselves for a few days now that I'm not breast feeding her anymore. It'll be fun, Tracy! You'll love this house! Do you remember Rachael talking about her friend, Mrs. Armerding? The one she sat by in church one Sunday who just happened to own all those beautiful Victorian houses, including the one I bought when I moved here from Colorado?"

"Vaguely. I thought she died not too long ago."

"Yes, she did. The house Barclay Alexander is renovating was hers. It's mission style, pure arts and crafts with beautiful, clean-cut oak woodwork and all the original light fixtures. Rachael closed the deal about a month ago. The house had been well maintained over the years but it needed plumbing and electrical work. Mr. Alexander has what seems to be fairly unlimited funds and he wanted to do a major facelift, so Rachael gave him my card. I was having the time of my life until last week when I started running into these glitches."

"I do remember hearing about this house now that you mention it. From the way Rae always gushed on and on about it, I always figured she and Mac would buy it when Mrs. Armerding passed on."

"I wondered if they wouldn't, too, but of course it wasn't available when they needed a place."

"They've put a lot of time and money into renovating the old farm house on the acreage they bought. I suppose they'd hate to have to start over again so soon."

"Now that Ian's getting older I think Mac is really hooked on the idea of him growing up in the country, having a dog and maybe a pony. You know how idealistic Mac can be. I doubt they'll ever move back into town, especially not on a busy street like this house sits on."

Tracy laughed. "He's a sweetheart, isn't he? And to think how furious Mom and Dad were when Rachael first announced they were getting married."

"Well, she was pregnant at the time and had just gotten her marriage to Luke annulled. Their first impressions of Mac were certainly formed under less than ideal circumstances. Of course, you have no idea what that feels like since you married the perfect man," Michelle quipped in jest.

Tracy froze. It wasn't Michelle's fault, she reminded herself. Her sister would never be so insensitive if she knew the truth.

"Seriously, you'll probably enjoy getting out of the house so much that you'll beg me to find you another job when this one is done, Tracy. I told you I think *The Handy Woman* is a natural. You'll have all kinds of freedom now that all three kids are in school and if you're like us, a little extra money never hurts."

"Speaking of..." Tracy didn't quite know how to broach the subject of payment. As a proper helpmeet to her husband, a pastor's wife was not supposed to make any money. If one actively sought to do so it connoted that the congregation, or worse yet God himself, wasn't adequately meeting their needs. In large part due to the commonly held attitude, and in no small measure thanks to her children, Tracy had done a lot of volunteer work over the years but, baby-sitting as a teenager aside, she'd never had a paying job.

"My contract with Mr. Alexander allows for twenty dollars an hour for sub-contract laborers. Of that, I keep twenty percent to cover my overhead, and in your case, tool rental. You're considered an independent contractor for income tax purposes so you'll be responsible for making your own estimated tax and social security payments and you won't qualify for unemployment when the job is done. I'll notify my workman's comp insurance carrier that you're to be covered under my policy for this job only. If you go on to become *The Handy Woman* you'll have to get your own."

"Wow, I'm impressed." Tracy knew nothing about such things, but sixteen dollars an hour sounded like a long way above minimum wage.

"I've had to develop the right side of my brain to some

extent no matter what you and the rest of the family may think," Michelle said smugly. "Now, when can you start?"

"Tuesday morning bright and early if you want."

"The sooner the better. I'll have all the paint, paper, and tools at the house. If you'd like to meet me at *The Painted Lady* at nine, we can ride over together."

"That sounds great," Tracy said solemnly. "Long story, but the money will come in handy. Thanks, Michelle. I'm glad you thought of me."

"So am I, baby sister. See you on Tuesday."

*****

"I can't keep living a lie." Trevor's voice sounded far away and tinny, maybe because her cell phone was the cheapest model on the market, and maybe because he was calling from California. Regardless, it didn't dampen the impact of his words.

It had been almost three years since Trevor had told her the truth, and she still had a hard time believing it.

"I can't keep pretending I'm someone who I'm not," Trevor said.

"You most certainly can. You have to." She lowered her voice for fear of waking the children. "If you can't do it for me, then do it for them."

She scooted Trevor's stiff-backed, navy blue leather swivel chair a little closer to the desk and dumped a few more M&Ms on the leather blotter.

"Fine," Trevor said. "I won't tell them I'm gay."

"The fact that we're getting a divorce is enough for them to deal with right now." All she needed was one more red M&M and the intricate arrangement of red, blue, green, yellow, and brown circles spread out in front of her would be perfect. She dumped the rest of the bag on the desktop and rifled through the remainder. Just one more measly red. No such luck. Tipping back her head, she swallowed one each of every color M&M except red and began the laborious task of devising a new design.

She sighed deeply. “You don’t realize how hard it is without you here. Theodora and I are always arguing about something these days. She practically lives in the bathtub – or would, if I let her. She’s more like Michelle with every day that passes and frankly, it’s driving me crazy.”

“Thank goodness we have two bathrooms in the parsonage, and not just one like your family had when you were growing up,” Trevor said. “It’s no wonder you three Jones girls quibbled so much when you were teenagers with only one measly bathroom for the whole family to share.”

“Michelle was always so afraid someone was going to see her. At least Theodora doesn’t have such a fanatical obsession with privacy.”

“See. She doesn’t have all Michelle’s traits. Just the good ones,” Trevor said.

Tracy shivered. Much as she hated the fact that Trevor was tearing their family apart, he was still her best friend. They had a history. She could talk to him. And because she felt so strongly that his sexual preference needed to remain a secret, he was the only one she could talk to honestly – unless you counted strangers in convenience stores. What was she going to do? Once Trevor’s epiphany became public, she and the children would be forced to move out of the parsonage. Where would they live? What would she do? Who knew what kind of situations they might find themselves in? The uncertainly of it had her stomach in knots.

“How did Titus’s first week of school go?”

She sighed and decided not to go into what had happened at the Budget Mart. “He slinks in the door without saying a word after Jason’s mother drops him off from soccer practice. I tried to get him to talk about his new teacher but he just won’t open up to me. He’s so sullen and withdrawn that it scares me. Were you like this when you were eleven?”

“He probably misses me,” Trevor said, sounding suddenly guilty.

Fine time to grow a conscience. Sadly, he was probably

right. Titus and Trevor had always been close.

"Sometimes I wonder if he doesn't... I mean, careful as we've been to discuss things when the kids were gone, I can't imagine Titus could have overheard us arguing, but..." She hoped he hadn't heard her crying into her pillow and feared the worse. Of all the children, Titus was the most intuitive.

Tracy fidgeted with the M&Ms on Trevor's desk, ate another round; first the brown, her least favorite color, then the yellow, red, and green. She fingered the blue candy for a second, swallowed tearfully, and tried in vain to make some sort of design out of the rest.

"Give him time. Boys are just different than girls. You can't expect him to jabber on and on about everything like Theodora does," Trevor said.

Like she did. She talked. Trevor listened. It was the glue that had cemented their relationship until... Their lives had been so orderly before Trevor had told her he was gay. Her poor babies. She'd tried to protect them from the cruelty and disappointments of the world as best she could, but that would all end when they found out she and Trevor were getting a divorce.

It was all so contradictory to everything Tracy had been raised to believe, to everything she had wanted for her family. Tracy stuffed the rest of the M&Ms in her mouth without rhyme or reason, lowered her head to the desk, and cried.

Chapter 5

"Wake up, sweetie." Tracy leaned over Timothy's inert form and brushed his hair back from his face. He didn't move. "It's time to go to the fair," she said a little more loudly. She moved a teddy bear and two stuffed bunny rabbits to the far side of the bed and jostled his shoulder. Timothy had told her just before he went to bed the night before that he had given his bunnies new names: Josh and Nate. She smiled. How could she regret anything that had happened between she and Trevor when their union had resulted in blessings as sweet as this?

A crack of sunlight peeped by the edge of the window shade. Timothy," she called in a sing-song voice. "Time to rise and shine."

She cringed involuntarily. She'd hated it when her mother used to tell her to rise and shine - and give God the glory. What was it about those mother-phrases that not only made them stick in your mind forever but spring forth from your very own mouth even though you never wanted to hear them voiced again?

She raised the shade with a whoosh. "C'mon sleepyhead! The merry-go-round will leave without us if we don't shake a leg!"

"Can I pick which horse I get to ride on, Mom?" Timothy sat up and rubbed his eyes with his fists. Tracy stooped over, gently removed the sleep from the corners of his eyes, and ran her fingers over the soft fringe of lashes on his cheek.

"I wish Daddy was here."

"I do, too. But we're going to have a great time with just Titus and Theodora and you and me. One nice thing about the fair is that it always stays the same no matter who you go with."

"Will you take me to see the big combines and four

wheel drive tractors?"

"We'll park right behind Machinery Hill like we always do and walk through the field on our way to see Theodora's dress at the 4-H building." Her daughter's purple championship ribbon at the Steele County fair had won her a showing at the Minnesota State Fair in the area of Clothing Construction.

"I don't like dresses. Girls are weird."

Tracy laughed. When Theodora had been chosen to play the role of Mary in the school's production of "Little House on the Prairie", it had seemed only natural to combine the need to sew a costume for the play with the opportunity to complete her 4-H project a few months ahead of schedule.

The combination of helping Theodora learn her role, making extra trips to and from Rice Lake for play rehearsals almost every night, and sewing the complicated, prairie-style dress, petticoat, and pinafore had been enough to throw the house into a continuous state of chaos for well over a month. Poor Timothy had been ignored on more than one occasion while they'd been in the throes of sewing. To make matters worse, the dress was a delicate pink flowered calico with enough ruffles and lace to make a boy nauseous.

"Up and at em', young man. I told you you'd be glad you had your bath last night. Now you can just slip into your jeans and pull your shirt right over your head like this," she said, half-dressing him in his semi-sleep. She could hear the other two children pattering about their rooms, toilets flushing, closet doors closing, drawers sliding open and shut.

It was tradition to leave for the fair at the first crack of dawn. *The early bird gets the worm,* her father always said, in this case a parking spot anywhere near the fairgrounds. She also liked enjoying the sights in the cooler morning hours before the sun got too hot. Whether she was gardening or sightseeing, her skin turned into a freckle free-for-all when she spent too much time in the hot afternoon sun.

"Will you ride the roller coaster with me, Mom?" Timothy queried hopefully.

"Um..." It had never bothered her when she was young,

as an adult she was scared to death of any ride that involved being upside down. Trevor, who loved wild rides, had always saved her the need to accompany the children on the Zipper, the Rocket, or the infamous Chicago Loop.

It was bad enough that she had to spend the day suffering from menstrual cramps. The very thought of being upside down on a roller coaster ride made her queasy.

"We'll see," she said obscurely, smug in her efforts to put him off - until she recognized her mother's voice again. "If you really need me to go with you, I will. But I'm sure Titus will want to go."

"Titus says I'm a baby. He'll tease me if I get scared."

"Titus gets scared sometimes, too. We all get scared. It's okay, you know. Everyone does."

Titus entered the room playing cool. "Me? Scared? Dude, I'm totally fearless."

Tracy gave him a withering look.

Titus ceased his taunts. "Theodora put the picnic basket and the cooler in the car like you said."

"Good. Do you have your backpack, Timothy?" She gave the room a quick once over to make sure they hadn't forgotten anything. "We're all set to go if you are."

*****

Barclay Alexander III stretched out one long leg just far enough to ease his clutch in, downshifted, and slowed his sleek, black Mercedes to a purr. The big engine rumbled its protest as he waited for the doorman to open the gate to the Humphreys' estate. The custom-built English Tudor perched at the crest of the hill shone like a jeweled crown on the head of a king in the late morning sunshine.

Barclay's Mercedes skimmed over the crisp new asphalt effortlessly as he wound his way up the steep, meandering incline. He'd made two trips to Iowa in the moving truck already this weekend. Although he was exhausted, he knew he'd receive no consolation from Lauren. A sympathetic nature was not one of his *fiancée's* strong points. Since his banishment to Iowa, their relationship had been particularly snappish.

One more reason that he needed to talk to her and put an end to this whole farce of an engagement. He'd been trying to let her down gently for weeks, but was at his wit's end trying to impress upon her that he had no intention of carrying through on their parents scheme to see their dynasties united. He felt no more ready to be married - most particularly not to Lauren - than Bret Favre was ready to retire. But it seemed one did not argue with Barclay Alexander II, his imperious wife, the one and only Elizabeth Dalton Alexander, or the Humphreys.

Barclay felt a familiar sinking sensation in the pit of his stomach as he thought about his parents. Shoving his regrets to the back of his mind, he approached the Humphreys' front door, rang the ornate brass doorbell, and waited for the doorman to summon Lauren from the opulent boudoir she occupied in the west wing.

"Darling," Lauren drawled. His *fiancée* coyly tilted her chin, raised her left cheek and eyebrow, and closed her eyes to await his greeting.

"Lauren." He placed a quick peck on her cheek. No, Barclay wasn't at all daunted by the fact that his *upcoming marriage* to Lauren was on indefinite hold. The whole thing hadn't even been an issue until Lauren had stopped seeing Henri a few months earlier. Granted, their parents had been plotting their union for years, but he'd never thought they would force the matter. He certainly hoped the Humphreys hadn't had anything to do with Henri's sudden desire to go back to France – alone.

His own father and mother had made their wishes on the subject clear long ago - on the night of Lauren's debutante ball - when they had rather pointedly suggested he escort Lauren instead of the shy young woman from Eden Prairie he'd been dating at the time. But Clay had not at any time agreed to their little plot - he had certainly never proposed. Until Henri had gone back to France, Lauren hadn't seemed interested either.

Lauren batted her lashes and tilted her head back for one carefully-calculated fraction of a second.

The fact that Lauren was almost ten years younger than he had delayed the inevitable for some time. Barclay supposed that now that Lauren was approaching thirty, there was pressure to complete the deal and produce an heir. Barclay sighed. Perhaps if he'd had someone else in mind to marry, he'd have been more inclined to fight his parents. Because Lauren was so devastated over Henri's betrayal, playing along until such time as she'd healed had seemed the right thing to do.

Handing him her wrap, Lauren twirled, executing a lissome pirouette. She shrugged into the tea-washed silk jacket he extended on cue with an artful grace. "Dispense with the suspense, dear. What sort of titillating adventure do you have in store for me today?"

Barclay's mind went blank. In the flurry of moving two truckloads of his necessities to his new home in Maple Valley, he'd forgotten to lay plans for the day.

"Well?" she queried disdainfully, immediately suspicious because he'd hesitated. "Do we have tickets? Reservations?"

"The State Fair," he blurted. He'd just heard an advertisement on the radio on the drive up Interstate 35. "It's the last day. I thought you'd enjoy a stroll around the grounds."

"Eew." She wrinkled up her nose. "I think they have pigs there. You've only been in Iowa for a few days and already you're content to spend an entire day looking at livestock and rubbing shoulders with carnies?"

Barclay resisted the impulse to turn and walk away. He was an expert at manipulating Lauren when he wanted to. It was disgustingly easy. As a result he very rarely had the urge. He was in the mood to have his own way today, however, no matter how spontaneous his suggestion that they go to the fair had been. "The State Fair is the most classic form of entertainment there is. It's an educational observation point, a mixing pot of ethnic and cultural diversity, a Garrison Keiloresque word picture waiting to be lived. Come on, Lauren. It'll be a hoot."

"Well, when you put it that way," she conceded. "I fear my attire may not be altogether appropriate for a fair."

"You'll be the belle of the ball just like you always are." Lauren was a lovely woman – if one admired her particular brand of brash sophistication.

She blushed, oblivious to his true feelings. "Fine. Is security such that your car will be safe on the grounds or shall we have Charles drop us off in the town car?"

"Let's drive." He tossed his keys a few feet into the air and caught them in one hand with a flourish. Lauren looked up at the delicate Bohemian crystal chandelier just over their heads, sideways at an heirloom mahogany entry table, and down at the Italian tiles beneath their feet, obviously appalled at the possibility that the keys might have nicked a crystal, gouged the gleaming surface of the table, or cracked a tile had Barclay miscalculated his aim. She would never have said so, but it was clear she feared that the Alexanders' efforts to instill a much needed sense of propriety in their son might backfire on them if he was allowed to live amongst the painfully rural, socially inept of Iowa for any great length of time.

*****

The Tomlinson family outing, less one father, was proceeding just about as well as one might expect under the circumstances. The children had all been wide awake by the time they reached the Cities and the decibel level in the car seemed to rise with the number of lanes and hundreds of cars on the interstate.

Titus had been itching for a wallop all week long. "Hey Theodora, remember the time we were invited to our neighbor's wedding at the Lutheran church and Timothy picked up that *balloon* that fell out of the groom's get-away car and put it in his suit pocket?" Titus snickered just about the time Tracy was trying to back the car into a painfully tight but perfectly situated parking spot along the curb. It was her third attempt.

"Mo-omm," Timothy wailed. "Titus is being mean."

"Titus," she threatened with as stern an inflection as she could manage under the duress of parallel parking.

Theodora made a face. "I can't believe he was sitting in the front row at church playing with a condom."

"Such a baby he doesn't know the difference between a condom and a balloon," Titus mimicked in an infantile voice.

"I'm not a baby." Timothy started to cry.

Tracy craned her neck around. The back tire of the car hit the curb with a thud. She could hear rubber chafing against cement as she straightened the tire, pulled forward ever so slightly, cramped the wheel, backed up a little, forced the wheel back again, and inched forward once more. She expelled a long sigh. Timothy's wails grew louder and she caught a glimpse of Titus pretending he was sucking his thumb in the rear view mirror.

"Titus, it's been less than twenty-four hours since I spoke to you about this. If I have to speak to you again you'll forfeit next week's allowance. Do you understand?"

"Yah, but it's not fair. If the little baby would just grow up, I wouldn't keep getting in trouble."

"Fine. You've lost next week's allowance. Now you're risking the week after next." She ignored his stricken look. "We're close enough to the front gate that we can walk back to the car and eat our lunch here. Let's get going while it's still nice and cool. I can't wait to see Theodora's 'Little House on the Prairie' dress hanging at the 4-H building."

"Look at those tires." Timothy's eyes lit up as he spied a giant of a tractor with earth moving equipment attached to the front end several hundred yards in the distance. He tugged at her hand. "That tire is so big I bet I can stand up inside it!"

"You're probably right, you little shrimp," his brother whispered none too wisely from behind.

"Spend your money carefully, Titus. It's very probably

the last cash you'll have for some time to come," Tracy said.

"I wish Daddy was here," Timothy said.

"Me, too," Theodora agreed. "The two T's are driving me crazy."

Lord, how Tracy hated having to play referee twenty-four hours a day. Couldn't they all get along for one day?

*****

It was nearing noon when Barclay Alexander pulled the convertible onto Snelling Avenue near the historic entrance to the Minnesota State Fair. A host of men dressed in black pants and orange vests were waving flags to direct traffic in the direction of the designated parking areas.

"Why don't I drop you off here, Lauren? I'm sure there's somewhere you can sit while I find a parking spot."

"You would really leave me here by myself?" She sputtered.

Barclay surveyed the colorfully clad fairgoers that paraded up and down the sidewalks in a merging jumble of shapes and color. What Lauren saw as a detriment filled him with the curiosity and excitement of a five year old. He had only been to the fair once before, when he was seven or eight. He had heard a group of Jamaicans playing the steel drums for the first and only time in his life. He could still feel the mesmerizing rhythms pounding through his veins. An intense longing to get out of the car that very moment and join the throng of energy and sound that pulsed around them nearly overpowered him.

"You can't be serious, Barclay."

"The alternative is walking nine or ten blocks, maybe more from what I can see." Barclay's finger hovered on the button that would lower the roof of the convertible while they waited at a temporarily placed stop sign on wheels. The urge to be a part of the carefully ordered chaos around them was strong and instinctual. "I was just thinking of your heels."

"Don't you dare!" Lauren screeched the second the roof

started to open.

Barclay removed his finger from the button. "It's a beautiful day, Lauren! Just enjoy it for once."

"The wind will ruin my hair and you know it, Barclay Alexander, and the sun beating down on this asphalt... I won't risk ruining my good silk wrap." She lowered her voice a few decibels. "You know how I love the combination of these smooth leather seats and the feel of ice cold air-conditioning blowing against my legs." She splayed her fingers over Barclay's thigh and swirled her hand in a sensuous circle.

He felt nothing but pity for the perfectly coifed woman beside him. Lauren would spend her whole life strutting vainly from one air-conditioned building to another if she had her way. She reveled in covered parking spots linked to condominiums by gleaming brass elevators, shopping and office complexes interconnected by glass walkways, a commonly practiced feature in Minnesota due to the severe winters, and houses inlaid with a vast network of passageways and well-shaded, walled courtyards.

"There's a security guard standing right beside the bench, Lauren. The left half is even in the shade. Grab your hat and jump out before we cause a major traffic jam, okay? I'll park the car and meet you here in fifteen minutes. Trust me. You'll be fine."

Lauren huffed loudly to emphasize her displeasure as she fumbled with the door, her purse, and a floppy straw hat with a magenta silk ribbon that matched the buttons on her dress. Lauren was not accustomed to managing heavy car doors by herself, nor disembarking unaided from a vehicle in the middle of a heavily trafficked intersection. She did not look back as she strode through the crowd to the bench, her shoulders squared, her jaw set to one side in a serious pout.

*****

Tracy took a deep breath and relaxed her shoulders. She and Timothy sat side by side on two dapple gray horses aboard the merry-go-round, she side-saddle, since she'd worn a cool, cotton sundress, he clinging protectively to a half-eaten swab of cotton candy with one hand and the horse's mane with the other. Titus and Theodora were awaiting their turn at a ride on the Chicago Loop. Tracy counted it as a small blessing that Timothy hadn't wanted to go on the more treacherous ride.

"Look, Mom, my horse is saying ne-eigh ..." Timothy nickered impressively and clamped his knees to the animal's firm belly. The gaily beribboned horse he perched on was posed with its head thrown back in some delightful if imaginary pursuit.

"Mine is racing the wind," she said, contentedly stroking the smooth-maned beast, whose tail streamed out behind him in permanently frozen abandon.

Tracy tried to remember the last time she had felt so carefree. The gentle refrains of the calliope always worked their magic on her heart, lulling her away from this world and into a whimsical fantasyland of princes and princesses, castles, dragons, and dashing knights in shining armor. Tall, fair-haired, Nordic-godlike knights, she thought dreamily, as her eyes began to focus at some unbidden point a third of the way around the ring.

"Mom, there's that man! You know, the one from the Budget Mart. See him?" Timothy was tugging at her skirt like a child possessed. "Remember? The one who talked to me about—"

Tracy reached over, clamped her hand over Timothy's mouth, and smiled reassuringly at the children around her.

Timothy wrenched her hand away from his mouth. "He's right there, on the white horse."

Clay. Her lips formed the word silently. Her eyes remained locked on his. "Please don't point, Timothy. It's not polite."

Her son dropped his hand for a second, thought, raised it again, and began to wave furiously from his perch atop the dapple gray horse. Clay raised one arm and sliced his fingers through the air in a silent greeting.

“It is him, Mom! He sees us! He waved at me, Mom!”

Tracy gave a timid wave from the level of her waist and perused the tall beauty seated on the bench next to Clay’s horse. Her son chattered away. Although the woman reached up and touched Clay possessively from time to time, she seemed unaware of the little drama that was unfolding a few feet away.

Tracy met Clay’s eyes, cocked her head, nodded in the direction of the woman, and raised one eyebrow.

Clay pointed one finger at his companion, pointed to his ring finger, and gave her the saddest look she’d ever seen.

Tracy ignored the little jab of pain that wrenched through her gut and nodded back at Clay. The woman did look a bit self-absorbed - and not at all dressed for the fair. Tracy squinted her eyes and looked a little closer to be sure she understood. The woman was too young to be his mother, too sensual in her attentions to be a sister. Only the obvious remained. As Tracy looked on, the flamboyantly clad woman flicked a strand of hair away from her face. Tracy saw the ring at once. Its facets caught and magnified the rays of sunlight filtering sideways across the merry-go-round. Tracy’s mouth drooped. His fiancée. Clay’s eyes met hers across the way. She looked away.

The merry-go-round started with a jolt. Tracy reached over to steady Timothy as their horses moved up and down in synchronized dis-rhythm. Her horse crested a swell as his dropped from sight. His rose with a flourish while hers lagged behind. Her son’s laughter floated on the wind. The breeze fluttered through her hair. The calliope wheezed out its melody. She assumed Clay had just moved to Minneapolis. From where, she wondered? Somewhere to the south. Not that it mattered, she reminded herself. He was engaged to that woman.

Barclay watched her from behind, his horse chasing hers but never quite catching up. He was vaguely aware of Lauren’s voice, but all he really heard was the boy’s giggles, the mother’s delighted laughter, and the calliope on the wind. The merry-go-round spun round and round and the fair whirled by until the wizened old man at the controls finally reined the horses in. The mother and son were the first to alight. Why couldn't he remember her name? Clay leaped down from his horse with a youthful enthusiasm he hadn't felt in months.

"Barclay, wait," Lauren's unwelcome intrusion cut through his reverie like a knife. "I've caught my purse strap on the stirrup of your horse and it won't come loose."

He turned away from his intention to follow the woman and her son reluctantly. "You what?"

"My favorite Gucci bag!" She wailed.

He worked to disengage the purse without saying a word.

"Be careful, Barclay. It's made from Italian leather."

The strap slipped loose and he turned, but the freckle-faced sprite of his dreams and her inquisitive young son had disappeared into the wandering throng of fairgoers.

Chapter 6

"Are you still here, Roger?" Barclay called out, noting the open window ventilating the parlor of the stately arts and crafts edifice he'd purchased several weeks prior. He knocked on the front door loudly more out of consideration for the painter inside than out of obligation. He stopped and attempted to juggle his briefcase so he could slip his key in the lock, but in the end, the door popped open of its own accord when he leaned against it to steady himself.

"Roger? It's me, Barclay. Didn't want to scare you..."

But it was he who was surprised when Michelle appeared from just inside the door.

"No need to worry about scaring me. We're pretty trusting here in Maple Valley," Michelle said. "The truth is, neighbors from miles around have been dropping by all day. Everyone's hot to see what's happening at Edith Armerding's old place. The only thing that caught me off guard was the racket you made. Everyone else just walks right in without knocking."

"I didn't expect to see you here today," he commented. He set down his briefcase and nodded appreciatively at the parlor. "Looks wonderful. The trim work is flawless. Is Roger done for the day or is he in back cleaning up?"

Michelle smoothed her paint-splattered hair and tugged at the old Red Oak High School T-shirt she was wearing. "Well, the truth is, Roger is laid up at home with a broken ankle."

"You can't be serious."

"Unfortunately, I am. It happened Saturday night at the gym. Pick up basketball. He's just sick about it, of course. He'll be laid up for at least a month."

"So Bud did all this?"

"No, I'd already switched Bud to a new job. Besides, I wouldn't have brought him back here without clearing it with you after what happened the other day."

"Thanks. You'll have to elaborate about this mystery crew you've been hiding up your sleeve then. I'm more than a little confused."

"I was just cleaning out the last of the brushes in the kitchen when I heard you at the door. Why don't we head back there and I'll explain?"

He followed her to the rear of the house.

"I know how eager you are to move in, Barclay, and your fiancée was so adamant about everything being done in three weeks - what with the invitations for the housewarming party already at the engravers."

He didn't think it worth the time or energy to try to explain the true nature of his relationship with Lauren, say nothing that it more or less defied description.

"So you're doing it yourself?"

"My crews are already stretched thin with the other two projects I've got underway. When Roger broke his ankle... Well, there simply wasn't anyone else available that I thought could do this house justice."

"I'm very appreciative of what you're doing and it's plain to see I couldn't be in better hands, but I can't help but be embarrassed at the sacrifice you're making on my account. Who's manning the shop?"

"Don't worry about it, Barclay. Laurie does a fine job of running things at the Painted Lady and Jake is wonderful about helping out with Sarah when I'm in a bind. I actually enjoyed myself today."

"You're gracious to say so, but I still feel responsible for the dilemma. It's pure foolishness to have to rush a job like this simply because Lauren's notion that proper etiquette demands I have a housewarming party within the month. It's so like her to rush in and take control of a situation she has no business being involved with in the first place."

"I thought perhaps the wedding date had been set and she was just trying to stay on schedule."

"Just being stubborn is more like it. Our wedding plans are sketchy at best. I'll admit I'm eager to move in but I could live without having a housewarming party anytime this century. Being the perfectionist I am, I'd much rather you take your time and do the job right."

"I feel the same. But it's not your fault Roger broke his ankle, Barclay. I made a commitment to have this job completed by a certain date and I intend to do my best to honor that obligation."

"I really do appreciate the lengths you've gone to expedite things. I just hope being here won't adversely affect your other duties."

"Not too worry. Besides, these things have a way of working out the way they're supposed to. I asked my younger sister to help me out with your house, thinking I was asking a great favor from her only to find out she's really in need of a job right now. She'll probably thank you when this whole thing is done. You never know when a crisis will turn out to be a blessing in disguise."

"Good. I'm relieved to hear you have help. If your sister is anything like you are, I'm sure she'll do an excellent job." He twisted his neck and looked through the door leading from the kitchen to the hall. "Is she still here?"

"She left about a half hour ago. She has school-aged children and I think she's afraid to leave them alone for too long after they get home - a phenomenon she assures me I'll understand when Sarah gets a little older."

"I'll look forward to meeting her." He reached into his pocket, pulled out the package of M&Ms he'd purchased earlier at the Budget Mart, tore open the top, and flipped a palm full of chocolate into his mouth. "I don't mean to be rude, but I missed lunch." He threw back his head and felt the starched shirt collar chafing against his five o'clock shadow as he repeated the motion. "I didn't realize there were other sisters in addition to Rae. Are there more still?"

"No, only three. There were many occasions when we were growing up that my mother would have said *three too many*."

"I can't imagine that having met two of the trio."

"Thank you, kind sir." Michelle curtsied impishly. "And

now I must finish cleaning my brushes and find some lotion or I shall have the hands of a peasant, and my husband, no supper, and there will be great unrest in the kingdom."

Barclay laughed and laid the empty M&M wrapper on the counter. He tried to imagine Lauren pitching in and doing whatever was needed to accomplish a goal no matter how undignified or beneath her the job. He couldn't.

*****

The next morning, Tracy pulled up in front of the Painted Lady and parked her car under a maple tree that was frosted in red. Michelle had called her just as she was leaving Blooming Prairie to tell her about a last minute meeting with Rae. Michelle wanted to show them a quilt their great-aunt Thelma had left to the three of them, and Rae evidently had some sort of announcement to make.

It had already occurred to her that if Rae had wanted her there, she would have called her herself, but Michelle had adamantly insisted that they all needed to be there to decide what to do with Aunt Thelma's quilt, and that Rae would certainly want Tracy to hear whatever news she wanted to share.

She locked the car and started up the cobblestone walkway to the house. She imagined the water lilies would be going inside for the winter before long. The Farmer's Almanac was predicting an early frost followed by a blustery winter.

Michelle met her at the door and shooed her inside. Rae was seated at a table, looking ecstatically happy – until she saw Tracy.

Tracy watched as an irritated look – not really a scowl, but almost – flashed across her oldest sister's face.

"Um, good to see you Rae," Tracy said, wishing she hadn't listened to Michelle.

"You, too." Rae cleared her throat. She looked at Michelle, her eyes shining with fondness once again. "I got my test results back from my twelve month check-up. I'm cancer free."

"Oh, Rae!" Michelle leaped up from her chair and hugged Rae while Tracy looked on.

"That's wonderful!" Tracy said.

Michelle motioned to Madeleine, the head cook. "We're going to celebrate with three pieces of Red Wine Truffle Cake with Dark Chocolate. It's healthy and decadent all at the same time."

"Sounds great!" Tracy said, feeling happy for Rae and horribly out of place.

Rae kept looking at Michelle, directing her comments to Michelle, smiling at Michelle.

"Mac must be so relieved." Tracy interjected.

"We all are," Rae said condescendingly, making it clear that "we" didn't include her.

She felt like an idiot. So she hadn't called Rae every other day after she'd gotten her diagnosis. So she hadn't sat and held Rae's hand during her chemo treatments. It had gone without saying that Rae wouldn't have wanted her to.

"Be nice, Rae," Michelle said, obviously aware of the tension that was mounting.

This was so unfair. She'd prayed for Rae morning and night when she'd had cancer. She'd put her on the prayer list at Fellowship. She'd bought daffodils and donated money to the American Cancer Society in her name. Theodora had donated her hair to Locks of Love. They'd even bought and lit a luminaria for Rae at the Steele County Walk for Life.

"Don't worry about it," Rae said, her implication very clearly being that Tracy had done something wrong.

"What?" Tracy said, the stress of the past few weeks finally getting the best of her. She didn't want to pick a fight, but she'd bitten her tongue for a whole year because Rae had cancer. Well, she didn't have to anymore. It was time to tell the insufferable prig just what she thought.

"I assume this is because I didn't have my head shaved when you got cancer like Michelle did," Tracy said.

"I never expected you to," Rae said. "I wouldn't have wanted you to."

"So it goes back even further? What, you're still holding a grudge about Mac?" Tracy said.

"It goes back much further than that," sweetheart," Rae countered.

"Stop it right now," Michelle said. "This is supposed to be a celebration."

Rae clicked her tongue. "It's a little hard to feel happy when I've got Miss 'My Life is Perfect in Every Way, and So Would Yours Be If You Had Only Tried A Little Harder To Find God's Perfect Will For Your Life Like I Did' sitting across the table."

Tracy's felt her face blanch. "Of all the..."

"Rachael MacKenzie," Michelle said. "You're supposed to be surrounding yourself with positive energy."

The split second of silence that followed was as cold and dark as a black hole in deep space.

"Just say it," Tracy said. Silence. "Fine, then I will."

Michelle glared at Rae. Rae looked at Michelle.

"Positive energy?" Tracy said. "Then what's she doing here?"

She wanted Michelle to defend her. She wanted Rae to apologize. She wanted them to gush over her, to say how wrong she was – to tell her how much they loved her.

No one said a word. When she realized they weren't going to, she burst into tears.

"I told you," Rae said to Michelle, as though Tracy wasn't even in the room. "This is why I don't invite her to parties. Because it doesn't matter what the celebration's about. Tracy always finds a way to make it about her. It's always about her."

"So you're going to pay her back for all the times she's hurt you and sat in judgment of you by doing the same thing to her?" Michelle said to Rae.

Ouch. That hurt. She knew she hadn't always been kind to her sisters, especially when they'd been single. But she'd really been trying these last couple of years. Rae hadn't even given her a chance when she'd moved back to Iowa. After awhile, she'd stopped trying.

"I'm not sitting in judgment of anyone!" she said in a hushed whisper, resisting the urge to scream. "And my life is not perfect."

"Not according to Mom," Rae said.

"Mom doesn't know the half of it," Tracy said, finally getting angry. Being held accountable for her own misdeeds was fine. She deserved that. But being taken to task for whatever it was that their mother said about her was another matter altogether. Her blood started to boil.

"You think Mom knows what's going on in my life? You think Mom knows anything about me? You honestly think that I confide my hopes and dreams and disappointments and failings with MOM?"

Madeleine whisked into the room and pulled the pocket doors between she and them closed without saying a word.

"She's right, you know," Michelle said. "I think a lot of the bad blood between you two is Mom's fault."

"Why can't you be more like Tracy?" Rae said, perfectly imitating their mother's voice.

"Tracy never gives me this kind of problem," Michelle said, a close second.

"I'm getting a divorce," Tracy said

Rae laughed, still on the subject of their mother, not even registering what she'd said. Michelle seemed not to have heard her either.

"Trevor and I are getting a divorce," she said again, this time a little louder.

"What?" Michelle said, a dazed look crossing her face.

"Trevor and I are getting a divorce," she said slowly and succinctly.

"You're kidding," Michelle said.

"You lie," Rae said.

"Nobody knows," Tracy whispered. "Not the kids, not the church. And you can't tell Mom and Dad."

"I don't believe you," Rae said, looking stunned.

"She wouldn't tease about something like this," Michelle said.

"What did you do?" Rae asked point blank. "I mean, we

all know Trevor's perfect, so—"

Tracy stood. "Michelle, if you don't mind, I'd like to get started on the Alexander house before it gets any later."

She saw the look that passed between Rae and Michelle, but didn't comment.

"Um, sure. Give me a minute to talk to Madeleine and I'll be over to unlock the door," Michelle said, looking as shocked as Tracy had when Trevor first said the word. "I suppose now's not a good time to talk about the quilt."

"Maybe another time," Tracy said. "Rae, I really am happy that you've been cancer free for a year. Congratulations. Michelle, thanks for including me in the celebration."

"She is kidding, isn't she?" Rae was saying as Tracy fled the room.

*****

Several long, tense hours later, Tracy left Maple Valley for Blooming Prairie. When Michelle had returned to the Alexander house, she'd been full of questions about her and Trevor's divorce. Thankfully, when Tracy had told her she didn't want to talk about it, Michelle had backed off and let the issue drop. For the time being. She had no doubt her sister would broach the subject again, and keep broaching it if necessary, until she got some answers.

She paused for a moment before exiting her car to polish off the last of a bag of M&Ms she'd grabbed from the Budget Mart on the way home from work. Home from work! The very phrase filled her with a sense of pride and accomplishment she hadn't felt in years.

Unfortunately, the knowledge that she'd have to face Trevor before the evening was over had made her crave chocolate despite her good cheer. She expected him before dark. Whether or not they would talk to the children tonight or tomorrow would depend on what time he arrived. At any rate, she had decided there was no longer any need to maintain propriety's sake. As of now, she wasn't going to allow Trevor to share her bed, even platonically.

"Hello, I'm home!" Tracy called out, expecting the children to greet her at the door. There was not a sound in response. "Hello? Anybody home? Theodora? Titus?" She was beginning to feel a momentary rush of panic when she heard the pattering of footsteps heading up the stairs from the basement. "What are you guys doing downstairs watching TV on such a beautiful day? Didn't you remember what I said about checking the garden?"

"Dad's home!" Titus's face shone as brightly as a jack-o-lantern's on Halloween. "He's home!"

Tracy struggled to find the words she needed. As much as she had tried to prepare herself for Trevor's return, she had not anticipated Titus's ecstatic reaction. She was completely undone in the face of his joy. Panic swept over her with a paralyzing force. "He's downstairs?"

"He has a DVD of this huge church in California where he went while he was attending the conference. It's so cool, Mom. You should see it. There are these huge palm trees and some kind of bougainvillea vines with bright red flowers and these high cliffs overlooking the ocean and everything. C'mon!" He tugged at her arm.

Theodora and Timothy were nowhere in sight. "Are your brother and sister downstairs, too?"

"Yeah. C'mon! We're missing it!"

Tracy, in a daze, let herself be led to the stairway door. She thought they had agreed not to let the children know the real nature of Trevor's business in California. How could he be showing them a DVD of the conference without divulging that it had been a seminar for gay men? Her insides roiled as she followed Titus hesitantly downstairs to the family room.

"Tracy! It's good to see you!" Trevor stood and caught her in a firm embrace.

Tracy turned her head away from him in one, quick, instinctive motion but his lips brushed against the corner of her mouth before she could move her face completely out of range.

"I was just showing the kids the retreat center where I

stayed in California."

"It's so beautiful, Mom." Theodora oohed dreamily. "Can we all go there sometime? I could really get into this beach thing."

Fear clutched at Tracy's gut. He was trying to take them away from her. He had promised her he wouldn't, but he was. It was all part of a perfectly-laid plan, a subtle plot to over-romanticize life in California, a cold, calculated maneuver on his part to lure their children into wanting to live with him. She wanted to scream.

"Look at that big wave!" Timothy squealed, stomping his feet on the soft sofa cushions.

"Sit down right now, Timothy! I've told you not to put your feet on the couch," Tracy snapped.

He ignored her.

"It's my fault." Trevor touched her arm.

She cringed.

"They're just excited to have me home."

"I know." She took a step back and glared at him from across the room. The tape continued to play. The video resounded with the echo of men and woman's voices chattering enthusiastically. Women? Who were they? Wives and mothers who were more accepting than she? Lesbians? Tracy shuddered. She had assumed the conference attendees would be men only. It was too much to take in. At once, she hated herself for being so naive and resented Trevor for forcing her to become otherwise.

She peered at the television screen. One would never guess to look that these were gay men and lesbian women. She chided herself silently. What had she expected? Men and women openly engaging in sexual acts in the middle of broad daylight? She took a deep breath.

"Don't look so worried," Trevor whispered. "It's a generic DVD designed to promote the conference center that adjoins the church."

Tracy knew if she was going make it through the next few days she was going to have to trust Trevor to act in the best interests of her and the children. She had no other choice.

Trevor turned off the television. “Well, that’s all folks. Did I hear your mother say something about gardening?”

“But, Dad—”

“No buts about it. I had a hankering for fresh green beans from the garden the whole time I was in California. Are they still producing? Theodora?”

“All right,” she groaned. “Dad, will you call me Teddy? Mom refuses even though I’ve asked her like a million times.”

“And me, Ty?” Titus added.

Tracy rolled her eyes. “C’mon you guys. Time to go.”

They watched unsympathetically as the children trudged up the stairs. An uncomfortable silence pervaded the room. Tracy listened carefully as their footsteps faded into the distance. The door clanged shut.

“So...” Trevor put his hands in his pockets.

“They’re so innocent. They’re not going to understand any of this.”

“You know it’s what I have to do.” Trevor’s voice softened. “You have to accept my decision on this, Tracy. I believe God is calling me to move to California. And while I don’t intend to indulge in sexual relations with another man, I can’t continue to live a lie. It’s not fair of me to ask you to continue to live without the benefit of physical relations in the marriage bed. You have needs just as I do, Tracy - needs I can no longer fulfill.”

“I know it. That doesn’t mean I like it.”

“I’ll do my best to make them understand.”

“What can you possibly say that will make it any easier?”

Trevor hung his head. “I could tell them the truth.”

“No. You promised me, Trevor. It will be hard enough for them as it is. Knowing the truth... It’s too much to ask of them. I can barely comprehend...”

“I know. I’m sorry.”

“Don’t be. I know it isn’t something you wished on yourself.”

"I'd give anything if it could be different."

"I know," she said.

"Keeping the truth from them will only make this harder on you, Tracy. If you let me assume the entire responsibility for what I'm about to do they'll put the blame on me and me alone. Which is as it should be."

"You needn't act like some sort of sacrificial lamb. You aren't purposely trying to do us wrong. And I don't want their pity."

"There are some who would say I should honor my commitment to my family no matter what the cost."

"I'm not asking you to do that." There had been a time when she'd wanted him to. She'd pleaded with him to stay, told him he never had to make love to her again if he would just leave things the way they were for the children's sake. She'd begged him not to wreak havoc on their families, their church, Theodora and Titus. Timothy. A part of her still hoped he would change his mind, to admit the whole awful thing had been some sort of phase he'd been going through.

Trevor reached for her hand. "The fewer facts we give them, the more likely they'll assume this was partly your decision."

"It is partly my decision. I told you you could go. I gave you my word we'd be fine without you."

"I still believe it's for the best," Trevor said.

"I know you do."

"You don't?" he asked.

"I believe it's best for you. And, in spite of everything, I still love you enough to want what's best for you."

"And for you?"

"Yes," she whispered. "Knowing what I know, it's what I would have chosen even if you hadn't. But for them... How can it be the best thing for them?"

A tremulous silence hung in the air.

"We should probably tell them as soon as we're done with supper."

"I'm supposed to take a cake to the Missionary Society meeting tonight but I'm sure Karen will swing by here and pick it up on her way if I call and tell her you've just gotten home. There'll never be a good time."

"No. It's going to be a shock no matter how or when we tell them. The kids said you'd been gone all day. Painting?"

"I'm helping Michelle out of a jam. The pay scale is surprisingly generous given my lack of experience. It could lead to more work if I play my cards right."

"Since when does it have anything to do with playing your cards right?"

"You'll always be a conservative minister at heart."

"I've been praying that God would lead you to something that would bring you a sense of purpose, some fulfillment."

"Something or someone?" She looked down to avoid his glance, but not before seeing the crushed look on his face. "I'm sorry, Trevor. This is hard for me, too."

"I know. I'll help you get supper together if you'll tell me what to do."

*****

Barclay cinched his belt around his robe and took the phone from Marianne Westheimer, the resident owner of the Mary Rose Manor Bed and Breakfast. "This had better be good, Lauren. I told you not to call me here unless there was an emergency."

"If having no caterer for a party that's only three weeks off isn't a crisis I don't know what is."

"Oh, Lauren. Please tell me it's something more pressing than that. I've already explained my cell phone doesn't get good reception here, and that there are no telephones in the rooms. The Westheimers live on the garden level and I'm on the third floor. Every time someone calls for me the poor woman has to run all up three flights of stairs and back down again say nothing about the fact that I have to get dressed and tromp all the way down to their office to use the phone."

"I refuse to be intimidated by your theatrics, Barclay. You make the place sound positively primitive. If I know you, you're wallowing in the lap of luxury even as we speak and just trying to make me feel guilty."

"I'm doing no such thing." Barclay looked over his shoulder. Marianne Westheimer had disappeared. "Please just tell me what the problem is, Lauren. I don't want to tie up their phone. This is their only line."

"I need the names of any caterers in the area you've managed to locate. If you think planning a party from over a hundred miles off if easy, you're sorely mistaken. It's essential that I contact whomever comes most highly recommended at once or you can be assured their calendar will be full and we'll be left high and dry."

"Fine," Barclay sighed. "The premier catering establishment in town is run by Michelle Sheffield. It's listed in the directory under The Painted Lady. The problem is, I happen to know the owner and she's extremely busy painting the interior of my house."

"How quaint."

He could almost envision Lauren looking down her nose, probably examining the cuticles of her nails and rating the efforts of her manicurist as she spoke. The gesture was so inherently imbedded in his mind that it didn't matter that she was miles away.

"The woman paints and cooks? I can only hope not simultaneously. Really," Lauren said. "The term *one horse town* takes on a host of new meanings now that you live in Maple Valley."

He refused to dignify her ravings with a response.

"What novel advertising possibilities it brings to mind. Is the food fit for human consumption?"

"Your scorn is unfounded, Lauren. The woman is a multi-talented wonder. Her specialty is interior design although she does not paint under normal conditions. She's doing me a great favor by heading up the renovations at my house personally because her painter broke his ankle. Rest assured she has a capable staff to manage the tea house and catering divisions of her small but admirable little empire."

"Then I fail to understand what you perceive to be the

problem."

"My point is simply that she is already overtaxed and may not react kindly to taking on another project of the magnitude you're most likely envisioning - especially one whose apex of activity would culminate at the precise moment she has to have the house finished. You have no idea what all is involved in an undertaking of this scale, Lauren. If you hadn't been so premature in scheduling the date for this housewarming affair we wouldn't be in such dire straits now, would we?"

"Barclay Alexander, I've half a mind to withdraw my services and leave you to your own devices where this party is concerned. It's obvious my efforts on your behalf are totally unappreciated."

"Ill timed, most certainly. And I've told you over and over again that I don't appreciate your intrusions on my new life here in Maple Valley. I've tried to be kind, Lauren, but this whole charade of an engagement has got to stop."

"The fact that I've got your grandmother's ring on my finger would prove otherwise."

"My mother gave it to you, not I. You know I never intended to act on their cockamamie scheme."

"Fine. Call the engagement off if that's what you want," she huffed.

"What I want is for you to be happy. I know Henri hurt you, but you will find someone who loves you the way you deserve to be loved, and you will find happiness again."

She laughed. A stilted apparition of the real thing, but a laugh nonetheless. "Mother never hinted that happiness was something I could expect to find in a marriage. I believe she did mentioned being well-provided for and sought-after socially, to which I might add occasionally bedded... with at least enough frequency to create a prodigy... sexually sated if was lucky. That's what I was led to believe I could expect from life as Mrs. Lauren Humphreys Alexander."

"And that doesn't bother you? No mention of love, joy, contentment?" He could have said more, but even he wasn't cad enough to force the issue over the telephone, in his robe, from the parlor of the Merry Rose Manor.

Lauren harrumphed. "You always have been an idealistic dreamer, Barclay. It's time for you to recognize a good thing when you see it, my dear, and snatch it up while you still can."

*****

Tracy settled into Trevor's big wingback chair and patted her lap. Timothy sprawled on top if her as limply as a sack of sugar. She wound her fingers through his hair absently. The boy was visibly sleepy, lulled into a false sense of security by the soothing touch of her hands.

She could hear Trevor in the next room saying, "Theodora, Titus, your mother and I would like you to join us in my office if you're done with the dishes. There's something we need to discuss as a family."

"Teddy, Dad. Remember?"

"And Ty," Titus said, his voice sounding a little lower than it had even that morning.

She heard a snap and shook her head. No doubt the very mature Titus/Ty, snapping a dishtowel in the direction of older sister Theodora/Teddy's derrière. He did it every night.

"Told ya." This from Titus.

"Told me what?" Theodora asked.

"We're moving to California."

"Shut up, brat."

"Theodora," Trevor said. "Titus. Now!"

The trio trudged into the office with Trevor bringing up the rear.

Timothy's little body suddenly felt like a great weight pressing down on her. When Trevor cleared his throat, he sounded miles away. Theodora was the first who seemed to feel the ominous silence that had settled over the room. She looked from her mother to her father and drew her breath in slowly. Tracy recognized the look of fear that flitted across her face, but there was nothing she could do to stop it.

Titus, normally tender Titus, was popping wisecracks

like a firecracker shooting off sparks. She was startled to recognize, after all these months, that it was his way of dealing with any stress too severe for his sensitive soul to encompass. She made a mental note that she would have to help him learn to express his emotions. She would have to teach him not to be afraid to feel.

"Your mother and I want you to know, first and foremost, that the decisions we make as adults in no way minimize our feelings for you, or how much we love each of you. You're very precious to us – both of us."

Titus grew quiet suddenly, as though he were living out some recurring nightmare he'd had in a previous life. Timothy shuffled in her lap, oblivious to the earth-shattering news about to be imparted. Theodora sat perfectly still.

Tracy took a moment to look each of them in the eye. "I want you to know that I will always be there for each of you. Nothing will change in that respect. Our lives will go on much the same as they always have."

She could see the effect that her words, designed to calm, actually had on her children. Their eyes grew wide with suspicion, then terror. Titus looked like he was ready to pounce on the first one to speak the words he feared would come.

Trevor cleared his throat again. "I know this is going to be very hard to understand. I take full responsibility for the choices I'm about to share with you. Your mother did not choose this course of action. She is blameless. She will need your support and understanding over the next few weeks."

Titus looked on, utterly, mortally horrified.

Theodora just sat, frozen by the bone-numbing silence. Neither child was stupid.

"I've accepted an assistant pastor's job in California at the church I was showing you earlier beginning later this month."

Titus was too shocked to say *I told you so.*

"Your mother and I have known for the last several years that the kind of love that is necessary for a marriage to survive no longer exists between the two of us." Trevor spoke gently, the way he did when he was giving the devotional for the children at Vacation Bible School. "We will always be your parents. We will both love each of you unconditionally for the rest of our lives. But we do not love each other in the way a married couple must."

"I know it will be very hard to have your Dad so far away," Tracy interjected.

"You're getting a divorce?" Theodora asked incredulously.

"What's a divorce again?" Timothy said, his bottom lip quivering. "Are Josh and Nate divorced?"

"You don't know anything. Uncle Jake is the one who's divorced from their mom, you moron." Titus said harshly.

Theodora froze. Timothy whimpered and tried to hide his face in Tracy's arm.

"Why don't you love her? What's wrong with you?" Titus yelled at his father.

"I do love her. I just don't love her the way a husband loves a wife." Trevor tried to rest his hands on Titus's shoulders but the boy pushed him away with a ferocity they had never witnessed. "There are things you don't understand, Titus. Things you won't understand until you're older," he said helplessly.

"It will be okay," Tracy said frantically. "We'll all be fine. It will take some getting used to but we'll all be fine."

Theodora was hugging her arms to herself like she wanted to block out the entire world. Timothy was crying. He probably didn't even know why.

"I'll visit just as often as I can and I'll be back for several weeks each year to spend time with you over summer vacation," Trevor said with tears streaming down his face. "You can phone me anytime you need to talk or e-mail me at my office computer. I know it won't be like having me here—"

"We don't want you here anyway," Titus said hatefully.

"Stop it!" Theodora shrieked. "Stop it, Titus! We do want you." She sobbed and turned to face Tracy. "This is your fault. What did you do to make him stop loving you?"

Tracy felt her face grow cold.

"She didn't do anything," Trevor took Theodora in his arms. "Your mother has done nothing wrong. This is my choice. This is all my doing."

"She said she wouldn't move to California." Theodora twisted her head around to glare at her mother. "Would you really ruin your marriage and split up our family just because you don't want to move? It wouldn't be that bad. Not as long as Dad was with us."

"This has nothing to do with California except that happens to be where I want to live right now. Your mother and I would be having this conversation with you whether or not I was moving."

"But Dad." She buried her face in his arms.

"I know it's hard to accept, honey." He turned to face his oldest son. Titus's normally serene face was twisted into a sneer. "Titus, your anger is justified. But it will destroy you unless you learn to deal with it and I can't stand by and watch that happen. I'd like to be able to talk to you man to man if you'll let me."

"Tracy, if you want to get Timothy ready for bed, I'll be up to read him a story in about fifteen minutes."

She nodded, helped her littlest to her feet, and met Trevor's eyes before she turned to leave the room. She looked back to face her children when she reached the door. "Theodora, Titus, I love both of you more than you'll ever know."

Neither child would meet her glance.

Chapter 7

Trevor watched as Timothy approached the hide-a-bed he'd pulled out in front of the television in the basement the night before. Timothy stopped short when he reached the edge of the thin mattress, rubbed his eyes, and looked down at his half-hidden form under the covers.

"Can I snuggle in bed with you while I watch Scooby Doo?" Timothy mumbled blearily.

"I don't think there are cartoons on Wednesday mornings. Don't you have to get ready for school?" He could sense the child's disorientation. "Is your mom awake yet?"

"No."

He wondered if Tracy had lain awake in bed three fourths of the night as he had. "C'mon, little man. Let's go see what we can wrestle up for breakfast and then I'll help you find some clothes to wear to school."

The sound of Timothy's giggles wafting through the kitchen walls filled Tracy with a much needed, if short-lived, sense of calm. Her composure turned to dread all too quickly, however, when she came face to face with Theodora in the hallway outside the bathroom door.

"Good morning," Tracy said in what she hoped was a normal voice.

Not only was there no reply, but her daughter made a specific point of walking around her in a circle wide enough to have prevented the transfer of a severe case of leprosy.

"Theodora, we can't survive living in the same house if we're not going to speak to one another."

"Fine. Maybe I should go live with Aunt Michelle and Uncle Jake in Maple Valley. She always says she wishes I lived closer so I could baby-sit Sarah. Besides, she understands me."

"What about your friends at school, your teachers, drama

club? Wouldn't you miss them?"

"Like I'll be able to show my face at school once everyone finds out you're getting a divorce."

"I'm sure there are other kids at school who live with just one parent."

"Yeah. Sure there are. Everyone treats them like some sort of freaks. And none of their fathers were ministers before they got divorced. They'll laugh me out of the place."

"Your father is still going to be a minister, Theodora. He's no less committed to serving God than he was before this happened. I hope when all is said and done you'll be proud of the way both of us have picked up the pieces and continued to live life to its fullest." Tracy touched Theodora's arm tentatively. "Brooke cares about you. It's fine with me if you want to confide in her. I think she'll be a good listener. I can't imagine her laughing about something this serious."

"If you say so."

Tracy ignored her sarcasm and continued to speak in a gentle voice. "If you don't mind, I thought I'd also call the school and ask to speak to the guidance counselor. That way if any of you need to talk to Mrs. Mittenwald you can feel comfortable going to the office." Tracy thought her daughter's expression softened a little. "This is going to be hard for all of us. I hope you'll feel free to come and talk to me if you have any questions."

A stagnant pause, ripe with the stench of waters that have not been stirred in far too long, filled Tracy's nostrils as she gauged her daughter's reaction. Tension gripped her chest until she could hardly inhale.

"Why didn't you say something sooner, Mom? If all this has been going on for two or three whole years why couldn't you have given us a little time to get used to the idea before now? How am I supposed to trust you with my feelings when I know you didn't trust me enough to be honest with me?"

"I'm sorry." Tracy's eyes filled with tears and her lungs felt like they would tear in two when she tried to breathe.

"I'm not a baby, Mom. I know about stuff. And I'm not stupid. I could see that things were different than they used to be. I can remember the days when you and Dad were, well, more affectionate with each other. And I know how Brooke's mom and dad are when they're together. It's kind of pathetic at times, but at least you can tell they're in love."

"I'm so sorry," Tracy stammered. "I still think of you as being my little girl and you're not. You're a beautiful young woman and I'll try to remember to respect that from now on."

Theodora looked at her as though to say *yeah, duh*.

"There will be times when I'll need to talk to someone, too," Tracy offered. "I'd like to know I can count on you to be there for me now that you do know what's going on."

Liar, liar, pants on fire. Tracy's sub-conscious taunted her. Theodora didn't have a clue what was really going on; nor would she ever.

"Well if you really want my opinion, I think you should probably warn Timothy's teacher and Mrs. Mittenwald both - unless you want the whole school to know. The kid's a blabbermouth. He'll be whining about the divorce before he even hits the building."

"That sounds like good advice."

"You need all the help you can get." Theodora rolled her eyes and proceeded to head down the hall.

Titus stumbled out of the room he shared with Timothy. He took one look at his mother and turned around to retreat into the safety of his room again.

"Hey, Titus! No good morning hug?" She extended her arms and watched as her older son turned and eyed her skeptically. "I already brushed my teeth so I don't even have morning breath."

"Aw, Mom." He hugged her quickly and then scooted back a few steps.

"You doing okay this morning?"

"Yeah. I guess so."

She stopped to weigh her words before she spoke. "I know you love your dad very much and that this hurts."

He looked down.

"I just want you to know that it's okay to keep loving him. It's okay to hate him or be mad at him, too - or at me - as long as you don't keep it inside and let it eat away at you. Promise me you'll talk to me or him or someone if you need to vent, all right?"

"Yeah. I guess so."

"I'm going to hold you to that. I love you, Titus."

"I know." He dangled his foot in circles that pulled the nap of the carpet this way and that.

She repeated her plan to tell the school counselor what was going on. "So you'll be all right at school today?"

"Yeah."

"Any soccer games this week?"

"A scrimmage on Thursday night after school. Mr. Bartholomew already said they'd give me a ride home."

"Good. I probably won't be able to come see you play. Maybe next week if things have calmed down a little." Tracy sighed. "Your dad will be around all week and part of next. Maybe he'd like to come to the game. Talk to him, okay?"

"I'll try."

"Thanks, sweetheart. Remember I love you."

"You already said that about ten times."

"I know. Well, we'd better both get a move on or we'll be late to school, work." She laughed. "I'm still not used to being a working woman."

He looked at her like she was crazy for being able to laugh. By the time she left the house, she wondered if he was right.

*****

It was with a huge sigh of relief that Tracy shut the station wagon door and navigated the driveway past the drainage ditch and onto the road. For the first time since she'd promised to help Michelle out, she felt no resentment in her mind about having to leave her family and go to work. Instead, what heaven to escape the house! It wasn't just that she wanted to keep her distance from Trevor. She was truly thrilled to have a new focus, a source of potential satisfaction and pride, a point of convergence in her life.

She had no intention of shirking her duties at home. It was clear the children would need her more than ever during the transition time that lay ahead. But her work was a welcome distraction. Her brain whirled with the realities of the financial obstacle course that lay ahead of her. She'd have to leave the parsonage soon now that Trevor had resigned, find a place for them to live, put down deposits on a rental house, put the utilities in her name, apply for new credit cards, and find out what her options were concerning health insurance.

Now that she had a job, even a temporary one, she could start to formulate a plan of action. It felt good. It wasn't just about the money. Knowing that what she was doing mattered to someone, even if only in the not so grand scheme of things, gave her an infusion of optimism that she sorely needed.

She didn't care one iota that she had only been asked to do the job because another painter had been clumsy enough to break his ankle, or that some rich woman had been stupid enough to plan a housewarming party so soon after her fiancé bought a house that needed renovating. Her newfound sense of self-importance was more significant than the events that precipitated it - an elixir that made the sky seem bluer, the sun brighter, the maple leaves that were starting to turn in the uppermost reaches of the trees in front of Barclay Alexander's house even more vibrant than they really were. She was on her way to somewhere, anywhere. After spinning her wheels and going in circles for almost three years, she was moving down the road.

Tracy pulled her station wagon into the driveway, gathered her small cache of supplies in her arms, disembarked from the car, and swung towards Barclay Alexander's house with a purposeful stride. She was wearing a pair of painter's pants that she'd dug out of the cedar chest during a bout of insomnia the night before, where they'd been since they'd fallen out of vogue sometime during her senior year. The crisp, white cotton pants were outfitted with tabs and loops for hammers, paint brushes, and assorted painting paraphernalia. Best of all, they still fit her like a charm.

She was proud, and rightfully so, that her waist was still as trim as it had been in high school, and after three children no less. The industrial strength front zipper of the painter's pants had firmed what little paunch she had in front and although the baggy legs would have camouflaged heavy thighs with ease, there was no need of that in her case.

She'd found just enough room to tuck in her shirt, an old teal green polo shirt of Trevor's with *LIFE UNDER CONSTRUCTION* imprinted on the lapel in letters formed by carpenter's squares, vertically placed screw drivers, a pipe wrench, and assorted two by fours with nails pounded in at strategic places. She'd helped him design the logo for a Christian men's retreat he'd headed up at Trail's End Lodge years earlier, never guessing how appropriate the intended meaning behind their artwork would feel today. The shirt was splattered with paint in the hues they'd used to freshen up the parsonage when they'd first moved in, unlike her pants, which had never been intended for work in the first place.

Michelle was prying open a five-gallon pail of paint with a screwdriver when Tracy walked in the door.

"Hello! Isn't it a glorious morning?" Tracy announced brightly as she bounced into the front room.

"My, aren't we chipper today?" Michelle looked at her curiously. "Hey! I remember those pants! They still fit you? You're absolutely sickening, you know."

Tracy beamed. "I brought each of us a hat so we wouldn't have to go home with our hair full of paint splatters again."

"Our hair?"

"Well, okay. So I didn't get any on myself. But you were right about the stiff neck, arms, and shoulders." Tracy bent over to peer at the wall where it met the craggy stone fireplace hugging the east side of the parlor. "Pretty fine trim work if I do say so myself. Who'd ever have guessed I'd have such a gift for painting around fossil rocks and agates?"

"I knew there was some sort of hidden talent buried under that fluff exterior you've managed to maintain all these years," Michelle teased. "Going down to the hardware store and buying a tiny artist's brush to trim around and about all the little recesses was a great idea."

"Thanks. Did the Lord of the Manor come by to inspect our work yet?" Tracy asked casually.

"He gave you rave reviews. He was shocked to hear you're just an amateur."

"Cool! Just what I wanted to hear."

"You're really enjoying this aren't you?"

"Yes! Last night when I couldn't get to sleep I actually sat down and charted out a schedule of sorts. Once I'd had the grand tour and seen how much we accomplished our first day out, I thought I ought to be able to put together some rough figures on how long the job should take to complete. Just to make sure we're staying on schedule and everything. Of course, wallpapering is still a relative unknown but I assume our speed will increase fairly consistently no matter what we're working on once we know what we're doing and get used to working together."

"I'm very impressed."

"Thank you." Tracy felt her cheeks heating up – a compliment from anyone who had grown up a Jones was a rare occurrence. "Is that the dining room paint you're stirring?"

"Dining room ceiling."

"Good. I'm hoping we can get the Frank Lloyd Wright wallpaper insert you were talking about yesterday hung before we leave today. It'll probably be a snap once we get started but I've never done anything like it before and it makes me nervous. I'm under enough stress right now that I'd just as soon get it over with so I can cross it off my list of things to worry about."

"That sounds great. I do have to leave a little early today. If it doesn't matter that I might have to go in the middle of things it would be great to get it over with. I've watched the guys work with these panels and they really don't look too hard."

"Good. Let's do it then."

They worked in silence for a few minutes, first trimming each corner, crease, and crevice with brushes, then rolling the smooth surfaces in between with extender poles attached to the roller handles.

Michelle stuffed a loose strand of hair back up under the cap Tracy had provided for her. "Speaking of stress, I expected you to be exhibiting a little more of it this morning. Did you not tell the kids after all?"

"No, we did. The experience certainly doesn't rank up there with the top ten high points of my life, but I'm relieved they finally know. Theodora was quick to point out that they might have appreciated a little warning instead of springing it on them all at once like we did."

"That's the Jones way. Cover up your adversities as long as you can in hopes that the problem will go away so you won't have to deal with it."

"You can laugh if you want." Tracy bent down to fill her roller with more paint. "The sad truth is, I've been in denial for almost three years. I spent months praying for a miracle before I finally admitted to myself that this was the road God intended we travel and there was nothing I could do but accept His will in the matter and move on."

"You don't have to defend your faith to me. I wouldn't let Rachael hear you talking about God's will for your life though, or you'll have quite a discussion on your hands."

"Thanks for the warning."

"So, how did the kids take the news?" Michelle asked.

"I should warn you that Theodora is planning to move in with you and Jake if the going gets too tough in Rice Lake. She's willing to baby-sit in lieu of paying room and board."

"Oh. I see." Michelle chuckled. "You'd know how tempting an offer that is if you'd had my string of bad luck with baby-sitters."

"Good. I may just take you up on the offer one of these

days. Remember how we got on our mother's nerves – and vice versa – when we were teenagers? Well, I'm here to tell you nothing has changed."

Michelle just laughed.

"I called Timothy's teacher and the guidance counselor at school this morning before I drove down. I'd given them Mom and Dad's number in case of an emergency since I'm so far away from Rice Lake but that wouldn't have worked today since Mom and Dad don't have a clue what's going on. Now that we've started telling people I'm anxious to finish so people don't start hearing it from the grape vine. You know how word gets around."

"Unfortunately, yes."

"Trevor's scheduled a meeting with the deacon board at six and then we're both going to go over to Mom and Dad's after supper."

"At least Trevor is sharing the responsibility of telling people. When Jacob and I decided to get a divorce I had to tell my parents and his both."

"Where was I when all this was happening? It seems like a million years ago now that you're with Jake."

"Things were different when Jacob and I got divorced. We lived so far away, and none of you were ever that close to Jacob. There weren't any children involved. I don't envy you that part."

"It adds a whole other dimension." Tracy made another swipe with the paint roller. "Now you've got me thinking about Jacob. How could he not tell his own parents?"

"It wasn't as though he didn't have plenty of opportunity. We maintained separate bedrooms in the same house for several months after we made the decision to split up, primarily for financial reasons. When his parents came to visit, his solution was to come crawling back to my bed at nine o'clock that evening rather than have to fess up to them about our sleeping arrangements."

Tracy shook her head.

"I didn't feel I should have to be the one to break the news so I kept quiet. Jacob still hadn't told them we were separating months later when he moved out and got an apartment. Every time his mother phoned I'd have to invent some excuse for him, then quickly call Jacob at his apartment and tell him to call his mother back before the night was over."

"Good grief. If cell phones had already been invented they probably still wouldn't know. How did the truth finally come out?"

"There was some sort of emergency and it was imperative his mother reach him immediately. She kept pressing me to tell her where he was and when he'd be home. I finally broke down and told her he hadn't lived at the house for over two months and gave her his new phone number. She was totally shocked and I cried myself silly when it was all over."

"Oh, Michelle. I'm embarrassed to say I never knew you went through any of this. I guess I was so involved with my own little life and the babies and church that I just didn't..."

"It's okay, Tracy. I wasn't trying to make you feel bad. I did my own part in shutting all of you out. I knew you and Trevor would disapprove. You always been so protective of the children and I didn't want to be a negative influence on them. My self-esteem was at such a low point that I just couldn't risk opening up to you for fear of how you'd react. So I never gave any of you the chance."

"Knowing what I know now, it's easy to say we would have risen to the occasion. I guess we'll never know."

"No. But we can be sure not to make the same mistake."

Tracy felt a tinge of guilt. She had already denied her family the opportunity to help her by keeping the truth about Trevor from them. By choosing not to reveal his new sexual preferences with them - or anyone else, she'd already cheated herself out of the benefit of their listening ears and supportive arms. Trevor was willing to be completely honest with their family and the church. Was her decision to withhold an essential part of the story really the right way to handle the situation or was she just letting her pride get in the way like she so often had in the past?

Chapter 8

The hours slipped by while Michelle and Tracy worked to finish the dining room ceiling and three out of the four walls, alternately engaging in conversation and lost in their own silent reveries.

Michelle paused long enough to flex her shoulders before dipping her roller in the tray of paint. "I think you'll get more support from the family than you think, Tracy. Even back when I was going through my divorce, Dad was really there for me. He used to call me when Mom was away at Missionary Society meetings and talk the whole time she was gone. It meant a lot to me to know that he was there if I needed him. Even Mom tried to understand."

"I had no idea," Tracy said.

"They did pretty well considering how they feel about divorce," Michelle inspected the southwest corner with a critical eye to make sure she hadn't missed any spots and moved to the opposite side of the room to continue rolling. "You and Trevor divorcing is going to be a lot harder for them though. I mean, they think you're perfect and they idolize Trevor."

"I know." Tracy grimaced at the irony. "They're very close to Trevor. They love him, and he they, like he was their own son. Even more so now that Trevor's parents are both gone."

"I don't envy you." Michelle paused with her elongated roller suspended in mid-air. "Oh my gosh! Is it really three o'clock already?"

"Talk about time flying! We've accomplished a lot though. I'm almost done over here. If you've got time to go over the directions for the wallpaper panel with me. I'd still like to try to get it done today if I can. It's just one small wall and then we'll be done with the whole room."

"Let me get the rollers soaking and we'll take a look.

The basic procedure is no different than any other wall-papering job, but the design will have to be centered in the middle of the wall both horizontally and vertically. I've got time to help measure, maybe even put up the first few panels before I leave if you don't mind finishing it up by yourself."

"You know how I hate math. If we can get the measuring done while you're still here I'll be fine. I can clean the paint rollers when I'm done so you can get out of here a little sooner. Now that Trevor's home I won't have to rush off quite so quickly in the afternoons."

Michelle read the directions aloud while Tracy pounded the covers back on the paint cans.

"So what is the design of anyway?" Tracy queried, peering over her shoulder at the series of parallel lines, quadrilateral shapes, and congruent circles that comprised the wallpaper inset.

"It's an exact replica of a famous stained glass window by Frank Lloyd Wright."

"Oh." Tracy stood back and scrutinized the pattern from a distance. "It looks like a nightmare I used to have when I was in tenth grade geometry with Mr. Zwicker."

"I liked that class."

"So what else is new? You were always good at math."

"I never thought of geometry so much as math, but art. The interrelation of space and forms and shape has always fascinated me. I'm not sure my fine arts professors would agree, but I found my background in math very helpful when it came to studying interior design and architecture."

"I'm glad one of us has a true appreciation for whatever it is this thing is supposed to look like." Tracy walked around the image and looked at it from this way and that as if trying to find something familiar ensconced in the abstract design. "This part looks like a head of wheat. See the grains? When I look at the motif closely I can almost see an American Indian influence."

"It's all part of the Prairie style of architectural design."

"It's a little too masculine for my tastes, although I do like the subtle colors."

"Again, the Prairie influence. It's very earthy."

"I'm really curious to see what you've got planned for the place when we're done painting, Michelle. It has such an austere feeling the way it is now." She shivered and hugged her arms around herself. "It makes me cold. I hope your concept of *earthy* includes a little sunshine and some flowers, or if we have to strictly adhere to the masculine persona, a colorful vegetable patch."

Michelle laughed. "I'll do my best." She crouched on her haunches and surveyed the plumb line she'd used to mark the wall. "I think I'm ready to hang the first strip if you've got the tools together."

Tracy stepped forward and handed Michelle a roller and a brush. "I've got the first two strips wet already. They're booked and resting."

"You'll have three plain panels on each side of the design and a part strip that will have to be trimmed in each corner when you're done," Michelle explained as she climbed up the ladder she'd positioned near the center of the wall.

"Is that the doorbell?" Tracy asked as she was about to hand Michelle the first strip of wallpaper.

"Maybe our fairy godmother sent a masseuse to give us neck and shoulder rubs." Michelle looked up doubtfully at the ten-foot high ceiling. "I'm beginning to understand why Roger's muscles are so well-developed. At any rate, you'll have to see who it is. I'm out the door the second this sheet is up."

"Don't do it until I get back, okay? I'd like to watch the first strip go up so I can make sure to use the same technique on each piece."

"Consistency is important. But you'll have to hurry. I've really got to be going or I'll be late for my meeting."

"I'll be right back." Tracy gingerly laid the wet roll she held in her hands on the sheet of plastic they were using to protect the floor, lifted her hat from her head, and flicked her fingers through her hair.

Michelle climbed down the stepladder, being careful to

avoid the water tray they were using to dampen the adhesive on the back of the panels and picked up the level. "I think I'll check the alignment of the chalk line one more time."

"Give me two seconds," Tracy said. She bobbed her shoulders and rotated her arms on the way to the door in an effort to ease the tension that had accumulated since morning, then swung the heavy door open with a burst of renewed energy.

A distinguished looking older couple was standing on the stoop. Her eyes went first to their mouths, the feature most near eye-level given her diminutive size. Her first impression was that of the man standing with his lips pursed in a petulant grimace. The woman's mouth was slightly agape as if to disagree.

"Can I help you?"

"You may if you know who the owner of the decrepit old station wagon that's blocking the driveway is." The man snorted.

"I'm s-sorry," Tracy stuttered. "I didn't know Mr. Alexander was expecting company."

"If you'd be so kind as to move the vehicle, we have a few small pieces of furniture and some boxes that need to be unloaded." He turned to the woman at his side. Her skin was flawless although aged, her hair carefully coifed and dyed to match her eyebrows. "Elizabeth, give the woman your keys so she can pull our car in to the driveway when she's finished moving hers."

Tracy wondered if she should curtsy before she left to comply with their wishes.

"No need to return empty handed." The man's suggestion followed her out the door like a kick in the rear.

She'd been given her second order, she realized with a start. The screen door twanged her from behind on her way out the door as if to second the motion.

Michelle was climbing into her vehicle when Tracy finished switching the cars. "I heard everything. I sneaked out the back door. I can't be late to this meeting."

"Traitor. Who are these people? Do you know them?"

"I think they're Barclay's parents. I've never met them before but they fit the description."

"Oh, good. What am I supposed to do now?"

"Stand up to them. Tell them you're in the middle of wallpapering and can't be disturbed."

Tracy could tell by her sympathetic look that however well intended, Michelle could no more have followed her own instructions than Tracy could.

"Have fun at your meeting."

"I'll make it up to you," her sister promised.

"Sure you will," Tracy said begrudgingly.

*****

Barclay stretched his legs out under his desk and leaned back against the old orange Herculon swivel chair, pushing it as far back as it would go. His office at Elk Creek Woolen Mills was furnished with a ragtag batch of furniture. Just like the factory, there wasn't a piece that hadn't seen better times.

Five file cabinets, all bulging at the seams, lined the west wall. That is was the west wall at all was only apparent to those that knew how the plant sat on the lot geographically. There were no windows in his office save one that opened up to the hall between his secretary's office and the plant itself.

A bevy of men and women crisscrossed the hall in front of him as the day shift began to wind down and the night shift started to filter in. A man lifted his hat or nodded, a woman occasionally waved as the employees streamed by. Anyone who had met him directly was put in the awkward position of not knowing whether to acknowledge his presence, or walk on by the open window as if he weren't right on the other side of the glass looking out.

He took a small piece of paper from the wallet in his back pocket, set it on the desk and tried not to dwell on the significance of the call he was about to make. He willed his muscles to relax as he dialed the number on the old rotary telephone, still sprawled out in a pose that was anything but rigid.

He'd always been one to pace back and forth while he carried on a conversation. The floor length windows that looked out over the Mississippi River from his office at the company headquarters in Minneapolis and a lightweight cell phone that he never went anywhere without had always made telephone consultations a pleasant aspect of his day. But his cell phone didn't work well at the factory and his desk phone felt like a lead weight, tethering him to his desk and dragging him down. There was not enough room in this office to pace.

He nuzzled the molded plastic piece attached to the heavy receiver against his shoulder blade and used his neck to tuck the phone in place. The hum of several dozen machines knitting their wares tinged the air with a static charge. He perched his hands, one on either armrest, until his lanky elbows bowed out on each side. His foot toyed with the underside of the desk as he listened to the phone ring once, then twice.

"Reverend Tomlinson speaking."

Crap. His muscles tensed and his feet hit the floor as the chair jerked back into an upright position. The woman at the Budget Mart had told him Tracy was married to a minister named Trevor Tomlinson. He'd known he might answer.

"May I speak to Tracy Tomlinson, please?"

"She's not home at the moment. May I tell her who called?"

Barclay's mind went blank. He'd rehearsed this very scenario at least half a dozen times in the last twenty-four hours. His answer had to be such that it wouldn't raise suspicion. *What if they had caller ID?* He didn't want to be the cause of any trouble when Tracy was going through so much already.

Barclay cleared his throat. "Um. Mrs. Tomlinson entered a drawing for a free carpet shampoo earlier this week at the State Fair and her name was selected to receive the grand prize. I was calling to try to schedule an appointment. I'm rather hard to reach. Will she be home later this evening?"

"Yes. No. I mean, she should be home from work any

moment now, but we have plans this evening. It might be better to try to reach her tomorrow evening - you should be safe if you wait until after six. She'll be very excited," Reverend Tomlinson promised pleasantly.

"Thank you, sir. And congratulations," Barclay added guiltily. Lying to a minister... one more black smudge behind his name come judgment day…

Barclay sighed. There was nothing he could do until tomorrow night. He'd just have to be patient. He stood, looked down at his watch, and decided that if he left immediately there was still time to make it downtown for the meeting at City Hall.

*****

The meeting had already begun by the time Michelle slipped into her chair. The Maple Valley Chamber of Commerce met once a month on a regular basis. Today's meeting had been convened at a special time for the purpose of planning for the arrival of 10,000 bicycle riders on the annual Des Moines Daily News' ride across Iowa come July of the following year. As a designated host community, the Maple Valley City Council and Chamber of Commerce would be responsible for supplying dinner, breakfast, camping or other overnight accommodations, and RV parking for two to three times the number of people who resided in their town.

The enormity of the task dictated that they begin planning months in advance. A representative from the Des Moines Daily News had traveled to Maple Valley at the request of the Mitchell County Messenger to impart the information needed for the merchants and city officials to carry out their task.

Michelle sought out the seat Rachael had promised to save for her from the back of the room and took advantage of a quick lull in the action to slip over some ten odd pairs of legs to reach her spot.

"I guess I should have found a seat on the isle," Rachael

whispered.

"You know you can always count on me to be at least five minutes late."

"You haven't missed anything important."

"I thought Mac would be here, too."

"He and Luke are sitting up in the front row. They must have gotten here a while before I did. Barclay Alexander is here, too." Rachael tilted her head in his direction.

Michelle nodded. "I'm glad to see he's getting involved with the Chamber. Elk Creek employs a lot of people in town. Who's watching Ian?"

"Luke's mom. I don't know what I'd do without her. Sarah?"

"She's still up in Austin with Jake's folks. They're loving it, but I'm starting to miss her."

"Things going well at Barclay's?"

"Very. Only two rooms down though. Ten to go. And most of the upstairs bedrooms and bathrooms have painted woodwork, so they're going to take a lot longer to do. We'll never be able to keep up this *room a day* pace. The kitchen needs a lot of work as well."

"We'll have to talk more after the meeting."

Michelle nodded and sat back in her chair to listen to the speaker's address.

*****

Tracy fumed all the way from Maple Valley to Blooming Prairie with hardly a break to come up for air. The nerve of them! The gall! Never before had she been treated so abominably. They hadn't even stopped bossing her around long enough to introduce themselves or ask her for her name.

Tracy pulled up into the garage, grabbed her purse, and slammed the car shut behind her. If Barclay Alexander III was cut from the same cloth as his parents it was a good thing she hadn't been there yesterday when he stopped by to inspect their work. She might not have come back.

"I'm sorry I'm late, Trevor," Tracy muttered as she entered the house. "Go ahead and go or you'll miss the deacon's meeting."

"That would be nice since it was me who called the meeting in the first place," Trevor answered.

"I know. I know. Everything was under control until the owner's parents showed up. I was right in the middle of putting up this intricate wallpaper design and Michelle had to leave and then these people started harassing me about everything under the sun. I've never met such condescending people, Trevor. You wouldn't have believed it. I knew I was running late by that time but I had to finish the wall and clean up the rollers before I left. It was a perfectly good day until they came along and ruined the whole thing." Tracy covered her eyes and burst into tears.

"Tracy Tomlinson, if I didn't know you better I'd think you—"

"Don't—don't call me that," she sobbed. "I'm not a Tomlinson anymore. You may as well get used to calling me T—Tracy Jones again..."

"Oh, sweetheart."

This time she didn't resist when he pulled her into his arms.

"Oh, Trevor, I hate this. I know I've led a sheltered life but no one has ever treated me with such disrespect. I'm used to people looking up to me, you know? I'm trying so hard to be upbeat and positive about going to work professionally but I'm so scared."

Her eyes were so blurred with tears that she barely noticed Theodora suddenly appearing at the top of the stairs, Titus poking his head around the corner, or Timothy creasing his eyebrows into a frown at the sight of his mother sobbing. It wouldn't have mattered if she had.

"I just don't know if I can face Mom and Dad tonight. It's just so much all at once."

"We have to do it tonight. They know too many people here in town and up at the school. If we don't tell them someone else is bound to. It wouldn't be right for them to hear it from anyone else but us."

"You're right," she sniffled, finally really noticing the children. "So you guys are all home."

Timothy nodded.

"Come here, honey. Your mommy needs a hug." She turned from Trevor and welcomed her youngest son to her chest. "I didn't mean to frighten you, sweetheart. I told you everyone gets scared sometimes." She gave him a tight squeeze and looked over her shoulder. "Right, Titus?"

"I guess so."

"You'd better get to the church, Trevor. I'll be fine."

"Are you sure?"

She nodded.

"I'll see you later then. Supper is ready. I've already eaten so we can leave for your folks as soon as I get home."

"Thanks. I'll be thinking of you, Trevor."

*****

Michelle clenched her abdominal muscles and coughed in a discreet attempt to muffle the rumbling of her stomach. If there was one thing inherently wrong with the democratic process, it was meetings that lasted too long. She supposed Jake was wondering what had become of her - unless he'd gone up to Austin to see Sarah and have supper with his folks like he'd talked about that morning.

The meeting ended just as she was trying to plot a graceful means of escape over the numerous legs between her and the isle.

Rachael took her arm and steered her outside the second they were free of the crowd. "So tell me, has Tracy told Mom and Dad yet?"

"She and Trevor are probably over there right now - or will be soon."

Rachael rolled her eyes. "So I've missed my chance to call Mom and accidentally let the news slip?"

"Rachael! You wouldn't have dared."

"After all the times Tracy's dropped hints to Mom about

what's going on in my life? And so blatantly that Mom would have had to be deaf and dumb not to figure out the truth? I could have done it without batting an eye. Not only that, but I would have paid money to be there when Mom and Dad find out. You've got to admit there's some sort of poetic justice in this situation."

"Rachael MacPhearson! How can you be so petty when you know how badly Tracy and the kids are hurting? This is going to break Mom and Dad's heart and you know it. You can't wish that on anyone."

"Oh, give me a break. I didn't wish anything on anybody. It just happened. The point is, it happened to Tracy and Trevor, the perfect child and her flawless husband. Can't you see the irony here?"

"I refuse to even think about it. Tracy's going through a rough time and she needs our support."

"I can't believe you're defending her! You're the one who ran away from home when you were six years old because Tracy tormented you so. And that's when she was only four. Need I go on to detail the numerous times our innocent little sister Tracy has screwed us both?"

"I remember each and every time quite vividly."

"Like the time she found the speeding ticket you'd gotten in Albert Lea in your purse and showed it to Mom? They never would have found out about it if Tracy hadn't been such a little tattletale."

"She wouldn't have been tempted to tell on me if I hadn't been speeding in the first place."

Rachael laughed. "Amazing! You guys must really be bonding over there at the Alexander house."

"Did I hear someone mention my name?" Barclay approached them from behind and put a hand on each of their shoulders. "How did things go over at the house today? I haven't had a chance to stop by."

"The dining room is nearly finished. The wall with the Frank Lloyd Wright panel was under way when I left to come over here."

"Great! I can't wait to see it." He turned to face Rachael.

"The panel is patterned after the Tree of Life Window in the Darwin Martin House in Buffalo - I was fortunate enough to see the real thing last time I was in New York."

"I toured Wright's home in Spring Green, Wisconsin last fall. I've always admired his work," Rachael said.

"The divergent lines in Wright's later works have always held more appeal to me than his turn of the century designs, but the subtle colors and symmetry in this particular piece are amazing." He turned to face Michelle once more. "I hope you'll enjoy decorating around the design."

"I'm looking forward to it. It's been a long time since I've gotten to do such a classic arts and crafts period house. I can't wait to get all this painting and wallpapering finished so I can put the icing on the cake."

"We'll have to spend some time going through the furniture I brought down last week so you know what we have to work with. Some of the fellows from the mill helped me unload everything in the carriage house. My parents called last night and said they were thinking of driving down with a few more accessory pieces sometime later this week."

"The doorbell rang at the house just as I was leaving."

"It's not like them to drop by unannounced."

"Tall, stately-looking couple driving a Lincoln Town Car?"

"That would be them." Barclay shook his head.

"My sister was helping them unload some things when I left."

"They're probably looking all over town for me. Either that or my father's at the mill going over the books."

"Sounds like a poignant reunion," Rachael teased him.

Barclay shrugged his shoulders. "You know how parents can be. I'd better go find them before they take hostages."

Rachael laughed. "We can relate."

Michelle felt a wave of guilt for leaving Tracy to face the lions alone.

Barclay nodded. "See you tomorrow, Michelle. Who knows? Maybe I'll even get to meet your elusive younger sister."

Chapter 9

Tracy paced the floor in front of the kitchen sink, ignoring Trevor, who had just returned from his meeting with the deacons and was waiting for her by the back door. Supper had settled in her stomach like a leaden lump.

"Are you sure you don't mind being left in charge on a school night, Theodora? The boys have to do their homework, and I expect them to be in bed when we get home."

"Teddy. And yes, I can handle it."

"Titus? Does Theodora have your cooperation?"

"Ty, Mom. And yes, I guess so."

"Timothy?"

"I wanna go to Grandpa's house with you."

"I'm sorry, honey. Your daddy and I need to talk to Grandma and Grandpa by ourselves."

"Are they getting a divorce, too?"

"No. Just Daddy and I. But Grandma and Grandpa will be sad when they hear the news just like you were and I want to be able to talk to them alone. Is that okay?"

"I guess so. Will we have to go live at Grandpa's house when we get divorced?"

Tracy knelt down in front of Timothy and adjusted his shirt collar. "No. You and Titus and Theodora and I will find a house that belongs to us right here in Minnesota. Your daddy will have a house in California. You can still go to Grandma and Grandpa's to stay overnight, but you'll live at my house with me."

"Can I go visit Daddy in California?"

Tracy drew in a sharp breath. "Daddy is going to come here to visit you as often as he can. Won't that be a fun thing to look forward to?"

"Yes." Her little boy nodded.

"Why can't we go there?" Titus asked.

"Well," Tracy said. "It's more expensive to fly three of you to California than it is to fly one of your Dad here."

"I can do some more baby-sitting to earn some extra money," Theodora said. "Ty could get a paper route."

Trevor looked like he was being strangled.

"Your Dad's apartment is very small. There's no place for you to sleep."

"It's a studio apartment," Trevor said. "It has a Murphy bed right in the middle of the living room that folds up into the wall during the daytime. It's very cramped, but it's all I can afford right now. Everything is more expensive in California."

"Now let me give you a good night kiss before we go. You run upstairs and jump in bed like a good boy when Theodora tells you it's time, okay?"

"Can I have a story?" Timothy asked.

"Theodora?"

"Sure, brat." She slung her arm around her little brother's shoulders.

"See you in the morning," Trevor said in a choked voice as they departed.

They rode in silence for the first few miles. Tracy blotted a tear from the corner of her eye. She could hear Trevor clearing his throat over and over again in the darkness of the car. The quiet was broken only by the sound of an occasional semi trailer whooshing past their car.

Tracy played with the buttons on her sweater. "How did the deacons react to the news?"

"They were disappointed to hear I was leaving and very saddened to hear about our separation."

"I bet old Mr. Klausen's teeth practically dropped out of his mouth."

"Pretty nearly."

"I'm sure Stu and Chuck couldn't wait to get home and tell their wives."

"You're probably right."

"I'll be all over town by nightfall."

"All the more reason we had to see your folks tonight."

Trevor braked, turned a neat left into the Jones' driveway, and let the car roll to a halt. "Do you want to be the one to actually tell them or should I?"

"I know they're my parents but..."

"It's my fault we're here in the first place."

"I didn't mean...

Trevor took her hand. "I don't mind as long as you're there with me."

Tracy made no effort to get out of the car. "I thought telling the kids would be the hardest thing."

"The kids have known something wasn't right between us for a very long time. Your parents don't have a clue."

"I know." Tracy unlatched the door and extended one leg. "I've been dreading this all day."

Her parents had seen their car drive up. They were waiting at the door.

"Come in! Come in! Good to see you Trevor," her Dad said.

Her mother leaned forward and gave Trevor a quick hug. "Oh, it's nice to have you home! We missed you last week at Ian's birthday party."

"Tracy said you were at a conference in California but she was sketchy on the details. Have a seat and tell us about it."

"Thanks." Trevor's face looked an uncustomary shade of gray as he went to the living room and took a seat at one end of the sofa. Tracy chose to sit in her mother's wooden rocking chair rather than arouse suspicion by sitting at the opposite end of the sofa from her husband.

Her mother joined Trevor on the couch. "Was the speaker at the conference someone famous, or was it a theme of some particular interest to you that took you all the way to California?"

"Well, it's a bit more complicated than that. I did attend a conference but I also looked at a church that has extended an invitation for me to join their staff as an assistant pastor."

James Jones jumped to his feet and crossed the room to shake Trevor's hand. "I was saying just the other night that a talented, hard-working young man like you could go a lot farther if he could just get himself hooked up with one of these big mega churches in the city. This congregation must be good-sized if it can support more than one minister."

"California?" Her mother looked as though someone had a stranglehold around her neck. "He didn't say he'd accepted the call, James."

"Don't worry, Mom," Tracy interjected. "We're not moving to California." The evening would hold enough disappointment for her parents as it was. Tracy would not sit by and let her mother think she was going to lose her grandchildren to a state two time zones removed.

Her mother looked visibly relieved. Her father looked confused.

"It's not quite that simple." Trevor gave Tracy a furtive look. "I have accepted the position at the church in California. It's a large interdenominational church. I'll be moving before the end of the month." Trevor gripped his hands together until his knuckles were white. "I don't want you to think this is a rash decision. Tracy and I have talked at length about the options available to us for a period of over two years. We've prayed together, searched our hearts, and looked to the Lord for guidance. We've agonized over the effect this will have on the children."

James Jones looked across the room at his wife and she back at him before they turned in unison to look at Tracy. She looked away.

"I love your daughter," Trevor looked down. "But not in the way a husband loves his wife. Not in the way Christ loves his bride, the Church."

Good grief. What was that about? Just say it. She gulped down the remnants of what seemed to be the last trace of air in the room. "Trevor filed for a divorce earlier today. Mom, Dad, I'm sorry. I know our decision will cause heartache for you as well as everyone else who cares about us. I know you think we're the perfect couple but we're not. I wish we were but we're not."

"I don't understand," her mother said obtusely.

"James..."

Her father groped for words. If any other man than Trevor had been standing before him, he would have been furious. But Trevor... her father loved Trevor like the son he'd never had. "But you know better than anyone what the scriptures say..."

"I'm assuming you would interpret the scriptures to say that Trevor and I should stay together even though he no longer wishes to be my husband," Tracy interrupted. "But I can't live that way. I don't want him to stay with me out of some misguided sense of responsibility. We'll all be better off in the long run if we part amicably now. We'll move on and rebuild our lives. There is no other choice."

The quiet desperation in her voice quelled their objections but not their concerns. The silence that followed was deafening.

Her mother moaned quietly. "I don't know what to think."

Her father nodded. "I'm at a loss for words."

Tracy stood. Her face felt cold and pale. "And I'm exhausted. It's been a long, hard day. The kids are home alone—"

"Have you told them yet?" her mother asked stonily.

"Yesterday," Trevor said. "I returned from a meeting with the board of deacons immediately before we came here."

"Lord have mercy."

"We can talk more later when we've all had time to think," Tracy insisted valiantly as she inched towards the door. She held her chin high. Her eyes blinked in rapid succession to hold back the tears. She hated this. How she hated this! "Trevor, please. I really think we should get home to the children."

"Will you tell Grandma Maddie or should I?" her mother pushed.

"I don't know, Mother. I can't think right now. It's been a long day."

"Let the poor girl be, Rebekah." Her father sounded a

hundred years older than he had a few moments ago.

"Michelle knows. You can call her if you need to talk to someone. I'm sorry, Mom. Really, truly sorry. I just can't... not now..."

"I just want to thank you for everything you've meant to me over the last twenty years," Trevor stuttered. "I hope you'll always be family to me."

Tracy's mother rose to meet his embrace. She sobbed against his shoulder, smoothed his hair away from his face just as Tracy sometimes did Timothy's.

"Trevor," Tracy insisted.

"We'll talk to you soon," her soon-to-be-ex-husband conceded.

Tracy's father stood at the far side of the room and watched as they fled.

*****

The sleepless nights were starting to take their toll. Tracy rolled over to the other side of the big brass bed she and Trevor had shared for sixteen years half expecting to find him there. An empty expanse was the only good morning to greet her.

Still half asleep, she raised her hand from the sheet and subconsciously grasped at the nothingness next to her. She no longer pined for Trevor the way she had when they'd first stopped making love, but she missed the emotional intimacy they'd shared and the physical presence of a man in her life more with every day that passed. She brought her fingers back to her side and slid her hand up to her breast with a resigned sigh. Her nipples stood erect, as if pouting from neglect.

Her mind flitted to the memory of the man she'd bumped into at the Budget Mart and then at the fair. Now that she knew he was engaged, however unhappily, she shouldn't even be thinking about him. But before she'd known... Good grief – even then, it had been ridiculous to think that anything would have come of some silly, chance encounter. He'd obviously been traveling through on his way to Minneapolis or St. Paul or some point further north. Even if he'd been moving to the Blooming area – I mean, how could she? Her stupid little fantasies were just that. She had no business, no right to dream of him as she had.

Still, to her, he represented a thin slice of hope in the muddled mess her life had become. To her, he had become the symbol of the hope she needed to survive, the belief, however futile, that another man would someday be interested in her and want to share her life - and the life of her children. She needed to believe that somewhere there was a man who was sensitive and caring enough to be there for her, someone who would make love to her with his heart and soul and mind, a man who truly wanted her.

In some ways, it helped knowing that the reason Trevor was leaving her had nothing to do with her or her lack of desirability as a woman. In another very real sense, knowing that Trevor didn't want to make love to her for whatever reason - that he preferred someone, no one, something, anything over her... had been a tremendous blow to her ego.

For a decade and a half, her self esteem had been subconsciously bolstered by the knowledge that she was loved, wanted as a wife and companion, and desired as a lover. Living with the converse situation for the previous three years had slowly but insidiously eroded her confidence to the point that Tracy sometimes questioned her very worthiness to be with a man. Her dating experiences as an energetic, self-confident, too-young-to-know-better teenager had done little to prepare her to reenter the world of dating as a middle-aged mother of three. Tracy fingered the tight knot of sensitive skin just around her nipples with an ever deepening sense of despair. She wondered if she would ever know the touch of a man's hands on her breasts again.

"Clay," Tracy moaned softly, dreaming of the solidness and sexiness and security the presence of a man represented in her life.

Her nipples were so hard they hurt. She jerked her hand away like she'd been bitten. What difference did it make anyway? Even if... her physical needs were just the tip of the iceberg, no pun intended. She had never worked professionally. She'd never had a job. She had never had to make the decisions that affected her family's livelihood, never even had a choice in the matter of where she would live. The board of trustees at church had not only paid their house payment, but utilities, insurance, and maintenance costs. She'd gone directly from having a father who took care of her needs to a husband and church that did the same.

The thought of having to come up with a security deposit for an apartment, first and last month's rent, and utility and telephone deposits within the month intimidated Tracy to the point of desperation.

The sense of shame that washed over her was becoming a more and more frequent visitor. Even her creative-to-the-point-of-being-addle-brained sister, Michelle, had mastered the art of being self-sufficient in a complex business world. Both she and Rae had survived on their own - without a man - for years before they'd met Jake and Mac. She had the same genes they did. How could she be so inept, so helpless when it came to the basic matters of survival?

She pulled herself out of bed with a groan and flitted past the mirror without even glancing at her reflection. What did it matter anyhow? No one cared how she looked. Besides, she deserved a little leeway. In the last forty-eight hours, she'd had to deal with the tension of Trevor's return, the indignities heaped on her by Barclay Alexander III's snooty parents, and heart-wrenching confrontations with her children and her own mom and dad.

She finally dared peek in the mirror. There were ominous smudges of bluish gray under each of her eyes.

She tried to be both quick and quiet as she showered and dressed. It would do Trevor good to have a little time alone with the kids. No sense imposing her gloomy mood on any of them.

She slipped into a second pair of painter's pants from high school and a faded tee shirt from nearly as long ago, but not even the trim fit of the pants managed to bolster her self-confidence as they had the day before. It was useless. She had failed her husband in the deepest sense of the word, failed her children, disappointed her parents, and humiliated herself before the entire community, both religious and secular.

Going to work at the Alexander house was the closest thing she had to be excited about. She grabbed a banana and a pack of M&Ms and slipped out of the house. A few minutes later, she backed the car out of the garage, turned on to the main road, and headed south. It would do her no good to sit around the house and mope away the day, although that was exactly what she felt like doing. These past few days with Michelle had done her good. Her compassion for what she knew of Tracy's predicament was obvious. Tracy longed for another dose of her encouragement more than she realized.

She accelerated as she drove past the Budget Mart and left the city limits, recalling her last conversation with Trevor. She'd been ready for bed, wrapped up tight in her terry cloth robe; Trevor, looking for a midnight snack.

"I forgot to tell you a man from a carpet company called to say you'd won a free carpet shampoo in some drawing you entered at the State Fair," Trevor had said out of the blue.

"The state fair? I don't remember registering for any thing to do with carpet cleaning," she'd claimed. "I didn't go anywhere near the Industrial Arts building this year. You know how antsy the kids get. It was all I could do to keep the boys interested in the 4-H displays."

"You must have signed up for something."

"Maybe it was a wrong number, or a scam. Some companies will do anything to get a foot in the door so they can sell you something."

"It would be nice to clean the carpets before we move out of the house so the ladies at the church don't have to do it. The timing seems providential."

"I think God has more important things to worry about than whether or not we get our carpets cleaned free of charge," she'd snapped. She'd always been irked by Trevor's propensity to assign each little quirk of fate to the Almighty. "Did you set up an appointment?"

Trevor had ignored her edginess. "The man seemed interested only in talking to you. I suppose it's only right since you were the one who won the contest."

"I didn't enter any contest!" she'd insisted. "Did the man leave his name? Did he tell you what company he works for?"

"No. I don't think he did come to think of it."

"Well, when he calls back, find out. In this day and age, you can't just assume an offer like this is on the up and up and invite some stranger into your home. It seems awfully odd that a company from the Cities would be so desperate for business that they'd drive all the way down here to clean someone's carpets."

She'd turned the light over the sink off, then paused. "I'm very impressed with the hardwood floors at the house I'm working on down in Maple Valley. Clean up is so easy. If I could find a rental place with..."

Trevor flinched as though he'd been slapped. "Sounds like a pretty impressive place."

"It is. You would have liked the Frank Lloyd Wright panel I hung yesterday. The lines and colors were very masculine. Kind of a geometric design, yet very graceful." She knew his tastes well after a decade and a half of marriage.

"They say Wright had a male lover," he'd said out of the blue. "They attribute the burning of Taliesin to a jealous rage that came about as a result of their relationship."

She'd probably looked as dumbfounded as she'd felt. "Is this another attempt on your part to justify your sexual orientation or why did you think I wanted to know that kind of information?" she'd asked in a hushed voice.

"I'm not attempting to justify anything. I'm just telling you what I heard."

"Is that all gay people talk about? How many of the world's most respected artists, musicians, athletes, and political leaders have reputedly been homosexual?"

"Of course not. You know it isn't like that."

"You know I love Elton John's voice, yet you feel compelled to remind me that he's gay every time Timothy watches the Lion King. Just yesterday you left an old copy of the Time magazine featuring the story about Drew Barrymore admitting she's bi-sexual on the coffee table where the kids could see it. You know Theodora loves "Ever After". She'd glared at him.

"I found it in the basement when I was packing. I was in the middle of the article when the phone rang."

"I'm not entirely naïve, Trevor. This is obviously a calculated, ongoing effort on your part to help you feel better about yourself and force us to become comfortable with the idea that being gay is okay."

"It's no such thing."

"Well, I don't want to hear about how many of you there are anymore!" she'd told him fiercely. "It doesn't make me feel any better. I don't want to be comfortable with same sex relationships. I just want to get things back to normal around here!"

"Same sex desires are normal for a gay person! It's time you let go of your superiority complex and admit it."

"I'll admit nothing of the sort! Your new lifestyle is NOT normal! If it weren't for us good old NORMAL heterosexuals having babies and propagating the human species, all of you ABNORMAL gay people wouldn't be around to scream about gay rights and whatever else is on your agenda. You're the one who's chosen to embrace this deviant behavior, Trevor. But it's my life that's very nearly been ruined!" she'd cried as she stormed up the stairs to their room. Her room, damn it! Was she ever going to start thinking of it as her room?

Chapter 10

Tracy was trying very hard to leave the past behind her and make a fresh start when she pulled up in front of the Alexander house. Michelle's car was blocked by a sleek black Mercedes convertible that she was sure she'd never seen before. A sense of anticipation shivered through her middle. Perhaps she was about to meet the owner of the house. Michelle had promised her this morning over the phone that Barclay was nothing like his parents. If so, she had nothing to fear from him.

Her work here, if anything, was the one thing Tracy could be proud of. Although she'd never met Barclay Alexander III, she'd painstakingly tried to please him. She'd worked hard, given her best, and she felt sure he'd be delighted at the progress she and Michelle had made in just a few short days.

She parked the car and walked towards the house. A few words of praise from Mr. Alexander might be just the boost her ravaged self concept needed today.

She heard voices as she neared the house and felt an odd sense of déjà vu. She couldn't make out what they were saying, but she could hear Michelle's soft voice followed by a louder, more passionate male voice that rang strangely familiar.

Her first thought was that the senior Alexanders had returned. *Just what she did not need.* She tried in vain to envision the stiff, rigid form of the man she'd met yesterday bending low enough to climb into a car so sleek. No possible way. She paused to listen more intently as she grew nearer. She had to give her sister credit for her professional demeanor. Although she couldn't yet make out the words, Michelle sounded so smooth that Tracy could have skipped a pebble across the surface of her words.

Tracy took a few more steps forward before the sound of

her sister's words made her freeze in her tracks. Michelle was apologizing! *For what, for heavens sake?* She pressed closer to the door and tried to hear what they were saying.

"The panel cost over $1000," the man said in his disconcertingly familiar voice. "It's basically ruined. It wouldn't be so bad if it wasn't the focal point of the entire first floor."

Panic coursed though her veins. She could hear the man's irritated exclamations continuing from where she stood on the porch, frozen to the wood slat decking.

"I appreciate your offer to pay for a replacement panel but there's no way it will arrive in time to correct the situation. I ordered it weeks ago so it would arrive in time to be installed before the housewarming party," he said. "It was on backorder for two months before it came."

Tracy's gut wrenched from where she stood eavesdropping. Ruined? It couldn't be! The panel had been fine when she left the house the night before. Still wet granted, but otherwise fine. Had the edges curled after she left?

"I'm so sorry, Barclay. I know it probably sounds trite to say so now, especially since she's my sister, but she's such a perfectionist – I just don't know what could have happened."

Tracy shuddered. She felt like she was about to be ill. Had the panel shrunk? They couldn't possibly blame her for that, could they? She'd probably left the wet panels booked for a few minutes longer than she'd needed to when the Alexanders had shown up, but if anything that should have helped eliminate a shrinkage problem, not added to it. She could only hope that whatever had happened would be classified as a manufacturer's defect. Where on earth would she ever get $1000 to pay for a replacement panel?

"The panels were clearly marked as to which end was up," he said. "There was an arrow on the back of each strip. Even if she wasn't familiar with the original design, I don't see how she could have missed something so obvious."

Tracy put her hand over her mouth to stifle a cry.

"It's my fault. I should have been here," Michelle said.

"If it was some abstract work I could probably live with it even if I knew it was on upside down, but the design is so well known. I mean, there's no way I can look at it day after day when I know it's wrong."

"Of course not," Michelle said. "No one expects you to. I don't know what could have happened. She had the panels laid out just the way they were supposed to be when I left. When your parents arrived I slipped out the back so I wouldn't be late for the Chamber meeting. She must have..."

Tracy shrunk back against the outer wall of the house. *It was her fault. Oh, God.*

"I know she's your sister, but my parents did mention that she was a little rude," the man said.

Tracy's eyes narrowed. She had been nothing of the sort! Why, the nerve of them! If they hadn't been there to distract her she never would have made such an error. It was no wonder she'd gotten flustered when they arrived. They'd treated her like some peasant girl instead of a paid professional with a job to do. She stormed through the front door.

"Excuse me." She let loose as she strode into the study. "But I parked their precious car and carried a whole carload of heavy boxes up to the third floor for them without so much as a *please* or *thank you* ever being uttered." She made contact with Michelle's eyes. "I'm eternally sorry about the panel."

Barclay Alexander stood stiffly, his back to her, still looking at the wallpaper panel.

"I can't imagine how I could have made such a mistake, Mr. Alexander, but I was not rude to your parents. Appalled at the way they treated me, maybe. But I was nothing but polite the whole time they were here. I was right in the middle of putting up the panel when they arrived. They ordered me around like I was some kind of poor white trash with a plague. But did I complain? No, I took it all in stride..." Her words froze in her mouth the second Barclay Alexander turned to face her.

"Tracy. Is that you?" He choked, staring at her as though

he had seen an apparition.

"Clay?" she stuttered. "What are you doing here?"

"You're Michelle's sister?" he asked incredulously.

"You're Barclay Alexander?"

"You two know each other?"

"No," Tracy stammered.

"Yes," he said simultaneously.

Michelle looked from one to the other.

Tracy turned her eyes from Clay's searching glance. She wished she could melt and disappear through the floor boards. "We talked for a few minutes one night up at the Budget Mart."

"And again at the State Fair."

"We never spoke at the fair. You were with your fiancée."

"Lauren. She's not my..." he stammered. "I tried to catch up with you after the merry-go-round stopped."

"Well, you didn't."

"I tried to find you. I stopped at the Budget Mart in Blooming Prairie and described you to the woman at the cash register earlier this week."

"You did?"

"I wanted to call you."

"Why?" she asked stupidly.

"I can't believe..." Clay looked dazed. He shook his head. "I have to get to work. I'm late for a meeting."

"I'll see what I can do about putting a rush order in for a new panel," Michelle offered.

"Thanks." Clay managed a smile that masked only a portion of the disgust Tracy was sure he must feel.

"I'm sorry," Tracy said again, really meaning it.

"My parents can be rather intimidating."

"I can be rather inept."

"Tracy. It was an accident," Michelle said succinctly. "A mistake anyone could have made, especially given the circumstances. If it's anyone's fault, it's mine. I should have skipped the meeting and stayed until the job was done."

Tracy closed her eyes and took a deep breath. If such a

thing was possible, it was more humiliating to have Michelle making excuses for her than it would have been to bear her shame without defense.

She could feel Clay's eyes on her even though her eyelids were pinched closed. How many times had she dreamed that the mysterious stranger who had been so gentle with her son would reenter her life by some divine stroke of fate? Oh, God, what she would give to wake up and discover this was just a dream turned nightmare and not the awful, unmitigated reality it truly was.

Clay turned as he reached the door. "Don't worry about the panel. It doesn't matter."

"That's not what you were saying when I came in. It most certainly does matter," Tracy said.

"I was simply venting my frustration. I shouldn't have lost my temper over something so trivial."

"It's obviously important to you," Tracy said. "And I intend to make it right."

Michelle donned her most conciliatory voice once more. "We'll all feel a lot better after I phone the manufacturer and find out what our options are as far as getting a replacement. I'll call you at the Mill as soon as I know anything, Barclay."

"I can stop back over the lunch hour and see if you've had any luck." Clay turned and focused his piercing blue eyes directly on Tracy. "Will you still be here, Tracy?"

She couldn't even look at him. Not now. She had humiliated herself one too many times in front of this man. To think that she had lain in bed this very morning fingering her own breasts and wondering if she had made as deep an impression on him as he had on her. Even before she'd known her fantasy and her employer were one and the same, she'd wanted nothing more than praise and adoration from each of them. Her eyelashes fluttered against the brazen heat of her cheeks as she stared down at the floor.

"I've been waiting to meet you all week," Barclay said quietly. "Both of you. Please, let's not let this get in the way..."

"Both of me?" she said, not understanding.

"The elusive youngest Jones sister and the mysterious woman from the merry-go-round. I've wanted to get to know both of you."

She raised her eyes. "Only to be disappointed in both respects."

"Not at all," Clay said.

Her eyes flitted reflexively to the wall. She had done a fine job of matching the three patterned panels despite the fact that the design was upside down. The seams where the horizontal intersecting lines came together were so perfectly aligned that the breaks were indistinguishable. "I guess you'll have to put up with me for at least as long as it takes me to earn enough money to pay for new wallpaper."

"We'll discuss that later."

"We certainly will." She finally looked him square in the face.

Clay met her glance with equal resolve. "Fine. I'll see you at noon." His eyes gleamed an even mix of irritation and amusement.

"I'll be here."

"Good." He backed stealthily towards the door, as she watched, unwilling to be the first to break the static charge that flashed from his eyes to hers.

He left in silence, his lips pursed and his nostrils slightly flared.

The echo of Barclay's car door smacking the steel frame of his auto resounded through the neighborhood.

Michelle looked at her in awe. "I feel like I've just witnessed some ancient mating ritual."

"Oh, stop it!" She paced the floor in front of the ill-fated design and turned to look at Michelle despairingly. "I've spent my whole life trying to avoid this kind of humiliation. You of all people should know that! I'm a master at covering my tracks, the proverbial one that always comes out smelling like a rose. Even now, my natural instinct is to make excuses and try to cast the blame elsewhere."

"I'm the one who sneaked out the back door and left you alone with those piranhas."

"Stop it right now, Michelle. You always find a way to blame yourself no matter what it is that's going wrong. You've tried to protect me from the time we were little kids. Well, it stops right here. I won't have it!

"I'm the one who put the wallpaper on upside down. I'm the one who broke Mom and Dad's heart last night. I'm the one who's just shattered her children's sense of security and well-being. I'm the one whose supposedly ideal marriage to the minister of the year has failed. I'm the one who has to admit her perfect little life is lying in shambles around her, and it's me and only me who needs to hold her head high and suck it up."

"Did you see the way Barclay was looking at you?"

"Michelle! Haven't you heard a word I'm saying?"

"Yes. It's just that I've never seen Barclay look so – rattled is the only word I can think to describe it. He's always so composed, so in control."

"Well, of course he's rattled. He knows his fiancée is going to kill him when she finds out the error can't be corrected before the party."

"Oh, I don't think he much cares what Lauren thinks these days. I don't think he cared about the wallpaper either after he saw you. What on earth could have happened between you two at the Budget Mart to have brought on a reaction like that?"

"Are you sure you really want to know?"

"Is it that bad?"

She grimaced. "Not really. We were both reaching for the M&Ms when we bumped into each other the first time."

"First? You did it more than once?"

"Well, I had my arms full of certain feminine supplies. Of course it all went flying when we collided. The second meeting occurred when we each reached for the above mentioned items." She touched her head gingerly as she recalled the way their heads had butted together.

Michelle threw her head back and laughed. "How embarrassing! What a way to begin a romance!"

"It's not a romance! Not that I didn't forget who I was

for the space of two or three seconds and start thinking along those lines - but then Timothy came into the store and jerked me back to reality."

"I suppose the kids were fighting in the car?"

"Kind of."

"Well, what?"

"You'll die."

"Tell me!"

"Timothy chose that precise moment to ask me, in a very loud voice, about a certain method of male masturbation. Of course, he had no idea what he was saying. He'd heard Titus use the phrase."

"You've got to be kidding."

"Would I joke about something like this?"

"How lovely." Michelle giggled. "What did Barclay do?"

"He handled it extremely well. If anything, it was that few minutes of conversation that kind of lit the spark between us."

"So you admit there's a spark!"

"He's engaged to some beautiful lady named Lauren if I'm not mistaken."

"I've never seen him look this way when he talks about her."

"So he has cold feet, or wants to have one last fling before she slips the noose around his neck. Tempting as a little romance sounds right now, I'm in no position to get involved in a mess like that. Besides—" She waved her arm in a half circle. "Look at all this. I'm no match for someone like him. And his parents," she sputtered. "Just the thought makes me ill."

"I see what you're saying."

Tracy, however, could see that she did not understand what she was trying to say at all. Not really. The wheels in her older sister's head were still spinning. And that could only mean one thing: trouble.

Chapter 11

The carefree banter of the last few days with Michelle now seemed a thing of the past. Although Tracy went about priming the walls of the master suite in her usual diligent manner, she spoke only to respond to the few specific questions her sister seemed bent on posing as the morning progressed.

Each time Michelle left to go downstairs to dial the 800 number listed on the packaging the wallpaper panel had come in, Tracy's stomach churned afresh. It only made matters worse when her sister returned time and time again with reports of continued busy signals.

It was eleven fifty-five when Michelle returned with the long-awaited news. "The phone finally rang through this time. I was able to speak to someone in customer service."

Tracy looked up, dreading her words.

"They promised me we'd have a new panel in two to four weeks."

"That's little better than a fifty-fifty chance it will get here in time to install before Clay's housewarming." Tracy moaned.

Michelle ignored her theatrics. Lord, sometimes she hated the cheerful, alien Michelle who had inhabited her sister's body ever since Jake Sheffield had come into her life.

"More good news!" Michelle beamed. "The woman from the wallpaper company offered me fifty percent off the price of replacing the panel when I explained what happened and said there's a very good chance that the paper will arrive in two weeks."

Tracy crouched low and resumed trimming around the baseboards. "Fine. Be optimistic. Your life is obviously charmed. With your luck the panel probably will come in on time."

"Listen, Tracy," Michelle said in a voice that she'd never heard before. I know you've had a particularly rough forty-eight hours. What's more, I'm thinking the odds are that you've been suffering silently for quite some time - in regard to exactly what, I don't know. I'm convinced there's more to this divorce thing than you're letting on. But I can't believe that you, of all people, would begrudge me the few short months of happiness I've been fortunate enough to find since Jake and I—"

"You're right, of course. I'm sorry."

"I do understand some of what you're going through. Life is a roller coaster ride. It's hard to believe things will get better when you're in the middle of a down cycle."

"So, what? I'm in the middle of the darkest night but dawn is coming soon?"

"Yes. I know it sounds trite, but I'm speaking from personal experience and it's true." Michelle picked up a roller and resumed painting. "Speaking of dawn, Mom woke me up very early this morning. She was full of questions I didn't have the answers to. I tried to calm her down as best I could."

Tracy paled. She couldn't help but think *better you than me*, but she kept her reaction to herself. "Thanks for trying. I know I'll have to give her more of an explanation before this is all over with but I just couldn't bear to talk to them any longer last night. It was too hard. You should have seen the looks on their faces."

Michelle knelt to refill her tray with paint. "So tell me about the church Trevor will be going to in California."

Tracy took a deep breath. "It's a big church. They have five or six ministers on staff. Trevor's title will be the Minister of Congregational Care."

"The name of the church is?"

Tracy cleared her throat. "The Metropolitan Community Church." Although the church was known worldwide amongst sympathizers as a haven for gays and lesbians, the title bore no overt reference to sexual orientation. Most people, especially those living in conservative small towns of the rural Midwest, had never heard of the liberal organization.

Tracy breathed a sigh of relief when Michelle's facial expression gave no hint of an adverse reaction, assuming her secret was safe. The two sisters continued to paint in silence, the quiet broken only by the occasional sound of a car driving by and the clucking of a squirrel rustling ambitiously about the maple tree outside the window.

Tracy was facing the window when Michelle finally broke the tenuous quiet. "My friend Dennis attended a church by the same name in Denver."

"Oh."

"Tracy..."

She looked at her sister, begging her not to voice the truth, however obvious.

But Michelle looked her straight in the eye. "Have you known Trevor is gay for some time now or did you just find out?"

Tracy's shoulders sagged in defeat. She stood frozen in place, a paint brush in one hand. "I've known for almost three years. And he's not a practicing gay, he just has gay inclinations."

Michelle closed her eyes and shook her head. "You could have told me. I could have been there for you."

"Finding out my husband is gay isn't something I felt like bragging about." The words slipped from her lips before she realized they were no longer alone.

"Barclay," Michelle stammered.

His hair looked almost white against the blush of his cheeks. His eyes sought Tracy's beseechingly. "I'm sorry. I didn't mean to eavesdrop."

"Oh, God," Tracy moaned. She turned her back to Clay, threw her head back, and looked at the ceiling.

Michelle looked from one to the other. No one spoke until she broke the silence. "I just remembered I promised to meet Jake for lunch today." Her hands flew as she wrapped her roller in plastic wrap to keep the paint from drying out. "I'll be back in forty-five minutes or an hour at most. I'll see you then, Tracy."

Michelle nodded at Barclay as she rushed towards the door, driven by some sixth sense or pure foolishness, Tracy didn't know or care.

Michelle was entering the hall when Tracy started to panic. She spun around, ignoring Clay. "Michelle, please don't tell anyone else. Not yet. Not even Jake. And especially not Rae. Please..."

"You have my word."

She turned again to face the canopy of maple branches framing the window. While her sister's footsteps faded in the distance, she felt Clay's lingering presence with every fiber of her being. She couldn't bear to look at him. Her right shoulder quivered involuntarily. She crossed her arms in front of her and clutched at her sides, trying desperately to contain the trembling before she gave into the panic she felt inside. Her efforts were in vain.

"Your secret's safe with me, too, Tracy."

"Which one?" she sniffled. "I seem to humiliate myself a little bit more each time I see you. The hole I'm digging seems to get deeper by the minute."

"Then you have a choice to make, don't you? You can wallow in the hole or you can climb out. Either way, I'll be waiting at the top."

She stared sightlessly out the window.

"Your ex-husband's sexual preferences are no reflection on you."

"Then why am I devastated by the thought of anyone knowing?"

"You're proud just like I am. Pride is a fragile thing."

"How would you know? You've got reason to be proud – a beautiful house, a gorgeous fiancée, a thriving business... I'm the one who keeps humiliating myself, most often in front of you." She turned tentatively towards him.

"Believe me... I mean... Yes, I'm very blessed. But you've met my parents. My whole existence is one long study in humiliation. I'm *engaged* to a woman I never proposed to, and the whole reason my father sent me to

Maple Valley in the first place is because I voted for a Republican in the last election." Clay said with conviction, "Is that humiliating enough for you?"

"Your father punished you for voting Republican?"

"I was banished from my former position at the company headquarters and sent down here to pay penance at the woolen factory."

She pursed her lips and nodded, still hesitant to look at him directly.

"I suppose you're a Republican."

"Yes." Her lips stretched at the edges to make way for a tiny smile.

Clay grinned. "I figured as much."

Tracy loosened her grip on her sides and looked timidly around the room. "If this house is supposed to be some sort of punishment I can't imagine what kind of things you must get when you've earned a reward."

Clay threw back his head and laughed.

The curls at his neck shifted enticingly with his laughter. She was so drawn to him. Everything about him was a bad idea, and yet, she couldn't keep her eyes off of him, her thoughts away from him, her mind...

Clay captured her glance and held her eyes in a firm lock with his. "Life with you would never be dull."

She flushed and looked away, shifting her toes back and forth over the smooth oak flooring. "Your fiancée is beautiful. At the very least you must be proud of her."

It was Clay's turn to look away. "You weren't exaggerating when you said you were an expert at humiliation."

"I didn't mean..."

"Yes you did. You put me in my place, and quite neatly if I do say so."

"I meant what I said. It's Lauren, isn't it? She looks like a lovely woman."

"She is. But I'm not engaged to her. I don't love her. She's never been and never will be any more to me than a friend. Another prime example of how I've always chosen to bow to my parent's wishes rather than stand up to them and do what's right."

Her eyes searched his for some explanation.

"Our parents let it be known years ago that they expected me and Lauren to marry. We joked and teased about it from the time we were little. I mean, we really never took it seriously, but it was always there, you know?

"When Lauren was twenty-one, she spent a summer in Paris and started dating a man named Henri. Our parents' arrangement was more or less forgotten until this spring when Henri broke things off. And suddenly, I'm in this horrible position of not wanting to hurt Lauren even more, but not wanting to marry her. It's a long story. Suffice it to say that if such a thing is possible, Lauren's pride is even more fragile than mine. What's keeping her going right now is clinging to the idea that we're going to be married. It would humiliate her terribly if I were to publicly denounce her. And my parents... her parents...

"It's a very complex situation. I've tried to convince Lauren that she deserves someone who is wildly, passionately in love with her, but all she wants at this point is to be with someone she trusts and feels safe with. She's known me from the day she was born. I'm ashamed to say I've let the illusion stand."

She exhaled loudly. "I see what you mean."

"About what?"

"You've got even more reason to be humiliated than I do. I mean, not to be rude, but why don't you just tell your father and mother how you feel?"

"I'm their only son, their only heir... You don't know what—"

"Unfortunately, I've got a pretty good idea."

"My father has so much anger inside. He was absolutely infuriated that I broke party lines and voted Republican. Can you imagine what he'd do if I told him there was no way on earth I'm going to marry Lauren? I'm afraid it will be something drastic – shut down the mill, fire all the employees... I don't know exactly what, just that a lot of people would be hurt."

She looked at him intently and sensed no duplicity on his part. "I appreciate your honesty. In a weird sort of way, knowing what you're going through makes me feel a little better. And I can't judge you for not standing up to your parents and telling them the truth. It's been over two years since Trevor and I stopped living together as man and wife and began perpetuating this charade, and I'm still not ready to be honest with anyone, least of all my parents."

His eyes glowed with warmth at her acceptance. For the first time in years, she felt like she could say what was in her heart. "I hated hurting my parents last night. Not that I haven't done things in the past that would have disappointed them greatly had they known about them, but this was different. Never before have I had to face them with the awareness that I was knowingly hurting them in a way not even time isn't likely to mend. It broke my heart."

"I know what you mean. My father is a bully, pure and simple, but he's still my dad, and I love him. Maybe I'm a coward, but it's not easy for me to intentionally do or say things that I know will cause his heart to ache."

"When we were teenagers, my sister Rae flaunted her rebellious behaviors in full view of my parents every chance she got. She still does when the mood strikes. Maybe it gave Rae some needed sense of being right or in control to do whatever she pleased and then brag about it – no matter how devastating her actions were to our folks. I don't know."

She sank to the floor, cross-legged, and kept talking. "I've always had differences with my parents, but I've never seen any possible good that could come from sparring with them about things that would hurt them deeply if they knew.

"When the three of us girls were teenagers, I was the one who sneaked out of the house dressed in a sweet, innocent-looking outfit, supposedly to work on a school project at a friend's house, then changed into a halter top and hot pants and partied all night. I'll admit that part of the reason I was so covert about my actions was that I was trying to save myself the embarrassment and wrath I would have incurred had my parents found out what I was up to. But I also cared enough about my parents to want to protect them from anything that would upset them. I saw the heartache and humiliation they endured at my older sister's hands. I never wanted to hurt them that way."

"Believe me, I know what you mean." Clay met her eyes and held them. "My tactic has always been to listen quietly, never quite agreeing, simply keeping my mouth shut when it served no point to disagree."

"Even now, when things come up with Mom and Dad, I'm content to sit back and let Rae be the warrior. Michelle does the same thing."

A look of pure compassion washed across Clay's perfect features. "I've thought about your little boy several times since that night at the Budget Mart. Is he doing okay? I've wondered how he would take the news that you're divorcing. Does he know yet?"

Perhaps it was by virtue of the fact that he cared not only about her but about her child, perhaps it was something as simple as the way he looked at her - as though she were some rare gemstone to be treasured and admired – but at his simple question her heart took flight and soared.

On an all time high,
We'll take on the world and wait.
So hold on tight, let the flight begin.
We're an all time high.

She struggled to collect her thoughts. She could feel her cheeks turning from pink to rosy red despite her efforts to douse the effects of her heightened senses. She held her breath until her pulse began to slow. "We told them a couple of nights ago. Timothy actually seems to be taking it better than Titus and Theodora, but then I don't think he fully understands what the implications of divorce are. He's just so happy to have his daddy home again. I'm afraid his heart will break when Trevor leaves for good next week and it finally dawns on him that he's not coming back except to visit once in awhile."

Clay nodded. "Maybe after Trevor's gone the three of us, five of us, I mean... could go do something special to take everyone's mind off his departure. I think the amusement park at Valley Fair is already closed for the season." He snapped his fingers. "Have you ever visited the antique carousel in Story City, Iowa? Timothy would love the horses on the merry-go-round and there's a great little tea house where we could all eat lunch."

"I could pack a picnic basket," she chimed in, forgetting that Clay didn't need to save money. Whatever – she felt excited about something for the first time in weeks.

"There are some great little boutiques in town – that is, assuming your daughter likes to shop. Is your older son, Titus, into golf by any chance? There's a course right beside the carousel..."

She could feel her face falling and see his disappointment rising as her attitude transformed from delighted to pensive. An awkward silence sprang up to replace their rapport. His words dwindled off.

"Titus and Theodora are acting a little hostile towards both Trevor and myself right now. I don't want to do anything that would make them feel more bitter than they already are. I've had over two years to adjust to the idea of Trevor's and I divorcing, but for them it's just so soon."

Clay cleared his throat. "I understand."

She could no more camouflage her disappointment than she had been able to hide her blush of moments earlier. "I'd love to see the old merry-go-round another time. If circumstances were different..."

"You don't need to say another word."

"Yes I do. Two words. Thank you."

"The pleasure's been mine." He turned to leave the room.

"Clay? I know facing your parents with words they don't want to hear isn't very fun, but I hope you find the courage to stand up to them - if you mean what you say about Lauren."

"You make it sound so simple."

"Isn't it?"

Clay's eyes sparkled until she felt the warmth they radiated. This time she was not afraid to hold his glance.

"I need to head back to the office, Tracy. Did you bring your lunch? You should have a bite before you go back to work."

"I didn't come until later this morning as you know. I'll probably take a break in an hour or two."

His face stretched taunt with concern. "Please forget what I said about the panel earlier. The more I think about it, the more I think it would be wonderful to have an excuse to cancel this housewarming altogether."

"Well I hate to disappoint you, but Michelle says there's a good chance the new panel will get here in time to be reinstalled before the party. The manufacturer wouldn't make any promises, but there's a very real possibility it might all work out."

"I imagine you'd feel better about the whole thing if it turned out that way."

"No doubt."

"Then I hope it does." His lips looped up in a smile. "Maybe I'll see you tomorrow."

"Maybe."

She could hear Clay's footsteps receding down the hall as she turned back to the wall and resumed trimming around the small-paned windows that faced west and south. She felt more lighthearted than she had in weeks. She was humming softly to herself when Michelle returned with Rachael in tow.

Neither of her sisters said a word about Clay or Trevor.

"Um. Tracy," Rachael began tentatively. "I know it's kind of late notice, but I'm having a little surprise get-together to celebrate Mac's birthday tomorrow night after work and I thought since you were going to be in town anyway, you might like to come. Michelle and Jake will be the only other family there. I hadn't planned on kids. It's more an adult thing - kind of an extended happy hour situation. I'm having it at the Painted Lady."

"Oh." Tracy didn't know what to say. If she knew her ultra-organized oldest sister, invitations for the party had gone out at least two weeks ago. It was obvious she was being included as an afterthought.

"It's really not necessary..."

"Mac would love it if you were there. I mean, he's not real big on surprises, and he's a little touchy about his age now that he's going to be fifty-five – I'm sure he'll appreciate all the moral support he can get."

"I don't know what I'd do about supper for the kids."

"Trevor should be able to manage without you for one night. I'll bet it's been ages since you've been to an honest to goodness party."

Tracy sucked in a deep breath. "I've been to my share of parties. Just because I didn't brag about my high school exploits all the time like you did doesn't mean I didn't have any."

"That's been close to twenty years ago," Michelle said tactfully.

"Yah, well, ministers and their wives aren't exactly on the top of most people's invitation lists when it comes to throwing big bashes. I'd probably just embarrass you if I came. I wouldn't know anyone—"

"They'd love you!" Michelle tried to reassure her. "There'll be enough people who know you at the party to make you feel comfortable-"

"And more importantly, almost no one who knows you're in the process of divorcing a minister." Rae turned her head and looked both ways. "My advice is to let that be our little secret."

Tracy met Michelle's eyes. Rachael had no idea how many *little secrets* she actually had.

"I'm not ashamed of my past, or of Trevor's profession," Tracy said.

"No. But you deserve to have a little uninhibited fun every once in a while and the fact is, some people just aren't comfortable being around – you know..."

"Christians?" Tracy said.

"Nothing kills a party faster than bringing up the subject of religion," Rae said, digging her hole a little deeper.

"Except, maybe, ah – cancer," Michelle said, looking disgusted.

"That's a low blow," Rae said.

"Well, it's true," Michelle said. "It's not like Tracy's going to be witnessing to people at the party."

"I know that," Rae said, starting to prickle. "I'm not saying you need to hide the fact that you've been a pastor's wife for the past fifteen years. Contrary to what we were taught as children, I just don't think what you think about the Bible needs to be the first thing people know about you."

"If I can't talk about the fifteen years you refer to so glibly, I may as well stay home. I'd have nothing to say."

"That's not true, Tracy," Michelle said. "You're well-read, involved in community affairs, and active in several volunteer organizations. You're a wonderful gardener and you've just embarked upon a new career. You'd find plenty to talk about. You never have any trouble making small talk at church, do you?"

"Your friends are evidently cut from a different cloth than the ones I meet at church."

Rachael snorted. "You're so used to those judgmental, holier-than-thou people you call friends that you've probably forgotten what fun normal people can be."

Michelle rolled her eyes. "Rachael, please."

"I'm serious. I'm not saying anything bad about the people you know up in Blooming Prairie, just that you're going to need a fresh start."

Tracy gave Rae a peeved look, not because it was the way she felt, but because it was what she and Rae did.

"I'd be the first to admit it took Mac and I a little while to break into the social scene here in Maple Valley," Rae said. "But now that we have I can attest to the fact that these people are some of the friendliest, most accepting folks I've ever met."

"She's right," Michelle said. "It would be good for you

to make a few new friends."

"Which is going to be impossible in Blooming Prairie with all the talk that's going around in your congregation," Rae said.

"If you come to Mac's surprise party, you can get your feet wet again on neutral ground."

"So why is my heart pounding at the very idea? And what would I wear?" Tracy said.

"You've got a closet full of beautiful dresses," Michelle insisted.

"With prim necklines and fussy lace collars. Nothing that's right for a party."

"Old lady dresses," Rachael commented. "Not the image you want to project at your first social event." She snapped her fingers. "Wait a minute. You've been flaunting the fact that you still fit into your clothes from high school all week. Wear a nice pair of blue jeans with some classy heels, a pretty sweater, and some jewelry. I can loan you something funky if you tell me what color you need."

"A sweater or jewelry?"

"Jewelry, of course." Rachael looked down at her own well-endowed chest for one brief moment before glancing pointedly at the miniature swells poking out from under Tracy's T-shirt.

"Brat," Tracy said.

"That's enough, you two." Michelle tried to intercede.

Rae grimaced. "Don't even think it."

"Give me some credit, Rae. I haven't called you *Big Squaw Wiggly Tits* in almost three decades," Tracy said staunchly. "You can't hold something against me that happened that many years ago, can you? I was only seven years old! Even the government has a statute of limitations!"

The two sisters, one the eldest, the other the baby of the family, stood facing each other, jaws set, breathing shallow, eyes glazed over with memories of vendettas long past.

"Oh, cut it out! Both of you! At least your nickname was never made public, Rae. No one ever knew but the three of us."

"Four. Rachael had to go and tattle to Mother," Tracy taunted in a sing-song voice.

"Who accused me of making the whole thing up just to get you in trouble because she didn't believe her little sweetheart, Tracy, could do anything wrong."

Tracy had to smile in spite of herself.

Rachael glowered back.

Michelle stomped her foot. "Neither of you has anything to complain about except being a little embarrassed in front of your own family! I was ribbed about my *little peanuts* for years at school and church because of you guys. Even Jake knew about that awful nickname. You told him what it meant!" She glared at Tracy. "I don't want to hear another word out of either of you if you know what's good for you!" She stomped her foot again for emphasis.

They each held their breath for one for one tense moment, then erupted into fits of giggling so unfettered that tears streamed down their faces.

"I was awful, wasn't I?" Tracy chortled.

"Yes!" Rachael and Michelle agreed a bit too emphatically.

They dissolved into another gale of laughter.

"Oh," Rachael gasped. "This feels so good!" She clutched her side. "I haven't laughed this hard since before I found out I had cancer."

"We should have done this years ago!"

Michelle was the first to give each of her sisters a hug, but it was at Rachael's tentative touch that Tracy burst into tears. Not only was a good laugh with her sister long overdue; a good cry was as well.

Chapter 12

Tracy wished more than once that she had never consented to go to Mac's birthday party, at no time more intensely than when she finally forced herself to rustle through the cedar chest in search of something to wear. She'd waited until the kids were in bed to avoid having to answer any questions. Trevor had already grilled her up one side and down the other when she'd told him she'd be late getting home.

Thankfully, she'd been so preoccupied with thoughts of Clay, the party, and upside-down wallpaper panels that Trevor's comments had hardly rattled her. As if it was any if his business where she went or what she did! The one redeeming factor Tracy could see in the chaos of the previous day's events was that now, when Trevor started to get on her nerves, all she had to do was think of Maple Valley and all that had transpired and suddenly, what Trevor said and did hardly mattered

She had no idea what someone like Clay would find so intriguing about someone like her, but as she mulled over his unexpected presence in her life, she grew more and more convinced that a frivolous friendship with someone like Clay was just the thing she needed to divert her attentions from her troubles at home.

Her friends from church certainly seemed to be keeping their distance. Even the telephone had stayed suspiciously quiet. Tracy knew very well that word of the Reverend and Mrs. Tomlinson's pending divorce had sped from one end of the tiny town to the other by now. Yet no one called to offer support or encouragement. And who could blame them? Who wants to learn that their pastor has been living a lie?

At least the kids hadn't protested when she'd told them she'd be late. Titus and Theodora had been too swamped with their own set of troubles in the form of homework galore to care when or if she came home at all. Timothy was thrilled that it would be Trevor who read him his bedtime story come tomorrow night.

Tracy tossed a blue M&M into her mouth. She'd broken into her private stash the second the door to her bedroom was closed. She felt a warm glow inside as the chocolate worked its magic on her psyche. She was smiling as she waded though twenty years of clothes and the memories that went along with them.

She'd soon found a classic pair of blue jeans that were perfect for the party. The legs were so fitted that a five inch zipper had been installed from calf to ankle on the outside of each leg to accommodate dressing and undressing. Now if she could just find a sweater that didn't accentuate her lack of blessings in the breast department.

Tossing articles of clothing left and right, she worked her way to the bottom of the cedar chest, lopping an old jumpsuit from her senior year across the back of her Grandma Maddie's antique rocking chair, then winging a print polyester knit jumper across the foot of the bed. Although Rachael had told her repeatedly that retro was in, the old clothes looked hopelessly outdated. She wished she had asked Rae if Clay was coming to the party. What she was wearing wouldn't have seemed half as important if she was sure she wouldn't be seeing him.

Her fingers lit upon the halter top she'd worn to her senior class picnic in Todd Park just as she was thinking of Clay. She had worn it only that once. Constructed of black bandannas tried together between the breasts, behind the neck, and across the back, she'd always felt it had accentuated her small but shapely bosoms to their best advantage. One particular young man had certainly thought so, she reminisced with a smile.

She took a second look at the halter. She couldn't. She wouldn't dare. She hadn't worn a piece of clothing so provocative for nearly two decades. Even when she was in high school she'd had to slip out from under her mother's watchful glare wearing a far more conservative tee-shirt, then change into the halter at her friend's house. She rustled through the pile of clothing once more, looking for something, anything else. Polyester was out. Smock tops were definitely not an option. A teenager might look darling wearing one, but such a blouse would make a woman her age would look suspiciously pregnant. She found a quiana knit dress that looked decidedly disco and ruled it out immediately.

Her eyes came back to rest on the halter top again. If only she had a nice, open front sweater to wear over it! The addition of a subtle wrap would tone the impact of her bare midriff down considerably. Tracy held the crisp cotton halter to her face. She was still tan from wearing a scoop-necked blouse to work in the garden. She pulled up the front of her shirt. Her midriff was a much lighter shade of pink, but only an inch or two would show anyway. What did would be shadowed. The September air would certainly be cool enough for a loose-fitting jacket by nightfall.

Ah ha! Tracy pulled down her blouse, opened the door, and exited into the now darkened hallway, creeping stealthily towards Theodora's room. The short-cropped, pearl button front, white, angora blend sweater she was looking for stood out against the dark recesses of Theodora's closet like a beacon in the night. It was perfect! The crowning touch! Tracy retreated to her room and donned the outfit with the first true enthusiasm she'd felt in weeks.

When she finally changed into her nightgown and crawled into bed, she slept like a baby.

*****

Clay checked the messages on his desk and frowned when he saw two from Lauren that had come in the previous afternoon after he'd left work. He dialed the number of the Mary Rose Manor B&B and booked the only room they had open for Lauren.

Lauren had no intention of ever living in Maple Valley, nor did she care to make friends in the tiny town, yet she'd made three trips south in the past two weeks. The woman was like a tomcat marking her territory.

"Mr. Alexander, could I speak with you?" The foreman of the night crew looked in on his way past Barclay's office. "I run the samples and the swatches you had made by the people in production, and they liked them a lot."

"Good," Barclay said. "Any adjustments they'd like to make? Recommendations on colors?"

"Yes, sir," the man said. "Just one. They think the weave of the new socks should be a little finer so they're not so bulky in the shoe."

"Good," Barclay said. "That's just the kind of feedback I was looking for. I'll have the computer programmers refine the settings and have another prototype for them to look at by tomorrow. Did they like the periwinkle blue or the cinnamon twist color better?"

"Periwinkle blue, sir, although they thought both colors would sell well. And sir?"

"Yes, Harold?"

"They really appreciated being asked. You know, their opinion."

"Well, they've been doing this a lot longer than I have."

"They think the fact that the new weave cuts the clothes drying time in half will mean a big boost in sales. People are getting more environmentally conscious all the time. And we all know that the less time our appliances are running, the lower our utility bills going to be."

"That was my theory," Barclay said.

"Well, my people are real pleased that you took the time to look into this new bamboo stuff and design a new product. The world's changing, and I guess if we want to keep the doors open, we need to keep up with the times."

"I appreciate hearing that, Harold." Barclay smiled and reached out to shake Harold's hand. The older man's grasp was firm, his fingers rough and chapped.

"Line two when you're free, Mr. Alexander," his secretary said from the cubby she occupied just outside his office.

"Thanks, Shirley." The only people who ever used the unlisted number were his father and Lauren.

*****

Tracy left the house quickly the next morning in hopes of continuing to avoid her mother. Her mother had phoned the house twice the day before while Tracy had been in Maple Valley and ended up talking to Trevor. She dallied only long enough to wash, dry and iron the halter top and place a quick telephone call to Michelle - who assured her she was welcome to shower and change for the party after work at her and Jake's place. Michelle agreed to meet her at Clay's house a half hour earlier than usual in hopes of accomplishing all they planned to despite the fact they'd be leaving early to get ready for the party.

The day sped by with a welcome dose of mediocrity. Tracy was thankful there were no repeats of the disaster of the day before. To her relief, Michelle didn't press her to talk about either Clay or Trevor. That didn't mean she didn't think about both.

She chided herself for staying inside for lunch on such a beautiful day, but feared she would miss Clay if she left to take a walk around the neighborhood as she had on days prior. She was more than a little disappointed when the day came to an end and there was still no sign of him.

Long shadows decorated the walls of the master suite. "Maybe we should try to get a little more done. Clay might think we're sloughing off if he stops by and finds us gone."

Michelle looked at her suspiciously. "I thought maybe he'd come by over his lunch hour again."

"He said he might."

"Well, I think he would have come by now if he was going to. And I promised Rachael I'd be on time for the party. She stressed the fact that everyone has to be there promptly at 5:30 p.m. if the surprise element is going to work. I'll never hear the end of it if I'm late."

"I'd be just as happy staying here and working."

"There's no way I'm letting you weasel out of coming to this party, Tracy Tomlinson, so forget your excuses right this minute and get started cleaning that brush!"

Tracy's stomach pitched alarmingly. Now that the appointed hour was actually at hand she was regretting not only her decision to attend, but her choice of clothing. What had she been thinking?

Michelle interrupted her mini panic attack with a jolt. "Barclay's fiancée phoned the Painted Lady yesterday asking for me. She wanted to discuss the possibility of me catering Barclay's housewarming party."

Tracy froze, remembering what Clay had said about Lauren, but declining to tell Michelle what she knew.

"She's s very demanding woman. Seems like the type who would want to micromanage every little detail."

Tracy tried to sound nonchalant. "Did you agree to work with her?"

"I quoted some prices over the phone and faxed a list of the various hors d'oeuvres that are available. She said she plans to be down in Maple Valley sometime this weekend and will try to touch bases with me to discuss the details."

"Oh." Tracy's stomach twisted into a knot.

"I suppose you may get to meet her if she stops by the house tomorrow." Michelle twirled the paint roller with a flourish and narrowly avoided a bank of built-in drawers finished in the same red oak woodwork that complimented the rooms downstairs. "It's a wonder Clay is as nice as he is with parents like his and a fiancée like Lauren."

"Not everyone turns out to be like their parents. We certainly didn't, at least in the ways that matter. And you all keep telling me that Trevor's choices are no reflection on me. I'm married to him. I don't think we should judge Clay on the basis of what his fiancée says or does either."

"No need to be so touchy. I meant it as a compliment to him. Your point is well taken though." Michelle added one last stroke before setting the roller down and stretching her arms high over her head, then to her sides. "Why don't we leave your car here when we head out to my place to shower so we both don't have to drive all the way out there and back to town again?" Michelle suggested innocently.

"Yeah. If I have my own car I might leave the party if I feel uncomfortable." Tracy called her on her plot.

"Fine." Her sister showed no hint of remorse. "I fully expect you to hate the whole thing for the first hour, but the only way that will change is if you stick it out. I know you'll have a great time if you just give these folks a chance."

Tracy couldn't help but marvel that the words she was hearing were being spoken by her notoriously shy, lacking in self-esteem sister, Michelle. "When did you become such a social butterfly?"

"Since a friend of mine refused to listen to my protests and insisted I go to my twenty year class reunion. I wouldn't be with Jake today if I hadn't listened to her."

"Oh." Michelle and Jake had known each other when they were in high school but had only admitted their fascination with one another after running into each other twenty long years later.

"I'll be busy helping with the food at the beginning but Jake said he'd look out for you until I'm free. He's looking forward to introducing you to all our friends." Michelle rinsed out the sink with a glass and turned to face her. "If you're done we can get going as soon as I find my keys."

"Okay," Tracy said, following her numbly to the door, then out to the car. "I'm feeling really uncomfortable about what I brought to wear. I wish we were the same size so I could borrow something of yours."

"Believe me, you don't wish you were my size."

Now that sounded more like the Michelle she knew.

"I'm sure you'll look wonderful," Michelle said a little while later, pulling away from the curb to start the five mile journey towards the Cedar River where she and Jake's home was located. "You always look lovely."

"Thanks." Tracy still felt less than enthusiastic but she obviously wasn't going to get any sympathy from Michelle.

The fact that autumn had arrived was more apparent the nearer they came to the river. The small willow and ash trees growing in hedgerows between the fields were already golden yellow. Several sprawling, hundred-foot-high sugar maples sported patches of brilliant reds and vivid orange.

Tracy rolled down her window a few inches and inhaled deeply as the faint odor of river and loamy black farm soil filled her nostrils. "Is Sarah still up at Jake's folks' in Austin?"

"Yes, but we're going to go pick her up tonight after the party if it doesn't get too late. I miss her too much to be without her for another day. Besides, I'm sure Grandma and Grandpa Sheffield have had their fill by now."

"She's such a sweet little thing. I don't know how anyone could ever get their fill."

"There were times when she was younger and I was severely sleep deprived from nursing her every two or three hours all night long that I would have loved a break." Michelle chuckled to herself. "Sometimes I'd sit in the rocking chair holding her, half asleep, yet too tired to stand up and put her back in her bassinet, wondering why I couldn't have had children when I was in my twenties like you did instead of waiting until I was almost forty."

"There are times when I've watched Rachael and Mac trying to keep up with Ian that I've wondered how they find the stamina to chase after him seven days a week. Especially when Rae was getting chemo. I suppose you have all of that to look forward to when Sarah starts to walk."

"Every blissful moment. It's easier now that she's sleeping through the night. And it's so fun to see signs of her own little personality emerging. I can hardly bear to be without her when I'm at work. She learns something new practically every day. Jake hates it when he has to be gone."

"It wasn't long ago that Timothy was a baby. Those were such happy days."

"There'll be more happy times ahead."

"I wonder sometimes."

Michelle just smiled. "I almost forgot to ask you what you wanted to do about tomorrow. Josh and Nate are going to be up for the weekend again – their mother is taking a class at the University of Minnesota. If you're game to work at Barclay's house, you could bring the kids down for the day so the boys could play. If Teddy, I mean Theodora," she glanced at Tracy sideways to see if her slip had caused a reaction, "wouldn't mind baby-sitting Sarah, Jake would be happy to tackle the responsibility of following the four boys around. He said something about building a raft."

"Oh, they'd love it! I had thought about trying to look at some rental properties with a Realtor Rae knows up in Blooming Prairie but I can put that off until Sunday or some evening next week. I'll have to check the schedule to make sure Titus doesn't have a soccer game but I think it would work. The boys had such fun together at Mom and Dad's. Timothy's mentioned the raft several times since then."

"I know Titus is a little more mature than Jake's boys, but they sure think the world of him."

"He likes them, too. It might be good for my kids to spend a little time with Josh and Nate now that they know that Trevor and I are getting a divorce. Josh and Nate are such happy, well adjusted kids. They seem to accept the fact that you and Jake... their mother is remarried, too, isn't she? Please don't take offense, but there just aren't many children of divorced couples at the Christian school. I think it would help my kids to be able to relate to and ask questions of other kids their own age who've been through the experience."

"Could be. Personally, I can't imagine the boys having much to say on the subject. They were so young when Jake got divorced. Other than the few bumps we had when Jake and I got married and he moved up here, it hasn't required much of an adjustment on their part. They grew up accepting the fact that their Mom and Dad live two separate lives."

"I'd be grateful if even a little of that acceptance rubbed off on my kids."

Michelle followed the long road as it wound past fields of corn and groves of oak, elm and walnut trees. "It doesn't look like Jake's home yet. There are plenty of towels on the wicker sideboard in the guest room. Make yourself at home and feel free to use the shampoo and toiletries in the basket."

"I will. Michelle?"

"Yes?"

"I might need to borrow a necklace if you have something black. Pearls would work, too. I thought Rachael was going to bring some by the house. I should have called her last night to remind her."

"I've got the perfect thing. I'll bring it in after I shower."

"Thanks." Tracy trembled involuntarily as she exited the car and wandered through the house to the guest room. She'd always felt relaxed in Michelle and Jake's home. Michelle herself was just so comfortable to be around that the picture perfect decor which might have been intimidating under different circumstances put one at ease instead.

But today her hands trembled as she unbuttoned her blouse. The pale cream sheers billowing gracefully before the open sliding screen doors leading to the patio only made her feel more clumsy and out of place. She was totally out of her class. Who was she, thinking that she could hobnob with people of Michelle and Jake's, Rachael and Mac's, and Clay Alexander's caliber? She moved to the mirror, unclasped her brassiere, and unbuttoned her pants, which slipped effortlessly over her slim hips to fall to the floor.

She surveyed her nude form in the mirror objectively. So she had the body of a twenty-five year old - one that most women in their thirties would be envious of. What did it matter when she didn't know how to use it? She was totally lacking in the social graces that women like Rachael and Michelle and Lauren had refined to perfection.

She felt comfortable in only one setting, and now only marginally so. The arena of the church was the solitary backdrop against which her adult life had played. Without it she was homeless. Her anchor was gone.

Tracy stared straight ahead, surveying the plump, richly fringed moiré pillows on the tall brass bed reflected behind her in the mirror. Her eyes roamed the length of the room, absorbing in one swift glance a contemporary quilt she knew Michelle had brought home from a trip to Santa Fe, a hand-loomed weaving looped in seemingly unplanned artistry over the bed, and a striking copper vase that looked like it was shimmering with sunshine.

How paltry her meager possessions must seem to her sisters. The late basement, early attic decor she'd struggled to perfect over the last decade couldn't hold a candle to the rich affects Michelle had achieved in the few short months she and Jake had lived in the home they'd inherited from Michelle's friend, the late Sarah MacKenzie Anderson.

And then there was Barclay. What could she possibly have in common with someone who would spend a thousand dollars on a wallpaper panel? How could she expect to hold her own in a friendship with a man who drove a Mercedes convertible? Tracy climbed in the shower and let the water pour over her shoulders. She was deluding herself if she thought the man would waste more than five minutes on a relationship with her, and that was assuming he broke off his "engagement".

Her hands were still shaking as she climbed out of the shower, toweled herself dry, and fluffed her hair with her fingers. She redid the knot that fastened the halter between her breasts five or six times before she felt moderately satisfied with the effect. Leaning at the hips, she bent to zip her jeans from calf to ankle. Even she had to admit the denim fit her like a charm. She lowered one shoulder at a time as she slipped into Theodora's bolero sweater. The hem of the white angora met her jeans exactly at her waist; the gap in front was just big enough to accentuate her halter.

The knock at the door broke the mesmerized stare that had her eyes riveted to the mirror.

"I have a couple of necklaces for you to look at if you're decent."

"C-come in." She wanted to hide. She wanted to run. She wanted to crawl under a rock and never come out.

"Tracy Tomlinson, you look darling!"

Her arms dangled uncomfortably from her shoulders. She flinched from pure nervousness. "You're my sister. You'd say that no matter what I was wearing."

"No, I wouldn't. And speaking as the older sister here,

and might I add, one who needs to lose some twenty odd pounds gained over the course of her recent pregnancy, it pains me greatly to admit how utterly, absolutely gorgeous you look. If you were anyone but my very own little sister, I'd spend the night at the exact opposite end of the room from you so no one could compare us. And I'd hate you for the rest of your life if Jake so much as glanced at you."

Tracy giggled.

Michelle stepped towards her with her arms outstretched and fastened a tiny necklace around her neck with one brisk motion. "Look in the mirror."

Tracy turned slowly. She caught her breath. The jet black crystals at the Y of the delicate chain dangled between the very tops of her breasts as though the necklace had been made with her in mind. A cluster of dainty fresh water pearls clinging to the chain a few inches up on each side were perfectly framed in the bronze oval of skin left exposed by her halter. Each tiny prism fluttered beguilingly as she arched her neck to glimpse the total effect.

"It's perfect."

"I told you it would be," Michelle said.

"You're sure?"

"You look lovely."

"Thanks." The words escaped her lips in a whisper.

"Ready to go, ladies?" Jake rapped lightly on the half-closed door to the guest room.

Michelle's face lit up in a smile that wreathed her whole countenance. "He slipped in just in time to share a shower," she whispered before turning to reach for the doorknob. "Come and see Tracy. You won't believe your eyes."

Her brother-in-law's low wolf whistle drowned out her embarrassed protests. "I'll be the envy of every man in the room tonight when I walk in with you two on my arms."

"Doesn't she look great?"

"If you two don't quit fussing over me right now I'm not setting foot outside this house!" Tracy insisted, scowling ferociously. But she secretly cherished their words.

Chapter 13

Tracy and the other thirty or so guests stood in the darkened front parlor of the Painted Lady waiting for Mac and Rachael to arrive. The air was so charged with electricity that she felt sure she'd get a shock if she moved. She couldn't wait to see the look on Mac's face. Mac was just the sort of man it was fun to surprise - unassuming, soft spoken, even reticent with folks he didn't know well. It was a perfect plan – Mac wouldn't suspect a thing when Rachael told him they needed to stop by the Painted Lady to pick up something from Michelle.

Tracy's stomach growled in anticipation just thinking about the buzz of activity going on in the kitchen of her sister's tea house. Michelle had probably declined her offers of help because she knew Tracy would snitch everything in sight. She'd taken a peek earlier and gotten a glimpse of platters laden with thick slabs of ham tucked into petite potato rolls, and mounds of fresh strawberries, melon, and grapes waiting to be dipped in a warm cinnamon sauce by any who wasn't watching their figure. Calico-lined baskets bulging with Mac's favorite homemade oatmeal butterscotch cookies were ready to be whisked outside to grace clusters of canopied patio tables illuminated by the rosy glow of sunset. The perfect menu!

The room grew quiet once more as the guests hovering in the entryway of the tall-ceilinged Victorian cut off their conversation and watched another car draw close, resuming their banter only when the car passed on down the street. To Tracy's relief, disappointment, or both, Clay was not among the party-goers. For better or worse, his absence freed her to concentrate on making the acquaintance of all the folks she had heard Rae and Michelle speak of over the last few years.

Michelle had been right in her estimation that she would enjoy herself after the first tense five or ten minutes of the party had passed. Jake had been kind enough to take her in tow, spoon-feeding her bits and pieces of information about the various people she was being introduced to. He had even been so thoughtful as to whisper the names of people she'd already met in her ear as they approached her to chat or ask her about her work on the Alexander house.

The crowd buzzed with merriment, alternately quieting, then erupting with spontaneous bursts of laughter, their eyes trained watchfully on the street. When one car in the string finally slowed and began a purposeful approach, they all seemed to realize it held Mac with a simultaneous sixth sense. The room had grown still before Rachael's metallic blue Mazda even rounded the bend.

The crowd sprang to life as they hurried to hide. Unfamiliar bodies pressed Tracy towards the wall with a sudden urgency as those who had been milling about stepped back to try to get away from the windows facing the street. The room had grown dim with nightfall and Tracy lost sight of Jake in the commotion. The unearthly silence seemed to deepen and Tracy had the distinct impression that everyone in the room was holding their breath.

"Is that your heart I feel pounding against my chest?" a deep, sensual voice whispered in her ear.

Alarmed, she tried to move away. Her heart nearly tripped over itself in that first startling moment when she realized she had backed squarely into the masculine frame of a man she couldn't see and probably didn't know from Adam. Who could tell? Shadowed forms pressed in on her from every side. Her heart beat even more wildly when she realized she was trapped.

She didn't dare say a word. She could hear a pair of mismatched footsteps tapping against the front porch just outside the door where she was wedged against the stranger, growing louder at every turn. Tracy held her breath and tried to turn.

The man put one hand on each of her shoulders to steady her and whispered, "Whoa. Not a good idea."

She realized too late that her hips were nudged firmly

against the midsection of the unknown man, her derriere nestled securely in what must have been his crotch.

She was thanking the Lord the room was dark enough that no one could see the blush staining her cheeks when the front door creaked open and Rae reached inside to flip on the lights.

“Surprise!” everyone but she yelled in unison. “Happy birthday!”

She caught one quick glimpse of Mac’s wide-eyed shock through a break in the crowd. The man caught behind her continued to rest his hands on her shoulders. She could feel the soft fibers of Theodora’s sweater slithering against her bare shoulders as he attempted to alter his position in order to see Mac’s entrance.

The knot of people clustered around them began to loosen as the first guests stepped forward to greet Mac. Still the stranger did not release his hold. She could feel his chest rising and falling as he pressed against her, knew that he held his breath as he gently swiveled her torso around to face him. But she didn’t receive the greeting she expected.

The man took one look at her and let her go like he’d touched a hot coal. “Tracy? Rae’s little sister, Tracy?”

“Luke?” she stammered, now facing him squarely. Her blush deepened. She’d never gotten to know Luke all that well – truth be told, she wasn’t even all that close to Rae and Mac. The whole little love triangle thing before Rachael and Mac had gotten married had always made her nervous, although everyone else in the family seemed to have forgotten Luke’s role in the whole mess. Rachael and Mac treated him like one of the family and regarded him as an adopted uncle to Ian.

Luke took in her uncustomary attire with an appreciative glance downward, then looked away with what she assumed to be embarrassment for both of them. “Sorry, Tracy. Rae told me you’ve been working over at Alexander’s house. I guess I shouldn’t be surprised to see you here.”

Tracy looked up at him with wide-eyed panic. She’d always thought of Luke as Rachael’s friend and business partner, never as a man. Looking at Luke through the eyes of an almost-single-again woman left her inexplicably tongue-tied. She tried to manage a smile, but all she could think about was how gauche she must look. What ever had possessed her to wear this stupid halter top?

Luke seemed disconcertingly aware of the effect he was having on her. "Wow. This is the first time... I mean, I've never see you looking so..."

"Ridiculous?" she found her tongue and queried dejectedly. Her shoulders slumped and she lowered her chin just far enough to avoid his glance.

"Just like Rae. Always trying to put words in my mouth." Luke teased.

She felt his eyes rake over her once again even though she wasn't looking at him directly.

"And no. Nothing ridiculous about you. You look frighteningly adorable." Luke twisted his neck down until she had no choice but to meet his eyes. He smiled endearingly.

"You really think it's okay? I mean, the top isn't too much?"

"Maybe too little." He laughed at his own joke. "No. Trust me. It's great just the way it is."

She felt the heat burning her cheeks creep down her neck all the way to her exposed cleavage.

He surprised her by turning a little red himself."Rae told me you're getting a divorce. I can't blame you for..." His hand waffled back and forth. "...whatever you're trying to do. Starting over, I guess." His eyes traveled the length of her torso once more. He looked pitifully apologetic. "It's hard for me not to think of you as a minister's wife."

"Shhhh." Tracy looked right, then left. The crowd had thinned enough to leave them in relative isolation. "Rae says I'm not supposed to let anyone know that I was, am, married to a minister until I'm a little better acquainted with them."

"Now that bit of wisdom sounds like classic Rae. Not that it probably isn't good advice. I just hope you don't listen to everything she tells you."

Tracy smiled. "I usually don't listen to *anything* she tells me, but this whole business of being single again has left me feeling kind of insecure. I mean, plop me down in the middle of a prayer meeting or a Sunday School picnic and I know exactly what to wear, do and say, but put me in a room with a few regular people at a simple birthday gathering and I don't have a clue how to act. My sisters are the experts at that, not me."

"Be careful. The things Rae's been through in the last few years have mellowed her a little bit, but she can still be as bossy as all get out."

"No need to tell me. I grew up with the woman."

"Not to sound obtuse, but the two of you are so different, I forget you're sisters. But it's obvious you've thought this through. You'll do fine." Luke nodded his approval.

"So you two were in on this whole sordid plot, too, eh?" Mac interrupted, loping one arm over each of their shoulders.

"So how does it feel to be a senior citizen?" Luke ribbed.

"Happy Birthday," Tracy said timidly, wondering afresh what her brother-in-law would think of her risqué attire.

The thought that it would never occur to Mac to judge someone on the basis of what they wore flashed through her mind. Sure enough, Mac said nothing, but responded with a bear hug the likes of which she hadn't had in months, scooping her nearly off the ground and enveloping her in his arms. Her first response was to hope her bandanna halter stayed in place, her second to give herself over to his grasp.

"I'm proud of you for being here, kid," Mac said gruffly. "I know it's not easy to put yourself out there and be social when you're going through a rough time. You've got guts."

Her eyes filled with tears as his cheek rubbed against hers. Oh, how she had needed this hug. She'd needed it for weeks and not known how to put it in words. Her body quivered against his. He pulled her even tighter. Mac. There was no one on earth whose understanding she deserved less than Mac McPhearson's. She had been so harsh in her judgment of this man, so vocal in her condemnation of his and

Rachael's actions before they were married.

If only she had known then what she knew now.

"Hang in there. Things can only get better."

"Thank you, Mac. I will."

He started to turn. She touched his sleeve.

"I always wished I had an older brother like you, Mac."

He appraised her silently for a moment as if gauging her sincerity. "Now you do."

She leaned forward and kissed him on the cheek. Luke was looking on warmly when she opened her eyes. Many of the guests were filtering outside to the front lawn. Colorful Chinese lanterns strung from one side of the wide porch to the other fluttered in the breeze. Several of Michelle's staff members rushed by with platters heaped with food.

And then she caught a glimpse of another familiar face. No, two. Tracy stiffened as Clay entered the room with the woman from the merry-go-round on his arm.

She chose to ignore the flood of emotions that poured over her at seeing Clay and turned back to Luke instead. "Rae tells me you have a beautiful voice, Luke. Maybe she's already recruited you to provide entertainment at the party tonight but if not, I know I'd love to hear you sing."

"Yeah, well, Rae tends to exaggerate."

Tracy could still see Clay out of the corner of her eye. His being here changed everything. Her heart was pounding, her hands were shaking. In two seconds she'd gone from feeling ridiculous to downright flummoxed. She forced herself to focus on Luke.

"Rae's always been picky about what kind of music she listens to. If she says you're wonderful, I'm sure you are."

"I actually did set up my keyboard out on the porch before you arrived. Rae has Mac's guitar in the trunk of her car. I brought two amps and a few mikes. A friend of ours was going to bring his drums." Luke looked over the top of her head and scanned the room. "I think I see him now as a matter of fact. If Rae can talk the old man into strumming along, we're set to jam."

"I've never heard Mac play either."

"I'm surprised to hear that. He's an excellent guitarist. I can't believe the licks he still has down after all these years."

"Sadly, the Jones family doesn't do guitar music, especially the amplified kind. Too jazzy for our conservative blood I suppose."

"Sounds like tonight's the night to set a new precedent."

"In a lot of ways." She smiled and tried to relax her shoulders. "Rae said you used to play with a great band in Colorado." Clay had spotted her now. She could feel his eyes moving over her. She felt like she could melt into the floor. "Um, Luke?" She fought her rising panic and glanced at Luke furtively. "Could you do me a really huge favor and pretend like we're together? Just for a few minutes? There's somebody here that I... I mean, I just don't want to look like I'm here alone."

"You got it," Luke said, slipping into his role like a natural. He smiled down at her encouragingly. "The Obsessions. That was the name of my band. I still miss playing with them. It helps to get to jam with these guys once in awhile."

"Um, what kind of music do you like to play?" Tracy said, feeling lame and pathetic and like she was in junior high all over again. She could see Clay speaking to a man she knew she'd met but whose name she couldn't remember. His fake fiancée looked just as out of place here as she had at the state fair – a bit too elegantly clad in clothes that were so well-designed they verged on pretentious. She had the same stiff, superior air about her Tracy remembered from the first time she'd seen her.

"Classic rock," Luke said. Then "If you want the guy to think we're together, you need to smile up at me and touch me every so often. It'll look more natural than the scared-half-to-death expression you're wearing."

Clay's focus begin to shift towards her again. Tracy turned her gaze away from him, leaned towards Luke and touched his bare arm tentatively. "Thanks. I'm not trying to make him jealous or anything. I just don't want him to feel sorry for me."

"Gotcha." Luke took her hand in his. "You have to stop shaking if you want him to think you're having a good time."

"I'll try. This whole divorce thing has all been so humiliating – I have to try to hang on to what few tattered shreds of pride I still have left."

"No problem." Luke lopped his arm around her and led her towards the front porch. "I have a special song I sing to all the girls when I want to make them swoon. Want to hear it?"

She giggled. Naturally. No act. "I'd like that."

Luke chuckled and nicked the underside of her chin with one crooked finger. "I'll be singing this one for you and no one else, sweetheart."

"Do you know any Rita Coolidge songs? She's always been my favorite."

"Sure. I do a fairly decent rendition of *Words*."

She locked her eyes with his. "I'll be listening."

Clay forced himself to look away from Tracy, and re-focused his attention on Lauren. The look of disdain on Lauren's face had to be evident to anyone within visual range.

"I thought you said this caterer specialized in planning sophisticated soirees for the discriminating. I was just offered an oatmeal butterscotch cookie." His *fiancée* wrinkled her nose at a waitress carrying a basket mounded high with the delectable morsels.

Clay reached out his arm and plucked another cookie before she retreated.

"Seems more appropriate for an after school snack than a hors d'oeuvre for a grown man's birthday party," Lauren said. "But then, this is Iowa. No one in the whole state seems to have the slightest bit of tact."

Clay riveted his glance away from Tracy. Again. He could only wish the woman at his side would exude some fraction of the warmth he had witnessed Tracy bestowing on Luke Zimmerman. He glared at Lauren. "I won't stand here and allow you to insult these people. I've grown very fond of Michelle Sheffield. In my opinion, the staff of the Painted Lady delivers an exceptional mix of professional service and delicious food. I've been at several elegant events catered by Michelle's firm and they've done an outstanding job at each. If Michelle and Rachael chose to serve cookies at tonight's festivities I can assure you there's not only a very good reason, but that they're the best damn cookies this side of the Mississippi."

Lauren rolled her eyes. "Really, Barclay."

Mac appeared from around the corner, his arm looped around Michelle's waist as if on cue. "These cookies are almost as good as Rachael's, which are damn near as good as the ones my dear departed mother used to have waiting for me every Friday afternoon after school got out..."

Barclay looked on smugly. "What a unique concept – a hostess who actually takes the preferences of the party's guest of honor into account when planning her menu."

"I suppose should we have children one day I can expect you to condone a bill of fare consisting of peanut butter and jelly sandwiches or macaroni and cheese just because our children prefer them to more socially acceptable options?"

Barclay's stomach rolled at the thought. "I'm sure no child of yours would ever dream of eating such a diet." A round of laughter drew his eyes across the room. He could see Luke leaning against the far wall, ankles crossed, a drink in one hand, the other slung casually around Tracy Tomlinson's slim waist. The cluster of people surrounding them laughed a second time.

Everyone within earshot heard Clay's sigh.

The kitchen was hot and smelled of melting butterscotch. A cluster of half-empty serving trays lined the counter where Rachael and Michelle stood refilling baskets with cookies still warm from the oven.

Rachael's face was a study in barely contained fury. "Did you see the way she's throwing herself at Luke? What the hell does the little tramp think she's doing anyway?"

Rachael exploded. "No one's that naive!"

Michelle glanced over her shoulder to make sure the kitchen door was still shut tightly. "Tracy, a tramp? She's done nothing that you haven't refined to an art form. Talk about the kettle calling the pot black!"

"I never came on to Luke so blatantly in all the months I dated him. Tracy hardly knows him!"

"He's been at practically every family function the Jones' have held over the past two years! I think it's great that she feels comfortable enough with him to let down her guard and flirt a little."

"She's never paid any attention to him before now."

"She was a married woman until now."

"The way she's throwing herself at him is disgusting."

"I should think you'd be happy they're having a good time and enjoying the party."

"I am," Rachael said begrudgingly. "I just don't understand why she had to single out Luke to bat her baby blues at."

"He's the only unmarried man here to the best of my knowledge except for Barclay Alexander – and he's with Lauren. It's only natural they would gravitate towards one another." Michelle stood facing her sister with her hands on her hips. "You're jealous! You've had both Mac and Luke at your beck and call for so long that you can't stand the idea of sharing the wealth, not even with your own sister."

"That is so not true," Rae sputtered.

"It is, too. Have a heart, Rae! You don't know half the hell Tracy's been through. And it hasn't been that long since you were alone. You ought to remember what a nice boost a little attention from a man can be when your self esteem is in the gutter. They're just engaging in a little harmless flirtation. It's nothing more than that."

"Don't even go there." Rae grimaced.

Michelle sighed. "I need to go and track down Barclay and Lauren. I had Madeleine put together some quotes for hors d'oeuvres for their housewarming party and I need to catch them before they slip away." She started to leave, then stopped. "Please stay out of trouble tonight, Rae. And give Tracy a break. It wouldn't hurt you to be nice to her just this once."

"I invited her to the party, didn't I?"

Clay didn't consciously decide to ignore his conscience and follow his instincts. He just did. The second Michelle and Lauren started discussing menu options for the housewarming, he made a beeline for Tracy's side. Trouble was, by that time, the position he'd hoped to fill was already taken.

"Oh, I love that song!" Tracy said, touching Luke's arm with the artless charm of a true ingénue.

"Hey, Mac! The lady has a request. Does that senior citizen's body of yours have enough strength left in it to lift a guitar out of the trunk or do you need some help?"

"Listen, punk..." Mac said.

"Okay. Time to take it outside, boys," Rae, who was standing beside him, interjected. She lowered her voice to a hushed whisper. "If I have to stand here and watch any more of my supposedly innocent little sister's coy moves, I won't be responsible for my actions."

Hmm, Clay thought. An interesting observation.

She flipped a switch and revved her voice up to its normal pitch. "I put your guitar on the porch earlier, Mac. Not because I didn't think you couldn't lift it yourself." She tilted her head back and looked up to meet Mac's eyes. "I know how much strength there still is in those old bones of yours."

Rae's words met with numerous hoots and cat calls from the crowd.

Clay took advantage of the movement of the crowd to inch a little closer to Tracy and Luke.

"Tell it like it is, doll," Mac said nonchalantly.

"My mother always said it's not polite to brag," Rae said, and gave Mac an exaggerated wink.

The crowd went wild while Clay moved close enough to eavesdrop on Tracy.

"Like she's ever listened to our mother," Tracy said to Luke.

Luke threw his head back and laughed. "That's an understatement."

Tracy laughed. "Better get your fingers warmed up before Mac changes his mind." She touched Luke's arm again as she moved away from him, seemingly unaware of Clay's presence.

"Don't forget you promised to make me swoon," she said, looking up at Luke again.

"I won't." Luke kissed her on the forehead.

Clay wouldn't have believed Tracy would behave in such a way if he hadn't witnessed it with his own two eyes. What on earth had come over her? The shy, fragile woman he'd spoken to yesterday seemed very at ease with Luke Zimmerman.

"Hi, Tracy," he said when Luke had gone, touching her lightly on her shoulder.

"Clay? Hello! I didn't know you'd be here tonight," she said, looking surprised although he was sure she'd seen him earlier.

"Luke's probably already told you how lovely you look tonight."

"He has. But it's nice to hear it from you, too."

"I don't want to hold you up if you want to step outside to hear the band."

"Thanks. Does Lauren like to dance?"

Clay flinched. "Her tastes gravitate more towards classical. She enjoys an occasional ballroom dance. Somehow I doubt that's what we can expect from the band tonight."

"I think you're right."

"I'd be delighted to dance with you if no one's spoken for the first round." He looked over his shoulder to make sure Lauren was still talking to Michelle.

Tracy blushed. "I'd like that – if Lauren doesn't mind."

"She won't," Clay said. "I wasn't sure... Do conservative, Republican, Fellowship minister's wives dance?"

"It has been quite a few years," she said, suddenly shy again. "I think I remember how. When I was in high school I used to ask permission to spend the night at a friend's house whenever there was a school dance so I could go. I guess I figured what my parent's didn't know wouldn't hurt them."

"That doesn't scare you to death now that you're the mother of a teenager?" Clay asked.

"That's why I have her enrolled in a Christian school. Not that there are any guarantees she won't get into trouble there, but I feel a little more secure knowing that she's sheltered from at least some of life's temptations."

Clay took her hand and led her outside to the front porch. "I've never known dancing to hurt anyone."

She laughed. "Me neither, although if I tried to do some of the dances I did back in the eighties I'd probably throw my back out or sprain something."

Clay squeezed her hand. "I'll bet you're more limber than most people half your age."

She had the grace to blush.

"Dancing is great exercise. I've never understood why some churches object to it," he said.

"They don't – as long as it's between married couples, behind closed doors, in one's own home," Tracy said.

"Seriously?"

Mac was tuning his guitar to Luke's keyboard when they reached the porch, the drummer inching a pair of snares this way and a set of cymbals that way. All were alternately tapping their mikes to test the sound.

"My soon-to-be-ex once described dancing as a sexual prelude in a sermon he was giving," Tracy said impishly.

Clay led her to center stage. "If that's how they view dancing it's no wonder they have a problem with it. I must say, however, that my interest in dancing with you has suddenly piqued."

He wrapped his arms around her before she could respond.

The band began with an Art Garfunkel hit Clay

remembered from junior high, "I Only Have Eyes For You."

Tracy kept her wits about her long enough to remember that Luke was probably searching her out, expecting her to swoon over him like they'd planned. She saw him trying to make eye contact with her out of the corner of her eye even as she gazed, mesmerized, into Clay Alexander's eyes. And then she lost herself in Clay's arms.

His hands held her at the waist but his fingers caressed her bare skin under the cover of Theodora's white cashmere sweater. She was not so naive that she couldn't guess the effect the rocking motion of their hips was having on Clay even before she felt the proof.

It was as though they were swirling alone in an alternate universe. The cool night air, music floating on the wind, the smell of hydrangea blossoms on the breeze, and the warm cocoon of air generated by their passion all added to the sensation of being swept away to another place and time – in her mind, a Rita Coolidge concert, just the two of them.

As pretty as you are,
you know you could have been a flower.
If good looks was a minute,
you know that you could be an hour.
Well, you could have been anything that you wanted to,
and I can tell the way you do the things you do.
The way you do the things you do...
The way you do the things you do...

Clay's eyes never left hers, their faces held apart by a mere fraction of an inch and kept apart by the nearly forgotten knowledge that people were watching. They danced through one song, the next, and then another. Her last semi-coherent thought was that maybe she should have listened to Trevor's sermon about the evils of dancing more carefully.

"So this is where you've been hiding all this time! I've been looking all over for you!" Lauren's shrill voice jerked them back to reality.

Chapter 14

Tracy pulled away from Clay. It took her eyes a minute to refocus – when they did, she was looking at Lauren, whose hands were on her hips, her lips etched into a pout.

"Sorry, Lauren," Clay said.

She watched as Clay struggled to regain his composure. His cheeks were flushed; probably her own were, too.

"I guess I lost track of time. You were so absorbed in finger foods and crudités, and then I started listening to the band..." Clay said to Lauren.

Luke, at least, was true to his word. The band was playing one Rita Coolidge song after another.

I can tell by your eyes that you've prob'bly been cryin' forever,

And the stars in the sky don't mean nothin' to you, they're a mirror.

I don't want to talk about it, how you broke my heart

If I stay here just a little bit longer,

If I stay here, won't you listen to my heart, whoa, my heart?

Tracy wanted to shrink into the wood slat floor boards.

"Honestly Barclay, I don't understand how you can stand to be out here. The air is so dank and humid. And the flies!" Lauren batted a bug away from her hair and sniffed the air. "With all the livestock farms in this area, it's no wonder they're so prolific. The whole community is probably nothing but one huge breeding ground. I don't even want to think about what other kind of vermin might be loitering around. Let's go back inside, Barclay."

"Certainly. Tracy, if you'll excuse me."

She nodded. Lauren had not acknowledged her presence. Under the circumstances, she was relieved Clay didn't attempt an introduction.

"Hey you!"

Tracy turned when she heard Luke's voice come over the loud speaker.

"Yeah, you. The groupie in the cute white sweater. This one's for you."

Tracy flattened herself against the wall. Luke looked across the porch at her with his fathomless blue eyes and held her gaze as his hands slid effortlessly across the keyboard. His smooth tenor voice made his rendition of "Maybe I'm Amazed" sound even better than Paul McCartney's. Michelle had told her once that Luke had sung this song to Rae before she'd met Mac, and that the way he sang it was the reason half the women in Maple Valley were in love with him. She could see why.

While the rest of the crowd danced on around her, Tracy was thankful for the diversion and relieved not to have to speak to anyone. When the song was over, she would thank Luke for his kindness and retreat to the kitchen to help Michelle clean up.

Luke played his heart out for her, looking for all the world as though nothing had changed. But she knew that everything had. At least to her, it felt like nothing would ever be the same.

*****

Sadly, she was right. Tracy may have thought her humiliation was complete when she left Mac's surprise party, but she had failed to anticipate the homecoming Trevor had planned for her when she arrived in Blooming Prairie. That was her first mistake. The second was that she didn't think to pull Theodora's sweater shut in front to hide her halter top before she walked in the house. It never occurred to her that her soon-to-be-ex-husband would be waiting for her right inside the door.

"Good Lord, Tracy, where have you been till all hours? And dressed like that?"

"I told you Rachael was having a surprise birthday party for Mac. I thought you understood I'd be late."

"Late as in seven or eight o'clock as opposed to six, yes. But to come tromping in at eleven-thirty at night? What was I supposed to think?"

"I really don't care what you think, Trevor." She flared. "What I do or when I do it is really none of your concern."

"I'm still your husband."

"Not for long."

Trevor's mouth gaped open. "This is just so unlike you."

"You know, you're absolutely right, Trevor. Everything about me is suddenly totally unlike the person I've been for all these years. And whose fault is that? I never asked for any of this. I was happy and contented with our lives. I loved being your wife and mother to our children. I'm not the one who decided to toss everything we'd worked for out the window and start all over again. Having to juggle a job and my duties as a mother was not my choice. Being forced to reenter the social scene at thirty some odd years was not my decision!"

"Shhhh. The children are trying to sleep."

"If you'll excuse me, I'd like to do the same." She clutched a handful of white angora to her chest and started to stomp from the room. "By the way, I'm planning on taking the children to Maple Valley with me tomorrow if Titus doesn't have a game. Jake is going to help Josh and Nate build a raft and he's invited the boys to join them. Michelle thought she and I could accomplish more at the Alexander house tomorrow if Theodora came along to baby-sit Sarah."

"The kids have been in school all week. Tomorrow is the last free day I'll have with them before I leave for California next week."

"You didn't seem worried about spending time with them last weekend when you decided not to come home in time to go to the State Fair with us."

Trevor cringed. "Is this how it's going to be between us from now on, Tracy?"

"Your decision to leave your family will never be regarded as a popular one in this household, Trevor. How you live with the repercussions of that choice is your problem, not mine."

Tracy left the room without saying another word. She was not in the mood to coddle Trevor. Let him call Kurt and cry on his shoulder, she thought bitterly. It was only nine-thirty in California.

Trevor caught up to her midway down the hall. "I can't help being gay, Tracy. This is not something I asked for either."

"No? You may not have chosen to be the way you are, Trevor, but it was you who chose to deceive me from the first time you met me. It was you who chose to involve me in perpetuating the lie you've lived all these years, and it is you who's chosen to leave your family in favor of embracing a gay lifestyle."

They stared at each other aghast with the sudden realization that they were speaking aloud of things that should only have been said in private.

"You'd better pray the kids are still asleep."

"You're the one who raised your voice," Trevor said accusingly.

"You're the one who keeps insisting we discuss this over and over again at all times of the day and night."

"And it's you who forbade me to be honest with the children in the first place. If you'd let me tell them the truth we wouldn't need to keep worrying about them overhearing conversations or figuring things out on their own. If you think I like being duplicitous with my own children you're sadly mistaken! I'm not ashamed of who I am!"

"So it was fine to lie to me and my family and your parishioners for over two decades but now its suddenly crucial that you be devastatingly, brutally honest with three innocent children who love you more than anything in the world?"

"That's exactly why I have to tell them the truth!"

A rustling sound from behind Timothy's door brought them back to their senses.

"He's awake," Tracy whispered.

"He might just be turning over in his sleep."

"I don't hear anything now," she said.

"I'll slip in and check on him."

"You won't say anything to him if he's awake, will you?"

"Of course not. I'd never tell them this way, not without you there."

"Promise me?"

"I may not agree with you, Tracy, but I'll continue to respect your wishes until I can convince you otherwise." She declined to thank him even though she supposed it might be appropriate. "I'll see you in the morning."

"Yes. Sleep well."

Of course, she didn't. Whether out of pure obstinacy or sheer panic, she didn't know. But when she awoke the next morning, having dreamed fitfully through the night of being safe in Clay Alexander's arms only to awaken to the nightmare of Lauren's shrill voice, it was as though she and Trevor's agitated conversation of the night prior had never taken place.

He'd told the children about Jake and Michelle's invitation before Tracy even showered and dressed. Timothy and Titus were obviously delighted, Theodora a bit less enthusiastic but willing nonetheless.

The sunshine streaming through every window in the house further enhanced the general feeling of optimism. Tracy was sure her daughter's occasionally surly behavior could be attributed to the general malice they'd all suffered since the announcement that Trevor and she were divorcing. An insightful, sensitive young woman of Theodora's age couldn't be expected to bounce back from news like that as fast as the boys. She could only hope that today's outing might be just the cure Theodora needed.

She took time to fix them all pancakes and sausage for breakfast before phoning the Realtor whose name Rachael had given her. Theodora and Trevor finished the dishes while she set up an appointment to look at duplexes and rental houses the next day after church. That would give Trevor the whole afternoon alone with the children.

She pushed thoughts of yesterday and tomorrow out of her mind as she helped the children pack their swimming suits and a change of clothes to take to Michelle and Jake's. She had hardly seen them all week. Even if she wouldn't be with them all day, the trip down and back would be a good way to catch up.

Timothy was bubbling over with reports of his first full week of school before she'd backed the car out of the driveway. "It's my turn to take cookies for our midday snack on Monday, Mom. Can we bake those cookies with the M&Ms in them?"

"Sure we can. Remind me to stop at the Budget Mart on the way home tonight and we'll pick up a big bag."

"Maybe we should buy two," Titus suggested.

"You know me too well." Tracy laughed.

"Do I have to go to church tomorrow?" Theodora interrupted.

The boys quit their banter. Tracy looked up long enough to glance in the rear view mirror. Pensive lines were etched across her daughter's face.

Tracy swallowed. "I'm a little nervous about facing everyone tomorrow, too – but I think it would mean a lot to your Dad to have us all there."

"What if I still don't want to?"

"I won't force you to go, but I will say that when the going gets tough the best course of action is to hold your head high and look your troubles straight in the eye. Staying away implies you have something to be ashamed of."

"Don't I?"

"Of course not! You aren't responsible for the choices your father and I have made. Our decision to get a divorce is no reflection on you, on any of you." Tracy swung her head around as much as driving would allow to make sure Titus and Timothy understood what she was saying as well.

"It doesn't feel that way." Theodora said sullenly.

"Benjy Morris says it's a sin to get a divorce," Timothy

piped up. "A really bad sin."

"There are some people who believe that," Tracy answered carefully, "and others who don't think of it quite that way. The important thing to remember is that we're all human. We all make mistakes. All any of us can do is to try our very best and know that God still loves us even when we do things that God isn't happy about."

"That's what I think," Timothy said contentedly. Titus and Theodora didn't look so easily convinced but Tracy didn't press the subject.

"Can I watch the Lion King on Josh and Nate's big screen TV when we get to Maple Valley, Mom?"

"I doubt you'll have time with all the fun things Uncle Jake has planned down by the river. Besides, it's too nice outside to spend the whole day cooped up in front of the television."

"Can I stay overnight with Josh and Nate if I promise to go to church with Uncle Jake and Aunt Michelle tomorrow?" Titus asked in a voice much too subtle not too arouse suspicion.

Tracy sighed. "I don't blame any of you for not wanting to go to church in Blooming Prairie tomorrow morning but your dad is looking forward to spending Sunday afternoon with you. It's the last time you'll be able to spend some quality time with him before he leaves for California next week."

"He could come down and pick us up after church," Titus suggested hopefully.

"I could help Aunt Michelle fix breakfast for everyone tomorrow morning," Theodora offered. "And catch up on laundry. She must have a lot to do since you've been painting all week."

"What would you wear?"

"We could save the extra clothes we brought for after swimming. We've hardly even worn the clothes we have on. If we put our swimming suits on as soon as we get to their house these will hardly get dirty."

"I'll think about it."

"Please," they begged.

"I need to talk to Jake and Michelle before I make a decision."

The kids were still clamoring and cajoling when they pulled up in front of Jake and Michelle's a few moments later.

Jake was in the front yard watering a cascade of morning glories that were climbing along a white-washed trellis to the west of the front door. Timothy and Titus spotted Josh and Nate in the back yard, jumped out of the car, and ran to join them before Tracy had even turned off the engine.

"Remember to put your swimming trunks on before you get your clothes dirty!" Tracy called after them.

Jake turned off the hose. "So, how do you feel about working by yourself today, Tracy? Michelle tried to call you earlier but you'd already left home."

"I hope nothing's wrong."

"Nothing drastic. Sarah woke up with a cold this morning and Michelle doesn't want to leave her." Jake glanced at Theodora with a warm smile. "Sarah can be a handful when she's not feeling well and Michelle's hardly seen her all week."

"I understand completely. There are plenty of things I can do at the house on my own. Are you sure my kids won't be in the way now that your plans have changed?"

"No. The raft building expedition will go on as planned and Michelle's looking forward to spending some time with Teddy." He turned to Theodora. "If you don't mind putting up with a cranky baby."

Theodora beamed. "No problem. One of the kids I babysit for in Blooming Prairie had chicken pox last week and Mom said I could still go over there because I had them when I was little. It was a little challenging at times because she wanted to scratch and I had to keep her hands away from the scabs. But I still managed just fine."

Tracy listened to her daughter with pride. Theodora had matured into a responsible young woman in what seemed like a matter of weeks. "Well, if you're sure it's okay I'll head back into town and get started on the house. Trevor packed some snacks in the cooler for the kids so I'll probably just work over the lunch hour if it's fine with you."

"Mom, what about? You know..."

"Maybe another time, sweetheart. I don't think it would be such a good idea with the baby not feeling up to par."

"But, Mom..."

"We can talk about it when I'm finished at the house. We'll see how Sarah's feeling later."

"All right." Theodora looked crestfallen.

Jake watched them with raised eyebrows but didn't inquire as to what they were talking about.

"I'll see you later, Jake. Thanks for including the boys in your adventure."

"It's my pleasure, Tracy. Say, I never got a chance to tell you how much fun it was having you at Mac's birthday party last night."

If her daughter saw her blushing she made no comment.

"Thanks for being so patient with me. I probably won't remember most of their names next time I see them but I had a good time meeting everyone."

Tracy nodded good-bye, got back in the car, and drove towards town, oblivious to the scenery now that the memory of dancing with Clay Alexander had been revived. The very thought of his arms around her stirred her senses so that she could think of little else.

She'd enjoyed talking to Luke. He was a very nice man and extremely good looking. She had no trouble understanding why so many women were taken with him, especially after hearing him sing. But with him it had just been a game. Her heart hadn't budged an inch in response to his flirtations. Of course, she'd known they were staged.

She felt a tinge of guilt. She'd been trying to get Clay's attention, and she had. She shivered involuntarily, remembering the sensations she'd experienced floating around the front porch in Clay's arms. His every word fascinated her, his smile made a merry-go-round of her heart, her body melted at his touch. She hadn't felt this way since high school. Something about Clay made her soul sing!

So then, why did she feel such a deep sense of shame and inappropriateness? She was no silly schoolgirl with a crush, Tracy reminded herself sternly. She was in her thirties, the mother of three children, and until recently, a minister's wife. She was in no position to enter into a new relationship – even if Clay Alexander had been available. The timing was all wrong. Her first and only priorities right now had to be her family, finding a new place to live, and bolstering her marketability as a painting and wallpapering pro.

She drove past barns and silos and oak groves, barely seeing the scenes that flashed by. What she needed was someone to talk to. Someone besides Clay. Someone who was wise, neutral, objective, candid but caring. Someone who didn't look at her like she could melt chocolate.

She needed a friend. She loved her sisters, but she just didn't have that kind of relationship with them. There was no way she could be honest with her mother, Theodora, or any of the woman at church, certainly not with Trevor. If she told a neighbor, the news would be all over town by nightfall. It was just too juicy, all of this happening to the pastor's wife that everyone thought was so perfect.

She'd had an imaginary friend when she was in grade school. Maybe that's what she needed now.

She turned on to the blacktop that ran from Saint Ansgar to Maple Valley, then a few miles later, east on Highway 9.

"You should see him, Elizabeth," she said, feeling silly but very justified. "His name is Clay and he's sooo dreamy."

You're not even divorced yet, her wise friend would say. *Just take it slow. It's going to time some time for you to heal.*

"It does still hurt. I mean, I'm trying to be understanding for the children's sake, but I feel like such a fool for believing Trevor's lies all these years."

You have every right to be cynical, sweetheart, her friend would say, and maybe even give her a hug. *You trusted him, and he betrayed you. Before you go getting involved with another man, you need to be sure he's what he says he is.*

"I don't want to be involved with him." Tracy sighed, thinking of Clay's parents and snippy Lauren and what her family – and his – would say if the two then ever got involved.

"What I need is someone to hold me." There. She'd said it. What she did need was someone to hold her. Dancing with Clay had sparked a need in her. So had Mac's hug, for that matter. A flood of longings so intense that she could hardly bear to acknowledge them even in the privacy of her own heart washed over her.

And you want that person to be Clay.

"I do," she whispered. "I know. It makes absolutely no sense." It was Clay she wanted to touch her.

She drove into Maple Valley and minutes later, pulled parallel to the curb in front of Clay's imposing house. The street was quiet at this time of day; the neighborhood, peaceful. For the first time in years, she felt at ease.

She told herself that she had parked on the street so that her car would be sheltered by the shade of the sprawling maple trees in the median, but the reality was... How could she even think about being intimate with a man whose family and friends were so intimidating that she was scared to park in the driveway? Everything she knew about Clay Alexander III should have sent her running.

Think about it this way for a second, her "new best friend" said. *Take Lauren and Clay's parents out of the equation for a minute. What's the first thing that comes to your mind when you think about Clay?*

"Well, he's gorgeous." She smiled to herself. "He's sweet and funny and kind. I feel like a princess when I'm with him. I'm intrigued by him... his interest in my children, his commitment to his employees and Maple Valley's future, the tenderness he's shown me."

A fun exercise, but reality intruded on her whimsy all too soon. Her mind drifted back to Lauren. The woman's social and economic status complimented Clay's perfectly from what she could tell, whereas Tracy had nothing to offer a man like Barclay Alexander but a passel of problems, a tarnished reputation, and an uncertain future.

She took her purse from the empty seat beside her and climbed out of the car. None of it made any sense. The bits and pieces of Clay's personal life that he'd shared with her seemed almost incongruent with what she had observed upon meeting his parents and Lauren. Perhaps she wasn't as good a judge of character as she thought she was. Perhaps Clay only appeared to be the caring, down-to-earth, hard-working man she believed him to be. And in the end, what did it matter? Because the only thing she could say with complete assurance was that Clay was not hers for the taking.

Chapter 15

Barclay looked across the breakfast table and watched as Lauren used the silver fork in her left hand to anchor the cinnamon roll on the plate in front of her. She cut the frosting-crowned morsel into eight, exactly even, bite-sized pieces.

Her hair was swept around her head in the elegant chignon she commonly used when she hadn't been to her hairdresser in a few days. Clay had seen the strappy, chemise-style blue silk dress she'd donned once before and remembered her mentioning a strapless, dyed-to-match lace bra she wore underneath.

"I still don't understand why I couldn't have stayed in your room last night, Barclay. I really didn't appreciate being relegated to that stuffy little servant's quarters the woman calls a room – especially knowing that your accommodations are infinitely more elegant."

"Lauren, I won't even touch on the many reasons it wouldn't be prudent for us to share a bed. As for your room, you're just lucky Mrs. Westheimer had one available. She's usually full both Friday and Saturday nights."

"I thought you'd be happy to see me," Lauren countered suggestively, leaning towards him and tilting her neck back to expose the flawless flair of her bosoms revealed by the low cut bodice of her dress. "We've hardly seen each other since you gave up your condo and took up residence in Iowa," she said, the purring quality of her voice changing gradually as she neared the reference to his place of his residence. She spat out the last word as if it tasted bad.

Clay looked around to see if the guests seated at the surrounding tables had heard Lauren's comments. If they had, they weren't letting on. He could feel his neck growing flushed and hot around the edge of his shirt collar. "Marianne Westheimer left the Twin Cities to invest her whole life's savings in the Mary Rose Manor. She personally renovated and decorated the entire B&B. She's been a very gracious hostess. Please don't offend her with unjust recriminations of a place you know nothing about."

"You're missing the point, Barclay. All I'm saying is that just because I don't care to live in this insufferable little point on the map doesn't mean I don't care to be with you occasionally. When I postponed our wedding date it was not with the intention of pledging my self to celibacy from now until we say our nuptials."

Clay tried not to grimace. It wasn't that Lauren wasn't beautiful. But he had no intention of marrying her, and thus, there was no way he was going to sleep with her.

"Well?" she said.

"Surely you've found ways of satisfying those needs among your more civilized acquaintances in the Cities."

Lauren patted the corner of her napkin to her mouth and glared at him indignantly. "You've come dangerously close to pushing me one step too far this time, Barclay. If I didn't know what stress you've been under these past few weeks - what with the horrendous conditions that exist at that God-forsaken factory your father owns, and the disappointing piece of real estate you've had to settle for in terms of living quarters, not to mention the second rate accommodations you've had to endure here at this ridiculous tribute to a more primitive time-"

Clay slid his chair back from the table with an abrupt jerk and rose to his full height of six foot one. His tone was quiet but firm. "I'm sorry if *I* offended *you.* Now listen to me, Lauren, and listen to me good. I can't marry you. I don't want to marry you. I won't marry you."

His eyes blazed into hers in such a way that there no mistaking his words.

Her face twisted into a hateful coil of wrath. "Oh, yes? We'll see what Daddy has to say about that!" She laughed a caustic rebuff.

She slid her chair back from the table but he stopped her from getting up. "Lauren, you were kind and sweet and gentle when you were with Henri. I know. I saw you together. You were happy. This person you've become – I won't stand by and enable this kind of behavior any longer. I won't condone your discourteous actions by my passivity. And I won't submit to an unhappy marriage just because it's what our parents dictate we do."

"You don't know..." Her voice faded.

He thought for a moment she might burst into tears – which probably would have been a good thing. The woman's emotions were no doubt a powder keg ready to blow. But what he glimpsed in her eyes was not sorrow, but hatred, bitterness and resentment. She abandoned her breakfast and strode from the room.

Clay took a deep breath and ran his fingers through his hair. He turned with no intent of following her but to make sure they hadn't disturbed any of the other guests. Marianne Westheimer was coming through the door that led from the dining room to the hall.

"I hope nothing's wrong," she said with a worried glance over her shoulder in the direction Lauren had disappeared.

"Nothing of your doing, Marianne. Breakfast was lovely as always." Clay stared vacantly through the door. "No, I think for the first time in a long while that everything is going to be just fine."

*****

Michelle tiptoed out of the baby's room and pulled the door shut ever so gently behind her. "Her poor little nose is so stuffed up. I hate knowing that she doesn't feel well when there's not a thing I can do about it."

Teddy went to the controls of the baby monitor sitting on the countertop and turned up the volume. "I want to make sure we can hear her over the dehumidifier if she cries."

"Thanks for all your help, Teddy. She adores you so much. If anything could make being sick a little bit of fun, it's a visit from you."

Her niece beamed appreciatively. "Thanks, Aunt

Michelle. I needed to hear that." Teddy's normally enthusiastic voice faltered for a minute. "This week has been so weird. My mom has been trying real hard to be nice to me, all of us kids, I mean, because of her and Dad getting a divorce. But I just can't talk to her about stuff like this and I'm too embarrassed to call Brooke or talk to my teachers. The last thing I want is for them to know what's going on in our family right now." The fifteen year old sighed as though she held the weight of the world on her shoulders.

"You know I'm always here for you, honey."

"Yes. I don't know what I'd do without you." Teddy's answer was punctuated by another sigh. "I'm glad Sarah fell asleep before the boys and Uncle Jake came back."

"Go ahead, sweetheart." Michelle could sense that it was with great difficulty that her only niece spoke. "I'm listening."

"Well, the thing is, I'm not sure I should even be talking to you about this. I mean, I trust you and all, but it's kind of personal, and I might have heard them wrong. So it might not even be true."

Michelle's heart skipped a beat.

"I tried to convince myself that there's no way. I mean, it's really unbelievable and I'm ninety percent sure it's not true. But on the other hand, it would explain a lot of things that just don't add up about this whole divorce thing and Dad's move to California. Then I think about it, and decide, n*o, I know my dad, and there's no way he would ever...*" Theodora looked up at her with big, tremulous eyes. "I can't even say it. I can't even think it."

"You need to talk about it if it's bothering you this much." Michelle spoke in carefully measured words. Fear clutched at her mid-region. She was strictly on her own here. She had kept the promise she'd made not to tell anyone about Trevor's admission of homosexuality, not even Jake.

"I think my Dad might be gay," the teenager whispered, her cheeks aflame, her eyes clouded with abject misery.

"Oh, honey." Michelle opened her arms.

Theodora threw herself into her embrace and dissolved

into tears upon impact.

"It's okay," Michelle repeated over and over in answer to the girl's sobs.

"It's- true, then?" Theodora gulped.

The girl broke into an even more heart-wrenching episode of sobbing when Michelle declined to answer.

"There, there, sweetheart. I won't lie to you. But you were right when you said this is a very personal matter. I think the thing you need to do is to talk to your Mom or Dad about this directly."

"But I can't!" Teddy choked over her words. "I could barely tell you."

Michelle smoothed the child's hair against her bosom. "Your mother loves you very much. This has been very hard for her as well. Did you ever stop to think that she might need to talk to you, too?"

"It's... just... so humiliating." Her sobs had started to lessen a little. "I love my dad. I don't understand how he could even think something like this."

"Your Mom is going to be working at the Alexander house all day. I could run you into town when Jake and the boys get back if you'd like to spend some time alone with her."

"But what, wh-what if she treats me like a k-kid and tells me to mind my own business, or j-just refuses to discuss it? We don't have a great track record when it comes to talking about things."

"This is different. I think you can trust your Mom to be very sensitive of your feelings when something this important is at stake." Michelle prayed that it was so.

"M-maybe I could borrow your bike and ride it into town?"

"It's an awfully long way and the first mile is gravel. Are you sure you want to?"

"It would give me a chance to think about what I'm going to say before I get there." Theodora pulled away from her and stood erect.

Michelle could see a faint glimmer of resolve through

the tears in her niece's eyes. "I think that would be a good idea."

"We don't have to tell her I'm coming, do we?"

"Not if you don't want me to."

"I think I'd rather just show up. That way she won't get all worked up before I get there."

"I'm fine with that." Michelle's heart went out to her sister. Tracy had been through a lot already this week. She didn't envy her the discussion she was about to have with her daughter.

"Do you think you can find the house?"

"I remember you pointed it out to me once back when Aunt Rachael's friend Mrs. Armerding lived there. I should probably write down the street address just in case."

"I'll get some paper."

Theodora copied down the address and tucked it in her pocket. "Thanks for being there for me, Aunt Michelle. I love you."

"Your mom needs to know that you love her, too." They stood in silence for a moment. "I'll help you get my bike down. It's hanging from the rafters in the garage."

*****

Tracy set the lid on top of the paint can, rapped it with a hammer eight or nine times, and headed downstairs to soak the brush she'd used to finish the trim in the master bedroom suite in water. There was plenty of time to start another room before it got too late. She vacillated between wanting to get the walls in the second bedroom scrubbed with TSP to prepare then for paint or using liquid sander to soften the old paint on the kitchen pantry so she could begin putting on the primer coat.

She was standing at the kitchen sink running warm water over the brush when she heard the doorknob jiggle behind her.

"Hello!" The door opened a crack. "It's me," Clay's distinctive voice rang through the kitchen.

"Hi," she greeted him, suddenly shy at the memory of the dances they'd shared.

"I saw your car out front."

"I hope you don't mind me being here on a Saturday. Michelle was going to be here, too, but Baby Sarah isn't feeling well."

"I'm glad to see you. I hope you didn't have to miss anything important to be here. The housewarming party has been called off, so we're not under nearly the time crunch I thought we were."

"Please tell me you didn't delay the party because of the wallpaper panel!"

"No. It has nothing to do with that."

Tracy raised her eyebrows and waited. "I see you had some furniture moved into the dining room sometime after we left yesterday afternoon."

"Just a few things so I'd have a place to sit down when I'm here. That's why I was late to the party last night. Well, that and Lauren showing up unexpectedly." Clay extended his arms backwards to meet the newly installed marble kitchen counter tops and leaned back against the cupboards. "I couldn't sleep last night so I came over here, built a fire in the fireplace, and crashed on the sofa for a few hours. I went back to the inn for breakfast this morning. Lauren was all bent out of shape because she had to sleep in a room that used to be the servant's quarters. We had a row and I finally put an end to our so-called engagement."

"I-I'm sorry."

"Don't be. I should have done it months ago."

She nodded sympathetically, not wanting to press for details but hoping he would offer.

"I still don't know what transpired between Lauren, Henri and the Humphreys. I hope to God my parents weren't involved in whatever happened. They and the Humphreys have been so bent on the two of us marrying that I wouldn't be surprised if Henri was – I don't know – offered a large sum of money to disappear, or something of the like.

"They would really do something like that?"

"I hope not. All I know is that the subject of me and Lauren getting married was never brought up while Henri was around. But as soon as he left, our parents spread the word near and far that Lauren and I would be marrying. Lauren is nearing thirty, and both sets of parents are adamant about wanting grandchildren, so suddenly, the pressure was on.

"I've tried to be kind while Lauren got over Henri, clinging to the hope that eventually, she would put an end to the ridiculous notion that we would actually marry and break things off with me.

"I don't want to humiliate Lauren, and contrary to what my parents think, I hate the thought of going against their wishes, but I realized today that I'm not helping anyone by continuing to play along with this charade."

"So you don't think she's really in love with you?"

"Perhaps she thinks so. Personally, I think it's more a matter of not wanting to be rejected again so soon after Henri."

Tracy felt a pang of sympathy for the other woman. "I don't know a woman on earth who wants to hear the words, *I don't want to be married to you* — whatever the reason might be."

"Of course. We all have our pride." Clay looked utterly anguished. "So what can I do to rectify things? I can see in retrospect that by biding my time rather than forcing Lauren – and our parents - to accept the truth, I've made an even bigger mess out of things. I suppose I haven't been very fair to any of them."

"Have you told them yet?"

"No. My cell phone gets horrible reception in Maple Valley and I haven't been to my office yet today. I fully expect them to disown me when I break the news."

"Well, that gives you something to look forward to."

He chuckled. "You have a knack for making me laugh in the midst of the direst circumstances."

"Just returning the favor."

"I appreciate it." Clay stepped forward, clasped both her

arms with his hands, and kissed her on the forehead.

Her breath caught in her throat.

He stood with his lips on her forehead and did not move away.

It had been so long – Clay was so different from anyone she had ever known. Uncertainties wafted through her mind, but only for a second. She shifted her weight and leaned deeper into his arms, letting him know that she welcomed his attentions.

He drew her closer. "You feel so good. I loved dancing with you last night."

She turned her head and timidly nuzzled it to the juncture of his neck and jaw. "It was heavenly."

Clay took a deep breath. "I'd better let go before we end up doing something we'll both regret."

She turned her face to look up at him. "You've made me feel good about myself for the first time in almost three years. I can't imagine that I'd regret anything I did with you."

"You don't understand..."

She looked up at him intently. "I may have spent the last fifteen years in the role of a minister's wife but I'm not so naive that I don't know exactly what you're talking about."

"Then you should know we're treading on dangerous ground."

"I trust you," she said, wondering if she really did. A surge of fear and heat and bravado and a million other indefinable emotions rushed through her consciousness. The only one she didn't trust was herself.

"You shouldn't," he said.

"I need to be held and I trust you to hold me. I want you to hold me."

He dropped his arms and stepped back from her. "I'm not at all sure that I can just *hold* you, Tracy. Knowing a woman – and her family - changes things. I value you and your friendship too much to risk the possibility of ruining our relationship by rushing into something you're not ready for."

"But it's because I know you that I trust you enough to hold me," Tracy said. "Would you rather I went to a bar and found some stranger to whom I mean nothing to be with?"

"No! Of course not." Clay rubbed his temples. "But you need to think about the ramifications of what you're suggesting. I couldn't live with myself if I thought I'd hurt you, however unintentionally. You told me yourself that you haven't made love to a man in almost three years. Your physical – and emotional - needs are probably as revved up as a Corvette at the starting line of a race. How can you be sure you're making a reasonable, rational decision given your circumstances?"

"I suppose I can't," she said quietly. She stood less than two feet from him, her shoulders drooped and her eyes downcast, so emotionally frail that it almost hurt.

"Your sisters are my business associates. You have three children. In the strictest sense of the word, you're still married." Clay rattled off one objection after another, the strangled voice in which he spoke the only clue to his turmoil. "You're beautiful, Tracy. You've opened a part of my heart that I didn't know existed. You have to know how deeply I feel about you."

Clay clutched his fists as though he were trying to restrain himself from touching her. "You don't know how it pains me to say this, but I respect you too much to throw it all to the wind for the sake of indulging in an impetuous..."

Tracy's eyes filled with tears. "So it's because you care for me that you're punishing me by withholding the one thing I need more than anything else in the world?"

"No!" He sighed. "But a woman like you should have a man who can give her certain assurances."

"I don't need assurances. I just want to touch you."

"I shouldn't even be entertaining the thought of doing this. You deserve to be with someone who's in a position to make a commitment to you."

"I didn't ask for a commitment. I just asked you to hold me."

A gust of wind flitted through the open window and

caught the curtain in its grasp. Clay took one step towards her, then fit his body to hers. The lace billowed and fluttered around them in a lithesome dance before falling back to hang limply in its place.

He pulled her closer and kissed the top of her head in surrender. "I can't believe I'm standing here trying to talk myself out of being with you. I've always thought I had a finely honed conscience and I've never in my life felt guilty about..."

"Shhh..."

"Tell me what to do. I won't do anything you don't want me to."

"I won't either," she promised. "I just need to feel your arms around me."

She reached around him to take two pillows and a throw from the newly delivered sofa. Clay crouched in front of the river rock hearth she had painted so painstakingly a few days before, gave her his hand, and drew her down to the floor in front of the fireplace. A few luminous embers still glowed in the soft light that ensconced the room. A log crackled into a quick burst of sparks as Clay lay down on the floor and took her in his arms.

Sighing contentedly, she snuggled against his chest and ran her fingers over his shirt, her touch as delicate as the maple leaves drifting down from the tree outside the window. Clay's chest rose and fell in perfect rhythm as he began to relax. Her fingertips traced circle eights around the muscular swells at his breasts. He took a deep breath and exhaled slowly.

Tracy fingered the smooth cotton knit of his shirt until she found what she was looking for. "Can I put my hand under your shirt?"

Prim, proper, pastor's wife – she fought the unwanted, no longer relevant expectations she'd held herself to for a decade and a half and moved her hand to his waist. She was a woman – a live, breathing woman with feelings, needs and desires. This was her reawakening. She was free to love, to feel, to taste. Her spirit soared as she mentally shed the plastic pretense of a life she'd been living.

Clay pulled his shirt out from his pants with his free hand, took hers, and guided it from his waist to his chest.

She inhaled slowly, in awe of the feel of his flesh, at once terrified and undaunted by what she was doing. Her fingers lingered over each peak and swell and indentation as she sought to learn the subtle nuances of the man who held her so tenderly. She moved against him without speaking, first discovering the soft, wispy hairs where his arms met his torso, then the secret hollow at his waist, the flawless symmetry of muscle, flesh, and man, all laid bare to her touch.

She fought back tears, feeling as reborn physically as she once had spiritually. "May I touch your face?"

His lips parted slightly and he drew in a breath. "Yes."

She traced his jaw line with her fingertips. The stubble of his beard was invisible to the eye yet she could feel the faint resistance meeting her fingers as they slid over his skin. She pressed lightly on each cheekbone, ran her finger down the bridge of his nose, and outlined his rounded lower lip.

He lay without moving, holding her glance, his eyes speaking more eloquently than the most carefully chosen words. She moved slowly at first, then let her fingers race as she explored the terrain of his features at will, caressing first his eyebrows, then his ears, and finally, the uneven line where his hair met his face.

"Your hair is thinning in a little spot right on the top of your head," she said gently. "You're so tall I never noticed it before."

He took her hand and kissed it, then lay quietly once more as she ran her fingers through the soft waves of hair. She cuddled into the crook of his left arm and he massaged her shoulder with his right.

"May I kiss you?" she whispered, suddenly timid again, and rested her lips on his earlobe. She slid her hands down his neck to the first of the curls that lapped at his throat without waiting for an answer.

He turned and found her lips in response.

Oh God. How could something that felt this divine, this heavenly, this magnificent, possibly be wrong? She let her lips melt into his, pausing only when she so hot and aroused and beside herself with lust that she could barely breathe.

We're just holding each other, she told herself. But she knew it was more than that. She didn't dare break the silence for fear he would tell her to stop.

Working her way down his torso, she pressed her open lips against his chest, pried each smooth nipple free from its nest of curls and circled it with the tip of her tongue. She buried her face in the fragrant pageantry laid out before her. His skin tasted faintly of almonds warmed by the sun, of everything earthy and masculine and good.

And then she nipped at his abdomen, using her fingers to tunnel a path through the curls that lined the way, working her way further and further down his body, tasting, tracing this impression and that with her tongue, enticing him with her lips.

Kissing, she thought dizzily. *All we're doing is kissing. All I'm doing is kissing him. He said it was fine if I kissed him.* She found more places to kiss him with every second that elapsed.

His breathing became shallow and his chest undulated under her fingertips, his body rising and falling at her touch in a dance as ancient as life itself. She very nearly dissolved when she realized how deeply her embraces were affecting him.

She was so caught up in the moment that she didn't realize she'd propped her elbow below his waist until she felt the first rhythm of his arousal throbbing under her arm.

Don't say a word, she thought. *No sudden movements or he'll come to his senses and tell me to stop.*

But he was already lost, and she knew it. Her mouth moved with greater speed. His shorts drooped further and further away from his abdomen as his breathing grew more shallow.

She descended on him with a flurry of passion.

"Oh, Clay," she moaned between kisses.

"Tracy," she heard him reply.

She felt his hands on her face, in her hair. Was it she or he who unbuttoned his pants? She didn't know. She didn't care.

And then it was done. She had done the unthinkable.

"Oh, Clay." She lay with her body draped over the lower half of his, lost in the joy of his release. She felt alive, free, renewed, as fresh as the first dew of spring.

She should say something. How could she express emotions so fragile, so sweet?

He spoke everything she was feeling when he reached for her and called her back into his arms. His cheeks were hopelessly flushed. She could feel his heart racing just beneath her cheek and he held her tight.

"What have you done to me, my sweet, little M&M loving mother of three?" He whispered into her hair.

"I have no idea." She giggled away the inhibitions, the almost-embarrassment that lay just beneath her glee.

Clay's laughter rumbled back from deep in his chest.

She pulled away and looked down at him hesitantly.

He reached for her hand. "My turn."

"Is it okay if I take off a few more clothes? I want you to touch my breasts."

He smiled, then laughed quietly.

She pulled her shirt over her head with an unapologetic tug. "I know they're small but I still like it when..."

"Come here, silly." He fit his face to hers and hugged her oh, so tenderly. "Did you think you still had to ask permission after all of this?"

"Those were the rules."

"If this were about following rules we wouldn't be here." He unclasped the brassiere that camouflaged her insanely small, sadly girlish breasts and pulled her down to meet his mouth.

"Oh, Clay." Her nipples grew until they ached. His hands. Oh. Dear. The room swirled around her until the Frank Lloyd Wright panel was sideways and right side up and upside down and moving round and round. A merry-go-round of emotions circled through her psyche as Clay's hands touched her breasts and rubbed her nipples, tasted the baby soft sweep of her skin.

His touch felt as gentle as butterfly wings one moment, as strong as a buffalo's the next, as soft as silk, rock solid the next. He revered her from eyelid to earlobe, from finger to foot, moving over her purposefully, with the grace of an eager-to-please paramour, and the intuitiveness of a devoted spouse, willing her to experience every pleasure known to him.

And then he parted her legs.

"You never asked if it was okay." She moaned when he used his lips to stir the nest of soft curls he found. He answered her with such delicate probes of his tongue that she could barely breathe. "No one's ever..."

The thought of such intimacy with someone she barely knew...

"If those little noises you're making are supposed to make me think you don't want me to keep touching you here you'll have to try something a bit more convincing," he mouthed before continuing his quest with the velvet smoothness of his tongue.

"Don't stop. Please... don't... stop."

And he didn't.

A million sensations swept over her when she orgasmed. Is this what it was like, being with a man who really wanted you? With Trevor, awkward teenage sex had morphed into awkward adult sex. Procreation had ruled over pleasure. But it was all she had ever known. This was... with Clay... feelings so sweet she could barely contain them caught her in their wake. She had dreamed of this moment for years. Clay was the one who had appeared to her time and time again in her fantasies. She hadn't known his name, but she had seen him just the same.

Her eyes grew misty. She trembled and felt Clay's arms tighten instinctively around her.

"Please, Clay. I need to feel you inside me. Now."

"It was a moment before he answered. "No. I mean...

sweetheart. No. It may kill me, but we're going to wait until next time for that."

She groaned.

"You'll thank me tomorrow."

Her moments ceased. She lay still in his arms.

"That's it. Settle down and just let me hold you. You're so beautiful. I just want to lay here and look at you." There were tears in his eyes.

She closed her eyes, wondering what she had started and where it would end. This was not a good idea on so many levels, yet nothing had ever felt so right. She could feel her breathing slowly returning to normal but she kept her eyes closed as though by refusing to look to the future, she could will this moment, her feelings, his tender embrace, to last forever.

Clay's lips fanned her cheeks with caresses so soothing that she grew drowsier and more contented with every brush of his eyelash against her cheek. And then she drifted off in his arms.

Chapter 16

The sun had tipped its hat to the top of the sky and started its decline. Theodora took in all kinds of sights and sounds as she rode her bike down Osage Avenue. People were busy mowing their yards and getting ready to eat. She could smell chicken, hamburgers and pork chops sizzling on grills, hear mothers calling their kids home for supper. She could see cars rushing here and there.

No one seemed to notice her. The curls around her face were sticking to the sweat on her skin, and she was tired from riding Michelle's slightly too big, balloon-tired bicycle. She was almost at the old Armerding house.

Her whole body felt weighted down from the worries of her parents' divorce and wondering what was up with her dad. The stress was really getting to her.

She was dreading this conversation with her mother more than anything she'd faced in her almost fifteen short years of living. If she hadn't promised her aunt she'd talk to her mother in the first place, she probably would have turned around a couple of miles ago and headed back to the river.

She was exhausted. The ride had only taken her little more than an hour but the sun was hot, and riding on gravel roads had been harder work than she had anticipated. Her mother had griped more than once that worrying about stuff and being under a lot of stress sapped her strength. For once, she guessed her mom was right.

She pulled up behind her mother's car with a mixture of emotions - gratefulness to have arrived at the Alexander house at last and dread of the questions she knew she had to ask her mother. A wave of nausea washed over her as the thought of her father *being with* another man hit her with sickening alacrity for the hundredth time that day.

She was grossed out enough by the thought of her mother and father doing it - anyone's parents for that matter.

She gripped the handlebars of Michelle's bike and climbed off. Last year, when Cassie's parents had announced they were going to have another baby, they'd all been shocked – no one had thought people *did it* anymore when they were as old as their parents were. It was pretty humiliating for Cassie to have to live with the proof that her parents had done it that recently. In the end Theodora and her other friends had calmed Cassie down by assuring her *the act* had to have been some sort of freak occurrence and not something her parents did on a regular basis, ancient as they were.

Theodora looked over the landscaping around the house and located a spot where she could tuck Michelle's bike so no one could see it from the street. She supposed Maple Valley was a lot like Blooming Prairie in that you really didn't have to worry about bikes being stolen but she didn't want to take any chances since the bike wasn't hers. Not with her mom and dad as broke as they seemed to be right now. They would kill her if she lost Michelle's bike.

She smiled. You knew things had to be pretty bad if she got turned on by thinking about her mom and dad yelling at her about losing a bike. But the scenario was at least familiar, and that made it strangely comforting to think about. *Brother.*

All this stuff about divorce and sex was stuff she'd hoped never to have to think about in terms of her own parents. It was confusing enough trying to figure out what she thought about it when she was reading about Brad Pitt and Angelina Jolie, and all the weird stuff that went on with people like that. But when it was your own parents - she wished the whole nightmarish situation would just go away.

Theodora winched the kickstand out with her toe and stepped back from the bush a few feet to make sure neither end of the bike was sticking out. When she was satisfied it was well-hidden, she headed towards the house. She didn't think twice about the black car sitting in the driveway, even when she had to walk around it to get to the back door.

She glanced at the front door but went with her instincts in the end. No one in their family used front entryways. Her grandmother's house hadn't even had steps leading to their front door until she was nine. When she and Titus were little they'd spent hours jumping out the front door and rolling in the grass at the bottom of the drop-off, pretending they were sky divers jumping out of an airplane thousands of feet above the ground instead of two.

Even Michelle and Jake didn't use their front door, and they had the coolest entryway ever - steps flanked by two stone lions and a pair of stained glass panels twined with water lilies running from floor to ceiling on either side of the door.

She smiled for the first time all day as she headed towards the back door of the Armerding house. She liked thinking about her family's little idiosyncrasies and some of the slightly zany things they'd done together over the years. *Little* and *slightly* being key. She so did not need a dad who was suddenly gay. Quirky she could handle. Kinky, she could not.

Tracy was telling cute Timothy stories and Clay was laughing out loud when Tracy thought she heard a noise. Clay said it was just the fireplace crackling and when he started to stroke her back in lazy circle eights, she forgot all about it.

She had a few more clothes on than Clay did, but they were still half naked and Tracy was thinking that she had to be the most blessed woman on earth to have found a man who liked to talk and snuggle and listen and cuddle.

She looked at Clay sitting on the floor buck naked except for a throw she'd tossed over his male parts a moment earlier and listened to him talk about the people who worked for him at Elk Creek Woolen Mills, how much he admired their dedication and their efforts to cut costs and conserve resources.

She'd chastised Rae once, when she'd been pregnant with Ian and in between marriages to Luke and Mac, when Rae had said she felt blessed. Sitting on the high horse that had always gone along with being a conservative minister's wife, Tracy hadn't thought that it was appropriate for Rae to talk about blessings, the implication being that they were from God, when she was pregnant with an illegitimately conceived child.

Now she was lying in the arms of a man she barely knew, and feeling so very blessed that she couldn't help but be humbled – and sorry she had ever criticized Rae. And then, Rita Coolidge was singing again.

All I wanted was a sweet distraction for an hour or two.
Had no intention to do the things we've done.
Funny how it always goes with love, when you don't look, you find.
But then we're two of a kind, we move as one.
We're an all time high,
We'll change all that's gone before.
Doing so much more than falling in love.
On an all time high,
We'll take on the world and wait.
So hold on tight, let the flight begin.

"Um, you don't happen to like Rita Coolidge's music, do you?" she asked Clay.

"Her rendition of *Fever* is one of my all time favorites. The band was playing a lot of her stuff the other night. I think I knew every one."

"You really like her?"

"I do. Do you?"

"From the time I was in junior high." She smiled. "My parents were very against rock music and wouldn't let us listen to the radio, but when I told them Rita Coolidge was a minister's daughter who learned to sing gospel in the church choir when she was growing up-"

"All of which is true," Clay interjected.

"They let me buy a cassette tape of her greatest hits. I hid the cover so they wouldn't see the song list. I guess I figured what they didn't know didn't hurt them. I mean, that's what headphones are for, right?"

Clay smiled and kissed her neck.

"Trevor hates her music. Too country for his tastes, he always said. After awhile, I stopped trying to convince him and let him pick the music he wanted to hear."

"You must have asked Luke and Mac to sing her stuff the night of Mac's surprise party."

"It seemed appropriate because I was starting over. The party was really a new beginning for me."

"I've very proud of the steps you've taken to get back on your feet, Tracy."

"Thank you. It's kind of like I have my life back. I mean, I'm not exactly free to do as I please because of the kids. But in a way, I am. I can listen to whomever I want to. I get to decide what time I come home. I can go to church, or not. It's like I suddenly have wings. I can fly."

"That's a beautiful way of putting it."

"I'm never going to let someone else decide what music I'm going to listen to again," Tracy said. "If I end up spending what's left of my life with someone else, they'll have to accept me the way I am."

"I can't imagine why anyone wouldn't love you just the way you are," Clay said.

"I'm far from perfect, but that doesn't mean I have to hide the real me."

"The real you is exquisite in every way, Tracy. I'm honored to have gotten a glimpse."

She smiled. "I know it sounds odd, but whenever something important happens to me, it's like she's there, singing one of her songs. But until the other night, I've been in playback mode. Mac's party was the first live performance I've heard in years. Ever since Trevor shut the radio off and I stopped listening to the music."

"Did he not like music at all, or just hers?"

"He loved Bette Midler."

Clay raised his eyebrows and shrugged.

"I know. It should have been a clue. I thought he liked her because she had big boobs."

Clay laughed and so did she. It all seemed so silly now.

The laughter brought her back to reality. "I need to go. My kids are at Michelle and Jake's and they're going to be wondering what happened to me if I don't get back there soon." Tracy left their warm cocoon, stood, then stooped to kiss him as she was buttoning the top button of her cotton shirt. "Would you believe I once tried to convince Trevor I was willing to give up sex altogether if he would just keep on pretending to keep our family intact? I prayed for months that he would see things my way and give up the notion of moving to California."

She had just admitted something about herself that was so ridiculous that she wanted to cry, yet with Clay smiling up at her, she felt so relaxed and accepted that it didn't even matter. After living a lifetime filled with futile efforts to be perfect, to please God, her husband, the board of deacons, and her mother, Tracy found the knowledge that she pleased Clay Alexander - just the way she was - exhilarating. He made everything else not matter.

Clay reached up with both hands to smooth her hair away from her face. "You can thank your lucky stars God didn't listen to that prayer request."

She reached down to palm his nipples and finger the satin smooth hair under his arms one last time before she left. "Oh, He was probably listening all the while. He just knew better than I what I needed. He knew about you."

Things might have started up all over again if a mysterious creaking noise from the direction of the side porch hadn't startled them.

Tracy stood and went to the window. "What was that?"

"I didn't hear anything." Clay pulled the throw around his hips like a loincloth and started to stand.

She held out her hand to caution him. "Stay down for a minute. I thought I heard footsteps on the porch." Tracy crept towards the door that led from the kitchen to the porch on tiptoe. She'd never realized that the doors leading from the kitchen to the dining room, and then to the parlor were all in exact alignment. She's been able to see all the way to the back yard the second she'd stood and looked to the rear of the house.

She didn't see anyone outside but she shut both doors behind her as she made her way back to the dining room.

"Was anyone there?" Clay cinched the makeshift wrap around his waist and started to stand again.

"Not that I could see. I was probably just imagining things. Even so, we'll have to be more careful next time."

Clay stroked her arms with his thumbs. "I'm already plotting what I'm going to do to you next time we're together."

She melted against him. "Don't be surprised if I have a few surprises hidden up my sleeve, too."

"Then you're going to have to find a new place to hide them," Clay said. "Because when I get done with you, you're not going to have anything on."

Theodora crouched behind a big lilac bush just to the left of the back door. Her haunches ached with the tension of being frozen in the same position for what seemed like an eternity. The breaths she drew were as short and shallow as a wild animal frantic to get out of a cage. Her mouth felt like it was full of cotton. Her stomach wretched. Theodora almost tipped over trying to clutch her side in an effort to ward off the pain.

"Oh, God," she mumbled over and over, more crying out to him than cursing. "Oh, God."

Her mother. First her father and now this. "Oh, God," she choked through her tears. Was this the reason her Dad had left her Mom and resigned his job as the pastor of their church? Had he found out she was having an affair? Maybe this wasn't even the first. For all she knew her mother had had numerous affairs.

Her heart momentarily soared to think that she may have been mistaken about her father being gay, then crashed to an even lower depth as the image of her mother leaning down to kiss some half-naked man replayed itself in her mind.

She wanted to puke. Theodora struggled to her feet and looked furtively in both directions before grabbing

Michelle's bicycle and making a mad dash for the street. She pedaled as fast as she could down Osage Avenue to Highway 9 and headed out of town at breakneck speed. If she hurried, maybe she could convince Michelle that she'd chickened out on the way to town, turned around, and come home before she'd ever made it to Maple Valley.

*****

Theodora barely made it back to Michelle and Jake's before her mother did. Thank goodness her mother hadn't seen her on the road.

She looked at her mom and tried not to roll her eyes. It was sickening the way she was acting all concerned about how they were getting along and how Sarah was feeling. Her mother hadn't taken two steps inside the house when she'd casually mentioned that Clay Alexander had stopped by the house to see how things were going.

Humph. He'd seen plenty more than how the house was doing. Her mother even looked like a tramp: shiny skin, hair slightly oily and pressed into some weird shape in the back, clothes rumpled, a sappy facial expression. How Michelle could not figure out what she'd been up to was beyond her.

It was a given her stupid brothers wouldn't have a clue, but she thought for sure Aunt Michelle would have put two and two together. It was totally obvious something had happened from the way her mother was gushing. God, it was sickening.

But Michelle seemed oblivious. The conversation had moved on to the topic of Teddy, Titus, and Timothy staying overnight at Jake and Michelle's house. "The baby seems to be feeling much better and the boys are getting on famously. Teddy has been a great help all day. I'd love to have them stay the night."

Theodora forced herself to address her mother. "I'll look after the boys. I promise we won't be any trouble."

"You really can't blame them for not wanting to go to church with you tomorrow, Tracy." Michelle had her hand held partially over her mouth but Theodora could still make out the words. "They've been through a lot already this week."

"You're right," her mother answered in a soft voice. "I can't fault them for feeling as they do. It's not going to be any fun. I wish I didn't have to be there."

Theodora stifled the urge to gag. She could just see her mother sitting in the front row at church tomorrow looking like the perfect pastor's wife when she'd been screwing this Clay somebody less than twenty-four hours earlier. She would have been sick for sure if she'd been forced to sit in church and watch that kind of spectacle. Her poor dad. She hoped her stupid mother wouldn't flaunt her latest indiscretion in her dad's face right before he had to get up in front of the congregation and announce his resignation.

"But you have to promise me you'll be ready for your Dad to pick you up by one o'clock," her mother was saying. "He'll never forgive me if he doesn't at least get to spend tomorrow afternoon with you guys."

You're worried about him not forgiving you for that? Theodora thought caustically. *I'd say you've got much bigger problems to worry about than whether or not he gets to spend a few hours alone with his kids.*

"I promise."

She was grateful when her mother turned away from her to face Michelle. Theodora honestly didn't know how long she could keep up this farce. Her face felt like it was permanently twisted into one big sneer from the inside out.

"I don't know what your plans are tomorrow, Michelle, but I'd be happy to come down and work on the house for a few hours later in the afternoon if my appointment with Jacobson Realty doesn't take too long."

"I need to spend some time at the office tomorrow but you can go ahead and come down if you don't mind working alone. I need to catch up on a few things over at the Painted Lady. Laurie's been doing a great job without me but there are a few bills to pay and some phone calls I need to return."

Isn't that convenient, Theodora thought. *Mom and Clay*

will have the whole house to themselves again and Dad will never be the wiser. The nagging memory of the conversation Theodora had overheard the night before reasserted itself in the forefront of her consciousness just long enough for her to feel a tinge of guilt at the way she was regarding her mother.

Theodora knew what she'd heard, and she supposed under the circumstances a woman might be driven to do what her mother had just done. That was assuming her Dad really was gay. There was no getting around what she'd heard. Aunt Michelle hadn't denied it either. Theodora had wanted her to. Oh, how she'd wanted her to. But she hadn't.

Teddy forced her suspicions about her dad out of her head and refocused her attention on the despicable stuff her mother had done. It was easier to be mad at her mother than her father. It always had been. It was what the mothers and daughters in their family did – the daughters blamed the mothers for everything that went wrong in their lives just the way their mothers and aunts and grandmothers had before them. It was a long-standing family tradition she hadn't picked up from strangers.

"I'll see how things go with the Realtor then and come down if I can," her mother was saying. "Thanks again for letting the kids spend the night. I know they appreciate it."

"No problem. I'll be thinking of you guys tomorrow."

"Thanks. Part of the reason I thought I'd like to work down here for awhile tomorrow is that I felt I might need an escape after dealing with everyone at church."

Right. Her mom probably had another sleazy rendezvous lined up with her boyfriend.

"Call me at the office if you need to talk." Michelle said.

"I will," her mother promised.

And then, something in Theodora's head clicked. Her dad couldn't be gay. He had kids, didn't he?

And then an even more horrible thought flickered through her mind.

What if her dad wasn't even her father? Who knew how many men her mother had slept with? She and Titus and Timothy might not even have the same dad.

Chapter 17

Michelle had been up to see the dawn on Sunday morning. Who knew that a tiny little baby could have such a huge influence on your daily routines and sleep patterns?

The air was crystal clear, the sky a radiant blue as Jake pulled into the church parking lot. It was too early to have to worry about the clouds of chaff that hovered over the countryside once harvest began, late enough in the season that the hot, heavy air of summer had dissipated.

All four boys – their two and Tracy's - clamored out of the Wagoneer as soon as Jake set the parking brake and popped open the locked doors from the panel by the driver's seat. Theodora stalled just long enough to peak in the rear view mirror while Michelle unstrapped baby Sarah from her car seat. Jake took off after the boys at a half run.

The little church sat at the top of a swell on the far west side of town. Jake and Michelle had been members of the small congregation since soon after they'd gotten married. Although Michelle had never openly flaunted her qualms with their strict upbringing the way Rachael had, neither she nor Jake had been interested in attending the conservative Fellowship Church on the other side of town. It was only logical, since she and Jake had been raised with different beliefs, that they would visit churches neutral to both of them until they found one where they both felt comfortable.

The little Swedish church had seemed like home the first time they'd walked in the front door. It still took her breath away when she walked into the church and saw the gothic design of the stained glass windows along each side, the vaulted ceiling, and hand carved oak pews accenting the serene little sanctuary. Jake had teased her on more than one occasion that the chapel even looked like a church an interior designer should attend. He was right.

They'd invited Rachael and Mac to come with them one

Sunday soon after Sarah was born. Michelle had hated to see her nephew grow up without the influence of any Sunday School training just because Rachael harbored a grudge against the church they'd grown up in. She'd known their young pastor's easy-going yet Biblically sound philosophies would appeal to Rae just as they had her and Jake.

Michelle had thought her parents would be happy Mac and Rae had started taking Ian somewhere besides the local grill for pancakes on Sunday mornings, but sadly, they'd failed to see it that way. Even now they seemed to view the little church as some subversive entity that had taken two out of their three children away from them.

Ian came bounding down the sidewalk just as she was thinking of him.

"Auntie Ell, Auntie Ell!"

"Ian!" She started to greet him with her usual, "How's my favorite boy?", then thought better of it when she remembered Josh, Nate, Titus, and Timothy were within ear-shot. "Oh, I've missed you, sweetie pie. Where has your mother been keeping you all week?"

"I go Gamma Z."

"Well aren't you a lucky boy." Michelle reached down and took her nephew's hand.

"I love Gamma Z and Uncle Uke."

"I know you do. And they love you. And so do I." Michelle stooped to give him a kiss.

She took no offense when he rubbed the spot where she'd kissed him with the back of his chubby hand. He was all boy, this one.

She could see Rae approaching at a fast clip. She slowed down and waved when she saw Michelle had Ian safely in tow.

Rachael got right to the point when she did catch up to them. "So what's this I hear about Trevor accepting a position at some Metropolitan Community Church in California? You know they're a church for gays and lesbians, don't you?"

"Shhh... Tracy's kids are here." She glanced over her

shoulder to make sure the kids weren't near enough to hear what they were saying. "Yes I know. How do you?"

"When Mac was working for the Minneapolis Post Dispatch he was assigned to take pictures for an article on the rapidly increasing membership of one of their churches up in the Cities. So you're saying it's true?"

"Where did you hear it anyway?"

"Mom told me."

"Mom knows?"

"She knows the name of the church. She doesn't have a clue about it being an organization for gays and their families. Neither did I until Mac told me."

"You didn't tell Mom, did you?" Michelle felt like she was going to hyperventilate.

"No, of course not. I mean, part of me would have loved to stick it to Tracy after all the times she's screwed me over, but I knew you'd never let me forget it if I was the one who let the cat out of the bag."

"Thank God."

"So I hate to harp on the obvious here, but does this mean our own sweet, perfect, little brother-in-law is gay or has he just taken a sudden interest in the cause?"

"I wish you wouldn't talk about my dad when he's not even here to defend himself." Theodora announced her presence in a stilted voice.

Rachael's face blanched red. "Theodora. I didn't know you were here."

"Obviously not," Michelle retorted. "They spent the night at our house. I'm so sorry, honey." Michelle moved to Teddy's side and put an arm around her shoulder. "I wish I could tell you that people aren't going to talk about this but they are. Minding other people's business is a temptation that's hard to resist. I'm afraid it's one unpleasant aspect of human nature that's not likely to change anytime in the near future." She glared at her older sister.

Teddy looked Rachael squarely in the eye. "You don't like my mom much, do you?"

"I like her just fine. She is my sister."

"But do you don't like her very well as a person, do you?"

"I'm sure she's a very good, very nice person. We've just never seen eye to eye on a lot of things, that's all."

Teddy sighed. "I don't blame you for not liking her. She wasn't very nice to you when you and Mac got married."

Rachael looked at Michelle with a touch of desperation in her eyes. *Help me,* her look pleaded. *Get me out of this!*

Michelle looked away. "All three of we Jones girls were raised to look at the world through very judgmental eyes, Teddy. Rachael and I learned some very tough lessons early on in our lives and as a result, we learned to look at things with a little more tolerance. Your mother has lived a very sheltered life. Until now, she's reacted to things in a very predictable way considering how we were brought up."

"She's trying very hard, Teddy," Rachael agreed. "I should give her more credit. She's doing amazingly well considering what she's going though. I'll admit I have a bad habit of poking fun at her. The truth is, she doesn't deserve the grief I give her. She may be my kid sister but she's really grown up these past few years. I was out of line and I'm sorry you had to hear what I said."

Michelle smiled warmly. "She and your dad have to have done something right to have raised a daughter as wonderful as you."

"Thanks." Their niece looked suddenly sad.

Rae and Michelle exchanged worried looks over the top of her head.

"So my dad really is gay, isn't he?"

There was a long, drawn-out silence. Both Rachael and Teddy were staring at her.

"I told you I wouldn't lie to you, Teddy. But I also promised your mother she could trust me to keep her confidence. I can't go back on my word to her. Like I said yesterday, you need to talk to your mom and dad."

"I guess I have my answer then. The only thing that could be so bad that you'd have to be sworn to secrecy is that my dad really is gay."

Michelle shook her head. She hated being put in this position. She rued the day Tracy had ever taken her into her confidence. “Teddy, listen to me. There’s a big difference between having sympathetic feelings towards and wanting to help gay people and actually having a physical relationship with a person of the same sex. To the best of my knowledge, your dad has not done any such thing. That’s all I’m going to say now and I want you to promise me you’ll talk to your mom and dad about this as soon as you get home.”

“Whatever,” Teddy responded in a resigned voice. “Is it okay if I go inside now?”

“Sure, honey. We’ll join you in a minute.”

Rachael watched her niece trudge across the parking lot and exhaled loudly. “Sorry I had to go and open my big mouth.”

“Me, too. It’s really not your fault though. She overheard Tracy and Trevor arguing a couple of nights ago and evidently one or the other of them said something in the heat of the moment that was not meant for her ears. I saw Tracy twice today but we were never alone so I couldn’t even warn her that Teddy knows. I feel just awful.”

“I can’t believe it’s really true. I thought Mom had screwed up the name of the church or something. It seemed pretty funny at the time,” Rae said.

“Tracy’s expended a great deal of energy trying to shelter her kids from knowing.”

“She’s sitting on top of a pretty big powder keg if you ask me.”

“I’m worried for all of them,” Michelle said.

“One of us better figure out a way to keep Mom from spreading the news about Trevor’s new employer all over town or it’s just a matter of time before everyone finds out,” Rae said.

“I agree,” Michelle said.

Church had dismissed and Teddy had gone half way to the car with the rest of the family when she realized she’d lost her headband. She was sure she’d had it on when they arrived which meant she must have left it inside the church.

Jake and Michelle were busy talking to some friends and the boys were playing kickball on the side yard. She knew no one would miss her if she slipped inside the church to have a look.

Clay didn't know why he'd had the urge to go to church that morning. Perhaps it was because he knew he had to speak to his parents about Lauren and his plans for the mill, perhaps because he was seeking guidance for the life-changing decisions he'd knew he'd be forced to make before the week was out. Or it might have been because he knew that Tracy was sitting by herself at church, albeit a different one, at the same moment. His presence here made him feel connected to her in some small way.

He started to make his way to the rear of the church. His father was going to go through the roof when he informed him that he'd broken the engagement they had masterminded. If Lauren had taken his edict seriously, which was definitely in question - he'd tried to let her down gently several times to no avail - and told the Humphreys, his parents might already know.

He was already being chastised for one transgression and it wasn't his father's style to resort to the same method of punishment twice. Clay was sure he'd be issued an ultimatum this time. And he could very nearly figure what it would be.

He'd taken the time to speak to the pastor for a few minutes following the service and was leaving the apse when he saw a curly-haired young woman reenter the sanctuary. His breath caught in his throat. He'd seen the girl earlier and known she must be Tracy's daughter. She had Michelle's build instead of Tracy's, but she looked just like her mother. He'd also spotted Timothy sitting with Jake and Michelle and Rachael and Mac. It hadn't taken him long to deduce that two of the other seven children in the pew were Tracy's.

He would have loved to meet Tracy's daughter and older son, but he'd held back purposely. He knew Timothy would recognize him instantly just as he had that day on the merry-go-round, and probably have given him a warm welcome. But he hadn't known what the two older children would make of Timothy's enthusiasm and decided it wasn't worth the risk of incurring their ire. Tracy had warned him they had reacted to their parents' separation with a great deal of bitterness. Clay didn't want to exacerbate the situation.

But the girl looked so sad, so discouraged, and so like Tracy. His heart went out to her. Perhaps he could say something to encourage her. Timothy was no where in sight. There was no reason the girl had to know Clay was even acquainted with her mother.

She seemed not to see him even though she was only an arm's length away from intersecting his path. She appeared to be looking for something. He cleared his throat.

When she looked up and saw him her face turned livid with anger. She swerved to avoid him.

Clay knew instantly that something was wrong - very wrong. Without thinking, he stopped and turned to face her.

Theodora's eyes narrowed. "What do you want?"

He momentarily choked on his confusion. The hate evident in her twisted face and icy eyes confounded him. "Do you know who I am?" It was a stupid thing to say. It was the only thing he could think to say. And he knew the answer before she said another word.

"Do I know you're my mother's lover? Yes." She looked at him as though he were the lowest form of slime on the planet. "You look a little different with your clothes on and your hair combed."

"H-how...?" His legs had turned to jelly.

"I rode my bike into town to talk to my mother and got a big surprise instead."

"Does your mother know you-?"

"What do you think I am, stupid?" She cut him off. "On second thought, that's an honor you and my mother seem to have reserved for yourselves."

"If you'd let me explain..."

"Sure. That's a story I'd love to hear. Come to think of

it, that's something you have in common with my mother. She tells some great stories - but only the parts she wants you to know. The rest is always her little secret."

Her bravado almost had him convinced until she turned so suddenly green that he thought she was going to faint or throw up or both.

"You're angry," he said. "If you could just try to..."

"What do you want me to say? First I find out my father is queer and now I find out my very own, sweet, supposedly perfect mother is nothing but a slut. What am I supposed to think?"

Clay felt his face growing hot. "Don't ever call her that. She's your mother. She loves you. And it wasn't like that!" He clutched his fist over the top of the nearest church pew and locked his knees.

Theodora knew about her father being gay, too? No wonder she was so inconsolable. His mind grappled for something he could do to make things better. "I care about your mother very deeply. She cares about me. I won't apologize for what we did. If I'm remembering correctly, you're not even fifteen yet. When you're a little older-"

"Oh, please," she said. Disgust dripped from her voice like acid leaking from a battery. "That crap may work on Timothy, but I'm hardly a baby anymore. I understand a lot more than you or Mom or anyone gives me credit for."

"You're seeing things in black and white. It's not that simple. There are grey areas and complex emotions at work here – things you can't possibly understand."

"Me? You hardly even know my mother! I've listened to her lectures for fourteen years, including the one about pre-marital sex. Plus, surprise, I'm old enough to read. I know what the Bible says. The thing you're guilty of is called fornication and I don't recall any circumstance under which it's allowable according to God."

"I refuse to feel guilty about something so..." he faltered, "so right. How do you know God didn't lead your mother and me..."

She looked at him with loathing. "Sounds like an excuse

one of my friends would come up with." Her face was livid with rage. "You're both such hypocrites. I'm not even allowed to watch *Glee* on TV because it contains *questionable subject matter and an over-abundance of sexual innuendoes*," she mimicked her mother. "You should have heard what Mom said when Aunt Michelle got pregnant before she and Uncle Jake got married. Talk about a different story."

"Your mother's been through a lot in the last two years. An experience as traumatic as learning that your husband... well, it's bound to change a person's outlook on some things. You can't fault her for that."

"Oh can't I? According to my calculations, Aunt Rachael and Uncle Mac had Ian about five months after they were married. But then, I'll never know for sure because my holier-than-thou mother didn't want us exposed to *that kind of thing*. We didn't even get to meet Uncle Mac or see baby Ian until they'd been married for over six months and Ian was a month old. She sure didn't show them any mercy. Why should I treat her any differently now?"

"Because she needs you. Because she loves you. Because none of us is perfect. She'd be the first to admit that she's only human. A work in progress just like the rest of us. Talk to her, Theodora. She deserves a little happiness in her life. Don't rob her, us, of the chance to find it together."

"Together?" Her look was one of utter mortification. "You and her? Why can't you just leave us alone? This whole thing is hard enough with you butting your nose in where it doesn't belong."

Clay closed his eyes and prayed for one hapless moment that this was all a bad dream. What else could he say? She was obviously beyond comforting, at least by him. If anything, he was intensifying her contempt for him with every word he uttered.

Still, he had to try. "I'm sorry."

She raked the length of his body with her eyes before she fled, a sneer plastered across her face in what could only be described as hatred. Pure, unadulterated hatred.

*****

The telephone was ringing when Tracy walked in the back door of the parsonage after church. Trevor had just dropped her off and was on his way to Maple Valley to pick up the children at Jake and Michelle's.

She was exhausted. Most people had gone out of their way to avoid her. A few had murmured sympathetic words but most had kept a carefully guarded distance - as though they feared what had happened to Trevor's and her marriage was contagious. She supposed it wasn't a wholly irrational fear; if it could happen to the minister and his wife – such a *perfect couple*, it could happen to anyone.

Harder still had been the feeling of hypocrisy that had hit her square in the face the moment she'd entered the church. The people at church would consider her an adulteress had they known what she'd done with Clay. She found it ironic that the only thing she felt guilty about was the lack of remorse she felt about Clay's and her time together.

But resolving that issue would have to wait until after she'd answered the phone. It was still ringing - as if whoever was calling thought they could make her answer by sheer determination. That was her first clue that it was her mother.

Not that it came as any surprise that her mother was trying to reach her. She'd been avoiding her all week. Trevor had spoken to her in Tracy's stead on three or four occasions. Theodora had intercepted two calls and Titus one that she knew of. She took a deep breath and picked up the receiver, supposing she had no choice but to face the music. "Hello?"

"Well it's about time! Where on earth have you been all week?"

"Hi, Mom."

"If I didn't know better I'd think you've been ignoring me."

"You know I've been working down in Maple Valley with Michelle."

"Yes," her mother sighed. "I certainly hope it's not

Michelle and Rachael who've been putting all these ideas in your head about divorcing Trevor."

"Mom. They didn't even know about it until a few days ago. Besides, I'm not divorcing Trevor. He's divorcing me."

"Well, I know they're my daughters and I love them both, but ever since they started attending that country church I think they've become more liberal than ever. I know the Fellowship Church in Maple Valley is American Fellowship and not Regular Fellowship, but no matter what conference they associate with, their doctrines would be more similar to what the girls grew up with than the ones you'd find in the church they go to."

"Michelle's never discussed it with me, Mom. I don't know what their reasons for choosing that particular church were." Tracy wasn't in the mood for a fight.

"All I know is that the world is spinning out of control. And it gets worse with every generation that passes. Why, when your father and I were young, divorce was practically unheard of. Those who did dare to entertain the notion knew exactly what kind of scandal they'd face if they went ahead and did it. Knowing they'd be shunned in their own family and in their community was a good deterrent."

"Well, this whole thing wouldn't have been my choice either, but-"

"I just worry about my grandchildren, Tracy. Look at the example you're setting for them. If you and Trevor go ahead with this divorce they'll grow up thinking split marriages are the norm, as commonplace as not. It just breaks my heart to think what this will do to them."

"It breaks my heart, too, Mom, but we are getting a divorce and there's nothing anyone can say to change..."

She was even more exhausted by the time she got off the phone. There was just enough time to grab a bite to eat and rush off to meet the Realtor. It would have been heaven to have the house to herself for an hour or two. A good long bubble bath sounded downright delicious.

A few minutes later, she'd rendezvoused with the Realtor and was looking at the first house on their list.

It was a cute little house, and the price was right, but sadly, it smelled like cat urine.

She politely declined the Realtor's offer to look at the basement and tried to keep a positive attitude. The last twenty-four hours were a jumble in her mind. Trevor had eyed her suspiciously when she'd come home from Maple Valley the night before but he hadn't dared ask her where she'd been after the scene his questions had caused the night prior. For that, at least, she was thankful.

She'd feared he would guess exactly what she'd been doing. It had been awhile, granted, but Trevor knew how her hair got when someone had been running their fingers through it repeatedly. He knew how she looked after sex, the scent of her, the sheen of her skin. He had seen it all.

A small part of her would have liked to have rubbed his face in it. But when it came down to it, the last thing she wanted was for Trevor to know. If she could just keep her secret for five more days, he would be gone and none the wiser about Clay. The only thing that would make her happier is if she never had to hear, see, or think about Trevor being with one of his male friends. Turnabout was only fair play.

She couldn't wait to find a place of her own. Once she'd moved out of the parsonage, she wouldn't be beholden to Trevor or the church. If she wanted to attend church in Blooming Prairie she would, if she wanted to find a new church in another town where she could escape the stigma of being the divorced wife of the old pastor, she could. She could do what she wanted to do, when she wanted to do it, with whom she wanted to do it, without feeling one tiny tinge of guilt.

Chapter 18

Clay looked up at the gothic windows in the little country church and stalled until he saw both the MacPhearson's and the Sheffield's cars pull out of the parking lot, glad in retrospect that he'd arrived late and been forced to park on the far west side of the church. With any luck at all, Theodora would continue to keep their secret and no one would ever find out what had transpired between them – or between he and Tracy the day before.

"Luck." He cursed under his breath. Tracy would die if she ever found out that Theodora had seen them. He didn't even want to know what they'd been doing at the time.

He wondered briefly if he should tell Tracy what had happened with Theodora. She'd probably hate him forever. He pushed the curses from his lips and looked up. Maybe God had been trying to tell them something. If that were the case, God should have punished him, not Tracy. He felt wholly responsible. Tracy was so vulnerable. He shouldn't have expected her to be the one to keep her head. It should have been him. He never should have given in to his emotions.

He slid under the steering wheel and turned the key. The engine sprang to life. Clay spun out of the parking lot and roared back into town.

His anger at himself had started to abate by the time he reached the center of town and with it, the speed at which he was driving. He knew what he had to do and he would do it like a man. He may have been a cad in some respects – he probably could have handled things with Lauren a lot better – but there was no way Barclay Alexander III would stoop so low as to come between a woman and her child.

Breaking things off with Tracy now, when he'd only just held her; now, when he'd only just tasted of her sweetness, would be the hardest thing he'd ever done. Clay waited out a traffic light with no small degree of impatience. It had to be. There was no other way. He could feel his heart sliding into a pit of bottomless remorse even as he considered how to do the inevitable. But with God as his witness, he could see no other way. Why should Tracy be put in the horrible position of having to choose between him and her daughter? If he were cruel enough to do that to her, she would choose her daughter and their relationship would be over anyway. No, it had to be him.

The last thing he expected to see was his parent's distinctive Lincoln Town Car parked in the driveway in front of his house. Their unannounced presence could mean only one thing.

"God help me," Clay mumbled. He braked sharply, executed a sharp U-turn, and slid the car up to the curb in front of the house. Within seconds he was walking up the front walk like a lamb being led to its slaughter.

*****

Tracy was ready to call it quits after only two hours of house shopping. House number two had been a hundred year old farm house that, unlike her sisters' vintage homes, hadn't been built well in the first place and certainly wasn't worth renovating. House number three had boasted carpeting that reeked and walls and draperies stained by cigarette smoke.

House number four was perfect except for like-new red and black wool shag carpeting that had been installed from wall to wall fifteen years earlier to compliment a tenant's Mediterranean decor. The owner was adamant that never again would he install new carpeting to suite a tenant's tastes, no matter how innocuous Tracy's preferences might have been. She'd known the second she'd seen it that she'd sooner live in the back seat of her car than wake up to that rug every morning.

House number five was a possibility – with at least enough good points to ward off the despair she felt after viewing the first four. Had the Realtor planned it that way to get her to make a fast decision? Tracy had to admit she might have ruled out this house, too, if she hadn't seen the others first. She'd have to ask Rachael if the tactic was a standard trick of the trade.

The house was small, and badly in need of fresh paint and some feminine touches, none of which daunted Tracy nearly as much as the Mediterranean Monstrosity. She'd pulled up a piece of the brown carpet where it bordered a heat register and discovered the floors of the little Cape Cod were solid heart of pine. Not quite as nice as oak, but probably the best she could do on her budget. Her Realtor thought the owner might be willing to let her pull up the carpet on the first floor and reimburse her for the cost of paint and some general repairs if Tracy provided the labor herself.

The boys would have to share a large bedroom upstairs, a decision she knew she might live to regret, but she and Theodora would each have a small room to themselves, hers on the first floor in what should have been a den. The basement was passable enough to accommodate a family room of the same basic configuration they currently had. The children were already used to watching television and entertaining their friends downstairs so little would change in that respect.

The house was in a neighborhood of houses better cared for than it was, an asset the Realtor had been quick to point out. With Titus's help on the yard, Tracy's green thumb in the garden, and a fresh coat of paint on the exterior, Tracy felt they could bring it up to par with the rest of the houses in no time.

Yes, the house had definite possibilities. If she worked all the hours she possibly could between now and the first of October, she should be able to save enough for the deposit and first month's rent.

Her heart was much lighter as she left Blooming Prairie and headed south to Maple Valley. Maybe it was true that the night was blackest just before the dawn. At any rate, the sky was finally starting to look a little brighter.

*****

Clay's mother's normally serene facial features were twisted into an expression that could best be described as something akin to the face of a gargoyle. His father was ruddy red with rage from the top of his head to the white collar where his stiffly starched shirt met his neck.

Clay's father's voice thundered out to greet him the moment he appeared at the door. "Well, you've really done it this time."

His mother's attempts to relax her face failed. "Lauren is simply devastated, Barclay. I don't know what you were thinking. Of course you'll marry her."

"We'll set the wedding date immediately to counteract any lingering doubts on the Humphreys' part." His father spoke in his most authoritative voice. "If we act quickly, we can probably still reserve the cathedral for the first or second weekend in December. We may have to settle for a Friday instead of a Saturday, but no matter - the church is beautifully decorated over the holidays. If all goes as planned people will be talking about this wedding for years to come."

Clay looked from one parent to the other in amazement.

"Lauren isn't quite ready to forgive you yet, but her parents both agree that she'll warm up to the idea of living here in Iowa once the renovations are completed and the house properly furnished." His mother tried to manage a smile. "I think it would be a nice gesture on your part to move this sofa into one of the smaller rooms to use as a study, and to encourage Lauren to decorate the main house the way she likes."

"I..."

His father's attention had honed in on the Frank Lloyd Wright panel. "It's upside down. Of all the-"

"It..."

Clay was only allowed to voice one syllable before his mother resumed her remunerations on Lauren's behalf.

"Granted, she's used to more opulent surroundings than you usually prefer, but I dare say a few crystal chandeliers and wall sconces, some fringed valances, and a Louis XVI sofa would go a long ways towards reconciling this little rift."

His father was pacing the floor in front of the Frank Lloyd Wright panel. "This wallpaper will have to go anyway. What kind of an idiot doesn't even know the top from the bottom when it comes to a world-renowned piece of artwork like the Tree of Life Window?"

"I'm sure Lauren would be delighted to send down her decorator from St. Paul to aid you in the necessary changes. She did such an excellent job on the west wing at the Humphreys'."

"I already have a decorator and I have no intention of letting Lauren aid me in anything. I'm not going to marry her. My decision is final."

His mother and father exchanged looks.

"Be reasonable, dear," his mother implored.

"I have no intention-" Clay started to say.

His father cleared his throat. "I've been looking over the books at the woolen mill, Clay. The restructuring efforts have progressed well ahead of the time frame I had envisioned when I originally sent you to Maple Valley."

"To your credit, darling," his mother stressed.

"Ted Johnson announced his retirement as Vice President of Consumer Affairs last Tuesday. Now I know you don't share the political aspirations your mother and I have always held for you, but this position is a highly visible one within the corporate structure and the perfect arena in which to hone your negotiating skills."

His father finished speaking without ever making eye contact with Clay.

"I'm sure you'll have no trouble selling the house. Barclay, dear?" His mother followed at his heels as Clay spun around and headed towards the door.

Clay gripped the polished brass doorknob in one hand and tried to assume a casual pose leaning against the door frame. He'd always been able to infuriate his father with a calm demeanor. Even as a boy, his father had always stopped spanking him the second he'd started to cry. As he'd aged, Clay had learned to clench his teeth and refuse to give his father the satisfaction of knowing he was hurting him. It was the fastest way Clay knew to make his father lose control. It had been worth a blistered butt to win the battle of wills even then.

He kept his voice was smooth and devoid of emotion. "I'm late for an appointment with my attorney. I've drawn up a rough proposal which I'll submit to the corporate office tomorrow before close of business. I regret to inform you that I've decided to terminate my employment with Alexander Industries. It's my intent to purchase Elk Creek Woolen Mills if we can come to terms on a price. If not, I plan to use my stock to stage a forced take over of the mill. I'll be making Maple Valley my permanent home."

His mother and father stood speechless with shock. Clay turned to leave. "I've asked my attorney to contact the Humphreys to relay my sincerest apologies for whatever grief I've caused Lauren and their family."

He left his mother with her mouth agape, his father looking like he could murder his only offspring without so much as batting an eye.

*****

Clay's car was not in front of his house when Tracy arrived in Maple Valley. She felt a momentary pang of disappointment. Clay had talked about next time they were together, she reminded herself – he hadn't said when that would be.

Besides, she tried to cheer herself up, she had come to Maple Valley to clock in a few hours of work. It was already four and she wanted to be home in time to make sure the kids had their homework done and a clean set of clothes to wear to school Monday morning. There really wasn't time to dally if she was going to get enough work done to make her trip worthwhile and still be home by eight thirty or nine o'clock.

She decided to finish priming the kitchen pantry, a job she thought she should be able to finish in the three hours or so she had to work. When she came in the morning she'd be able to start right in on the first coat of semi-gloss.

She worked diligently until about six thirty. Tracy knew the second she heard footsteps on the porch that Clay had come after all. Her heart quickened when she saw him walking from the dining room to the kitchen.

"Hello," he said, the study of nonchalance.

"Hi," she said, recognizing instantly that something was wrong. Wasn't he excited to see her? Why did he look so unhappy? Didn't he want to kiss her as badly as she did him? She was walking on air. Clay looked as though he'd just walked across a bed of nails.

Clay fought to control the flood of emotions that washed over him at the sight of Tracy's freckled nose and shining smile. Why did she have to look so damn happy to see him? Her enthusiastic expressions weren't making this any easier.

He looked at the floor. Her naiveté would be the end of him yet. The woman didn't have a coy bone in her. He swallowed hard and continued to avoid her eyes. He knew he had to play it cool or she would see right through him.

"I stopped and got some pizza. There's plenty if you want some," she said, looking like she was finally getting the message that all was not well.

"Thanks."

Clay tossed two packages of M&Ms on the countertop.

"You remembered." Her face lit up with relief.

Okay. So the M&Ms had been a mistake. But then, he wasn't out to devastate her, just discourage her a bit. He wanted to remain on friendly terms. He wanted their working relationship to remain intact. He wanted... hell, he wanted her. He wanted her now. He wanted to make good on his promise to make love to her. He wanted her like he had never wanted anyone before.

"How did church go this morning?" He couldn't just

launch right into the kind of news he had to impart. He knew she'd been nervous about facing everyone at church and he had to break the ice somehow.

"A few people spoke to me. Trevor did as well with the sermon as could be expected under the circumstances. I mean, he didn't try to make a lot of flimsy excuses or justify his actions. That would have made it worse." Tracy tore open a bag of M&Ms and spread them out on the counter. She began making a row of each color, probably without even realizing she was doing it.

He was so damn attracted to her he could barely stand it.

"It was very difficult for me. But I had to be there. I had to give some kind of closure to the past decade and a half of our lives." She sought out his eyes. "I wish there was some way I felt we could continue to attend church there for the children's sake. It's the only church they've ever known and all their friends..."

God. He hated it that she was treating him like a friend, confiding in him, looking at him as though she trusted him implicitly. For a moment he wondered if he could actually proceed with his plan. And then he remembered the hatred, the scorn, the hurt he'd seen in Theodora's eyes. He couldn't bear to know that because of him, Tracy might have to endure that kind of pain. He had no choice but to break things off.

"Tracy," he began, when she had finished. "We need to talk."

She looked up at him as though startled by his announcement. She had to have been able to tell by his voice that something was wrong.

And those words. She'd no doubt heard them before. So innocuous. So cruel.

He swallowed the bile in his throat and forged on. "Now that we've both had a chance to cool down a bit, I'm sure you'll probably agree with me when I say that what happened yesterday was, well, a mistake." He managed a smile that had to look feeble at best.

She stared at him dumbly. She was hurt. He could see

she was hurt. But this hurt was nothing compared to the pain she would feel if her own daughter rejected her.

"You're a beautiful woman, Tracy, and I have the utmost respect for you. I just don't have the kind of feelings for you that you seem to have for me." He panicked. He hadn't meant to say that. He hadn't wanted to humiliate her. "It has nothing to do with you. I'm just not the kind of man who would ever be able to make a commitment to you and I don't want to start something I can't finish."

It hadn't occurred to him that she might cry. For a moment, it looked as though she was going to. While he watched, her expression went from heartbroken to indignant. God, he loved that she was feisty and brave and not afraid to let him have it.

But he couldn't – could not – absolutely could not-

She refused to look away. "I don't believe you could have done what we did with someone you don't have feelings for. I won't believe that of you, Clay. I was there. I felt you."

His response was dispassionate. "Men are very different than women. What can I say? We can perform physically without the emotional involvement that women obviously feel."

God, he hated this, hated himself.

"What happened yesterday felt good. It was a physical release. That's all." He shrugged. He could see she wasn't convinced. "Good Lord, Tracy. You were married to a homosexual for how many years and didn't even know it? You of all people should know that men are great actors when it comes to sex. The act means little to us emotionally. It's all physical. We take it when and however we can get it. I am sorry if my greediness for sex hurt you in any way."

She stared at him with unmasked disbelief. "No. I can't accept that. It was more than that." Her face was ashen. "If you had wanted to use me you would have done a quick slam, bam, thank you, ma'am and sent me packing. You held me in your arms for hours, Clay. You laughed, you cried with me. You felt it, too. I know you did!" she said frantically.

"It's a lot more complicated than that and you know it." He stared at her with no trace of a smile, which wasn't hard at this point. He felt ill. But he had to do this. He had no choice.

Her eyes filled with tears.

"Damn it, Tracy. I told you this would happen!"

Her lips were trembling so blatantly she could hardly form words. "Fine. I was warned. Now I'm warning you. Don't ever come near me or my children again. Stay out of my life. And don't ever swear at me again!" Tears streamed down her face.

He stared at her a moment longer, turned, and walked away.

"Clay," she cried piteously.

He paused when she called out and stood with his hand on the door for one second, then two. But he never looked back.

Chapter 19

All Tracy knew for sure is that she couldn't seem to stop crying. Her tears probably came as no surprise to those who knew her considering what she'd been through in the last several days. Some probably wrote it off to the stress of moving, others to grief over the end of her marriage, others still to the simple fact that she was a woman. Her mother was certain that shedding copious tears was just one of many dire things a person could expect to endure when they blatantly chose to disregard God's Perfect Will for their lives and divorced their husband.

Theodora was evidently refusing to think about it at all in favor of another option - ignoring her completely. Titus reacted as men usually do to tears - by fleeing to the far opposite end of the house and staying there until she stopped. Timothy came and gave her a hug, which made her cry more.

Trevor was assuming it was just that time of month. Only she, and, of course, Clay, would have known that her blessed time of the month was just past and not due again for at least two weeks.

Rachael and Michelle were most concerned, having witnessed firsthand the fortitude with which she had been handling the divorce proceedings up until now. Neither of them had a clue as to what had happened to change her tenuously held hopefulness for the future to the abject pessimism she seemed so suddenly caught up in.

Even Rita Coolidge weighed in with a sympathetic shoulder and some words of advice.

Baby cried the day the circus came to town
'cause she didn't want parades just passin' by her
So she painted on a smile and took up with some clown
While she danced without a net upon the wire...

Don't cry out loud
Just keep it inside, learn how to hide your feelings
Fly high and proud
And if you should fall, remember you almost had it all
Baby saw that when they pulled that big top down
They left behind her dreams among the litter
The different kind of love she thought she'd found
There was nothin' left but sawdust and some glitter
Don't cry out loud
Just keep it inside and learn how to hide your feelings
Fly high and proud
And if you should fall, remember you almost had it all.

Tracy tried not to let her tears impede her work. She had no doubt that Clay would keep his distance while she was painting at the house. She was right. Michelle brought up the subject once or twice to mention that Clay was keeping in touch with her via the telephone in the evenings when she was home. His excuse that things had been extremely busy at work seemed sufficient enough to allay Michelle's suspicions about why he hadn't stopped by to see how they were progressing during the day.

Sometimes in the mornings when Tracy first arrived at work she could see that Clay had been there – boxes half unpacked, remnants of a fire in the grate, rumpled pillows on the floor, the afghan he had used to cover his nakedness strewn carelessly over the back of the sofa. One morning it looked as though he had spent the night curled up on the floor in front of the fireplace in the same spot where they...

All the more evidence that what had happened between them had meant nothing to him. She was convinced he had probably forgotten all about it by now – whereas she could hardly bear to enter the room. Michelle thought she avoided the place to steer clear of the upside down wallpaper panel. How relieved she was that Michelle didn't know the truth.

But life went on. On Monday morning of the next week, Tracy received her first paycheck, a miracle for which she was not ungrateful. On Monday evening she took the children to see the house she'd chosen as their new home and made the first installment on the deposit - even though their begrudgingly-given approval was less than enthusiastic.

Tracy tried to be upbeat and reassuring, to allay their concerns about the transitions ahead and set their minds at ease, but she was in such a stupor she didn't even care. How could she expect them to exhibit any kind of eagerness about the months to come when she herself couldn't muster a single positive thought?

Tuesday evening she and Trevor met with their attorney and hammered out an uncontested divorce and child custody settlement. They had not argued. Still, the act of dissolving a union she had expected to be until death do us part left her drained and exhausted.

Trevor left for California the next morning, on Wednesday of that week. He drove this time, pulling a U-Haul trailer full of his clothes, books, a few personal possessions, and two photo albums with pictures of the children. The children handled it better than Tracy did. A few weeks earlier, she would have easily admitted that she couldn't wait for Trevor to leave. Living in the limbo land of pretending to be a happy couple, but knowing it just wasn't so, had been stressful. But at least she'd known what and what not to expect from Trevor. In that respect, his presence had always been a comforting constant.

But now she was spooked. Her first attempt at trusting another man had resulted in an outcome just as devastating as the culmination of her relationship with Trevor. She'd wanted flowers from Clay, an invitation for a nice dinner out together, some words of appreciation at the very least. When she thought of how intimate they'd been, remembered how free she'd been with him, the humiliation was almost more than she could bear.

At least she hadn't wasted another fifteen years of her life before learning that Clay Alexander was just as big a jerk as Trevor Tomlinson was.

Trying to detest the men she had made love to with her heart and soul and body was the only way she could think to soothe her ruffled feathers. But in her mind, ah... in her mind... what she thought of still was the way Clay had held her. So tenderly, so worshipfully. And try as she might, she couldn't forget the way he'd caressed her skin, the way he'd quivered when she first touched her lips to him, the way he'd laughed and teased and snuggled with her, the caring way in which he'd listened to her, the comfortableness she'd felt with him.

He had opened the door to her heart. It was still ajar, open to the chill winds of autumn, frost rimed-nights, and cold rainy days that had descended uninvited on the towns of Blooming Prairie, Minnesota, and Maple Valley, Iowa.

She had thought the weekend would help, spending time with the children, being busy packing, not having to go near his house for two days. She had entertained high hopes that Saturday would be ever so much better than the long week that had just passed.

She lay in bed listening to the rustling sounds of the children waking up, the sheets cool and crisp against the heat of her body. Timothy had climbed into bed to snuggle with her a little after eight.

"Mommy, will you read me a story?"

His tousle-haired, sleepy-eyed innocence was enough to make her want to weep again. "How 'bout some *Winnie the Pooh*?" She felt like Eeyore today. A story about Eeyore might be just what she needed.

"Titus says Pooh is for babies."

She'd noticed Timothy had been sleeping with his Power Ranger instead of the nearly threadbare, half-empty-of-its-stuffing old Pooh bear he'd had since he was a baby. "A person's never too old for Pooh."

Except, perhaps, Theodora. She appeared in the doorway of Tracy's bedroom halfway through the tale in which Eeyore loses a tail. Tracy was using her best gloomy voice, which was in prime form for obvious reasons.

Her daughter's attire, or the fact that she suddenly looked like thirty instead of almost fifteen should have clued her in that there was a problem. But Timothy was pressing his snugly, pajama-clad body into the crook of her arm and giggling, and she had just smiled for the first time since last Monday. She hadn't wanted there to be another problem ever again.

Theodora wasted no time in shattering that little fantasy.

"Staci Slattery asked me to stay over at her house tonight so I won't be home until tomorrow afternoon," she announced while chanking on a wad of gum the size of a walnut.

Something about the way her daughter told her instead of asking her rubbed her wrong from the start. "I thought you were going over to Brooke's house to work on your science project with some of your friends from school."

"Hardly."

"I hope that means your project is finished."

"It's not due until Monday. I'll do it tomorrow night."

It was typical Theodora to put things off to the last minute, yet she always pulled things off without a hitch in the end. She was her Aunt Michelle all over again. Tracy knew better than to try to win that particular battle. She decided to try another tack.

"When did you get to be so chummy with Staci? I thought you didn't even like her." Staci lived with her mother and two older brothers on the east side of the tracks. The kids had come to Sunday School when they were little, but hadn't attended for years. "When I suggested you invite Staci to Teen Night at church last month you rolled your eyes and pouted and made an awful fuss."

"Yeah, well, a lot of things have changed in the past month."

Tracy looked at her oldest child sharply. "All the more reason to stick by those tried and true friends who really care about you. In light of all the changes that are going on in your life already, you may find that now isn't the best time to start making a lot of changes in your circle of friends."

"Look who's talking," Theodora retorted.

Tracy recognized a challenge when she saw one even though she didn't know exactly what had prompted

Theodora's belligerence.

"I'm serious. It wasn't easy for me to admit to my family that your Dad and I were divorcing. It's pretty humiliating to have to face your sisters with that kind of news, but at least I know they care about me and have my best interests at heart."

"I meant your new male friend."

Tracy blanched.

"Theodora thinks Staci's big brother is really cute," Timothy piped up out of the blue.

Neither she nor Theodora said a word.

"Does Eeyore ever get his tail back, Mom?" Timothy said in a vulnerable little voice.

Tracy's heart pounded furiously. She could feel the pulse point in her neck swelling with anxiety. Theodora couldn't possibly know what she had done with Clay. She hadn't told anyone, not even Michelle.

Tracy took a deep breath. Half of Maple Valley had seen her pretending to flirt with Luke, on the other hand. Theodora could have overheard a careless remark from Mac, Jake, either of her sisters, or any of their friends while she was with Michelle and Jake last Saturday and Sunday.

She decided to ignore the quip. Whom she'd spoken to at Mac's birthday party was none of her daughter's business. She met Theodora's eyes undaunted. "Staci's youngest brother just graduated from high school this year, didn't he?"

"What of it?"

Tracy tried to remain nonchalant. A sudden desperate sense of déjà vu swept over her. She could almost see herself, at barely fifteen, sneaking out to meet friends, going places her parents never would have approved of. "I'm just surprised you know Staci's brothers since you don't go to their school."

"It's a small town." Theodora glared belligerently.

Another memory flashed before her eyes, this one of Rachael standing before their own mother, eyes flashing, fists clenched, arguing her case.

"You were my age when you started dating Dad. He was

eighteen."

"I knew your Dad from church. His parents and mine had been close friends for years." She didn't need to tell Theodora what kind of folks the Slatterys were. She knew. Everyone in the whole town knew about Mr. Slattery's drunken brawls and abusive behaviors towards his wife and children. Just because his wife had finally kicked him out didn't mean his children hadn't learned a lot at his hand before he left.

If they were even his children. Rumor had it each of the three Slattery children came from a different gene pool.

"And we know how wonderfully your perfect little life turned out because you married a boy from church, don't we?" Theodora taunted her.

Her face must have registered shock. *No*, her heart cried out. *Not my daughter, not my daughter, too.*

"I want to know if Eeyore finds his tail." Timothy tugged at her arm. "Mommy."

She couldn't answer him. Not yet.

Timothy turned from his mother to his sister. "You're bad. I don't like you anymore."

"Ask me if I care, you little brat."

And with that, Theodora was gone.

*****

Michelle had already been painting for two hours when Tracy arrived in Maple Valley Monday morning. She was very pleased with their progress. They had made definite, visible headway over the past two weeks. The first floor was finished, from the lowest floorboard in the kitchen pantry to the highest cornice in the drawing room. The master suite and one guest room were almost done - their completion hinged on the appearance of a carpenter. They had primed the hallways and two remaining bedrooms on the second floor before leaving on Friday afternoon.

"Sorry I'm late!" Tracy breezed in and grabbed a paintbrush without even taking time to catch her breath.

"Theodora has been giving me fits all weekend. This morning was the worst yet. I finally called Trevor in California. He was able to talk her into going to school but by that time Brooke's mother had left with the other kids and I had to drive her to Rice Lake myself. I don't know what Trevor said to her but I've never been so relieved in my life. I was at my wit's end."

"Teddy?" Michelle tried not to let her fears seem too evident. "What's wrong?"

"I hope it's just a reaction to the divorce and if so, that she gets over it in time. She spent all weekend at the Slattery's house. I guess they're nice enough folks in their way but they live a very troubled existence. They're not the kind of people I'd have chosen to be influencing her right now when she's so vulnerable."

Michelle froze. She'd waited all week for Tracy to confide in her about the conversation Teddy had promised to have with her mom. She hadn't wanted to betray Teddy's confidence by telling Tracy that her daughter had found out Trevor was gay. Teddy had promised her she would talk to her mom and Michelle had trusted her to follow through on that promise.

Tracy paced the floor in front of her. "What really scares me to death is that Theodora seems to have a thing for one of the older brothers. They're good looking boys. For all I know they don't even know Theodora exists. At least, I hope neither of them returns her sentiments. Michelle, I'm just so scared for her. I hardly slept last night or the night before worrying about her. Theodora will hardly acknowledge me. I don't know what to do."

Michelle had tried to be sensitive to Tracy's moods all last week. It was obvious her sister was struggling. She'd reassured Tracy countless times that she could talk to her about anything. She'd hoped Tracy would confide in her - especially where Theodora was concerned. She cared very deeply for her niece.

She'd also tried to be very careful not to pry or butt into Tracy's business. Tracy had made it very clear that Trevor's homosexuality was not something she wished to talk about, but now... She couldn't hold her tongue any longer now that Teddy's welfare was involved. "Tracy, has Theodora told you she knows Trevor is gay?"

"No." Tracy's eyes filled with disbelief, fear, then pure panic. "She knows? How?"

"She evidently overheard something you and Trevor said and put two and two together."

"She told you? Oh, good Lord. Did you confirm her suspicions?"

"I couldn't lie to her, Tracy. I didn't confirm or deny anything. She promised me she would talk to you and Trevor about it and I believed her."

"Oh, God," Tracy moaned, hugging her arms tightly around herself. "I didn't want them to know."

"I'm sorry I didn't tell you before. I kept hoping you would bring it up so I would know that the situation had been resolved. I didn't know what to do and you've been so touchy..."

"I guess it's good that Theodora feels she can confide in you," Tracy stumbled to speak. "I've tried to let her know she can talk to me about anything."

"It has to be a two way street, Tracy. I understand your need to try to protect your kids from certain things you'd rather they didn't know. But if you keep secrets from them they're bound to do the same thing."

Tracy looked even more anguished than she had before. "Theodora tried to tell me the same thing when she first found out about the divorce. She had already figured out we weren't in love any more and she was hurt we hadn't been honest about our feelings before then."

Michelle didn't say anything else. She didn't need to.

"I'll talk to her as soon as she gets home from school. I'll be as honest as I can be." A tear trembled on Tracy's eyelash. "I don't know that I'll be much good here today but I'd like to try to paint for awhile. I need to be busy."

"Whatever you feel comfortable with. There's really no rush to get the house done now that Clay's called off the housewarming party."

"He must still be eager to move in."

Michelle nodded. "I keep forgetting you haven't talked to him in awhile. I brought a copy of this morning's paper so you could read the article about his attempted takeover of Elk Creek Mills. It sounds like he's going to be so busy dealing with corporate attorneys and stock brokers that I doubt he'll have time to move for awhile - although he does keep bringing things into the house a little at a time."

Tracy's mind whirled as she digested Michelle's news. "Why is Clay trying to take over the mill? I thought his father owned the business."

"He doesn't work for his father anymore."

"Since when?"

"About two weeks, I guess. Today's article was the first formal announcement that's been made but Rachael got wind of it earlier this week from a friend of hers that's in management at the mill. I guess Clay and his father had a falling out."

It wasn't hard for Tracy to figure out that Clay's terminating his engagement to Lauren was somehow involved. Her stomach churned just thinking about the courage and resolve Clay had to have mustered to stand up to his father. Despite the horrible way he'd treated her, she felt an overwhelming sense of pride in him.

If Clay could be honest with his parents – stand up to them, why couldn't she do the same? What a colossal mess she'd made of things! She'd almost lost Theodora because of her duplicity. She'd forced Trevor to withhold an important truth from their children, her parents, and a host of other people who honestly cared about both of them – in theory, to protect her children – in fact, to protect her own pride.

Michelle looked at her intently. "I'm sure Clay will be fine. He's one determined man."

"He knows what he wants, and isn't afraid to go after it."

Michelle must have been realized this wasn't about Clay anymore, although, of course, part of it certainly was.

"Don't be so hard on yourself, Tracy," Michelle tried again. "We all make mistakes. This whole situation involves things that none of us could possibly be equipped to deal with. I mean, who would have ever in a million years imagined that Trevor was gay or that you two wouldn't be together for the rest of your lives?"

"Thanks. I have no idea what I'll say but I'll still feel a lot better once I've had a chance to talk to Theodora. Do you mind if I leave in time to meet her right after school?"

"I think that's exactly the right thing to do. And now that I know you're leaving early I won't feel guilty telling you about my noon appointment," Michelle confessed. "I have some new clients who were recommended by my friend Deb. I've put them off twice already and I just couldn't do it again. I'm sure I won't get back here at all today. But I will be here again first thing tomorrow morning."

"No problem," Tracy said. "I promise I won't touch any more wallpaper panels while you're gone."

They were still smiling when Michelle left.

They'd finished putting the first coat of paint on the second floor hallway earlier that day. Although the surface area itself was insignificant, the eight doors leading to and from the hallway had required an excessive amount of trim work. The first thing Tracy did once Michelle had gone was to scan the area around the numerous door frames for drips.

She lingered for a second when she reached the door to the master bedroom suite while she tried to decide what job to start next. Theodora's school got out at three-thirty. She would have to leave Maple Valley by two fifteen if she wanted to be there to pick her up. She was still mulling over her options when she wandered into the bedroom.

The antique oak bedstead angled out from the southwest corner of the room hadn't been there before. The rest of the suite was bare except for the bed and a solitary stack of linens in the center of the mattress.

She didn't set out to make the bed with any purpose in mind. It was more a mother's instinct than anything. The bed needed to be made so she made it.

The sheets were smoother than any she had ever felt, perhaps the Egyptian cotton she'd seen advertised in catalogs. The fabric was the color of the wood violets she'd picked as a girl. She found herself wondering if the sheets were some Clay already owned or part of Michelle's sanctioned decorating scheme.

Perhaps she'd been spending too much time with Michelle, but she found herself wondering if this room was hers to decorate, what would she do to enhance the prairie motif? Perhaps an oriental rug of deep purples, russet reds, and copper tones at the foot of the bed with a matching runner along the side so one wouldn't have to step out onto a cold floor in the winter. She stretched the bottom sheet over the two corners nearest her and walked to the other side of the bed.

It was easy to think like her sister after spending the last few weeks listening to her decorator lingo. Her eyes traced a path to the fireplace as she bent to tuck in the top sheet at the foot of the bed. Something bold and masculine was obviously called for over the mantel, but with graceful lines and colors to keep the mood light. She envisioned a multi-dimensional wall sculpture of some sort, perhaps something in a striking enameled copper, some purple clematis trailing the length of a trellis made from craggy branches...

Tracy laughed aloud. She'd definitely been spending too much time with Michelle. She tucked the blanket under the deep cuff of the sheet with an experienced flick of her wrist and slid each pillow into a case, fluffing as she went.

Thinking about the fact that these were Clay's sheets in what was soon to be Clay's bedroom would have taken her to a place she didn't want to go, so she didn't - although she did feel a little like Goldilocks eating the mama bear's porridge.

She turned, ready to put the foolish thoughts she'd been thinking out of her head and get back to work.

Clay was standing squarely in her path. Her first thought was that she'd conjured up a vision.

Chapter 20

But this was no dream. She could smell Clay's aftershave, see the stubble of his beard. He was so near she could have touched him, but of course, she didn't.

He didn't say a word. A ray of sunshine filtered through the maple trees outside the window and shone in his hair until the blond tresses around his face looked almost iridescent. He was dressed in his suit pants but his jacket was gone, his sleeves rolled up and collar pulled open at the neck. His face was full of longing.

Every sense in her body swept into high gear. Clay had come for her. Her car was out in front; Michelle's wasn't. He had come for her. Their eyes locked with the intensity of two heat-seeking missiles locking in on their targets.

She could see moisture in the corners of his eyes and decided it was all the apology she needed. Clay opened his arms to her and she slipped into the fold of his hug.

She could feel his heart pounding against hers, but it was his kiss that said what he could not. He held her head with the tips of his fingers, guiding her gently in one direction and then another while he pressed his lips to hers, caressing her mouth with warm sensations.

She took in the sweetness of each kiss like a fragile flower that had somehow survived a draught. It had only been two weeks and a day since they had been together, only a few days, really. But when he crushed her mouth to his and deepened the kiss, she pressed back with an intensity that seemed born of years of waiting.

He paused when he felt her respond, as though he had stopped to thank the stars above that she had welcomed him. And then he showered her with another kiss, more reverent still, and another, as light as butterfly wings.

Her knees weakened and she gave herself over to kissing him with her mind and heart and soul. She thought she had lost him forever, and now, he was found.

She found the buttons on his shirt, he, the waistband of her painter's pants. And then they were lying between the sheets that she had lovingly smoothed over the bed just moments earlier.

It didn't matter what the future held. All she wanted was to feel and know and experience him now.

"Please forgive me," he said.

"I do."

Neither of them spoke again except to murmur the others name or cry out in response to feelings so exquisitely created by the other that they had to be acknowledged. There were fewer surprises this time as they explored each other's bodies. She welcomed him like a cherished friend returning home for the holidays, sensing his frustrations and ridding him of his fears with every loving stroke to his skin.

He had not forgotten how to please her, remembering each and every thing that had elicited the panting, gasping, moans of wonderment that had so delighted hertheir first time together.

This time when Tracy shyly spread her legs and looked up at him with all the love in the world, Clay rolled under her and lifted her over his hips. She fit her hands under his arms and let her thumbs rove over his chest. As he lay looking up at her breasts, those tiny but perfectly shaped breasts she felt so hesitant about, and cupped their dangling points in the palms of his hands, all he could think about was how much he adored her.

Her children, his parents, her sisters, the mess at the factory, the board of directors at Alexander Industries – none of it mattered.

"How I love you, Tracy," he whispered. "Please believe that I love you," he said again, sighing, his breaths ragged and urgent. What he would give if he could only be with her like this, every day for the rest of his life.

When he raised her up, intending to reposition her so that she could take him in, she sighed delightedly. How exactly she did it, he didn't know, but she made him feel like the most cherished man on earth. And that was why he couldn't – wouldn't...

She squirmed against him, trying to align her body to fit his. She was so willing, so wet, so ready... and all he could think about was the words Theodora had spoken.

He moved her forward a good foot. "Not until we're married," he whispered, feeling exactly like the fool he was. He desperately wanted to be one with her, however ironically, in the Biblical sense. But how could he with thoughts of being a good example and words like sin and fornication rumbling around in his head? He supposed it was nit picking given their intimate pose, but someday he wanted to be able to look Theodora in the eye and say that he and her mother hadn't had intercourse until they were married.

Tracy moaned her frustration, bent down to kiss him, and then moved on to a Plan B so pleasurable that anything he might have been missing out on was soon forgotten.

When they had pulled every last bit of pleasure from the other, she let her breasts melt into the curls on his chest and continued to caress him. She looked so peaceful – so content – so trusting - that it almost broke his heart. He rolled with her until they faced one another, and held her until she fell asleep in his arms.

Tracy woke with a start from a sleep so deep it took her a moment to realize what year it was, what planet she was on, and in whose bed she found herself. Clay was gone.

The warm languor she'd felt upon waking quickly disappeared. Clay had pulled the sheets up around her shoulders so she wouldn't get chilled. Had he thought she wouldn't mind waking up without his arms around her if he cushioned the blow with silky sheets and a blanket tucked in tight? Tracy didn't know. She didn't know anything.

She sat up timidly and swung her legs over the edge of the bed, using the sheets to shield her nakedness. The fault was no one's but her own. She hadn't asked. She hadn't cared about anything except being with him again.

There's a name for girls like you, a voice not unlike her mother's flashed in her head. *Stop it,* she willed the voice. Clay loved her. Just because he had said it in the throes of passion, instead of over a more conventional dinner for two, didn't mean it wasn't so. She believed him. Why and what was keeping him from her, she could only guess. But he did love her. She might be naïve, but she trusted him enough to believe that his reasons were noble. They had to be.

She grabbed her clothes and hurriedly slipped her pants on, then her blouse.

She hadn't asked Clay for a commitment. And yet, the unspoken truth of it was that there were plenty of things she wanted from him.

Good grief. First she'd had to create an imaginary girlfriend to confide in. Now she was pretending she had a boyfriend.

"I want you to be considerate of my feelings," she said to the walls she'd painted earlier in the week. "I want you to be faithful to me for as long as we're sleeping together." Imaginary Clay was offended she'd even thought she had to ask. "I want you to share your thoughts, to be honest and truthful with me."

Imaginary Clay looked a little guilty and said he would try to be more forthcoming, but that it was difficult, given the circumstances.

"What circumstances?" she asked pointedly. "Because I'd really like to know."

Imaginary Clay looked distressed but said nothing.

Tracy clasped her bra in front, twisted the hooks around to the back, and slipped one arm under each strap.

The real words Real Clay had spoken the last time they'd been together took up residence in her mind like an unwanted squatter. She evicted the thoughts and invited the fantasy of a future with Clay to move back in.

Still, some small part of her mind remained coherent enough to sense danger. And for that reason there was one more thing she wanted from him. She looked Imaginary Clay straight in the eyes and said, "I want you to feel free to confront me when there's a problem – with me, with you, with us. Most importantly, if and when you don't want to see me any more, you have to promise to talk to me face to face, to care about me enough to work through a peaceful parting of ways. None of this disappearing stuff, okay?"

The irony that her greatest wish, regardless of the outcome of their relationship, was for intimate conversation with him, and the fact that they had just made love with barely a word being uttered, almost passed her by. Yet even as she thought through her list of wishes she knew that she was taking one very important fact for granted. She was assuming Clay wanted an ongoing relationship with her at all. She didn't want to think about the possibility that all Clay Alexander III had wanted was to sleep with her once or twice. Not with his kisses so vivid in her mind, not with the sting of his whiskers still raw on her thighs, not with the heat of his hands still fresh on her breasts.

*****

Clay drummed on the Formica desktop in his over-crowded office, trying in vain to erase the memory of Tracy lying naked on his bed. Much as he would have liked to savor the memory of the time they'd shared together - her sweet, fresh-faced innocence, her tender willingness to bare her soul to him, and the feminine mysteries of a body he could spend the rest of his life trying to unravel only to be more intrigued with every attempt - he had no choice but to get down to business. He needed his wits about him like never before if he was going to garner enough votes to gain the controlling vote on the forced sale of Elk Creek Woolen Mills. His holdings alone would not be enough to out-vote his father's controlling interest in Alexander Industries. He desperately needed to rally all the support he could find.

He had to forget about Tracy and focus on the matter at hand. What good would it do to moon over her anyway? Tracy's daughter still hated him. He would not come between them. He should never have stopped at the house in the first place when he'd known she was there alone. Making love to her was an exercise in futility. He had tried his best to dissuade her last week. What the hell was a man supposed to do when a woman was so sweet, so blindly accepting, so eager...

"Paul Eberhart speaking."

Clay sat up straight and jerked to attention. His feet hit the floor. "Hello, Paul. Clay Alexander here. Thanks for taking my call."

"I'm talking to you at all against my better judgment, young man. I'm sure you don't need me to point out to you that it's a hell of a position you're putting me in here."

"We go back a lot of years, Paul."

"Yeah, yeah. And your daddy and I go back a decade further than that."

"I only thought to call you because we've been of like mind on so many issues in the past. I know you of all people have known this was coming. I'd like to know I can count on your vote this Friday." Clay swallowed hard. "We've all known this was just a matter of time."

"All of us except your daddy."

"Then he's been living in a dream world. Hell, Paul. I'm not trying to take over the damn company. I just want my freedom."

"So why not move to Timbuktu and buy a gold mine? Why butt heads with your daddy over an insignificant piece-of-shit company like this woolen mill?"

"This is where I want to settle. I've grown fond of the people in Maple Valley." Clay cleared his throat. "The house I'm renovating holds certain sentimental attachments, and the icing on the cake is that I've already boosted profits at Elk Creek by twenty percent. You know the mill is nothing but a tax write-off to my father. He'll tire of it one day soon and shut the whole place down. He would have closed it down a few months ago if sending me here hadn't been such a convenient way to punish me."

"Your father's a wise man. His decisions have always stood the test of time. He's earned many a man's respect by having an uncanny knack for making the right decision at the right time."

"How could closing the mill ever be the right decision for anyone but my father? This company may be small potatoes to him but the jobs it generates are a major source of this town's sustenance. I won't stand by and see these people get caught up in his vendetta against me."

"Business decisions aren't made using prerogatives like fondness for a house, or even people. Only a fool lets sentiment get in the way of good business sense."

"You know I'm no fool. But this is not just business we're talking about here. It's my life. I know it's all one in the same to my father but I can't live my life the way he has. I've seen what it does to a man." Clay propped the phone to his ear with one elbow and raked his fingers through his hair with the hand that was free. "All I'm asking for is the chance to start making a few of my own decisions. I'm nearing forty, Paul. How will I ever know if I have a knack for business if I don't take control of my own life and start making some of my own damn decisions?"

"Your Daddy's a hard man when it comes to business matters. If you proceed with this he may never welcome you back into the business."

"Or the family." *Especially not if he finds out I've fallen in love with a Republican, ex-minister's wife with three children,* Clay thought to himself. "You think I don't know what's at stake here? Let me assure you that I'm well aware of the risks that are involved and I'm committed to proceeding as planned. Can I count on your support, Paul?"

Not a shred of evidence existed to belie the turmoil Clay felt inside. His voice was firm and unruffled, the silence as he waited for a response, unshakable.

He could hear the older man's sigh over the phone. "I may regret this for the rest of my life, but yes, you'll have my vote come Friday."

"I appreciate that, Paul. I'll do my best to make sure you never regret your decision."

"You damn well better."

Clay left the phone at his ear when Paul had hung up and dialed the next number on the long list of stockholders in front of him. His father and mother combined held forty percent of the stock in Alexander Industries, and Lauren's father, three percent. Clay controlled just twenty-five percent. If only eight percent of the additional stock holders voted with his father, a likelihood that was almost inevitable, Clay could be ousted from the woolen mill before the end of the week, and the doors of the long-stable vestige of Maple Valley's economy closed before Christmas.

*****

Tracy sat parked just outside of the front door of The Fellowship Christian Academy in Rice Lake, Minnesota with both front windows rolled down waiting for Theodora to exit the building. There hadn't been enough time to start another painting project after Clay had stopped by. She'd driven home to shower instead, then proceeded directly to the school to meet Theodora.

The euphoria of being with Clay again made it hard for Tracy to stay focused on anything else. She would have liked to languish in Clay's bed all day, savoring the feelings he had evoked in her, and replaying the memory of his lips moving over her as he touched her.

Stop it! She had no choice but to set aside her fantasies for now. Theodora needed her. And she had decisions to make. She'd mulled over her options all day as she'd worked and again as she'd driven north, not knowing whether to be honest with all of the children now that Theodora knew or whether she could trust her daughter to keep the secret between themselves.

She felt another flash of anger towards Trevor. This was his secret to divulge, his responsibility, his nightmare - not hers. He was the one who should have been here to deal with it.

I mean, who talked to their kids about their sex lives? Tracy would certainly never tell Theodora the truth about her own dabbles with teenage sex - not just with Trevor, but with the two or three other boys she'd dated when Trevor had first gone off to Bible college and seminary. There was no way a mother could answer a child's questions honestly and then tell them not to try the same thing themselves. Theodora would spot that kind of hypocrisy a mile away. No, sometimes a person just had to bend the truth a little.

Sadly, it appeared that there was no longer any way to hide what was going on in Trevor's life. She felt almost ill, trying to decide what to say, thinking about what words she would use and imagining Theodora's reactions.

She was a master at slight of hand living. This being honest about things that she'd been taught not to discuss was the most terrifying thing she'd ever had to do.

Her mind flashed to her oldest sister. Rae and Mac would probably tell Ian he had been conceived before they were married as soon as it was appropriate. She could just imagine the two of them sitting down with him to explain that although they wouldn't recommend he follow the same timetable in his relationships, they were happy God had worked things out to His good in their circumstance.

She knew it was good to talk about things and be up front about what was going on in your life. On the other hand, in some ways, she couldn't help but long for the good old days when everything was swept under the carpet and left alone.

A smattering of children started to filter out the door of the school. She glanced nervously in her rear view mirror. Brooke's mother was waiting behind her in her van. Gloria Adams had known something was wrong that morning when Theodora refused to go to school and missed her ride, so she hadn't seemed surprised when Tracy had pulled up in front of the school and rolled down her window to tell her that she needed to talk to Theodora alone and to ask if the boys could still ride home with her.

Brooke walked out of the building with a close cluster of girls, and a few seconds later, climbed into her mother's van, waving good-bye to her friends. Theodora and Brooke had always been so close. The two girls had spent countless hours playing together even as children and had been inseparable until now.

Tracy's interactions with Gloria and Howard Adams had been awkward and strained since the news about her and Trevor's divorce had come out, just as they had been with everyone else from church. Still, she trusted them implicitly when it came to her daughter's best interests. The Adamses loved Theodora nearly as much as they did their own daughter.

Tracy's eyes met Theodora's the second she exited the massive oak paneled doorway to the lawn. She was walking alone, her head held high, her books clutched tightly to her waist as though they were a shield she wanted to hide behind. She looked away from her mother but continued to walk down the sidewalk towards the car.

Tracy didn't want to embarrass Theodora by getting out of the car so she sat and hoped her daughter would climb in the auto. She did. The door slammed shut after her. Tracy pulled away from the curb before either Titus or Timothy exited the building.

Neither mother nor daughter said a word until they were several blocks from the school.

Tracy looked over at her daughter nervously. "How was school?"

"About as fun as being stuck in a room with thirty people that hate your guts gets."

"They don't hate you, Theodora. Why would you think such a thing?"

"Excuse me," she said sassily. "I guess they act like I have the plague because they like me so much."

"I'm sorry you have to go through this, sweetheart, sorry they're treating you badly because your Dad and I are divorcing. It's not fair. But look at the bright side... by next week they'll have forgotten all about it and moved on to tormenting someone else."

Theodora glowered skeptically from the far side of the seat.

"Just make sure it's not you who's shutting them out, Theodora. Especially not Brooke and the others who really do care about you. Don't punish them just because some of the others are acting immaturely."

"You're the expert on immature behavior," her daughter snipped sullenly.

Tracy tried to ignore her tone but she could feel her heartbeat quicken and a bead of sweat break out on her brow. She couldn't pretend to understand Theodora's behavior or what it would feel like to have learned, as a vulnerable teenager, that your father was gay.

"Theodora – Teddy." Fighting over a silly thing like a nickname suddenly didn't seem worth the energy it took to argue. "I wanted to talk to you alone... um... because... um... it's come to my attention that you overheard a discussion your father and I had last week."

Theodora slid over until she was hugging the door on her side of the car. She gripped the armrest and stared straight ahead. "So she told you. I figured she'd rat on me sooner or later. I guess I can't trust anyone, can I?" she asked dejectedly.

"This is not about Michelle. You know she'd do anything for you."

"Except keep her mouth shut when I ask her to."

"Except sit by and watch you self-destruct. She loves you too much."

Their silence sizzled like a hot ember on the seat between them. Tracy made a sharp left onto a gravel road and drove until they came to a field driveway on the far side of a hedgerow of ash trees. The car was hidden out of view of anyone driving down the highway when she pulled into the dirt lane.

"So it's true?" Theodora's voice squeaked out.

"Yes." Tracy's eyes filled with tears. Her nose was suddenly so stuffed up that she had to breathe through her mouth to keep from hyperventilating.

"He's g-gay?"

"Well, he thinks he'd like to be. He hasn't actually...

there's a big difference... the church he's going to is a place where gay people..." Tracy's voice broke off. Sobs clutched at her side. It always felt so much worse when she had to say it out loud. "I haven't told anyone else except Michelle," Tracy sobbed. "It's still hard... I'm sorry. I didn't mean to... I never wanted you to know."

Theodora looked ill. "I didn't believe it at first."

"Neither did I."

"I have to change schools, Mom. People are going to find out. I can't go there anymore. Please." Her daughter's eyes were haunted with fear.

Her first thought was how immature it was for Theodora's first reaction to be about how her peers would react and not how the truth would affect their family. Then she remembered that she had spent the last two years fretting about what her parents and the people from church would think if they knew, worrying that they would pity her, knowing that she and Trevor would be the cause of tongues wagging all over town, fearing the rejection that would ensue once people found out. How could she expect her daughter to be any less concerned about those things than she was?

"School is something we'll have to consider very carefully when we've all had time to adjust to the changes that are going on in our lives. I won't make any rash decisions now but I will promise to listen to your thoughts and consider your wishes as much as I can when the time is right. Your dad's only a phone call away if you want to talk to him, Teddy."

"I don't think I could. I, I wouldn't know what to say." Her daughter hung her head and looked out the window. "This changes everything."

"Yes, and no." Tracy dabbed at her tears with a napkin she'd found in the glove compartment. "Your Dad's the same person he's always been except for this one thing. And in a very true sense, he's always been gay in his heart. So the only thing that's really changed is that he's decided to be honest about the way he feels."

"So, when he was just a normal father and husband - that was all a lie?" Theodora's lower lip quivered.

"No! He loves you so much, Teddy. The boys, too. That part has never been a lie. Your father has always been as honest as he felt he could be - even in our marriage. I know that being gay is still not regarded as an acceptable lifestyle alternative here in the circles we're part of in Blooming Prairie, but the movement has gained a lot of acceptance on the national level in the past few years. It's still hard to deal with the truth, but you can imagine how scared your dad was to admit his true feelings twenty years ago when no one was openly admitting to being gay."

"So you're saying if our culture hadn't changed so much he might still be here with us and we'd never have found out he was gay?" Theodora sniffled and wiped her eyes with one balled up fist. "Then I wish no one had ever talked about it in the first place or made it okay to be gay because then I'd still have normal parents."

"Oh, sweetheart. A person can't live their life with nothing more than the goal of trying to be normal to guide them," Tracy cautioned. "You have to be true to yourself, and follow your heart no matter what anybody thinks. But I think I know what you mean. There was something comforting about the old days when everyone just stuffed their feelings in a box and did what was expected of them."

She could see Theodora's lips turning up at the corners of her mouth at her statement and decided to continue. "No one had to worry about being honest or saying what you really thought about anything. We all just wanted to fit in so bad that we didn't dare rock the boat."

"Now you sound like Grandma."

Tracy could see her daughter's lips, still slightly upturned. "I was trying to sound like Grandma. I just want you to understand that with the good comes some bad. I've always thought it was a good thing that each new generation was more honest than the last. Kids your age are so much more willing to confront issues and talk about their problems and ideas than the kids from my generation were."

"But then we have to deal with the effects of that honesty."

"Whether we like it or not, the definition of normal will keep getting stretched in all kinds of new directions as time goes by," Tracy said.

"And people will just have to get used to it," Teddy said tentatively.

"If we didn't learn to go with the flow, everybody would be fighting all the time. Not to say that each of us shouldn't still form our own opinions and beliefs and then stand up for what we feel is right."

"Because the Bible says all kinds of bad things about being gay," Teddy said quietly.

"The Bible says all kinds of things are bad. The thing to remember is that we all do things that God says are wrong. Some Christians like to think that they're the ones who get to say which sins are really, really horrible, and which ones are really not all that bad. You know that's not the way it works, right, sweetheart?"

"Yes. So it's okay to love Dad even though I hate what he's doing?"

"Absolutely."

"Because even if somebody is doing something that we don't believe in, we still have to care about them and accept them even though they're different from us. Right?" Teddy asked.

"Churches aren't hotels for saints, they're hospitals for sinners." The space in the car fell silent. "And we're all sinners." Tracy felt tears welling up in her eyes. "I'm very proud of you, Teddy. You've grown up to be a very intelligent, very thoughtful young woman."

There was no response from the other side of the car.

"Is there anything else we need to talk about, sweetheart?"

The silence that followed was ominously long.

"No."

Tracy swallowed nervously. "I'd like to be able to tell your Dad that you know. He wanted to tell you all but I thought it would be best... Whether I was right or wrong in insisting he keep the truth from you, I'd still like it if you wouldn't tell anyone else, especially not the boys, at least until I've had a chance to talk to your father and decide when and how to tell them. Is that okay with you?"

Theodora sighed deeply and looked away. "I guess so."

Tracy could feel her daughter retreating back into the impenetrable shell of hostility she'd wrapped herself in for the past few days. She was helpless to stop it.

"Your dad will want to talk to you. I hope you will when you feel ready."

Silence.

"Now that we've talked I'm sure Michelle would be happy to talk to you, too. If you need someone else to confide in."

"I guess so."

"I promise not to put any perimeters on what she can discuss with you this time. When I asked her to keep my confidence before I never dreamed that it would get in the way of your relationship with her. I never intended that. I know what the two of you have is very special."

Teddy fiddled with the hem of her blouse. "Used to be. When I was younger, you weren't very close to her. She seemed more like my friend than your sister. Now that you guys are working together..." Theodora sighed deeply.

"A lot of things are changing all at once. It's been hard for me, too."

"We better get home before Titus starts teasing Timothy or it's going to be a long night. Without me there to referee, the little brat's probably already in tears."

Tracy laughed out loud in spite of herself. She looked over her shoulder before backing the car out of the field driveway and on to the road, shifted into first gear, and headed south for Blooming Prairie.

Chapter 21

The first thing Clay planned to do when and if the office he'd been occupying at Elk Creek Woolen Mills was officially his was to buy some new file cabinets. Some modern track lights would do wonders. And if Tracy would paint the walls...

He definitely needed something – or someone - to cheer him up. The walls suddenly looked so dingy and lack-luster, the cabinets so dull and worn that he knew he couldn't stand the dreary, closed in office for another moment without laying plans to remedy the situation.

He felt quite confident that the next board member on his list would side with him. Jonathan Fitzgerald was only five years older than Clay. They'd been neighbors and played together as boys. Jonathan had inherited his stock in Alexander Industries when his father had died of a sudden, massive heart attack two years earlier.

"It's great to hear your voice, Clay." Jonathan greeted him enthusiastically.

"Yours, too. I'm sorry I haven't been at the club much lately. I think that tennis match we talked about last spring is long overdue."

"It's never too late to reschedule. You and Lauren should join Sandy and me for brunch one day."

"I'd like that," Clay said. "Lauren and I have gone our separate ways, but if don't mind just me..." When he was growing up, Jonathan had been like the older brother he'd never had.

"We're always happy to see you, Clay. Sorry about you and Lauren."

Clay asked about Jonathan and Sandy's children and they chatted pleasantly for several minutes before Clay broached the subject of his plans to take over Elk Creek

Woolen Mills.

Jonathan didn't respond as he'd anticipated from the start. Instead of being persuaded by Clay's arguments, Jonathan's reticence grew more apparent with every word that passed between them.

"I'm going to give you some advice, Clay," Jonathan finally said.

"Okay," Clay said, not knowing what to expect.

"The only person I know who's more controlling and dictatorial than my father was is yours."

"You think you're telling me something I don't already know?"

"What you don't know is that five, ten, or twenty years from now, when he's dead, you'll look back on these supposedly huge differences you had and realize how trivial they were."

"But-" Clay started to say.

"I'd give anything in the world to be able to tell my Dad how much I respected him," Jonathan said. "You're his son. He's going to do things that piss you off. You're going to have disagreements. But if you sever the cord you'll regret it for the rest of your life."

"I do respect him," Clay said. "But I can't stand by and let him close Elk Creek Woolen Mills just to spite me. There's too much at stake, too many people who would be hurt."

"I'm sorry, Clay. I love you like a brother and I'd like to help you out – I really would. But I won't cross your father."

Clay hung up the phone fifteen minutes later, his spirit shaken and his hopes dashed. He had only one more person to call, and he knew that his chances of succeeding with Stan Carlson were almost nil.

He dialed the last number and was promptly put on hold. He tried to stretch his legs out under his desk and tried to think positive thoughts. He'd already waited almost five minutes, a portent he didn't take as a good sign. The bastard was probably hoping he'd get frustrated and hang up. Well, annoyed as he was, he'd be damned before he'd let another of his father's lackeys off the hook.

This was more than some damn pissing contest. If he wasn't successful in securing Stan Carlson's vote he'd fall short of the shares he needed to buy Elk Creek by one stupid percent. He was so close. He'd spent the whole week working his way down the list of Alexander Industries stockholders, calling them one by one to plead his case. He'd used every argument imaginable to try to convince his father's business associates that his plan was economically sound. He'd done everything but grovel. Fine, he'd done that, too.

Unfortunately, only a handful of the stockholders had been willing to go against his father no matter how convincing Clay had been or how much sense his proposal had made.

Stan was his last and only hope. There was no other way to save the mill. His father was adamant in his desire to squelch Clay's show of independence by closing the factory. His mother had taken to her bed again and wouldn't accept his calls. It was a given Lauren's father would never cross his long time friend, Barclay Alexander II, in favor of the rogue who had just dumped his precious daughter.

His only hope lay in convincing Stan Carlson to vote his way.

Clay cleared his throat nervously and stared up at the ceiling. An old rust colored water stain spread across the far corner of the office, no doubt the result of an old roof leak or burst radiator. He shook his head. Maybe he was as big a fool as his father claimed he was. Despite his recent attempts to upgrade and modernize Elk Creek's products, colors, and styles, the equipment at the mill was as outmoded as the office itself, the factory so far from being equipped for the twenty-first century it was laughable.

Clay heard his adversary's sigh over his end of the telephone line before the other gentleman uttered a word. He straightened involuntarily in his chair and waited for his father's friend and business associate of thirty years to speak.

"This had better be important, young man," the older

man said tersely. "I was in the middle of a very important meeting." The irritation in his voice was unmistakable.

"Thank you for taking the time to speak to me, Stan." Clay tried his best to mask his cynicism. The call was pointless and he knew it. But he had to try. He wouldn't be able to live with himself if he didn't try every option he could think of.

"I'm calling in reference to the proposal I submitted in regard to the purchase of Elk Creek Woolen Mills. I think you'll find the price I've offered to be more than generous given current market conditions, and the terms of the sale decidedly advantageous to Alexander Industries. I'd like to know I can count on your vote come Friday."

"You can stop wasting your breath right there, young man. Your daddy's beat you to the punch. Called me last night at home. My money and my vote are on him."

"Did my father mention that he plans to close the mill? Or that his chosen course of action will result not only in a major loss of revenue for Alexander Industries, but that three hundred people will be put out of work, a move that will likely send a town the size of Maple Valley into an economic tailspin?"

"No, he didn't." The man snorted. "He didn't have to. Your father knows I trust his business acumen implicitly. Damn it, Barclay, even you can't be so naive as to think that your father's decisions have never put people out of work before. And you know damn well that taking a calculated loss for any number of reasons is standard practice in the business world.

"Your father deals in life changing commodities on a daily basis. If he wasted his time fretting about each and every man, woman, and child who was going to be affected in some small way by the decisions he makes..." The man guffawed loudly. "Well, quite simply put, chaos would prevail. You've got to start looking at the big picture, son. The big picture." The older man laughed loudly, obviously of the mind set that the situation was somehow amusing.

Amusing as hell. Clay closed his eyes and moaned. He

rolled his eyes and looked heavenward. It was hopeless. He'd taken his best shot and he'd failed.

"I appreciate your concerns, Stan." Clay's voice broke as the full implications of his failure to win the man over started to sink in. "But I still intend to purchase Elk Creek Woolen Mills. If you reconsider, you know where to reach me."

He could hear Stan Carlson's chuckles fading into the distance as he placed the telephone back on the receiver. Damn! He pounded his fist against the desk. Damn it all.

*****

Tracy followed Theodora in to the house and put the mail on the kitchen table. The boys had obviously arrived home ahead of them - an open jar of peanut butter, a half empty bag of Wonder bread and a dirty knife littered the kitchen counter like debris left strewn behind a storm. Although Titus and Timothy were nowhere in sight, the sound of the television blaring from the lower level provided a blatant clue to their whereabouts.

"Hello!" Tracy called down the stairs. "Homework done already?" Her children all knew the rules about not watching television until their chores and schoolwork were done. "There are leaves that need to be raked before it gets dark. If you hurry we can make a bonfire and roast marshmallows after supper."

She heard the click of the TV being turned off a second before Titus bounded up the stairs. "Mom. You're home early."

"Surprised?" Tracy smiled smugly.

"I was working on my homework down in the rec room," Titus claimed. "Timothy must have turned on the TV. I guess I was concentrating so hard that I didn't even notice."

His guilty-looking attempt at a smile betrayed the truth of the matter even before she spotted the stack of schoolbooks he'd tossed on the kitchen table before retreating to the basement.

"Sure, Titus. Doing research for a project on the *Flintstone's*? Where's your little brother?"

"Asleep on the davenport in the basement. He was out like a light the second his head hit the pillow."

Tracy's eyebrows arched upward. She'd heard Timothy tossing and turning in the middle of the night for the past few- well, ever since Trevor had left for California. Her heart skipped a beat. Her poor baby. How could he possibly understand why his daddy would leave them for a place halfway across the continent? He was only five years old.

She made a mental note to be sure she snuggled with him and read him a bedtime story. He probably had questions and she'd been so busy - so preoccupied with her own concerns, moving, and Theodora that she'd hardly-

"Do I still have to put the chicken in the oven since you're home early?" Theodora's voice interrupted her thoughts. "Staci said I could work on my science project over at her house tonight."

Staci doesn't live in a house. It's a trailer sitting on cement blocks in the middle of a trailer park. Tracy struggled to keep her thoughts to herself "What's your project about? Couldn't you work on it better here where you have all the things you need?"

Her suggestion was met by a blank stare.

"I'm assuming you'll need some materials or the encyclopedias or the internet for research. You're welcome to invite Staci over here if she wants to help you."

Theodora looked at her mother like she was a complete idiot. The telephone rang just as Tracy heard her mutter something about having to put up with the brat brigade. She reached for the phone. In the second it took her to reach for the receiver, her daughter disappeared, the screen door left to slam against its frame in her wake. She caught one quick glimpse of Titus bounding stealthily back downstairs to the basement.

"Teddy! Titus!"

"Tracy, is that you?" The familiar voice cut her off in

mid sentence.

"Mom?"

"Is something wrong? Is Theodora going somewhere? I thought you didn't allow her to go out on school nights."

"She's just going over to a friend's house to work on a science project."

"Someone she knows from church?"

"Well, not exactly." Tracy feigned a cough. "Did you need something, Mom? I was about to get supper going for the boys."

"You sound like you're coming down with a cold, sweetheart. Your father and I worry that you're not taking care of yourself with all this running back and forth to Maple Valley every day. It just seems to us that you should be at home with the children right now. I'm sure you all miss Trevor terribly. Wouldn't it be easier for all of you-"

"I'm fine, Mom. The kids are only alone for an hour or two after school until I get home from work."

"Yes, but how can you spend any time with them when you've got to fix supper, get groceries, do the laundry, iron, and pack their lunches for the next day all in one short evening? When you three girls were growing up I worked hard to finish my chores before you got home from school so I was free to help you with your homework, enjoy a leisurely dinner with the whole family, and relax in the evenings."

"I know, Mom, and I wish things could be that way here, but I have to work right now. Michelle's given me a great opportunity to earn the money I need to pay the bills until Trevor gets his first pay check."

Tracy stopped and caught her breath. Trevor had a lot of expenses right now, too. She hated being dependent on him. She had no qualms about letting him pay for the children's schooling and clothes, but she wanted to be able to pay her own way financially. "I really have no choice but to work right now. The kids have been great about pitching in and helping around the house. We're getting along just fine."

"Well, you know I don't like driving much once winter comes, but I would be happy to come up to Blooming Prairie every night until it snows to help you catch up on some laundry and take care of the kids until you get home from work. I could make up some casseroles and put them in the freezer so all you'd have to do when you get home is-"

"No, Mom, please. We need to get used to being on our own. This is the way it's going to be from now on. There's no sense putting off the inevitable. It won't hurt the kids to become a little more self-sufficient and help with things around the house, and I'll learn to juggle my time like a million other working mothers do every day. We'll be fine."

Tracy stretched the telephone cord over to the stove and used one hand to open the oven door. She went to the refrigerator and took out a pan of cream chicken she'd assembled the night before and carefully placed it in the oven, her mother's voice fading in and out of one ear as she went about her work. All she had to do now was to add the milk to the dry biscuit ingredients and drop the dough on top of the casserole when it was hot.

She started to shuffle through the mail she'd laid on the countertop a few minutes prior while she continued to talk. "No, Mom, Trevor hasn't decided he misses me and no, he doesn't want me to move to California."

Her mother dismissed her protestations like it was only a matter of time. "Not to worry, darling. All men may think they want their freedom at some point in their lives but it doesn't take long before they tire of having to do for themselves and start to appreciate all the little things a woman does for them around the house. You mark my word, Trevor will get sick of TV dinners and having to iron his own shirts before long. If there's one thing we women can count on in this life it's that men need us around for more than one thing!"

Tracy sighed. If she was alluding to the fact that Trevor would miss her in bed, well, Tracy knew better than that, but she certainly couldn't tell her mother the truth of that situation.

Her fingers flew through the pile of mail as she listened, sorting the bills into one pile and the magazines and catalogs into another. She propped the phone into the crook of her neck and started to tear open the envelopes one by one. Utilities. That one would go to the church. She put the telephone bill into a second stack of bills she had to pay herself. She turned the next envelope over without looking at the front, ran her finger under the flap to open it, and pulled the single piece of paper from its cocoon, assuming it was another bill.

Dear Trevor, the letter began. She should have refolded it and returned it to its envelope immediately. She knew that. She flipped the envelope over and looked at it more closely. It was addressed to Rev. Trevor Tomlinson. But it was already open. Trevor would think she'd read it even if she hadn't. If she was going to get blamed for it, she may as well do it. She let her eyes roam over the first few sentences while her mother droned on.

Dear Trevor, I know you told me that it wouldn't be safe to contact you at this address but I've tried calling the work number you gave me repeatedly over the past two weeks and have not been able to reach you. Four years have passed since we met at the Minister's Conference in Tulsa, but I still think of you often, and didn't want to lose touch. I am getting ready to move and wanted to inform you of my new address in hopes that our paths will cross again one day.

Tracy clutched the letter in one hand. "Mom, I really have to go right now if I'm going to have everything ready in time for supper."

"Oh, that reminds me." Her mother laughed. "I almost forgot to tell you the reason I called."

Tracy moaned silently.

"A friend of mine from church who lives in Hayfield is looking for someone to repaint and paper her living room, dining room, and kitchen. I told her I thought you'd be done with the house down in Maple Valley in another week or so. She was delighted to hear you might be available."

An irrational wave of nervousness gripped at Tracy's

stomach. She needed another job. That was certain. And it really was sweet of her mother to have recommended her to her friend. But the thought of working without the comforting umbrella of Michelle's expertise and professional confidence to shelter her left her petrified.

"I still don't like you working at all, Tracy, but Hayfield is three times as close as Maple Valley and Myrtle said she wouldn't mind if you only worked until three o'clock so you could be home when the children got out of school."

"Thanks, Mom." Tracy hurriedly scribbled down the woman's name, address, and phone number. The letter to Trevor lay unread but not forgotten on the countertop.

"I'll talk to you later then, sweetheart," her mother said. "Remember what I said about church. I still think you'd feel more comfortable attending down here until this whole situation with Trevor is resolved."

The situation with Trevor is resolved, Tracy wanted to remind her. But she kept quiet. Contrary to what Rachael had always assumed, it did no good to argue with their mother.

"I don't want the kids to miss Sunday School just because it's awkward for them to go to church in Blooming Prairie."

"I understand what you're saying, Mom. We'll talk to you soon. Bye for now!"

The forced cheeriness in her tone did nothing to dispel the dreadful sense of foreboding that was chasing her stomach around in circles. She remembered well the minister's conference Trevor had attended at Tulsa. She had always gone to conferences with him - their trips had been an excuse to leave the children with Grandma and Grandpa and be Trevor and Tracy instead of Mom and Dad or Pastor and Mrs. Tomlinson.

She had always looked forward to their conferences, from socializing with other couples who regarded them as peers and not religious icons, to the inspirational music and messages, to going off to shop with the other wives while the men were in meetings. But most of all, she had loved spending time alone with Trevor without constantly being interrupted by the children, her parents, or an emergency phone call from a parishioner.

But this time, Trevor had insisted he go alone. Tracy's lip trembled. She hadn't known that Trevor was gay yet when he'd suddenly announced that he wanted to go to Tulsa by himself. She had been very hurt that he hadn't wanted her to come along.

She spread the letter out flat on the countertop and continued to read, feeling many emotions, not one of them guilt.

I have always believed that the random stroke of fate that resulted in us ending up as roommates that weekend was actually the hand of God at work in our lives, Trevor's friend continued. *I can imagine what you must think of my theory in light of what happened between us that weekend, but before you toss my letter in the trash, please let me explain.*

Tracy gripped the countertop and read on.

I know you probably still believe that what happened between the two of us that night was a grievous sin. I, too, have questioned whether either of us was really ready for a physical dalliance yet at that time. But what we did that night changed my life. Honestly expressing my physical passions for another man for the first time gave me the courage to be honest with my family and friends, to embrace the gay lifestyle and to seek out a ministry among gay men and women in the Dallas/Fort Worth area in which I am still actively involved.

Tracy fought back waves of nausea.

Because of you, I'm finally living a lifestyle true to my heart as well as to my beliefs. At the risk of incurring your judgment, I must also confess that I am living with a man who has become very dear to me. I pray you will be happy for me, Trevor. I owe you a world of thanks for being the catalyst by which I first realized and admitted my gay leanings. I will close with one last thought: nothing is worse than living a lie. Yes, being honest with my family was difficult, and being asked to leave the parish I had served for seven years was devastating. But nothing I've endured has been as bad as the day to day deceitfulness involved living a lie.

Tracy's hands shook at the realization that Trevor had been unfaithful to her. He had lied to her. She had accepted his explanation without question when he had told her why he made married and had children with her. But to know that Trevor had slept with a man, then made love to her again at least once or twice before finally admitting he was gay - the thought sickened and infuriated her.

For the first time since Trevor's admission, hate welled up inside her. Trevor had used her one too many times. She had been nothing but a pawn in his grand plan to hide his homosexuality. She had given him her life and her love, and he had used her to convince his family and peers that he was a man with a normal lust for women. Tracy laid her head down on the countertop beside the bowl of biscuit mix and a half-empty carton of milk and wept.

Chapter 22

The door to Clay's office was closed but the glass walls surrounding his cubicle of space left little room for privacy. He couldn't curse. He couldn't rant or rave. They were watching, turning their heads in cursory glances as they walked by, changed shifts, went to, and returned from breaks.

He sat at his desk and stared blankly at a paper, shuffling inanely through a stack of memos just often enough to allay suspicions that he was doing nothing, that the neat, orderly little world he had wanted for himself in the town of Maple Valley wasn't crumbling down around him.

He felt numb and defeated. The bitterness would come later - perhaps when he had to say good-bye to the employees and managers he had come to respect so greatly over the past few months, or when he had to put his house on the market, pack up his things, and leave town for lack of any purpose to stay.

He had failed. It was over. He could only hope his father would leave the factory open until after Christmas. He couldn't stand the thought of the dedicated staff and crew who worked at Elk Creek Woolen Mills being put out of work only a few weeks before Christmas. With the busy fall and holiday season upon them, the only reason his father could have for closing the mill before business slowed down in the spring was spite, pure and simple.

His lethargy was interrupted by a knock at the door to his office. Clay rose from his desk and crossed the short space to the door. A cluster of floor managers, all three with grim faces and letters clutched in their hands, stood half visible through the glass partition. His stomach sank.

The stockiest of the three, a woman, was the first to speak. "Mr. Alexander, sorry to bother you, but, um, we thought you ought to know that someone was just down from corporate headquarters and put one of these letters in everyone's mailbox."

He knew without asking what the letters were. His worst nightmare come to life.

"Says here the factory will be closing in two weeks," the second, a man, spoke up in an accusing tone. "That after working here for over twenty year, we got two lousy weeks to find another job."

"Yeah. They say that they'll be happy to give us letters of recommendation upon request. Now ain't that just dandy. They lay me off after nineteen years and I have to make a long distance phone call to request a damn letter of recommendation for my file," another man, the taller, leaner of the three, spoke up.

Clay's head reeled back as though he'd been slapped. "I'm sorry," he stammered. "As I told you last week, I've been doing everything in my power to avoid this very situation. I know that's small consolation when you're the ones standing there holding letters terminating your employment."

Clay ran his fingers through his hair in a disconcerted effort to think. The managers stared at him expectantly. They were counting on him. Their futures, the future health of this community, and the welfare of each family represented here was in his hands. He could not, would not let them down.

"My father had no right to issue these letters until Friday's stockholder meeting when the vote has been tabulated," Clay said decisively. "I'm not finished yet. Disregard the letters. Let your people know that no word is final until Monday. I won't lie to you and tell you there's no cause for concern. But if and when there are any layoffs to be made, I'll be the one to inform you." He looked behind the three managers to the crowd that had gathered in the secretary's office to their rear, each face etched with concern. "Until such time, I want everyone here working at top capacity. We're not done fighting yet!"

A murmur of voices rose from the congregation of workers in the foyer. The woman in the front row shook his hand. "We're counting on you, Mr. Alexander. I've got two kids in college and two more still at home. Johnson here just got married three months ago. He just bought a house and his wife's expecting. None of us has ever been on unemployment a day in our lives, nor our daddies before us. I can't afford to lose this job and neither can they."

"I'll do my best, Karen. I promise you all I'll do my best." Clay shook hand after hand as the crowd thinned out. They approached him one by one, their eyes locking with his in a silent plea for his success. He saw tears in some, fear in others, a tinge of resentment in a few. It was his father that was closing the mill. The company his family had owned for three generation that had betrayed them.

"Don't worry, Gladys," he assured an older woman who had worked at the mill for over two decades. "I promise you I'll find a way to keep the doors open."

His mind leaped from one possibility to another, working furiously to find some previously untried solution. A brave, determined smile lit his face. But God help him, he couldn't think of anything he hadn't already tried. He'd begged, pleaded, and cajoled everyone on the list. Everyone but Lauren's father.

Clay sighed. He knew Mr. Humphreys well. Well enough to know that unless he made good on his original intent to marry Lauren, there'd be no talking to the man. He was as arrogant a man as he'd ever known. In fact, Clay had fully expected to hear from him immediately upon his hearing the news of Clay's decision to break off his and Lauren's *engagement*. It wasn't Mr. Humphreys' style to sit back and do nothing when the happiness and well-being of one of his family was threatened.

"Hold my calls for the rest of the day," Clay instructed his secretary when the crowd had finally dispersed. "And put out a memo to all the employees telling them to disregard the notices they received earlier today. I'm going to do whatever it takes to keep this factory open." Clay clenched his teeth in a foreboding grimace.

*****

Tracy tossed and turned in her bed, the sheets wrapped around her like an octopus' tentacles. An unwelcome stream of sunshine speared into her bedroom window from either side of the inexpensive mini blind she'd purchased years earlier at the five and dime.

She'd hardly slept a wink for visions of Trevor and the man he'd met in Tulsa (doing things she could only imagine) floating through her head. She had tried not to think about it, tried to forget that a man she had thought was her loving, dedicated, and faithful husband had made himself at home inside the most private parts of her body after he had betrayed her with a man.

She'd trusted Trevor to be honest with her. It was the one thing she had always felt sure about, that Trevor had been absolutely and totally honest with her, that he would never ever lie to her. And now she knew that he had.

She had to assume he had lied to her about other things to. Wondering which of their life's events he had falsified and to what extent he had gone to cover up the truth shook her to her very core. The only way she had managed to deal with this whole humiliating episode to date was to believe that Trevor was telling her the truth - that he was only inclined towards homosexuality, and not a practicing gay.

Now that she knew differently, how could she possibly believe that he and Kurt weren't sharing a bed? And even if that had been the case at first, how long would their good intentions keep them from consummating their attraction for each other?

It's none of your business, she tried to remind herself. Her and Trevor's lives were going in separate directions. That was what divorcing meant. Trevor would be free to do whatever he wanted with whomever he wanted and there wasn't a damn thing she could do about it.

"Mommy?" Timothy's voice cut through her reverie like a bolt of lightning. "Can I come snuggle?"

Oh, Lord. What if there had been others? Did she need to be tested for HIV? A shock ran the length of her body.

She held out her arms to Timothy and patted the empty pillow beside her.

He snuggled sleepily into her outstretched arms and laid his tousled head on her breast. Love welled up in her heart as she petted her youngest child's head absently, tears overflowing her eyes. She had to stop being so naïve, so gullible. She'd been stupid to trust Trevor – and Clay.

How could she have? What had she done?

She'd not only bared her soul to Clay, she'd given him the most intimate parts of her body. She'd given him the gift of her self. The private thoughts and hopes and aspirations that she so rarely shared with anyone were already his. She could not take back the intimacy they had shared.

Doubts and fears crashed over her like waves on a rocky shoreline.

A simple blood test would buy her peace of mind and solve the newest of her problems where Trevor was concerned.

But with Clay... Clay had never even called her on the phone, taken her out to dinner, or eaten a meal with her. He had never watched the sun set while holding her hand or seen where she lived. She had made love to him with her whole heart and mind and soul. He had not even called her the next morning to tell her she was beautiful. Tracy started to quiver. Timothy had gone back to sleep. She clutched a clump of twisted bedclothes in her hand and tried to steady herself, tried to stop shaking. And couldn't.

She needed the truth from Clay - what she was to him, what their lovemaking had meant to him, why he had sought her out a second time, then left without a word. She needed the truth, no matter how painful it might be.

*****

The sun was rising over the hills framing Maple Valley when Clay glided into the parking lot at Elk Creek Woolen Mills. A few stubborn patches of fog still clung to the river, valleys, and ditches. The air felt heavy and humid despite the slight breeze that was beginning to chase the low-lying clouds from their hiding places.

Clay flicked the long, heavy door of his sports car closed with one quick motion and strode the short distance from his parking space to the front door. The lobby was open. He used his key to access the inner offices - at least his father hadn't sent in a locksmith to change the locks.

He could hear the low drone of the knitting machines immediately upon unlocking the door to the floor, the clatter of the guillotine like device that cut the threads, and the occasional voice of a third shift manager shouting instructions over the din.

He went directly to his telephone. He wouldn't have been so presumptuous as to call most people at this hour, but he knew the habits of this person well.

The phone rang twice before it was answered by a member of the staff whose voice he didn't recognize. Probably just as well that it wasn't someone who knew him. He had failed to acknowledge the possibility that the servants might have been instructed not to take his calls.

Clay identified himself in a curt voice. There was no sense pretending this call was anything other than what it was... a desperate, last ditch effort to save Elk Creek Woolen Mills by selling his soul.

"I'm sorry, Mr. Alexander," the staff member informed him courteously, "but he and the Mrs. are still in Europe. They won't be back for another two weeks. If it's imperative that you speak to them immediately I can check their itinerary. I'm sure the concierge at their hotel in Munich would be happy to leave them a message."

"Thank you, but that won't be necessary," Clay interrupted her. He knew this couple almost as well as he knew his own parents. More importantly, he knew who held their proxy when they were out of the country.

Clay took a deep breath. If he was going to deal with the devil, he might as well jump in with both feet. He let Tracy's face float in front of his eyes for one poignant second. And then he asked to speak to Lauren.

*****

The sound of the paint roller swishing up and over the wall of the southeast corner bedroom was almost mesmerizing. Tracy was glad she had cut in around the white, painted window and door frames the afternoon before, an exacting art that required at least minimal concentration. Her mind was elsewhere today.

Preoccupied as she was, it was probably a good thing that she had a relatively mindless task to perform. There was something almost soothing about the repetitive motion of rolling out the denim-blue colored walls.

She was finishing the east corner bedroom. Michelle was priming the master bathroom suite. Tracy had made up an excuse about getting twice as much done in half the time if they split up and attacked the job on two different fronts, but really, she'd just needed some time alone to unravel the tangled web that had become her life. And she hadn't wanted to go anywhere near the master suite.

She squinted against the glare of the sunshine. The splotches of sunshine and shadows filtering in through the maple trees made it difficult to focus. Her eyes were so tired.

Her eyes were so blinded by the light that she didn't even see Rae and Michelle when they first entered the room.

Her first thought was that they had found out about her and Clay and had come to do an intervention.

"I asked Rae to stop by because I have the quilt from Aunt Thelma I was telling you about last week. The one she left to the three of us in her will," Michelle said. "I thought if we could decide together who gets to keep it, one of us might as well be enjoying it."

Okay, so she was feeling a little paranoid.

"No sense leaving it in a sack in the basement for all eternity," Rae said, her cynical look implying that that was probably exactly where it belonged.

Tracy smiled in spite of herself. This time, she was actually inclined to side with Rae. Michelle claimed the quilt was pretty, but with Michelle, that could mean anything. Michelle would never speak ill of anyone, especially the dead.

If Aunt Thelma was anything like their mother, the quilt was probably made from scraps of polyester double knit left over from the seventies that she couldn't bear to part with because they were so good and warm. It could have been orange, purple and chartreuse and Michelle still would have found something nice to say about it.

Rae looked bored and just as skeptical as Tracy. "So why didn't she just make a quilt for each of us?" Rae said. "Or just pick one of us. I mean, what are we supposed to do – cut the thing in thirds?"

"A lady from our church used to take old quilts and make teddy bears out of them. If we did something like that, we could each have something to remember her by," Tracy said.

Rae gave her a withering look.

"Aunt Thelma loved us like we were the children she never had. She never missed one of our birthdays in all of her 93 years," Michelle said.

Well, Michelle was right about that, Tracy acknowledged, feeling a pang of guilt that she hadn't been better about visiting Aunt Thelma.

And then, Michelle pulled the quilt out of the bag.

Rae jerked to attention and sat with her mouth gaping. "It's beautiful."

Michelle flicked the quilt open with a snap of her wrists and Tracy blinked as the pattern took shape. The pastel colors gleamed like prisms in the sunlight, swirling to a pinwheel in the center like a merry-go-round twirling round and round.

"Isn't it beautiful?" Michelle asked dreamily.

If the look in her eyes was any indication, she already had an entire room decorated around the color theme.

"I know you're not a fan of pastels, Rae. But I wanted you to at least see the quilt. Both of you. I mean, it wouldn't have been right of me just to assume that I, I mean, because

I've been the one who's been in touch with Aunt Thelma all these years."

"What were her instructions again?" Rae said, looking like an eagle that had just spotted a rabbit in a field.

"That it was up to the three of us to decide who got the quilt."

"I love the colors," Tracy said, trying to be subtle.

"Well, since there's no clear cut way to decide, I suppose since I'm the oldest daughter of the oldest daughter of the oldest daughter of the oldest daughter – isn't it seven generations now?" Rae said, obviously having the same thoughts she was. "That I should take it."

I should take it? Really. Like it was some sort of duty on her part. Yeah, right. Rae wanted that quilt.

"It's actually eight," Tracy said. "But Theodora is the oldest daughter of the next generation, so shouldn't she have it? I mean, if you really want to continue with the tradition of things being passed down to the oldest daughter."

"So I'll leave it to her in my will," Rae said.

"Right," Tracy said. "By that time, Ian will be married, and his wife will have decorated her whole bedroom around the quilt, and you're going to say, 'Oops! Sorry! Give it to Theodora. I promised.' Except you won't be around to tell them it's Theodora's because you'll be dead."

"I don't mean to sound self-righteous," Michelle said, "but I wrote Auntie Thelma a letter almost every week the whole time I lived in Colorado. Since I moved back here, I've visited her at least once a month. Did either of you ever go to see her?"

"I know I took by each of the kids when they were babies," Tracy said, figuring she still had Rae beat by a mile.

"If you were so close to her, why didn't she just give it to you?" Rae said to Michelle.

"Maybe because she wasn't one to play favorites," Michelle said. "Not that you'd know."

"I knew the two of you would turn on each other one of these days," Tracy said, feeling very, very smug. "And listen to you! Rae, you have the rainbow quilt – the one and only quilt Grandma Jones made before she died."

"Which should tell you something," Rae said. "Grandma Jones would never have done something as ridiculous as leaving one quilt to three sisters. The woman had favorites and wasn't afraid to admit it."

"And you were it," Tracy said.

Rae just smiled.

"Michelle, you have that gorgeous doll quilt that Grandma Maddie made for you when you were ten, and the water lily quilt Sarah MacKenzie Anderson made for you before she died," Tracy said, for once, not afraid to stand up for herself.

"And you have the quilt Fellowship Church made for you and Trevor when they celebrated your ten year anniversary of serving the church," Rae said. "Mom gushed about it for weeks."

"Trevor took it to California," Tracy said. "Like I would have wanted to sleep under *it* for the rest of my life."

"So I'm not allowed to have two quilts?" Rae said.

"I'm the one who's trying to make a new start here," Tracy said. "I'm going to be moving into a new house, starting over from scratch. As fate would have it, I threw my old sheets, pillowcases and bedspread in the dumpster this morning. I had to. Anything that Trevor touched in that house just fills me with revulsion right now. Can you understand that?"

Michelle nodded. "I certainly can."

"Soft-hearted, Michelle," Rae said scornfully. "You always were a pushover."

"I am not," Michelle said, with an unaccustomed show of anger. "All I'm saying is that I understand how Tracy feels. I still think I should get the quilt. I helped Aunt Thelma pick out the colors. She bought the fabric at the Painted Lady. I recommended a woman to do the quilting when she finished piecing it and didn't feel like she had the energy to finish it herself."

"Fine," Rae said, usurping control. "Here it is in a nutshell. All three of us want the quilt. All three of us were equally related to Aunt Thelma. As the oldest, it falls to me to make a decision that I think is fair to everyone, and I've decided we stick to tradition. I'm the oldest daughter, so I get the quilt. I'll give it to Theodora on her wedding day."

Tracy turned and looked out the window. What was wrong with her anyway? She hadn't even thought about getting a new quilt until she'd seen the thing. Then suddenly, one look later, she felt like she couldn't live without it.

There were plenty of old blankets in the linen closet at the parsonage that were perfectly fine. But there was something about that quilt. The design, the colors... just one look, one taste, and the quilt had called out to her, touched her heart - as though it had been pieced together with her in mind. Why she felt so strongly about it, she didn't understand, but she knew it, just like she knew that Clay Alexander had been made for her, and only her.

A few minutes later, Rae left with the quilt. And there wasn't one damn thing she could do about it.

Chapter 23

After Rae left, Michelle resumed what she had been doing and Tracy started rolling again.

Forget about the quilt. *You didn't even know it existed until a few minutes ago*, she reminded herself. Besides, she had plenty of other things to worry about.

"Hi again," Michelle poked her head around the corner, the angst over the quilt already fading from her eyes. "I just finished priming the walls in the bathroom. Between old walls and new walls and patches and seams, it looked like a crazy quilt in there until I got the first coat on. Come see how smooth the walls look now."

Tracy had to smile. In the short time since Michelle had relocated from Colorado to Iowa, she had come to be regarded as one of the best interior designers in the whole Midwest. She had routinely masterminded projects whose budgets totaled in the hundreds of thousands of dollars. To think she could find such simple, childlike pleasure in the transformation of a mere wall, and a piecemeal one at that. Tracy admired her attitude greatly but did not attempt to put her feelings into words.

But she couldn't help chuckling as she laid the paint roller in the tray and followed her sister. She tried not to wince as she walked into the master suite. She had been so euphoric after they'd been together that she hadn't even noticed that Clay hadn't called or stopped by to see her again. And then - as time had passed - seeing the bed where they had lain together was just too painful.

She forced herself to ignore the bed, now stripped of its sheets and covered with a drop cloth, and looked towards the newly added glass blocks Michelle was so excited about.

The opalescent half wall shimmered in the morning light. Sunshine streamed through the thick, teal-hued squares and glinted off the reflection of a shiny new Jacuzzi for two.

Ceramic tiled steps led the way to the slightly raised platform. It had been Michelle's idea to open up two rooms to make a master suite large enough to accommodate the new whirlpool for two.

"It was a stroke of genius on your part to put a Jacuzzi in the bay," Tracy admitted admiringly. Michelle needed a pat on the back, and it was only fair Tracy give credit where credit was due. Her sister knew nothing of what had transpired just a few feet from where they were standing, had no way of knowing the flood of emotions that were sweeping over Tracy.

Her older sister blushed at her compliment like a school girl. "I could see it in my mind's eye all along, but now it finally looks the way I envisioned it. Don't you love it?"

She remembered the passion she'd felt as she'd lain with Clay and shivered with trepidation wondering when - or if - she would see him again. She felt a sickening premonition that she'd made an utter fool of herself... again.

"Yes," Tracy stuttered. "It's perfect. You did a great job."

"You don't think it minimizes the original appeal of the room or detracts from the builder's intent?"

"No! The tiny room you sacrificed was too cramped and dark to be usable anyway. I know you wanted to stay as true to the original floor plan as you could, but having a master bath and additional closet space makes the room a lot more functional." Tracy turned to sweep her eyes from one end of the room to the other. "I love the way the glass wall sweeps down and around the whirlpool. And tucking the shower and commode behind the solid wall next to the closets was a perfect idea. It's wonderful."

Michelle beamed. "I hope Barclay likes it as well as you. I've hardly spoken to him all week, so I don't know if he's seen the glass wall or the tile work yet."

"I should get back to my roller," Tracy said feebly.

Michelle didn't intentionally ignore her attempt to escape, but her face was etched with concern and it was obvious she wanted to talk. Her sister swept her arm around the room with a disparaging look. "It would break my heart if Clay was ousted from his position at the Mill and had to leave Maple Valley now, after all this."

Tracy knew she didn't know the half of it.

"I'm sure his only concern is for the employees who will lose their jobs if the plant closes," Michelle continued, "but I know he'll be devastated if he has to give up this house after all it's come to mean to him."

Tracy's heart started to pound. Maybe Clay wasn't avoiding her. He was obviously going through a difficult time. Maybe it was she who should be reaching out to him. Maybe he'd been waiting for her to call him all this time. Her heart leaped with renewed hope at the prospect.

Michelle pondered aloud. "I thought maybe his enthusiasm for the house would wane when he broke off his engagement to Lauren."

"And you don't think that's the case?"

"No." Michelle answered. "If you want the truth, he seemed visibly relieved after the break-up. As I think back now, I realize he never seemed particularly concerned with her preferences anyway, even in the beginning. I thought it was a bit odd at the time, but who was I to judge? I don't know either of them all that well, say nothing about the nature of their relationship."

"That was my impression, too," Tracy said, trying to camouflage the squeak in her voice.

"What's even odder is that the evening we got together to finalize the plans for the master bath, Clay suddenly changed all the colors he'd selected for the bedrooms. I haven't even told you this, but he selected a very pale mauve rose paint and a wallpaper border with antique carousel for the attic. I couldn't help but think it was an unusual choice for a single man with no children but who am I to question..." She stopped abruptly mid-sentence. "So you haven't heard from him either, I take it?"

Tracy could feel her cheeks heating up. She looked away quickly in hopes that Michelle wouldn't notice. "No."

"I'm sorry to hear that. I think each of you could use a

friend right now. It seemed like things were really clicking between you. It's none of my business... I just thought maybe..."

Tracy turned abruptly and took two steps towards the door. "I'd better get back to work before my roller dries out. I didn't cover it."

Michelle was quicker to take the hint this time.

*****

The next morning, she had finally drifted back to sleep after Timothy had appeared for his early morning snuggle - blessed, coveted sleep – when the telephone rang and awoke both her and Timothy. She kept one arm around her son and blindly reached in the direction of the noise, groping and fumbling with the receiver before she finally found her ear. Timothy lifted his head for a second and then burrowed back under the bedspread.

"Hello?" she mumbled groggily.

"Happy Birthday, Tracy! I hope we didn't wake you!"

"Michelle?"

"And Jake," a second, much deeper voice chimed in cheerily.

"Oh," she groaned. "I forgot all about..."

"We did wake you. I'm sorry, Tracy. I thought with the kids..."

"It's okay," she mumbled. "The alarm would have gone off in a second. It's my birthday? I talked to Mom yesterday. She never said a word."

"She'll probably call before the end of the day. Either that or she's planning a surprise party and didn't mention it on purpose."

"Oh, Lord, I hope not." She could hear Jake laughing in the background. The sound of his masculine inflections made her grimace in spite of herself.

"Hey – Jake and I want to take you out for lunch today. If you'll bring one of those sweet little pastor's wife dresses you own to change into, I thought we could gussy ourselves up over the noon hour and have a nice, relaxed lunch at The Painted Lady."

"The owner gives her a great discount," Jake said good-naturedly.

"She'd better," Michelle teased.

"I'm going to work on the computer from home this morning so I can join you," Jake added. "I hope you like smothered pork chops with mashed potatoes and sage gravy because I've been promised they'll be on the menu."

"Those girls spoil him rotten." Michelle laughed. "He'll weigh more than I do before long if he doesn't watch out."

"I already weigh more than you do," Jake reminded his wife from his extension.

"Which sounds great unless you consider the fact that you're six inches taller than I am and solid muscle."

"When it comes to being in bed with the woman I love, I'll take soft and fleshy over muscular and bony any day of the week."

"Every day of the week when it comes to you, Jake Sheffield."

Tracy could hear Michelle giggling.

"Okay, you two, cut it out," Tracy ended their banter with a loud voice. "I'm a sex-deprived single woman now," she whispered into the receiver. "I can't take this so early in the morning."

"Was that deprived or depraved you said, Tracy?"

"Jake!" She and Michelle's voices rang out in simultaneous protest a second before both Sheffields dissolved in laughter. Tracy made a noise into the receiver just to be social but she couldn't find it in her heart to laugh.

"Maybe you two should go to lunch without me," she said feebly.

"No way, Tracy."

"We're sorry. I promise we'll be good." Jake chuckled into the receiver.

Tracy's clock radio blared out loudly.

"I hear your alarm. We'll let you go. See you in a bit."

"Happy Birthday!"

She hung up the phone with a sigh. Her birthday. She hadn't even remembered in all the chaos. She doubted the children would either. Trevor had always helped them plan something special. Her mother and father hadn't fussed much over any of their children's birthdays once they'd each married and had spouses to take over the honors. It was nice of Michelle and Jake to have called. It really was.

"Time to rise and shine, Timothy." She tugged at the covers until her tousle-haired son reappeared.

"You musta been tossing and turning all night, Mom. This bed is a mess!" her littlest claimed knowingly.

"I didn't sleep very well last night," she answered thoughtfully. "Do you want to know a secret, Timothy?"

His eyes lit up. "Yes."

"You have to promise not to tell Titus or Theodora."

He nodded his head furiously.

"You look like a cute little puppy dog waiting for a bone when you do that." Tracy laughed. "The secret is," she said dramatically, raising one eyebrow. "Today is my birthday."

"Your birthday?" he said, awestruck as only a five year old boy can be.

"Yes."

"I wish I could bake you a cake with lots of candles," Timothy thought out loud, "but all we have at school is a pretend kitchen."

"Maybe after school. It would take a lot of candles."

"I know what I want to get you for a present," he said smugly.

"You do?"

"Uh, huh," he nodded, his blue eyes shining like stars.

"What's that?"

"It's a surprise."

"I suppose you want me to be patient then," she said.

He bounced his head up and down. "My teacher might let me make a card for you in school."

"You're a sweetheart, Timothy." She leaned down and kissed the top of his head. "Now go get dressed for school quick like a rabbit. And don't forget to use the bathroom -

hurry up before Theodora gets in there. I'll go down and make us some pancakes for breakfast."

"Cause it's your birthday?"

"Yes. But remember, don't tell any one else. It's our secret."

"Okay, Mom." His eyes shone as he darted out of the room.

Her eyes lingered on him lovingly. It felt good to smile.

*****

A few hours later, Tracy was at Clay's house, painting her heart out, when Michelle poked her head in to see how she was doing. "Are you getting close to a place where you could break for lunch? I made our reservation for eleven-thirty but I told Madeleine we might be a few minutes late depending on how things went this morning."

"I'm almost done with the first coat."

"You've got paint speckles on your nose," Michelle said.

"How can you tell with all my freckles? I'll wipe them off when I get cleaned up."

"You remembered to bring a dress?"

"Yes. One of the many sweet, prim, proper little pastor's wife dresses hanging in my closet which I now have no place to wear."

"You always did look darling in those dresses. I know it's probably not what you want to hear right now, but Trevor used to look so proud of you when you were by his side."

"Sure he did. A lovely, adoring wife like me was exactly what Trevor needed. I enabled him to hide his true colors and I was a nice boost to his ego besides."

"You don't really think that, do you, Tracy?" Michelle said. "I've always thought Trevor loved you very deeply. His sexual preferences don't preclude the fact that he probably still loves you even now."

"So he says," she answered curtly.

"I hate to see you swallowed up in sarcasm, Tracy."

"So turn off the television if you don't want to watch." She knew how horrid and unappreciative the words sounded the second they came out of her mouth. She whirled around to face her sister. "I'm sorry, Michelle."

"Don't worry about me. I've got thick skin."

"Yeah, right," she said. "You're not the one I should be taking out my frustrations on."

"That's the hard part about being alone. The frustrations mount up inside you until you feel like you're going to explode. Sooner or later it comes out despite your best efforts to keep it all in. It has to. As depression for those of us who are into repressing our emotions, as bitterness or cynicism for the ones who aren't afraid to say what they think. I've always thought that Rachael's rough edges are probably the result of all the years she spent alone."

"I'm sorry I wasn't more understanding when the two of you were single. If I had known then what I know now..."

"There was no way you could have."

"I could have shown a little more empathy even if I didn't have any first hand experience with what you were struggling with. I could have been more supportive. I don't know what I could have said to make it any easier, but at the very least, I shouldn't have judged you until I'd taken a few steps in your shoes."

"Thanks. Truly. But I don't want you to worry about that now. I just want you to quit agonizing over Trevor and enjoy your birthday for a little bit. I'll get my brush cleaned out while you finish rolling, okay?"

Tracy turned and trudged back to the denim-blue bedroom. The roller had slid to the bottom of the tray, its furry surface soaked through with thick, heavy blue paint. She used a paint stirrer to skim off the excess before grasping the handle with one hand and raising the roller high above her head to the last unpainted section of the wall.

Of course Michelle would think she was agonizing over Trevor. She had no idea what had happened with her and Clay, or that it was his rejection that she was feeling so acutely.

Chapter 24

The soaring maple trees that lined the streets of Maple Valley were still primarily green, but wanton splashes of red and orange burnished the very tips of their leaves like starbursts streaming across the sky on the Fourth of July.

The festivities repeated themselves yearly as the trees performed their grand finale, one last brilliant display just as their season was destined to close. Tracy thought the colors seemed even brighter this year, the lighting more intense, each and every leaf more vivid in passing.

She smiled as she and Michelle drove by the Mary Rose Manor and down Osage Avenue en-route to the Painted Lady. Cars of every make and year, many if not most with Minnesota license plates, lined the streets.

"Care to share the joke?" Michelle asked.

"The fall colors are twice as beautiful here in Iowa as they are in Minnesota, but no self-respecting Minnesotan would ever admit it."

Michelle laughed. "Jake and I boated down the Mississippi from Red Wing to Prarie Du Chein in mid October last year with my friend Deb and her husband. When we got home and drove up in front of the Painted Lady, we both agreed that the colors that were right here in our own backyard were prettier than anything we'd seen on the trip."

Tracy looked up at the beautiful Victorian facade of the Painted Lady as they turned up the drive that led to the top of the hill. It felt good to be dressed up and out on an adventure, away from the children, the houses that alternately reminded her of Clay or Trevor, and the disappointment associated with each.

Michelle parked the car in back. "You don't mind walking around to the front do you?"

"No, I love the sound of leaves crunching under my feet.

Autumn smells so wonderful."

Michelle smiled. "It's good to see you looking a little more relaxed."

"Thanks for the invitation. I suppose I would have remembered it was my birthday eventually, but with as wild as things have been..."

"Theodora must know what day it is. Didn't she say anything this morning?"

"No. Timothy was snuggling in my bed when you called so I told him, but I swore him to secrecy. Titus might remember before the day's up, but Theodora... Things seemed a little better between us after we talked about Trevor, but she's back to acting like she absolutely detests me again. I doubt she'd give me the satisfaction of saying anything even if she does remember."

"I don't understand why she's acting so hostile towards you when it's Trevor that..."

"That's the big mystery. I don't understand it either."

"Happy Birthday!" Jake greeted Tracy with a hug and his wife with a kiss as they rounded the corner and ascended the steps to the front porch. "Madeleine has our table all ready." He extended an elbow to each woman.

Tracy couldn't help but smile. Their merriment was infectious.

"Psst, Tracy. Over here!"

She heard a low voice beckoning to her in a hushed stage whisper from the direction of the wood colonnade on her left. "Surprise!"

Michelle clutched her elbow from behind. "I hope you don't mind," she whispered. "Luke was at the office when I stopped by Wild Rose Realty to invite Rachael and Mac. He more or less invited himself. I didn't think you'd mind."

"Of course not," Tracy murmured after flashing a quick smile of greeting at the three additional revelers. Truth was, she was relieved that she wouldn't have to spend the whole lunch hour watching Jake and Michelle moon over each other like two love sick...

"To be honest, I thought about calling Clay, too, but I

wasn't sure..."

"It's probably better that you didn't," Tracy said quietly. At the very least it was good to know Clay hadn't declined an invitation to help celebrate her birthday. She turned to the table with a smile. "Thank you all for coming. I feel so honored."

A round of greeting cards and two beribboned boxes appeared out of nowhere. Luke leaped to his feet and nearly collided with Jake in an effort to help her with her chair.

She was just about to take a seat when her eyes locked with the bluest set of eyes she'd ever seen. She knew immediately where and when she had seen them last. It had been at very close range.

Her first thought was that Michelle had been teasing her a moment earlier - that Clay was yet another surprise in a long, always wondering-what-was-next string of birthday surprises.

The fact that there were no empty chairs at their table registered in her brain just one brief second before she saw the sveltely manicured, slender-fingered, still-diamond-studded hand clinging to Clay's arm.

"Oh, darling, a table by the window. You've thought of everything," Lauren was purring in a voice that turned Tracy's stomach.

Tracy's lips parted and she drew in one staccato breath.

Clay's eyes shone back at her for a one heartbreaking moment before the light was snuffed from his smile. In an instant, his look changed from one of tender devotion to one of non-recognition. It was as though his love for her had simply died, right before her eyes. No sun-drenched summer skies, no sunshine dancing on waves, no impossible to dim lover's intimacy reflecting brazenly back at her. Nothing.

Tracy sat dumbfounded, unable to stop staring, as Clay helped Lauren with her coat, removed her sweater, and extended his arms to pull out her chair.

She could feel her mouth standing agape, the group around her murmuring in hushed tones, then falling quiet. She finally managed to turn and smile at the ring of faces trained on hers.

"Wow. A real, honest to goodness party. I'm nearly speechless." She tipped her head and forced another smile. "You guys are great! I... thank you... I mean..." Her eyes filled with tears. She felt them coming but could do nothing to stop them. "I appreciate... if you'll excuse me for a moment. I just need to duck into the ladies room."

She was up and out of her seat before Luke or any of the others could stand to get her chair.

Michelle looked at Jake and sighed.

Rachael was the first to speak, her lip curled in a surprised look. "What's wrong this time? Maybe you should go after her, Michelle."

Mac laid a hand on Rachael's shoulder as if warning an eagle away from its prey.

"She's been having a rough time again lately. The kids have been a handful. I'm not sure what else. She's been touchy at work, too. I wish I knew what was wrong."

"Give her a minute alone," Mac suggested in his classic low rumble. "Maybe she really does need to use the ladies room."

"Sure." Rae looked dubious.

"Hey, isn't that Clay and Lauren over by the window?" Jake interrupted. "I didn't see them come in."

"Too busy making goo goo eyes at your wife when they made their grand entrance to notice anything else," Rae teased, eyeing Jake suspiciously before she turned to her sister. "You're not pregnant again, are you, Michelle?"

Michelle could feel the blush creep from the V of her neckline, past her cheeks, and up to her forehead, hopefully to disappear in the frenzy of curls surrounding her face.

Jake laughed out loud. "I told you they'd figure it out."

"Jake!" Michelle protested weakly, her fingers pressed to her throat.

"Hell, I'm not going to lie about it." Jake said with a low chuckle. He looked around the table, meeting one set of eyes at a time. "We're due in April and we're thrilled. Just hadn't planned on taking the wind out of Tracy's sails on her birthday, that's all."

Congratulations rang out from every corner of the table.

"Shhh..." Michelle cautioned them. "We haven't told Madeleine or Laurie and I don't think I want to quite yet. They fuss over me so much when I'm pregnant."

Tracy could hear the enthusiastic chatter emanating from the corner where their table of six was nestled as she made her way back across the room. Relieved that the others seemed not to have noticed she was upset, she plastered a smile on her face and kept walking. She was careful not to look in the direction of the table Clay shared with Lauren.

"The birthday girl returns." Luke sprang from his seat and took her elbow the second he saw her approach. The others sat in place, looking at one another like a circle of cats who have just swallowed a cage full of canaries.

"It's a birthday surprise, Tracy." Michelle's face shone. "You're going to be an Auntie again."

"Well that explains a lot," Tracy said dryly. "You two have been acting like a pair of love birds for weeks."

Rachael and Mac laughed in unison. Tracy saw Mac reach for Rae's hand under the table.

Couples. She detested them. Every last one of them. Thank God Luke was there to lend her support.

"Congratulations, Michelle, Jake," she smiled as happily as she could stand to, looking at each of them. "I'm very happy for you. No wonder you've been painting with the windows wide open on all these forty degree mornings, Michelle!"

"I thought maybe you'd already figured it out and were just trying to be polite until I 'fessed up."

"I didn't have a clue. Guess my mind has been on other things." Tracy felt the circle grew as suddenly quiet as it had jubilant.

"Yeah, leave it to my big mouth to blow your cover," Rae said without the slightest hint of embarrassment.

Tracy said a silent prayer of thanks that her older sister

had shifted the focus away from her again, whether inadvertently or on purpose. The conversation moved on around her. She stole futile glances at Clay as often as she dared. There was no sign that he was even cognizant of the fact she was in the room.

Her birthday! Clay's heart pounded inside his chest as he sat across the table from Lauren, consciously willing himself to forget about Tracy. He reluctantly mustered what he hoped was passion enough to melt a rock and gazed into Lauren's eyes.

His eyes blinked rebelliously. This was wrong. His instincts hammered out conflicting messages inside his head. He was listening to Lauren's gushing words, but his heart was with Tracy. He thought of their lovemaking and remembered the things about her that had made her so precious to him - from her embarrassing repartee with Timothy to her anguish over Theodora - dozens of times every hour. He relived the sensation of her soft skin against his and imagined her naked beside him with every breath that he drew. Even now, he sat wondering what she was thinking. Knowing he had hurt her, and on her birthday at that, made it all the worse.

Clay grimaced, momentarily swept away by the increasingly familiar revulsion he felt for himself. He was using Lauren in the most heinous way imaginable. The very things he'd always abhorred about the corporate moguls that had been pecking away at him for years, he was now guilty of himself. They'd finally gotten what they wanted. He had stooped to his father's level. He had used whatever means he needed to accomplish his business goals.

And the means to the end he desired was Lauren.

Things would have been so much simpler had he been in love with Lauren. In his heart of hearts, he perceived the tastefully groomed, finely made up woman seated across from him to be as lackluster as he knew Lauren thought Tracy to be. But in all the years he'd known Lauren, she had never given him any cause to disdain her other than being herself. And that, Lauren couldn't help any more than he could.

He had no wish to hurt either Lauren or Tracy, but he had just hurt them both, say nothing of the fact that his own heart was being wrenched in two.

Barclay cleared his throat and reached for Lauren's hand. "I appreciate the fact that you agreed to drive down here today. I know Maple Valley isn't your favorite place."

Lauren smiled sweetly.

"Things are so volatile at the mill right now because of the rumors in regard to the impending closing that I hated to be out of town even for a few hours." Clay fingered the pager clipped under his jacket with his free hand. If marrying Lauren was the price he had to pay to secure her proxy and save Elk Creek Woolen Mills, he would do so. And he would be the best damn husband to her he could be. Lauren deserved that much.

"I didn't mind a bit, Barclay," the new, sweeter, more considerate Lauren purred, squeezing his hand across the table. "I suppose I'm so accustomed to and happy with my own little world that that I have absolutely no motivation to try to adapt to a new setting. It was boorish of me to have been so critical of this town when I knew how fond you've become of the people here."

Clay sucked in a deep breath. He could hardly believe his ears.

"Aren't those some of your friends over behind the colonnade, darling?" Lauren craned her neck enough to catch Michelle's eye and fluttered her fingertips at the table that included Tracy. "If you'd like to say hello, I'm sure we have time to wander over to their table before our food arrives."

Clay nodded at Michelle and Rachael and the others while muttering a hurried protest. "No. This is our day. I have so little time with you today as it is, what with the upheaval at the Mill. I'm more than content to spend what time we do have alone."

"I assume those are the other two Jones sisters you've

spoken of so admiringly," Lauren said. "The three of them each make such a handsome couple sitting there with their respective spouses. I've never met the youngest. She has such a fragile quality about her."

"She's soon-to-be divorced. The gentleman beside her is Rachael's business partner, Luke Zimmerman. I believe you met them both at Mac's surprise birthday party."

"I was in such a dither that night worrying about the housewarming that I can remember very little of whom I was introduced to or what went on."

Clay remembered his dance with Tracy that night with photographic accuracy – although it seemed forever ago. Again, he willed himself to replace thoughts of one woman with the other. He was at Lauren's mercy. Even if he could get her to sympathize with the plight of the Elk Creek employees, she could decide to vote against keeping the factory open for no other reason than to strip him of his reason for settling in Maple Valley. She had been very vocal about her displeasure in regard to his choice of residences. Nothing would suit her more than to have him back in the Cities where she believed he belonged.

"The whole concept of rushing into purchasing a home here in Maple Valley was probably ill-fated on my part to begin with, Lauren." And then, at least one thing he could say in truth. "I'm sorry you got caught in the crossfire."

"But I was, wasn't I?" Lauren murmured. "And still am."

Lauren was nothing if not astute.

"This situation at the mill has turned into out and out warfare between you and your father. It breaks my heart to see the two of you pledged to opposing factions in regard to closing the facility," Lauren said.

The pretty pout she was so adept at wielding played on her lips until Clay couldn't resist a quick smile. He struggled to keep his voice from betraying the desperation he felt in his heart.

"The mill is so much more than a facility, Lauren." He leaned forward in his chair. His thumb toyed with her diamond and he wondered briefly if she had continued to wear it the whole time they'd been estranged of if she'd just put it back on today. "The Mill is a second home to over 300 dedicated employees, many of whom have worked there a dozen or more years. It's part of the life breath of this community. It's a vital, profitable, business concern in its field. It's a living, breathing entity that affects the lives of thousands of people. To shut the doors just like that after these people have poured their hearts and souls and energy into this place for decades..."

"I overheard my father saying that more than eighty percent of the employees at the mill are women. Aren't you being a little melodramatic to assume that people are going to go hungry if the doors close, Clay? Granted, there may be a few families who won't have as much leisure income at their disposal if both spouses aren't working, but the town will hardly wither up and die."

Clay shook his head. "Your father is correct in his reasoning except for one crucial point. These are not women of leisure who have chosen to work so they can buy a few extra baubles for themselves. These are single mothers whose ex-husbands don't know the meaning of child support, wives whose husbands are stuck in menial jobs that pay barely more than minimum wage with families that rely on a double income to make ends meet, and sole wage earners with no savings accounts that wouldn't be able to keep the utilities paid for a month without their weekly paycheck coming in."

Lauren looked serious for one brief second. "And is it also your father's fault that these people haven't set aside some money for a rainy day? Besides, there are agencies designated to help people in temporary distress. It's not like anyone will actually suffer."

Clay shook his head. She simply didn't understand. She couldn't. She had lived her whole life safely nestled in a world so free from financial hardship that her perspective could be nothing other than what it was. If he was going to get through to her he would have to try another tack. "I gave these people my word, Lauren. You know I'm a man who keeps his promises." He looked at her expectantly. He was only here today because he was a man true to his word. He knew it, and on some level, she knew it.

"You scarcely know these people."

"Whether or not I owe any of these people anything, I gave them my word. Whether I ultimately secure the Mill myself, see it sold to some third party, or convince my father to keep it open; whether I stay in Maple Valley or move back to Minneapolis tomorrow, I gave these people my word that I would not stand by and watch them lose their jobs."

"With Daddy's three percent..." Lauren cleared her throat nervously. "Would you have enough stock to gain control of the Mill with my vote tomorrow?"

"Yes."

"It seemed more than a little coincidental that you chose yesterday to call me after days with no word."

Clay held her hand in his but said nothing. He did not wish to hurt her; neither would he defend himself with lies. Yet he knew that his choice of words could undoubtedly affect the lives of hundreds of people. "I've been stubborn and selfish and preoccupied. Can you forgive me?"

"You're glossing over the issues, Barclay. I'm not an idiot. My pretty little brain is plenty big enough to figure that you wanted me to vote my proxy in your favor when you called this morning."

Clay tried to think of a response and could only stammer a nonsensical word or two in reply.

Lauren's eyes did all but bore a hole through him. "Quite frankly," she finally said in clipped, but sweetly uttered tones, "my first response was to tell you to go to hell. But on second thought, it occurred to me that this might be just the opportunity I've needed to clear the air between us, and of course, to straighten out the whole unfortunate misunderstanding that occurred in regard to our engagement."

Barclay sat dumbfounded, staring at the woman across the table from him.

"Let's lay our cards on the table, shall we, Barclay?" Lauren tilted her head and pursed her lips. "You want my vote tomorrow. I want a Christmas wedding at St. Mark's Cathedral in downtown Minneapolis. And I do mean this December, not next."

Clay's eyes opened wide with sheer surprise.

"It's your turn now, dear." Lauren curled her fingers and examined her nails nonchalantly. "Spell out your terms."

"I've always been partial to holly. And you do look lovely in red." He elicited no response. Clay raised one eyebrow. "The only thing I ask is that my father not know of our re-engagement until after the board meeting tomorrow. The alliances I'm depending on to sway tomorrow's vote are tenuous at best. If my father were somehow alerted to the fact that I have the votes I need, the house of cards could easily collapse."

"Enough said. Now, let's be perfectly candid, shall we, dearest?" Lauren's eyes were as cold as steel. "I've always assumed you broke off our engagement because you'd taken in some trollop on the side and fancied yourself in love with her. And just so you know, Barclay, I no longer care. I won't even insist that you give her up."

"How generous of you." He knew he was taking a risk – a huge risk - yet he continued. "She's not a trollop, dear Lauren, nor would she ever consent to live her life as my mistress."

"How quaint." Lauren didn't bat an eyelash. "By the way, I took the liberty of checking with the rector before I left town this morning, and there just happens to be one December date open due to a recent cancellation. Mother will throw fits when I tell her she has no more than two months to plan her only daughter's wedding, but the way it appears, it's December tenth or nothing. Are you free?"

"Of course I am, Lauren," Clay could barely mask his resignation. He had known his freedom was the price he would pay for Lauren's cooperation, but to hear the words said aloud in such a calculated manner was another matter entirely.

He resisted the impulse to renounce her, to get up, and walk away once and for all. “December tenth works fine for me if it does for you. Shall I contact Rachael and tell her I’ve decided to put my house on the market?” He was unable to hide the trace of bitterness that crept into his voice.

“I’ve given considerable thought to the matter of our mutual abodes, Barclay, and I see no reason why we can’t maintain separate residences for a period of, shall we say one year? I’ve assumed you would insist on staying in Iowa to nurse your little factory along, especially now that you’ll own the building. Yet try as I might, I just can’t envision myself living in Maple Valley. If you’re willing to spend weekends in Minneapolis, I feel quite sure I can occupy myself without you during the week.”

“How magnanimous of you.” Clay’s fingers cradled his chin. He tapped one finger against his lips with a listless but inferred compliance. “I guess it’s all settled then. Or are there other things we need to discuss?”

“Not unless there’s something else on your mind, dearest.”

“No.” Clay choked out the word. “I think we’ve said all there is to say. Shall I pick you up on my way to corporate headquarters tomorrow morning, say about half past nine?”

“Wouldn’t it be better if we arrived in separate cars?” Lauren asked sagely.

Clay nodded and lifted his glass to toast hers.

Lauren smiled like a cat sitting in front of a bowl of cream. “Now let’s set business aside for a moment and enjoy our lunch. Shall we?”

Chapter 25

The sounds of the tea house – waitresses, customers, a telephone ringing in the distance - swirled around the lace-covered table for six at Tracy's thoughtfully planned, but ill-conceived birthday extravaganza.

"The pork chops were as wonderful as Jake claimed they'd be," Tracy stammered, trying not to appear ungracious.

Michelle gave Rachael a pointed look. Tracy had barely uttered two words through the entire lunch.

"You two must be nearly finished at the Alexander house," Rae said in a cheerful attempt to draw Tracy out. Michelle declined to answer in hopes that Tracy would take the bait.

The waitress brought their desserts, and with it a candle for Tracy to blow out.

Rae cleared her throat when Tracy remained quiet. "I ran into a subcontractor over at the Johnson house yesterday and he mentioned that he'd lain some glass blocks at Barclay's place earlier this week. I can't wait to see the master suite. It sounds absolutely spectacular."

"Aren't you going to make a wish and blow out your candle, Tracy?" Michelle asked.

"Sure," Tracy said, after another awkward moment had passed. "I think I'd like a new quilt. Maybe that's what I'll wish for."

Mac and Jake looked visibly tense. They'd obviously both heard their respective wives' versions of what happened with Aunt Thelma's quilt.

She saw Michelle give Rae the evil eye. "You'll have to stop by sometime before the end of the week and see what we've accomplished, Rae," Michelle said. "We should have all the loose ends tied up by the end of this week. With any luck, Clay will be able to move in next Monday. We have just one more floor to go."

"And one upside down wallpaper panel to re-hang when the replacement we ordered finally arrives," Tracy said, then blew out the candle in her cheesecake.

Michelle paused and gave her a vexed look. "There are always a few finishing touches that have to be done at the last minute. I was just telling Tracy earlier that Clay is doing the attic like an old-fashioned flat. Very quaint and feminine - it's almost like he has a specific use in mind for the area, but I haven't a clue what it is."

"Now you've made me curious," Rae said with forced gaiety.

Mac looked gently at Tracy, as though he knew what her sisters were up to and sympathized. Mac was not known to pussyfoot around, and today was no exception. Her brother-in-law knew how to cut through the chaff. "Have you decided if you'll continue on with painting and wallpapering once you're finished with the Alexander house, Tracy?"

Jake interjected his opinion, assuming Tracy would evade Mac's question, however direct. "Michelle feels Tracy could make a generous salary if she chooses to pursue even a fraction of the painting business that's out there. You never know what talents are going to come in handy when you're faced with a crisis and forced to consider the options. Simpler things have turned into lucrative careers for many of my friends."

Five pairs of eyes were trained on Tracy.

"Mom mentioned a friend of hers up in Hayfield last week who plans on redoing her house this winter. Not that I haven't loved working in Maple Valley. I mean, I appreciate Michelle giving me the chance to-"

"It was you who got me out of a bind when you agreed to help me with Clay's house. I couldn't have done it without you!"

"I just worry about driving so far to work every day once the weather gets bad. If it weren't for the kids... But it would be awful if I got all the way down here and then got stranded and couldn't get back to Blooming Prairie in an ice or snow storm. I just can't take the risk of them being alone."

"It sounds like you've made a wise decision, Tracy." Mac rumbled his approval.

"As long as you remember that I've got plenty of work lined up for the spring," Michelle piped up. "Say nothing about the fact that I'm going to miss working with you."

"I'll miss you, too," Tracy said weakly. It was all decided then. She wouldn't be seeing Michelle or Clay or any of the people she had come to rely on after another week or two of painting in Clay's attic. She bit her lip to keep it from trembling.

"Speaking of work," Rachael grumbled. "I guess it's time I said my farewells and headed back to the office. Luke and I have a showing at one thirty."

Luke nodded and pushed his chair back form the table. "Enjoy the rest of your birthday, Tracy. Hot plans tonight?"

"No," she stammered. "Just supper with the kids, homework, the usual laundry, and lunch bags to pack."

Luke laughed. "It actually sounds like fun to me."

"We should trade shoes for a day. I guarantee you'd be singing a different song."

Luke smiled and bent to hug her goodbye. When she turned, she could see Clay and Lauren locked in earnest conversation at their table for two by the window.

Rachael, Mac and Jake also left to make their ways back to their respective places of employment after another quick round of hugs. Michelle excused herself to have a quick word with her assistant, Laurie, on the third floor. Tracy was standing in the foyer with her back to the dining room entrance when she heard a voice behind her.

"I couldn't help but overhear that it's your birthday, Tracy. May I add my best wishes?"

Clay swept her into his arms and kissed her ever so gently before she could say a word. Her eyes filled with tears.

"I'm sorry, Tracy." Clay's fingers lingered on her skin a moment longer than was proper as he brushed a stray hair back from her face. "I know you've been getting a lot of mixed messages from me over the past few weeks. I want you to know that I've been trying to work things out so we could be together. I'm reluctant to say what seemed like an impossible situation in the first place has just taken a turn for the worse."

She could see the lines etched at his temples, the deeply printed fatigue taxing his face. She took his hand. Her thoughts came out in a rush. "Michelle has been filling me in on the crisis at the factory. You've been on my mind every second of every day since we... I didn't know if I could call you there, or if you even wanted to talk to me. Are you okay? Have you succeeded in keeping the factory from closing?"

He nodded. "Yes, if all goes as planned tomorrow. The resolution to the problem came at a very high price." He glanced over his shoulder to make sure they were still alone. "I don't have long Tracy. Lauren's waiting." He looked directly into her eyes. "The board meeting is tomorrow. Please know that whatever happens next, I love you. Promise me that you'll always remember that, Tracy."

"You're scaring me, Clay."

"I've never felt the way I feel about you , Tracy. You're very precious to me."

His features took on a new edge, a fierceness, a determination she had never before glimpsed in him.

"And you to me, Clay Alexander." Her bottom lip quivered.

"I don't know what you wished for when you blew out your birthday candle."

"A new quilt," she said wryly. "Private joke. Seriously, if I tell you what I really wished for, it won't come true."

"Shhh... I want all your dreams to come true, and mine."

"Oh, how I hope they will!" She pressed her palm into his.

"I feel like I'm spinning my wheels, going around and around in some huge, unending circle where the scenery never changes. Tomorrow when the board votes in my favor and my father is forced to sell the factory to me, it will seem like I've won. But the fact is, he'll have gotten exactly what he wanted in the first place. He never cared about the factory. He still doesn't. He just wants me to do what he thinks I should. And now, I have.

"I don't know what the next few weeks will hold, but I haven't given up on being with you, Tracy. Will you believe me when I say that? No matter what you hear or see in the next few weeks?"

"Yes. I promise." A tear escaped her eyelashes and rolled down her cheeks.

He ducked to kiss it away. "I love you, Tracy Jones."

"And I love you, Clay Alexander."

*****

Tracy worked with renewed vigor throughout the afternoon. They had finished the top coat in the master bedroom by the time she pulled out of the driveway and left for home. Self-satisfied and happily tired for the first time in days, Tracy had almost forgotten it was her birthday when she arrived in Blooming Prairie.

"Surprise, Mommy!" Timothy's voice rang out to greet her the second she stepped out of her car. "Happy Birthday!"

"Surprise!"

"Surprise!"

Theodora and Titus's faces were sporting smiles big enough to rival Timothy's usually cherubic expression. "Hey, you guys. What's all this?"

"I didn't tell anybody just like you said, Mommy. But Teddy already knew." Timothy informed her seriously.

"Dad called as soon as we got home from school and reminded me," Theodora confessed. "All I did was make some dinner and send Ty uptown for a card." The teenager shrugged.

"I got her a gift, too, stupid." Titus glared at his sister.

"And flowers came, too, Mommy! Hundreds and hundreds of red flowers in a tall vase with some white stuff called baby's teeth," Timothy said.

"Baby's breath, you idiot."

"Well, thank you! All of you!" Tracy resisted the urge to reprimand Titus for calling his brother stupid. Her eyes filled with tears for the second or third time that day. "I love you guys so much, do you know that?"

"Yeah, so you keep claiming," Titus mumbled with a chagrined glance from beneath his bangs. He smiled again.

Tracy pinched his cheek. "You're such a cutie when you smile, Titus. You'll have all the girls swooning if you keep grinning like that."

His ears turned beet red.

"Come and see what we got for you, Mommy! Come on! The flowers are in here! Teddy said they're from A Touch of Charm."

Tracy let herself be tugged into the kitchen. "Swedish meatballs! My favorite! Thank you, Teddy. This means a lot to me."

"Well it is your birthday, and we had to eat something."

Tracy looped her arm around Theodora's shoulders, half expecting her to recoil. But for once, the teenager let herself be hugged.

"If you turkeys go wash your hands and get cleaned up a little, we can eat already," Theodora told the boys, pulling out of the quick embrace. "I'm going to start dishing up the mashed potatoes as soon as you scram."

"Whatever you say, boss." Titus couldn't resist. They clamored downstairs to the washroom.

Tracy turned to face her oldest. "Thanks again, sweetheart. This is the best birthday present of all."

"Well, I figured I kind of owed you since I've been so hard on you. Aren't you going to look at your roses? I put them in the living room by the window."

Tracy walked through the dining room to the parlor. While Timothy's estimate proved a bit high, there looked to be at least two-dozen long stemmed red roses towering up from a cut crystal vase sitting on a doily on her grandmother's cherry parlor table. "Oh, honey, you kids shouldn't have spent this kind of money..."

"Get a life, Mom. We don't have that kind of money to spend if we'd wanted to. And Dad said he didn't do it either. Maybe they're from that Alexander guy you've been seeing."

Tracy caught her breath and looked at Theodora intently. "You know about Clay?"

"Doesn't everybody by now?"

"I haven't told anyone. Not even Michelle... how could you possibly...?"

"I saw the two of you locked in some hot embrace the day I was down in Maple Valley baby-sitting for Michelle."

Tracy stared at her daughter in shock. "But you were at Jake and Michelle's. You were out in the country..." She was horrified to think what Theodora might have seen.

"I rode my bike into town," Theodora confessed, conveniently avoiding her glance by turning away.

Tracy couldn't have looked her in the eye at that moment even if her daughter had dared.

"I've been thinking, Mom. I mean, I was pretty upset with you at first. I guess I always thought it must have been you that broke up with Dad, and when I saw you with this Alexander guy, I just figured that you'd been cheating on Dad all the while. I was pretty bummed."

"Oh, Theodora..." Tracy caught a sob in her throat.

Her daughter continued to stare out the window while she spoke. "Once I calmed down I figured out that I probably had it wrong but I was still too peeved at you to admit it. I mean, now that I know what I know about Dad, I guess I can kind of understand why you did what you did."

Theodora paused. Tracy could hear the Power Rangers theme song playing faintly from below and prayed that the boys had gotten distracted when they left the bathroom.

"Today when I was talking to Dad, I started to think about what it must have been like for you to find out about... well, after all those years and having three kids with him and everything. Sometimes I just hate him, Mom, and then I think I should be mad at him, not you, but when I was talking to him today, I just thought, what's the use? I can't spend the rest of my life being mad all the time."

"I don't know what to say except that I'm sorry you've had to deal with any of this."

"I bet you never had this kind of talk with Grandma, huh?" Theodora turned around and gave her an impish look.

"No," she stammered resoundingly. Taken back as she was, it was at that precise moment Tracy knew everything was going to be fine.

"Can I ask you one more thing, Mom?"

"Sure," she said, thinking *God help me.*

"Were you totally naive and innocent when you were my age or did you go out with boys and stuff?"

Tracy first blanched and then turned red, making her discomfort all the more obvious to her daughter.

"I thought so," Theodora said, knowing full well she had the upper hand and relishing every last minute of it. Her daughter spun on her heel and faced her squarely. "You see, the way I have it figured, there are two kinds of kids at school. There are a few kids who really are naive about sex and stuff. Personally, I don't know how they can escape it. Maybe they aren't allowed to watch TV or go to the mall.

"Anyway, the second kind are the wild kids that pretend to be perfect. And I mean wild, Mom. Their parents don't have a clue what they're doing, and they act like such little angels in front of the teachers that it's sickening."

Tracy gulped. "So do I dare ask where you fit into the picture?"

"That's just the point, Mom! I don't! Well, before all this stuff started happening with you and Dad I suppose I was one of the more naive ones. Brooke still is, but I can't pretend that I have my head in the sand any more, and although it was tempting at the beginning to go out, forget about my troubles, and get rowdy with the wild kids, I just didn't have the stomach for it."

"I'm relieved to hear that, Teddy. I wasn't sure..."

"Well, I am, Mom. I hate going to school in Rice Lake. The only friend I'm really comfortable with right now is

Staci Slattery. Her life hasn't been that great, but she's got a good attitude about it. I mean, she's just a normal person like I am who's trying to figure out the best thing to do in the middle of some pretty weird situations."

"I think I understand."

"My faith is important to me, Mom. Really it is. All I want is the freedom to figure out what I believe about stuff instead of getting somebody else's interpretation shoved down my throat all the time. Do you know what I mean?"

"Yes, I do. I think you've done a pretty good job of that already. I'm very proud of you."

"You already promised me that you'd think about letting me switch to public school. Staci says the new semester starts right after Christmas. I'd really like to make the switch then if you say it's okay."

"It's okay." Tracy said quietly.

"Seriously?" Theodora looked at her incredulously.

"Seriously. And Teddy, thanks for being honest with me about Clay."

"I guess I was pretty rude to him, too."

"You talked to him?"

"He never told you? I saw him at Michelle and Jake's church the Sunday after it happened. Sorry if I wrecked things up for you or anything like that."

Tracy was speechless. Theodora's admission explained a lot. My, the day certainly had been full of surprises.

"So are you going to open the card and see who sent you the roses or what?"

"Sure." Her fingers fumbled with the card as she removed it from the envelope. She felt suddenly timid.

Teddy moved towards the dining room. "I'll check the gravy and see if it's thick enough."

"Thanks, sweetheart."

The message on the card was printed in a bold, but artistic script. "Tracy, Promises and commitments are not mine to give, but I can pledge to you what's in my heart - my undying love. You are the love of my life." The card was simply signed "Clay".

Chapter 26

Tracy walked on air for the rest of the night and flew to work the next morning on a cloud of euphoria that nothing could diminish – not gay ex-husbands, squabbling children, or quilt-hoarding older sisters. When she arrived at Clay's house, she stood in the center of the master bedroom suite and twirled around and around with her arms outstretched, for once, confident in the love she felt for him.

She reminded herself that she might not see him again for a long, long time. Still, her happiness could not be squelched. He'd said he loved her! She went to the third floor and busied herself poking around the spacious sanctuary where they'd be working next.

She finally heard Michelle coming up the stairs. Her sister was out of breath when she appeared on the landing, a portable TV tucked under her arm.

"I'm sorry I'm late again, Tracy. First Sarah sobbed and sobbed when I dropped her off at Luke's mother's house this morning, and then it was so hectic at the office when I stopped by to get my messages I thought I'd never get out of there."

"Don't worry about it. I've been scoping things out a bit - trying to envision how the wallpaper border will work with the slant of the ceiling. I've got the primer all ready to go, too."

Michelle set the TV on the floor and took off her jacket. "Rae called. Mac is up at the Alexander Industries corporate headquarters in Minneapolis right now waiting for their board meeting to adjourn. Channel Three has a crew on stand-by to give live coverage of Clay's attempted forced sale of Elk Creek Woolen Mills. There's supposed to be some sort of formal announcement as soon as the board members exit the meeting."

"I've been thinking about Clay all morning. I didn't

realize..."

"The whole county is buzzing. Rachael told me the Mitchell County Messenger and KIMT both have camera crews at the factory waiting to interview some of the workers when the verdict is announced."

"If he fails, I suppose the effects will spiral on down through the whole area."

"Yes." Michelle sighed. "I've been praying all morning that things will go Clay's way."

Tracy found a plug-in while Michelle fiddled with the rabbit ears.

"I talked to Clay for a few minutes yesterday while you were up on the third floor talking to Laurie," Tracy mentioned casually.

"You did? Why didn't you say something earlier? I kept thinking I should go over to his table and say hello before we left, but he and Lauren looked so deep in conversation I assumed they didn't want to be interrupted. Did he say anything?"

"He seemed fairly positive that the vote was going to go his way, but he said something about having to pay a high price for his victory."

"I wonder what he meant by that?"

"I'm not sure." Tracy tried to swallow away the lump in her throat. "He did say something about his father winning after all."

"I wonder if he's had to agree to move back to Minneapolis to work for his father again in return for keeping the factory open."

"I suppose that's a possibility." Tracy clenched her hands. She had another theory, but she couldn't bear to say it aloud. Not yet. Not to anyone. But she couldn't erase the image of the huge diamond engagement ring glistening on Lauren's left hand from her mind.

*****

Barclay Alexander II also noticed that Lauren's ring was

back on her finger. He made note of it when she and Clay had walked into the board room just seconds apart. The careless, if non-verbal announcement of their new alliance was a tactical error on the younger Barclays' part that could have cost him the vote had he been playing in the big leagues, but this was, after all, just a minor family matter.

The senior Alexander's eyes glinted... just one more piece of evidence that his son was simply not cut from the same cloth as he was. Clay's instincts had always been off. He had never been able to go for the kill. Then to develop a conscious on top of it all - that had been the real cincher.

Barclay Alexander II shook his head in disgust. Word had it that Barclay had persuaded his old friend, Paul Eberhart, to vote his way. He could have chosen to pull the man aside and call in a favor if he had wanted to. Barclay Alexander II made it a priority to know certain things about his friends, especially his board members. He regarded the practice as nothing more than an efficient way to preclude dissension among the ranks. At any rate, if he had wanted to force the issue, he could have uttered one significant word in Paul's direction and the man wouldn't have dared oppose him.

But he sat back in his chair, content to watch the chips fall as they may. He had no real desire to own the woolen mill any longer. There were other tax write-offs to be had. What he did want was Clay married to Lauren and back in the fold. With Lauren pressuring Barclay to move back to the Cities, and Clay beholden to her for saving the mill, it wouldn't take long before all would be well and an heir on the way. He suppressed a chuckle. The factory Barclay was determined to save had turned out to be a gargantuan noose around his neck. He couldn't have orchestrated a better end to his problems with his son if he'd tried.

Barclay acknowledged him briefly. "Father."

"Barclay." He nodded in return. "Lauren. Any word from your parents?" His purposeful referral to them was a subtle effort to intimidate her.

"I spoke to them yesterday. They should be luxuriating

at their spa in Baden Baden if I'm calculating the time difference correctly."

"Give them my best next time you speak to them."

"I will." Lauren turned away with an almost imperceptible wince.

He resisted the impulse to smirk. Barclay and Lauren, together again. One was as bad as the other. Neither one of them had a shred of loyalty to their parents. He could well imagine how furious his friend of many years would be upon learning that Lauren had betrayed his wishes and voted in favor of selling the mill to Clay. Maybe if his insipid son did marry her some of her savvy would rub off on him. The lady had balls thinking she could cross her father and get away with it. Either that or she was a bigger fool than he thought she was.

The crowd swelled through the narrow recess of the door and flooded around the table like water bursting through a hole in a damn.

The senior Barclay seated himself and called the meeting to order with one curt motion of his head. A part of him was sorely tempted to put Clay in his place, to cut him down to size right here and now in front of every last one of their business associates and his pretty little fiancée. He opted instead to let the vote get under way immediately, before he followed through on his baser instincts and left his son with no pride at all. He knew the limits of his own restraint. The youth was still his spawn after all. He chuckled to himself. He'd have to answer to the boy's mother if he didn't let their son leave today's proceedings with his some small shred of his pride still intact.

Barclay Alexander II felt almost jovial at the possibilities, but he kept his emotions to himself and led the meeting with a deft, defiant air, clipping through Robert's rules of order with an air born of experience. He looked Paul Eberhart and each of the other dissenters directly in the eye when they voted against him, and raised one eyebrow when Lauren cinched the sale of Elk Creek Woolen Mills to Clay with the votes she'd stolen from her father. Except for one, brief cynical smile, he kept his features free of any visible emotion.

Later, he would pride himself on being kind enough to have called a recess when the vote was finished and Clay declared the victor. He could have gone on to cover the other business at hand without giving Clay and his little fiancée the chance to gloat, shake hands, or preen for the pathetic little television crew that was waiting outside the door of the board room. Instead he deduced that the shaggy-haired camera crew had driven all the way up here from the booming metropolis of Mason City, Iowa, and supposed the sooner they got whatever crumbs they'd come for, the sooner they'd leave.

He did chuckle as his son stepped up to the microphone and held up one palm to quiet the audience. Fool.

*****

"Tracy! Come quick! The board members are filing out of the conference room! I think they're going to make an announcement! I see Clay. He's smiling. If that's any indication... Shhhh..."

Tracy toyed with her paintbrush as she looked over Michelle's shoulder at the television screen - she felt an ever deepening dread as she watched Clay step up to the microphone. She was prepared for the announcement that Elk Creek Woolen Mills was soon to be the sole property of Barclay Alexander III, pending papers to be drawn up and the transfer of deeds. She had always had an implicit, childlike trust in Clay, an unshakable confidence that he would make things work somehow, some way.

No, it wasn't the fate of the mill that held her spellbound, it was the suited blond woman that clung to Clay's arm.

"Ladies and gentleman."

She heard Clay's voice and saw him standing with the backdrop of the Minneapolis skyline behind him, visible through a wall of sheer glass. The man before her looked comfortingly familiar yet disturbingly different. His voice sounded slightly distorted and his face looked a tad longer than she remembered, but his jaw... and the way his Adam's apple bobbed when he spoke...

"Thank God," she heard Michelle breathe deeply beside her. "The factory is Clay's."

"...no plans to close the factory now, or at any time in the future..."

"He did it!" Michelle crowed.

"Oh, Clay!" Tracy exulted aloud.

"Will you be the sole owner of the Mill, Mr. Alexander?" a reporter asked. The camera panned out, and there was Mac, honing in on the couple. The video zoomed in for a close up of Lauren. "Or will there be other partners involved that may affect the long term future of Elk Creek?"

"That all depends on the ifs, ands, or buts of our prenuptial agreement, doesn't it, Barclay, dear?" Lauren interjected in her usually charming manner.

Tracy froze.

"Is this an announcement?" the reporter from Channel Three asked excitedly, eager to see his scoop do double duty. The young man held the microphone to Clay's lips once again.

Clay cleared his throat. Lauren arched her neck back in a gesture of apparent modesty and giggled like a teenager.

"Miss Humphreys and I are engaged to be married on December tenth of this year, however, Elk Creek Woolen Mills will remain my sole property," Clay announced with a dreadful finality.

And then he looked directly at Tracy, looked at her right through the television screen. "I'm sorry." He mouthed so imperceptibly that only she could see. So very, very sorry.

*****

Tracy hadn't seen or talked to Clay since that early October day. He'd tried to phone her but she hadn't picked up. There was nothing he could have said or done to change things between them and Tracy knew herself well enough to know that she would have been tempted to make love to him once more had they seen each other again. And she would not, could not be a man's mistress. That much she knew.

She had sent him a thank you note for the roses – a simple note in which she had told him that she returned his feelings, and more importantly, that she understood. She understood only too well. Even if it weren't for the mill, there were Clay's parents and her children and a million other reasons they weren't meant to be together.

She'd been so starry-eyed over Clay Alexander that she'd thought meeting him had been some sort of divine plan. Now that she had her feet planted firmly on the ground again, she could see that the whole thing had been a huge mistake.

Then she had shed her tears, and confessed to Theodora that she had made an unwise decision when she had chosen to share herself with Clay, one she hoped her daughter would be spared.

And then a kind of numbness had settled in upon her, a numbness perpetuated by the dismal, foggy days of October. In her mind, the sodden mounds of damp leaves clumped along the street sides lay heavily on her soul. An entire week went by in which she could not seem to get warm. She took to wearing heavy sweaters and thick socks that, ironically, had come from Elk Creek Woolen Mill.

But life went on. She and Michelle had finished the third floor attic of the Alexander house a few days after Clay's big announcement. She tried always to think of it as the Alexander house now, rather than Clay's personally. It was easier that way. There was still the matter of the upside down wallpaper panel, but it was still on backorder. She'd wanted to strip the paper and re-prep the wall before she left Maple Valley, but Michelle had been adamant about Clay wanting it left the way it was until the replacement panel arrived. It would have been nice to be completely, irreversibly finished with the Alexander house – and Clay – and the whole town of Maple Valley - but she couldn't fix what she didn't have.

The day after they'd finished the Alexander house, she'd gone to work for her mother's friend in Hayfield, Minnesota.

It hadn't taken Tracy ten minutes of painting at Myrtle Puttweiler's house to discover how much she missed the easy camaraderie of working with a partner, her sister in particular, or the pure joy of working on a structure of the caliber of the Alexander house.

She had made a daily ritual out of reminding herself that the plan from the very beginning had been for Michelle to go back to designing interiors – not painting them - as soon as Clay's house was finished, that if she only worked on houses with as much character as Clay Alexander's that she'd be unemployed ninety percent of the time, and that she couldn't expect there to be a handsome bachelor with whom to fall in love at every house she worked.

Even more depressing than her lackluster new job was the dismal little rental house she'd leased in Blooming Prairie.

She'd rarely had to deal with change in her life. She was trying her best to adapt, but this round and round and up and down existence she'd been thrust into hadn't been easy.

She walked in a circle, eyeing the patch of vanilla ice cream colored paint she'd just painted on the wall of the house that would soon be their home. Mrs. Puttweiler had used it for the tiny bathroom at her house in Hayfield and it had looked just fine. She tried to imagine how it would look covering the walls of the equally tiny living room of her new rental house.

She had her answer before she'd rinsed out the foam applicator in the kitchen sink. Boring. Bland. Uninspired.

Mrs. Puttweiler had said she could have what was left in the can, which should have been enough to do the job. Free paint was a good thing, but if she didn't have walls that were positive and cheery, she didn't see how she would be able to face coming home every night.

She'd had a garage sale and sold many of the things that had belonged to her and Trevor – in part to raise money, and in part, because she needed a fresh start, a life that didn't pay tribute to her failed marriage, but to a bright, new beginning.

She was making a fan out of the paint swatches and twirling them around like a never-ending rainbow when she heard a timid knock on the door. She peeked out the window and saw her sister.

"Rae?" She opened the door. "Is every thing okay?"

"Sure. Oh, no. I mean, yes, everything is fine." Rae stammered.

"Is Michelle with you?" It was weird – extremely weird – to be alone with Rae. Michelle had been a cushion to their sharp edges for years.

Rae shook her head.

"Mac?"

"No. I'm by myself. And no, I wasn't forced, blackmailed, or otherwise coerced into coming."

Well, to be honest, it had crossed her mind. "How did you find me?"

"Mom."

Neither of them said a word.

Rae thrust out her arm and handed her a plump garbage sack. "It's a housewarming present."

"It is?" Tracy felt her eyes open wide.

"I should have given it to you the other day," Rae said. "You were right about..." Her voice cracked.

Tracy looked in the bag and pulled out The Quilt. *Okay. Wow.* "I'll put it somewhere safe until Theodora..."

"It's not for Theodora. It's for you," Rae said.

"It is?" Tears started to slip down Tracy's cheeks. She took the quilt from the bag and spread it over the back of a chair. "Thank you."

She was so happy, so dazed, that the whole room felt like it was swirling, the house, suddenly alive – with color, with motion, with energy. She grabbed the paint book and flipped through the colors until she found a leaf green that matched the quilt perfectly.

"If it weren't for the boys, I might use this one," she said, pointing at a shade of rose called Mulberry Mauve.

"This one is nice with the quilt, too." Rae flipped back a couple of inches to the blue section.

"Some sky blue pillows on the sofa would be nice," Tracy said.

"Some rose colored ones, too. I'm great at slipcovers," Rae said. "I could help you make one for the sofa. Maybe the same shade of leaf green as the paint, but darker. Oh, and Mac is great at things like hanging quilts – I mean, if you want the quilt on the wall."

"Oh, I can't wait! It's going to be beautiful!" Tracy said, her eyes growing misty. "I've been a having such a hard time focusing – on anything – least of all, moving into this house."

"Look at us," Rae said. "Who would have thought..."

"It is kind of surprising."

"Shocking is probably more like it."

Tracy said nothing.

Rae looked her in the eye for a mere fraction of a second. "I'm sorry. I sincerely regret the wise cracks - and giving you a bad time - and not being more supportive."

"Thank you," Tracy said. "I know I haven't always been the kindest to you either. There are a lot of things I've said that I wish I could take back. A lot of times I should have said things, stuck up for you – but I didn't."

"I guess in a way, I owe you – if it weren't for you, I might have ended up with Trevor," Rae said.

Tracy gloated silently. Just a little. She couldn't help herself.

"I can see you smirking," Rae said.

"I wasn't wishing Trevor on you – really. I was trying to envision you as a pastor's wife."

"Lord, the very thought makes my stomach heave."

"The two of you wouldn't have lasted ten minutes," Tracy said. "Trust me."

"I do," Rae said. "I really do." She reached out her arms, took one halting step forward, and stopped.

Tracy eyed her from the short distance between them, then stepped into Rae's embrace. A brief, somewhat awkward pat on the back later, Rae stepped away.

"Michelle would be beside herself with joy if she could see the two of us." Tracy said. "Do we have to tell her?" Rae looked over her shoulder. "Does she really need to know?"

Tracy laughed. Rae looked offended at first. Then she started to laugh. Tracy laughed even harder. So did Rae.

"We should have done this a long time ago," Tracy said.

"The important thing is that we did it now," Rae said.

"You know," Rae said. "Mom has really mellowed out since you and Trevor... I mean, she's at least trying."

"Maybe the four of us should have lunch at the Painted Lady sometime," Tracy said.

"Good idea."

Rae smiled.

Tracy smiled.

Rae got out her cell phone. "What's your number? I'm going to add you to my contacts."

Tracy got out her cell phone and did the same.

"I hope you'll come back to Maple Valley and work at least once in awhile next spring. I'd like Ian to get to know you and his cousins a little better. I mean, it's ridiculous, us living so close and hardly ever seeing each other."

That was when Tracy started blubbering. Seriously blubbering.

Rae got her some tissues and acted ill at ease. But it was a start. A long overdue start.

*****

One thing Tracy didn't miss about working in Maple Valley was the hour-long drive. Tracy felt much more in touch with her children now that she was taking her turn carpooling again. It was amazing the things that one could learn just by listening to the chatter that went on between the Adam's children and hers in the back of the station wagon. She found comfort in the fact that she was within quick driving distance of the school should a problem arise, although, thankfully, none ever had. It was nice to be able to attend Titus's weekly soccer games again, better yet just to be home when the children came home from school every afternoon.

She and Theodora had taken to fixing supper together many nights, talking and chatting as they worked. Her daughter was still seeing more of Staci Slattery - and her cute, older brothers - than Tracy would have liked, but she had learned to keep her thoughts on the matter to herself in favor of maintaining the trust that had developed between them. There were bigger issues at stake than fleeting teenage friendships and crushes, and she coveted the new closeness with her daughter above all else.

She had already enrolled Teddy in the Blooming Prairie Public School system for the second semester, set to begin immediately after Christmas vacation. She was still undecided about what to do about Ty and Timothy. Trevor had assured her that her child support payments would remain the same whether or not she chose to keep the remaining two children in private school or transfer them to Blooming Prairie. She couldn't deny that the extra money would comc in handy. And the children could walk to school from the street where their rental house was located.

Whatever she decided, her children would not be without the influence of Christian teaching in their lives. They had started to attend a small, interdenominational church she had discovered in Hayfield the first time she'd met Mrs. Puttweiler. The short drive was a small price to pay in return for the added anonymity they had gained by avoiding the local churches, and with it the stigma of being the ex-wife and children of the previous minister of the Fellowship church. They had all taken to the non-judgmental, loving attitudes that prevailed at the little church in Hayfield. The children loved their Sunday School teachers, and were making more new friends with every week that passed.

She still worried about rumors getting out, and how they

might affect her children. Trevor had made no effort to defend himself to those former parishioners who had researched the Metropolitan Community Church he was pastoring in California. As far as Tracy was concerned, their family's only salvation was that Trevor's questionable sexual orientation was as big of an embarrassment to the church he had led for years as it would have been to them, had it been made common knowledge.

Still, Tracy and Trevor had spoken at length, and agreed that Trevor should speak with Titus over Christmas vacation. She was both dreading the holidays and relieved that the matter would be taken care of in a few short weeks. They were in total agreement that Timothy would be told nothing until he was older, unless he posed questions of his own accord first. The truth would be hard enough for Titus to understand.

She had continued to keep in touch with Mac and Rae and Michelle and Jake by phone. She knew without a doubt that the closer relationship and deeper understanding that had been forged during the time she and Michelle had worked together in Maple Valley would last regardless of whether or not they ever worked together again. Thus, she hadn't been surprised when Michelle had called from her office at the Painted Lady.

Chapter 27

Tracy had almost forgotten that the upside down Frank Lloyd Wright wallpaper panel still needed to be replaced. She had wondered about it once or twice and assumed that this time, perhaps Michelle had decided to re-hang it herself – perhaps to make sure it got done right. Not that she would have been offended if Michelle had taken care of it without bothering to call her. It would have been a relief in a way.

But Michelle knew she was the kind of person who liked to follow through on what she started, and she had called her the second the panel had arrived. Of course, there was still the matter of Clay. But Michelle had spoken to that objection before she'd even had a chance to voice it, almost as though she knew more than she was letting on. Her sister had started out by saying that Clay was going to be out of town for a few days and that's why it would be a convenient time to re-hang the wallpaper.

What viable excuse had that left Tracy? Michelle was pregnant and trying to run a business. It would have been ridiculous to call in another painter, even though Roger, Michelle's regular painter, was now recovered and back at work. It was Tracy who had made the error in the first place. It was her responsibility to correct the problem. She let Michelle know right off that she wasn't going to accept a dime for her time. The paper wouldn't have needed re-hanging at all if she hadn't been so careless in the first place.

Tracy was glad the sun was shining when she pulled up in front of the Alexander house. She instinctually avoided the driveway, not wanting to be hemmed in should there be any surprise visitors while she was working.

Michelle had said the house would be open, and it was. Her emotions were on high alert as she went to the back door and peered inside. It went without saying that she would never be able to look at the place where she and Clay had lain on the floor and snuggled without her heart filling with joy, then freefalling to a crash landing on the rocky shore of reality below. But it didn't matter, because this was the last time she would ever be in this house. Life moved on, and in this case, it had taken Clay in one direction, and her in another. Even if they'd been on the same merry-go-round at the same time, in the same place like they had been the day of the Minnesota State Fair, her horse never would have caught up to his, nor his to hers. Because of her faith, she would always believe in miracles, but she was also a realist. Clearly, she and Clay would forever be on opposite sides of the merry-go-round, going round and round for eternity, their paths doomed never to intersect.

Her eyes filled with tears as she stood in the center of the room. Not only were Michelle's finishing touches in evidence throughout, but the house had a lived-in quality that had been missing before. Books and art deco pottery, most of which she recognized as Red Wing, lined the built-in shelves in the sitting room. A leather folder with a pen tossed hurriedly atop it sat by the phone. Clay's presence was everywhere, from the masculine scents of vanilla and sandalwood that wafted through the rooms, to the carelessly strewn pillows and magazines tossed about.

She steeled herself from thinking about Clay, the man, and tried to think of him as a stern employer who deserved customer satisfaction and a job completed. She was actually very thankful to have been given this chance to find closure. Coming here, today, by herself, was a way to find atonement. Not that she'd doubted for a minute that she would survive her unfortunate tryst with Clay – even thrive – once enough time had passed.

Her emotions shifted again, and her heart filled with sorrow, just thinking about a life that didn't include Clay.

No. He had done what he needed to do, and so had she. He was with Lauren. She had Theodora, Titus and Timothy. In time, everything would be fine.

She found the rolls of wallpaper still in the box and the tools she needed in a neat pile, then a tray to fill with water so she could wet the wallpaper panels. She filled the tray and soon had the strips cut to the right lengths. Case closed.

She was willing her mind to move on to other things when she heard a noise from upstairs. What on earth? Had the door to the balcony blown open? The unmistakable sound of footsteps resounded through the quiet house. She flattened herself against the wall. What if it was Lauren? She'd confirmed the date and time she was scheduled to arrive with Michelle just last night. It would be just her luck to have made another mistake while trying to repair the first.

The other option – an intruder – while scary, wasn't half as intimidating as the thought of coming face to face with Lauren, Clay's parents, or even Clay.

She looked through the clear glass panes of the French door she was hiding behind.

Great choice. She couldn't have been near a solid door?

"Tracy?"

Her heart hit her chest with a thud. *Clay.*

"Tracy? Is that you?"

Good grief. He was going to see her in ten seconds, like it or not. And even if she found a better hiding spot, her car was parked in front of the house. It wasn't like he was going to be fooled.

Fool that I am, fool that I may be
When will I ever know what's true?
And if I found out differently
Would I still love you?

Stop it.

She kept her hand on the doorknob for support, tried to ignore Rita, and stepped out from behind the door just as Clay rounded the corner. He was dressed in blue jeans and a lavender polo shirt. He looked relaxed.

"Tracy." He sounded so relieved that her heart could have melted like M&Ms all over again. But it didn't. She grabbed a couple of big chunks of ice from the jam of memories piled up in the back of her brain and packed them tightly around her heart.

"You're supposed to be out of town."

"I came home early."

Because I knew you'd be here. He didn't say it, but it was pretty obvious.

"Listen, Clay," she said, feeling terribly empowered for maybe the first time in her life. "I've made it very clear that I don't want to talk to you. Number one, what happened between us never should have happened in the first place. Number two, it's ancient history. You've obviously moved on and so have I." She stuck her chin in the air. "Number three..." Her mind went blank. She looked into Clay's eyes. Her head emptied of everything she knew was right. And wrong. And in between. Until all that mattered was Clay.

This had to stop. "Number three..." She tried again. "Number three..."

"There is no number three."

"There is, too. I just - forgot what I was going to say. Besides, numbers one and two are reason enough to-"

"I love you," Clay said, very quietly, his voice firm with understated conviction.

"So did Trevor." Her eyes filled with tears. "Yet there are a million kazillion reasons we shouldn't be together."

"Just as there are a million kazillion reasons we *should* be together," Clay responded.

"*Shouldn't*," she said. "Lauren-"

"Lauren and I are through. She knows I'm in love with you."

"The wedding is off?"

"Permanently."

She struggled to maintain her composure. "How? When? Why?"

"You really want to know?"

"Yes."

"Fine. Lauren's father and mother came home from Germany exactly two weeks ago today. As expected, her father was outraged that she had used his proxy to vote in favor of selling the factory to me. Votes without which I could not have accomplished my goal."

"I knew it." Tracy let out a long breath. "I understood, Clay, I really did. If all of those people had lost their jobs because of me, because of us... I couldn't have lived with myself."

"I know. And I loved you even more for being so brave and gallant about the whole thing."

"I wasn't," she said. "My heart was breaking when you announced... even though I knew..."

"Of course it was. Mine was as well."

"I still don't understand, Clay. Lauren had to have anticipated that her father would be upset with her for going against his wishes and siding with you."

"She did to some extent. I don't think either of us was totally prepared for his reaction."

She looked at him quizzically.

"He accused Lauren of using his proxy to blackmail me into marrying her."

"Isn't that fairly close to the truth?"

"Of course it was. But I think Lauren thought that her father would somehow approve of the underhanded methods she used to gain the advantage in what she saw only as a little lover's spat. Her father is, after all, known for being able to justify any means to the ends he desires."

"And that wasn't the case?"

"No, most surprisingly not."

"She was expecting a pat on the back for proving she was a chip off the old block."

"Instead, her father turned on her. He threatened to disinherit her if he ever found out that she had done what he suspected."

Tracy's eyes opened wide. "What did you do?"

"Her father confronted me right then and there. Asked me point blank if I was marrying his daughter for love, or if she had blackmailed me by promising me her vote in return for setting a wedding date."

"And?"

"I couldn't betray her that way - turn against her with her

father standing there in such a rage. Besides, I was as much to blame for what happened as she was. We both made a pact with the devil when we agreed to do what we did."

"But you had no other choice!"

"No. I was desperate. And so was she. Maybe that's what her father found so despicable that he couldn't bear to witness it in his only child."

"What did you tell him?"

"I told him I loved his daughter and that I was marrying her of my own accord. I told him he was wrong."

"And he forgave her?"

"Yes. He did."

"Then why aren't you in Minneapolis living happily ever after with Lauren?"

"You don't know how close I came. Thankfully, I hadn't given Lauren enough credit. As it turned out, she was very deeply touched by my willingness to come to her defense. Knowing I chose to defend her when I could have stood by and watched her lose everything, say nothing about being freed from the farce of marrying her, changed her mind about a lot of things."

"Oh, Clay." Tracy's heart swelled with thankfulness.

"She came to me a few days later and told me that her father was right, that it was beneath her to marry someone who was in love with someone else. She admitted that she had never really been in love with me either, that marrying me was more a matter of pride than love."

Tracy shook her head. "There it is."

"What?"

"That word again."

"Pride?"

"Yes. That one little word has gotten me into such trouble over the years."

"Me, too." Clay smiled. "But all that is behind us now. So you see? There's nothing to keep us apart now that-"

"Except your parents." She said first.

"And yours." He said second.

Okay, so there were going to be parent problems no

matter what. She smiled. Faintly.

"Your daughter wasn't too happy when she first found out about me," Clay said.

She grimaced. "I heard about that."

"Then you know that those things I said – about what happened that day not meaning anything-"

"You thought it was better to lose me than to come between me and my daughter."

Clay looked at her and held her glance with eyes that were molten hot and magnetic.

"Do you love me?" He asked. Simply. Humbly.

"Yes."

"Then why-"

"First, because my whole life has just been turned upside down, and I have to learn how to take care of myself before I can-"

"So we'll take it slow."

She ignored him and kept talking. "Second, because I have to give my kids time to adjust to their new lives before I pull the rug out from under them again."

"So we'll take it easy. Let them get to know me, a little at a time."

"Third, because..." She couldn't take her eyes off of him.

"There is no number three."

"There is, too." She smiled. "I just forgot what I was going to say."

"Well, I didn't," Clay said. "I love you, Tracy Jones. I want to spend the rest of my life with you. I will do whatever it takes to make you happy, whatever it takes to help you to become the woman you were meant to be, whatever it takes to make all your dreams come true – the ones you've had for years, the ones you're thinking of for the first time, right this minute, and the ones you haven't even dreamed up yet."

He looked so proud of himself. "So?"

"So, I'm thinking about it," she said. "And to be honest, I was thinking that right now, I'm dreaming of getting these wallpaper panels hung."

Clay threw his head back and laughed. "And here I've

been thinking that maybe I should leave it the way it is."

"You're kidding."

"No. It's symbolic. You've turned my life upside down, and I think I like it."

"But to me, it's a glaring reminder of a huge mistake."

"But-"

Men were so clueless.

Clay must have interpreted the look on her face correctly. "Then we'll change it."

"We'll?"

"I'll help."

She tried not to laugh. She really did. "Have you ever wallpapered?"

"No, but I'm sure I can learn."

"So being from a family that pays other people to do their home improvement tasks - and I'm guessing everything else, you've probably never heard the old adage about wallpapering together being a sure way to wreck a marriage."

Now it was his turn to laugh. "So - if being able to wallpaper together is the standard by which a good or bad marriage is defined, does that mean if we're able to successfully complete this wallpapering task – together - that you'll marry me?"

"No. I might let you take me on a date."

Clay got a silly grin on his face. "Glad you mentioned it, actually. Because as fate would have it, there's a limo waiting outside to take us on our first date."

"Oh, really?" She smiled, climbed on the stepstool in the corner of the room and ripped off the first length of the upside down wallpaper. "A limo."

"Yes. I can do that." Clay reached up, found the corner of the next panel and stripped it off the wall. "So, do you think we can be done in an hour if we work together? I was presumptuous and made reservations."

She left him to remove the rest of the design and picked up the first length of wallpaper to roll it with the bottom side up.

Clay finished his task, then picked up a roll and tried to imitate her motions with a few clumsy chops of his hands.

"You're very sweet, Clay. But unless you were also presumptuous enough to find someone to pick my kids up at school and fix them dinner, I really can't-"

"It's all arranged. Michelle put me in touch with Teddy, who thankfully, appears to have forgiven me. She spoke to Brooke's mother, who has taken care of everything."

Wow. This was serious. She was trying to play it cool, but her heart had started doing a happy dance and there was nothing she could do but groove to the music.

Your love is liftin' me higher,
Than I've ever been lifted before.
So keep it up, quench my desire.
And I'll be at your side forever more.
Now once, I was downhearted.
Disappointment was my closest friend.
But you came, he soon departed
And he never showed his face again
Ooh, I'm so glad I finally found you.
You're that one in a million man.
When you wrap your lovin' arms around me,
I can stand up and face the world again.

She tried to wipe the silly grin off of her face and dipped the first roll in the tray of water.

"I saw that look," Clay said. "You can't hide it. All Time High?"

"Your Love Has Lifted Me Higher."

He smiled.

A few dozen bubbles spurted up from the inside of the rolled up wallpaper, reminding her to glance at the clock, and mentally start the countdown. She had to get a grip.

"I hope you're not planning anything fancy. Look at me. I'm dressed in blue jeans, an old T-shirt, and splattered tennis shoes."

"Michelle said I should buy you a dress – something

about you feeling like a fuddy dud in your pastor's wife dresses? But she was busy, so Rae met me at Flannery's and helped me pick something that she thought you'd like."

"The two of you did that for me?" She closed her eyes and the music started up again.

Baby you're so sweet,
You know you should have been some honey.
Well you could have been anything that you want to
And I can tell - the way you do the things you do.
You really sweep me off my feet.
You make my life complete.
You make my life so bright.
You make me feel alright.
The way you do the things you do.

She opened her eyes, lined the first strip of wallpaper up to the chalk line and started to smooth it with a brush.

"If you don't mind positioning the pieces, I can do that." Clay put his hand over hers and slowed the brush to a gentle halt. He was standing just inches away, looking down at her with all the love in the world.

"Um, you'll have to get all the bubbles out and roll the seams flat before I can do the next piece." And then she rose up on her toes, put one hand on each of his cheeks, and kissed him. "You Alexanders you – distracting me when I'm trying to concentrate on my work."

"In a good way this time. At least I hope."

"A very good way."

Forty-five minutes and not a single tense word later, the wallpaper panels were all hung – right side up. That was when she noticed a little piece of paper on the floor next to – of all things – a brown M&M. Clay was in the kitchen, rinsing the wallpaper glue out the brush and washing the tray.

She unfolded the note. *You melt me, the* note said in Clay's distinctive scrawl. *Like Hansel and Gretel, this is your fairy tale, but instead of bread crumbs, follow brown*

M&Ms.

She saw the M&Ms trailing out of the parlor and up the stairs the second she looked down. How could she have missed them before? Of course, she wouldn't have had he used any color but brown. Tracy smiled at the thought of Barclay Alexander III sorting through untold bags of M&Ms until he had enough brown ones to make a nicely camouflaged trail. How could she not play along?

She started up the stairs, eating an occasional M&M as she went. The trail wound down the hall to the master suite. The door was ajar and the room looked warm and inviting. She smelled the scent of flowers before she found the rose strewn on the corner of the bed - one red rose nestled in a posy of baby's breath and toile, a gift-wrapped box with her name on it, and a second note. *The gingerbread house is yours.*

She tore open the box and found a dress made from vintage tea-dyed lace on a bed of tissue paper. She lifted it gently from the box. The neckline looked low and sexy, and a long bodice lined with silk moiré met a two-tiered skirt that flounced at the bottom, flapper style.

A pair of lace panties, a low cut, strapless brassiere, silk slip, and stockings lay tucked under the dress. A long strand of pearls and two dainty droplets for her ears were curled in tissue paper at the bottom of the box. She looked down at her paint splattered tennis shoes and saw a pair of off-white slippers placed toe in by the bed.

She read aloud from a second note, fingering the pearls. They were probably real. *Your coach awaits you, Cinderella.* She ran to the window. A white limousine was parked under the maple tree in front of the house. She'd thought he was teasing!

She slipped out of her clothes, freshened up in the master bath, and dressed. The gown fit her perfectly. When she looked in the mirror, she hardly recognized herself. With a sigh, she looked around the room one last time, took her rose posy in one hand and went to the bottom of the stairs.

A white-bearded driver was standing at the front door.

"May I?" Clay had changed into a tuxedo, and was holding an ecru poodle hair jacket for her to slip into. Fitted at the shoulders, wide and swirling at the base - it was a perfect fit.

"Tracy, this is Niles. Niles, Tracy."

The driver nodded and opened the door.

Clay took her elbow and helped her to the curb.

"We have a bit of a drive ahead of us, ma'am," the driver announced as Clay helped her into the limousine. "I've opened a bottle of Asti Spumante for you to enjoy on the trip."

A basket of ripe, red strawberries dipped in white and dark chocolate, and a delicate crystal bowl filled to the rim with every color of M&M but brown sat on a tray beside the champagne. Tracy giggled in spite of herself.

"May I ask where we're going?"

"It's a surprise," Clay said.

She looked at Niles. "Niles?"

"I'm under orders to be as secretive as possible without unduly alarming you," the older man looked over his shoulder and smiled at her in the rear view mirror. "You aren't feeling alarmed at present, are you, ma'am?"

"No." Tracy laughed. "Curious. I'll be patient."

"Thank you, ma'am. We'll be on our way then, if you have no objections."

"None at all." She smiled at Clay and he squeezed her hand.

"Enjoy the refreshments, Ma'am. Sir."

"Thank you, Niles."

The windows of the sleek vehicle were blackened. By the time she felt the transmission shift into high gear, she had lost track of which direction they were headed. She deduced after a time that they were on the interstate heading either north or south, for the powerful automobile was clipping along at a brisk pace, rarely breaking or slowing.

She and Clay spoke quietly, serious one minute and silly the next. She marveled again at the feeling that she always had when she was with him – that somehow, she had known him forever. He held her left hand. With her right, she made swirling designs from red, green, blue, yellow and orange M&Ms. Before long, the limo came to a gentle halt.

She heard the faint strains of the calliope the second the driver opened the door. The merry-go-round was storybook-like in its perfection, the horses magnificently carved and delicately colored, the tremolo of the music still strong after nearly a century of playing for beribboned little boys and girls and hand-holding lovers alike.

"Are we in Story City?"

Clay nodded, helped her out of the limousine, and kissed her more times than she could count. And then he swirled her gently to the music as they danced round and round on the planked flooring of the old merry-go-round.

The famous antique carousel was a glory to behold. A round table covered with a moiré cloth was set up on the far side of the carousel. A caterer's van with The Cottage at Story City painted on the side was parked nearby, and a waiter in a white vest stood ready to serve them. The summerlike sunshine warmed her to the core.

The carousel moved round and round in soothing circles while the horses moved up and down in a melodic accompaniment.

Clay laughed. "I love you, Tracy." He tweaked her chin and kissed her reverently, their clasped hands rising and falling in time with the merry-go-round.

Tracy simply smiled. "I love you, Clay."

"I have one last surprise," he said.

"You're going to sing to me," she said.

"Who told you?" He said it tongue in cheek, but he picked up a microphone that was hooked up to a karaoke machine and started to croon nonetheless.

Once a story's told, it can't help but grow old
Roses do - Lovers too
So cast your seasons to the wind
And hold me dear, oh, hold me dear
Close the window, calm the light

And it will be alright
No need to bother now
Let it out, let it all begin
All's forgotten now
We're all alone, oh-oh, we're all alone.

"We won't be for long," she said, listening to the music fade.

"What? Alone?"

"My kids, your parents..."

"Your parents..."

"Your factory..."

"Your sisters..."

She smiled. "I can sing, too."

"So do."

"It's not Rita Coolidge, but it works." She sang, "Drop all your troubles by the river side. Catch a painted pony on the spinning wheel ride."

Clay's face lit up. "You mean it? You're ready to hop on and take a spin?"

"What's a little ride on the merry-go-round? We survived wallpapering, didn't we?"

Also from Second Wind Publishing by Sherrie Hansen:

Stormy Weather

Maple Valley Book 1

An ill wind is brewing up a storm and as usual, Rachael Jones is in the middle of the fray. If the local banker succeeds in bulldozing the Victorian houses she's trying to save, she's in for yet another rough time before the skies clear. The only bright spots on the horizon are her friendship with Luke... and her secret rendezvous with Mac... Is Rachael meant to weather the storm with Luke, who touches her heart and soul so intimately, or with Mac, who knows each sweet secret of her body?

Water Lily

Maple Valley Book 2

Once upon a very long time ago, Jake Sheffield and Michelle Jones graduated from the same high school. Jake can't wait to take a trip down memory lane at their 20th class reunion. The last thing Michelle wants to do is dredge up a lot of old memories and relive a part of her past that wasn't that great in the first place. Will the murky waters of the past destroy their dreams for the future, or will a water lily rise from the depths and bloom?

Night and Day

It's midnight in Minnesota and Jensen Marie Christiansen is dreaming of a rosy future. It's daybreak in Denmark and Anders Westerlund is waking up to a world full of stark realities. When parchment paper and faded ink meet computer screens and fax machines, the old-fashioned magic of a great-grandmother's letters sets the stage for a steamy Internet romance...

Additional titles from other talented Second Wind Publishing authors:

Fate and Destiny
Claire Collins

A romantic thriller set on a snowy mountaintop. During a blizzard, Andrew's dog, Shadow, finds Destiny;a beautiful woman left for dead, but very much alive. With her she brings mystery, danger and passion to the little cabin.

Finding Madelyn
Suzette Vaughn

Galen lost her. Somewhere along the journey of their life, which started at such a tender age, he'd lost her. After three years in Europe, fighting a war that wasn't personally his, he came home to fight for what he lost. Madelyn Murphy enjoyed her new life far away from memories of her drunk father, runaway mother, and the love that left her. Until that love sits down in her diner and everything she ran from rushes back to haunt her. With memories of growing up and dreams of growing old together bombarding them, they have to find the truth amid a history of lies and decide if they can even trust each other.

Pure is The Heart
Amy De Trempe

A Christian romance set in the 18th century, Pure is the Heart has the ability to draw out the lover and the faithful spirit in every soul.

www.secondwindpublishing.com

8451243R0

Made in the USA
Charleston, SC
11 June 2011